This story covers a wide canvas, peopled by vivid and distinctive characters, the passionate Leah, the gentle Rachel, the placid Isaac, the ambitious Judah, the incorruptible Joseph, and their hopes and despairs, passions and dangers are woven into the pattern of which the central theme is the complex and frustrated character of Jacob himself. Was he truly the thief and supplanter, unworthily taking the great birthright of his brother, or was he one who patiently and honourably sought the Divine inheritance—the promise of Shiloh? To this and many other questions, this novel gives an exciting immediacy.

JEAN REES

JACOB

HAVE

I

LOVED

The Prophet Malachi
(Ch. 1, v. 2)

Wm. B. Eerdmans Publishing Company
Grand Rapids, Michigan

AUTHOR'S NOTE

WHEN preparing to write this book, I followed my usual custom, and spent some months researching on the historical background, living in libraries, including the British Museum. I found that these, together with my visits to the Near East, threw great light upon the story, but most of all I read and re-read the story of Genesis, until the pages of my Bible have become quite transparent! I have tried to adhere as closely as possible to the ancient record, and to develop what is told there, rather than to invent new situations. There is little need for invention; the biblical story is a concentrated record, portraying in terse language passionate love, treachery, human tenderness, intrigue, bitterness and triumph. I have tried to live in the characters, and find out the reasons behind their actions and sayings.

I was astonished to find how much my conception of Jacob had been overlaid by tradition. The accepted teaching of sermons, commentaries and devotional books appears to be far from the actual historical facts. Just as Sir Thomas More and Shakespeare have portrayed Richard III as the wicked uncle, deceiving people for many generations, until recent historians have disclosed the facts, so Jacob has been a much maligned man. The mean little twister, trying to defraud his handsome, strong brother, is a positive travesty of the facts. True, I see him as a frustrated young man, developing the inferiority complex inevitable in one so palpably not his father's favourite: I deplore his methods of obtaining what was actually his by promise and purchase: but a study of the facts, and not sermonising fiction, quite explodes the picture of Jacob, the cheat, banished from his father's house. In actual fact, he was sent to seek a wife, with full parental approval and blessing. The picture of him bargaining with God, and cheating his father-in-law arise, if the first case, from a wrong understanding of the word 'if' instead of 'since' in the Authorised Version, and a deliberate ignoring of Jacob's integrity when, after twenty years of servitude, Laban was unable to refute Jacob's declaration of his honesty and diligence.

The story is a fascinating one. A man who could arouse such passionate love in his wives, and who could be so considerate to his children, (". . . the children are tender . . . I will lead on softly . . . and the children will be able to endure." Gen. 33.13, 14) could hardly be the mean twister of whom we have heard. It was only Esau, in his rage, who called him 'thief and supplanter', as he, Esau, tried to steal the blessing he had sold to Jacob. Jacob was later called 'prince with God'—a fit name for the progenitor of Israel.

The story of his son Joseph in Egypt is an enthralling one, and has required many months of research into customs and Egyptian history.

Jean A. Rees

1

JACOB crouched down beside the panting ewe. His fine garments of dyed wool, and the blue mantle decorated with white needlework, had been carefully laid aside and hung over the roots of a stunted acacia nearby. The garments for the family festival of mourning were not suitable for a shepherd about to assist at the birth of a ewe's first lambs. Even while talking with his cousins, the sons of Ishmael, Jacob had noticed this one ewe wandering a little way from the rest of the flock in evident distress. With the briefest explanation, he had run up the hillside and prepared to carry out the instructions given to him by that wise man, Miram, chief shepherd of the flocks of Isaac.

The ewe was quiet again, lying down, gaining strength.

"I wonder what you are thinking?" Jacob asked the ewe. "No one can tell you what to expect, and suddenly this thing 'birth' is upon you, and has you in its terrifying grasp."

The ewe stood up again, and restlessly walked about. Fifteen-year-old Jacob stretched himself and allowed his mind to look back over the epoch-making events of the past few days. Abraham was dead. His grandfather, the head of the tribe, the father of nations, had been gathered to his fathers. What a meeting it had been at the cave of Machpelah, that place which Abraham had bought as a burying-place for his beloved wife, Sarah. Jacob had never seen her. She died even before his parents had been married, but the stories of her beauty and goodness were still told around the firesides, and the poets sang songs praising her. His mother, Rebekah, was beautiful too. Some said not as lovely as Sarah, but to him she was the most beautiful person in the world, and Jacob hugged the thought to himself that she loved *him* best. She would never admit it, but it was true, she loved him best, just as Isaac loved handsome Esau. Everyone else seemed to like Esau best. His father's preference had been obvious ever since they were small boys. Esau was a mighty hunter. He loved going out with the men for exhausting days, coming home at night with venison to make the savoury meat his father loved. Always it was the same. The men would regale his father with stories of Esau's skill. He could shoot straighter and farther than men twice his age. He, Jacob, could find no pleasure in this hounding animals to their death, coming home physically spent, suffering hunger and thirst. He loved animals, and to care for them, relieve their suffering and ease their way into the world was the life he loved. He wished he could do something to please his father as Esau could. A day's hunting to Esau meant a dish of venison that excited his father's anticipation all day, and made him praise Esau from sundown to darkness. No, there was nothing he could do to please his father. The fact remained that Isaac loved Esau best. But Jacob shrugged his shoulders, and turned his attention to the ewe. She had lain down again, straining rhythmically. Gently Jacob sought to help, speaking soothing words to this ewe which had never lambed before. He could do nothing to help yet. No little hooves were visible to make assistance possible. He wished he had brought some of the pig lard Miram used to ease the delivery.

Jacob's mind went back again to the exciting doings of the day. Yes, everyone liked Esau. His easy manner and friendliness won his way with the many cousins who had gathered to do homage to the memory of their grandfather. Esau seemed to find much to discuss with them and to talk about. Even Ishmael, his father's mysterious brother, known as a mighty hunter, had spoken kindly to Esau, having heard of his prowess. He had spoken strange words too. He had said, " So you are the heir, and in the sacred line of promise." Esau had looked a little surprised at something in Ishmael's tone, and Jacob had pricked up his ears as their uncle continued, " Watch out that your younger brother does not usurp your place. It has been done before." What could he have meant? Esau never analysed anything like that, or thought to question what he heard. He had just smiled his broad pleasant smile, and asked his uncle a question about hunting. But there was something mysterious about this uncle Ishmael. As a child Jacob had asked his mother once or twice, " Why do we never see Uncle Ishmael's sons? Why do they call him a bastard? And why are he and Father not friendly like other brothers? " Rebekah, his mother, had told him that he was too young to understand, and to remember that father knew best. Always a maddening thing to be told, thought Jacob, calculated to drive you to seek information from other, less reliable, sources. Some said that Ishmael had tried to kill his father, others said that he had tried to lame him, but no one really knew. All he could find out was that Ishmael, son of his grandfather's Egyptian concubine, had been banished with scant ceremony. But death seemed to cancel everything, and today his father Isaac, with all the dignity of the new chief and inherited position of priest to the tribe had, together with his half-brother, Ishmael, performed the burial rites and ceremonies with honour due to such an illustrious father.

Certainly the cousins were not poverty-stricken. Indeed, people said that Ishmael's sons were clothed and behaved like princes. The three he had talked with had a lordly manner, and boasted of their possessions. Mishma, Duma and Massa their names were. " Hear ", " Keep silence " and " Bear " these names meant, but they had hardly lived up to them. It was amazing the great stress they constantly laid on being of the seed of Abraham. " Sons as we are of the great Abraham's firstborn, Ishmael . . ." Duma had declared, while his brothers said the same. Esau had in his friendly way disarmed them, and asked them of their other brothers, and looked with interest at their sisters, especially one, Mahalath. Though this was not surprising, Jacob smiled to himself. Esau, even at fifteen, looked with interest at *anyone's* sister, if she had flashing black eyes and shining braided hair!

Then Jacob forgot his cousins and his brother in caring for the ewe. She was straining and panting and, seeing at last the tiny hooves, Jacob gently held these as Miram had taught him, and worked rhythmically with the ewe, each contraction bringing the tiny head into nearer view.

9

"Come along, not long now," Jacob whispered encouragingly, convinced that the ewe understood.

At last with one final effort, emitting a bleat of distress, the ewe brought the lamb to birth. What strange instinct was it, thought Jacob, that this ewe, with no wise person to instruct her, no mother to teach her, should instantly stand to her feet, forgetting the pain and effort, and feverishly lick the little lamb clean? But for the ewe all was not over, for it was evident that her anguish must begin all over again, and another lamb was born in a very short time. Soon the twin lambs, licked clean by their mother, had risen to their feet and were staggering about, knock-kneed, drunkenly falling but rising again, each one going unerringly to the udders of the ewe for milk with that same uncanny instinct that had taught the ewe to care for her young.

"Twins," said Jacob aloud. "So little time between, but what a world of difference those few minutes can make!"

He sank his chin into his chest, thinking deeply, only to be aroused by the voice of Miram, the chief shepherd.

"Well done, Jacob. I expected we'd have trouble with her," he said. "I thought to find you feasting with the mourners, not caring for the sheep."

"I caught sight of her going off alone, and thought she might be in trouble," Jacob told him. Then he looked up at Miram and asked, "How does she know what to do when it's her first time?"

"God tells them," said the shepherd simply. "He reveals many secrets to His creatures, more to the dumb creation than to those who depend on hearing and learning, and reading the stars."

Miram was an old man, especially in Jacob's eyes, but magnificently fit. He stretched himself and looked out over the distant horizon.

"I know many secrets, Jacob," he said. "Secrets that are revealed to me as I sit under the stars. You have the gift, you care for the sheep as a real shepherd, not as a hireling. Some day I will tell you my secrets."

"Tell me them now," pleaded Jacob. "I am fifteen, I have been a man these three years."

"I will teach you my craft, and as years go by I will reveal many secrets. One ancient secret is known only to me. It was told me by Father, who had it from one of Shem's children. A man who lives alone, away from the cities, under God's heaven, learns many things not revealed to those who spend their life with merchandise and commerce. But never fear, I will teach you. Your grandfather Abraham left the city, they say, at the call of God to found a great nation."

Miram was surprised at the reaction his words caused.

"Don't speak of it to me. Don't tantalise me with it. I know it all. I have sat and listened to my grandfather talk and tell of the promise of founding a great nation, and that one day of one of his descendants would come . . ." Jacob paused. What he was about to utter was strangely magic, mysterious and holy. His voice changed to one of awe, ". . . will come SHILOH. I know little of what is meant by this, but when my grandfather spoke his whole face seemed to be lit from an inner light, and he spoke more like a god than a man. 'You must keep yourself pure,' he told me, 'different from the heathen nations round about, whose base ideas and customs are a sin against the God Who made them.' He kept telling me all this, and all the time my heart responded and I caught something of the glory of it all. 'See that you marry a wife worthy to bear you sons, of whom might be born SHILOH' he told me. 'I had my Sarah, and your father has his lovely Rebekah. Chose wisely, my son.'" Jacob paused, and then said bitterly, "Think of it—all because of a few minutes, just like these two lambs. Look at them now, both so alike, feeding equally strongly, but just because Esau, even as a baby, pushed right to the front to be the first to see the light of day, born a few minutes before I was, all these words are empty." He looked up at Miram. "Why did he speak like that to *me*?" he asked urgently.

Miram looked thoughtfully at the lad, who was standing with his fists clenched. What a handsome boy he was, to be sure—tall as Esau, but slight, his smooth skin tanned with the sun to which he was so often exposed. He spoke cautiously. "Your parents have never said anything to you about which of you will inherit?" he asked.

"Of course not," said Jacob, "but Esau has the birthright, and if it were a case of preference, isn't it known throughout the tribe that Esau's little finger is to my father Isaac as my loins?"

Miram could not refute this, but his mind went back fifteen years to something he had heard from his wife, Deborah, who was Rebekah's nurse. She had travelled all the way from Haran when Rebekah had been brought to be the bride for Isaac, and she knew her mistress's mind like her own. There had been much secrecy over the birth of the twins, and talk of a vision concerning the younger taking precedence over the elder. But nothing more had been said, and everyone knew that Esau was the apple of his father's eye and could do no wrong.

As if reading Miram's thoughts, Jacob continued, "Esau, of course, can do no wrong in my father's eyes, but I know that he goes with the hunters and consorts with the Hittites. I hear them making their lewd jokes about the daughters of Heth. If my father knew this, he might think differently. I know that Esau cares nothing for his birthright or the promise of SHILOH. or any of the things about which Abraham told us as children."

Miram looked intently at Jacob. "Has it ever occurred to you," he said, "seeing you want this birthright so much, that you could purchase it from Esau?"

Jacob looked at him quickly. "Buy it?" he said. "Can a man buy a birthright?"

"Certainly," Miram told him, "a birthright is negotiable. according to the ancient laws. Many an elder son, caring nothing for the position, has sold it for so many shekels of silver or so many hundreds of sheep—whatever price he puts upon it."

Jacob's eyes were alight with hope and desire. "Esau cares little for his birthright. Maybe he would sell it to me. My father allows me to build my own flock, and each year it increases. One day I will go to Esau and I will offer him my best, and maybe he will sell me his birthright." Jacob had already begun to dream. If he were to be the heir, how he would prepare himself, he thought. He would learn all that the ancients could teach him of God and of the promise. He would choose a wife worthy to follow Sarah and Rebekah, and one who would be worthy to be the mother, grandmother or ancestress of . . . Again his voice changed, " . . . of SHILOH ".

.   .   .   .

Ishmael, gorgeously attired in a woven red cloak gaily embroidered in a manner his brother Isaac privately thought rather vulgar, stood facing him. His handsome face, with luxuriant beard, wore an amused expression as he looked at Isaac through half-closed eyes.

"Well, brother," he said, "we all pay homage to you today. It has come about as you hoped. You are the sheik, priest, and lord of all the tribe of Abraham. May you prove a worthy successor to such a father."

The mockery in the tone was unmistakable. Why did Ishmael invariably give him this sense of inferiority and futility, thought Isaac. He never knew how to answer these rapier-like thrusts. He looked around, hoping his wife Rebekah was near. She had a quick wit and a ready tongue, and on Ishmael's previous visit, shortly before Abraham's death, had been his equal in the wordy dual.

"You have a fine son, Isaac," Ishmael told him.

Isaac's eyes lighted up.

"I have indeed," he said, and started to recount to Ishmael some of Esau's many successes on the hunting field.

"A fine fellow, brother, a fine fellow," said Ishmael, breaking into the discourse, "But how came you to beget such a lad? He is more like a son of mine than yours. Maybe I did not inherit all my wild ways and love of hunting from my Egyptian forbears. Perhaps the sons of Terah had more spirit than I thought."

Isaac answered his brother with some heat.

"Have you forgotten how my father led three hundred men against Chedorlaomer and his confederates, and utterly routed them, leading the charge himself? "

Ishmael inclined his head.

13

"In sooth, brother, I had almost forgotten. How wise of you to remind me! But you yourself are a man of peace, only eating of the venison and growing portly in your middle years."

Isaac was again filled with that impotent feeling Ishmael aroused in him. The worst of it was that there was an element of truth in it. Beside Ishmael's lean figure with no ounce of surplus flesh upon it, it was evident that Isaac had lived well and enjoyed the good things of life. He wished that Ishmael would cut his farewells short and cease his sarcastic comments. But there was more to come.

"You feel confident, dear brother, that Esau will follow in your father's footsteps, and will value . . . what was it called? . . . the promise our father spoke of? What does friend Eliezer think of him? Or is he too old to beat young Esau into shape, as he did me in my youth, much to my mother's wrath? Is Esau worthy to be the family priest as well as its leader?"

Isaac murmured a few non-committal comments about Esau being young yet, and wished Ishmael a long life and prosperity, with a fervent hope that their families would always be at peace.

"Long life," said Ishmael. "Ah, that is in the hands of the gods. Prosperity? Our father Abraham has graciously made that possible. But as for peace between the sons of Ishmael and the sons of Isaac, only the scribes of future history will be able to say whether our children's children will live at peace."

And with a low mocking bow Ishmael rode off, taking with him his twelve sons, his wives and his daughters, leaving with all the pomp and circumstance of an oriental king.

Isaac was left, following with his eyes the progress of his half-brother as he went. Yes, Abraham, in his wisdom, had made him prosperous. When the old man had realised that his end was near he had not left his estate for his son Isaac to dispense, but had called his many sons together, Ishmael, estranged from him for so long, together with the sons of Keturah, the concubine-wife of his old age, and had given each his portion. In a statesmanlike manner he had dealt in such a way that all felt was just. Ishmael cared nothing for the promise of his fathers, only for

14

material prosperity. Abraham, whom God had made rich, gave Ishmael great wealth and sent him away, far from Isaac, but not far enough to prevent his descendants, the Arabs, being at enmity with Isaac's descendants even to this day. The six sons of Keturah, Midian, Zimran and others, were given their portion and sent off to the east—sons of the east, or Saracens, as they came to be called.

Only Isaac was left. He was to rule the tribe, now numbering some thousands. He was to be the priest to hear the voice of God, and to interpret it to the people as Patriarch. He was to judge and dispense justice. Best of all, Abraham gave Isaac his blessing. It had been a solemn moment as he knelt in Abraham's presence. How conscious he had been that this was no empty ceremony! Three days and nights his father had fasted and prayed in his holy place before presuming to be the vehicle of God's blessing to his son. He could still hear his father's voice:

"May the God of our fathers lift up the light of His countenance upon thee, and give thee peace. May He make of thee a great nation. To thee and thy seed will God perform all His promises."

And much more that was stored in the annals of Isaac's memory.

Isaac pulled himself up. He was now the sheik. No more could he lean upon his father. He felt as if a mighty rock upon which he had leaned had been removed.

.   .   .   .

Rebekah was sitting at the door of her tent with Deborah, her old nurse, who was also her friend and confidante. Deborah was a privileged person. She could say things to her master and mistress no one else dare utter. She had helped to bring Rebekah into the world, and when the day came for Rebekah to leave her father, Bethuel, her mother and her brother, Laban, Deborah had been allowed to accompany her. She was by rank a slave, and as such could only marry if her mistress were so disposed. Soon after her own marriage, Rebekah had given Deborah to

Miram the shepherd, and having no children they loved Jacob and Esau as if they were their own sons.

There was a clatter and sound of the departing cavalcade as Ishmael and his family went their way.

"Let's hope that's the last we see of *them*," said Deborah in her downright manner.

Rebekah would have rebuked anyone else but Deborah for presuming to speak so of her husband's kinsmen. But Deborah was allowed a little latitude.

"All show and talk, throwing their weight about, calling themselves the sons of Abraham with every other breath—for fear all the servants here didn't know. One of those young princes was demanding more melons to quench his thirst, and Coniah the steward got impatient and said many older people were to be given their wine, and he would have to wait. And then his lordship sticks his nose in the air and says, 'A grandson of Abraham does not wait,' and Coniah . . ." and here Deborah rocked herself with laughing, ". . . Coniah forgot himself and said, 'No, but the grandson of Hagar, the Egyptian slave, does have to wait.' Young lord Mishema, or whatever his name is, stalked off in a rage to his father, and Coniah kept out of sight for some time."

Rebekah, pretending to be very shocked, changed the subject, saying that Coniah and the servants had prepared a feast of which none of them need be ashamed. Deborah agreed, and the two women saw again in their memory the feast of good things, the fatlings that had been killed and stewed, the savoury meats that had been prepared, the loaves made with oil, the cakes sweetened with honey and aromatic seeds. The fruit had been piled high—pomegranates, melons, grapes, figs, nuts and raisins in abundance. An especially large quantity of shekah had been prepared from fermented pomegranate juice, steeped in dates and barley and sweetened with honey. All had feasted well.

Rebekah and Deborah were tired, and sat happily while the old nurse passed judgment on all the guests and relations, and told Rebekah of various crises behind the scenes, of which she had not been aware.

Then Deborah shuffled comfortably on her cushions, murmuring, "All's well that ends well."

They sat in companionable silence.

"So after all these years our lord Isaac is the sheik," said Deborah. "Do you remember our first sight of him, walking in the fields at sunset?"

Rebekah nodded, her eyes soft.

"Mind, I admit I was in a real worry all the way on those camels, what he'd be like. It seemed a risk to go and marry a man you'd never seen. When I wasn't worried about the motion of the camels, rolling me around till my inside was in a turmoil, I was thinking, what if my nursling's come all this way to marry a man like Nebo the Syrian? And then we saw him, and that was enough," Deborah finished in satisfaction.

Yes, thought Rebekah, that was enough. She could still recall the thrill when, living in bondage to her mean over-bearing brother Laban, the messenger from Abraham had come. He had given her golden earrings and bracelets. When Laban had seen the golden bracelets he had welcomed the messenger, and miracle of miracles, she had been allowed to set off the very next day to be a bride for Isaac.

She too could remember seeing him walking in the fields. Although custom had demanded she should cover her face immediately, it was not before she had seen the tall figure, his handsome regal bearing and, above all, his kind eyes. If anyone had asked her what she appreciated most about Isaac, she would have said his kindness. After Laban's utter lack of consideration, his cruelty and almost sadistic behaviour, to belong to a man who treated her with reverence and love was overwhelming. She lived again that day of triumph when he had taken her round to the tribe, to be shown off as Sarah's worthy successor.

As years rolled on, she found herself loving Isaac, not only as a wife, but as a mother. He roused her maternal instincts, he turned to her for advice and comfort.

Abraham, her father-in-law, was a man amongst men. How she had respected and loved him! He had taught her so many things, and imparted to her so much of his wisdom. He comforted

her too when year after year she had no child. He told her of
the years of waiting that he and Sarah had endured, and how
in the end the promise was fulfilled in the birth of Isaac.
It was his suggestion that she and Isaac should fast and pray
and go to his holy place and entreat the Lord to give her a
child.

Deborah seemed to have arrived at the same place in reminis-
cence.

"Mind you," she said, using her favourite expression, "I
always say those love-apples I got had a lot to do with you
becoming pregnant."

Rebekah gave a low laugh.

"My dear Deborah, you talk like a superstitious old witch.
Just because Miram found some mandrakes and I ate them has
nothing to do with the end of my barrenness. It was entirely
due to our seeking the blessing of Abraham's God in his holy
place."

"Agreed," said Deborah, nodding sagely. "But doesn't the
great God use His creation to answer the cries of His people?
When men are thirsty, they pray to Him to give them drink, and
He sends down the rain from heaven. They don't find a goatskin
full of shekah. And He uses nature. Now my man Miram, he
knows secrets. He knew that if he could find a love-apple, or
mandrake as you call it, he could prepare it so that a barren
woman could become the mother of children."

Rebekah could remember the triumph of Deborah when sixteen years ago she had brought the orange-coloured berry from
the mandrake, that plant with fleshy roots that groans like a
human being when pulled out of the ground.

"I well know," said Deborah, "that many witches and
workers of iniquity use the mandrake, but to my mind your
prayer was answered by my man finding the mandrakes. But
that's neither here nor there. The twins are born, and what I
want to know is—when are they going to be *told?* "

Rebekah looked a little startled at Deborah's emphatic tone.

"Told? " she asked. "Told what? "

"My mistress, you know well enough. My lord Abraham is

18

dead, and my lord Isaac is his heir. Who comes next? When are the boys going to be *told*? You know well enough the vision you and your lord Isaac were vouchsafed. Abraham knew before they were conceived in the womb. It was the first time you had actually heard the voice of the Lord God of Abraham. I remember it as if it were yesterday. You sitting where you are, telling me word for word all about it. 'We knelt,' you said, 'in the holy place, and we prayed and we pleaded, and then the great God spoke to us, and said we were to be fruitful.' And then it was later that you got the real message, wasn't it?"

Deborah paused, while Rebekah waited.

"What a time you had! I've never seen a woman with child so treated by her unborn children. You were nearly torn to pieces by them. You thought you'd die. And the other midwives said they'd never seen anything like it either. Such turmoil and wrangling!"

"Yes, I remember," said Rebekah. "It was beyond bearing. And Isaac and I enquired of the Lord again.'

"Yes," said Deborah, with quiet emphasis. "And this time He spoke, and what did He say, mistress, tell me that—*what did He say?*"

"He said two nations were in my womb, two manner of people."

"And what else?" persisted Deborah.

"He said the elder would serve the younger."

Deborah let out a deep breath.

"That's what I'm getting at. That's what I mean. When are the boys going to be told?"

Rebekah stirred uneasily.

"It's very difficult, Deborah," she said. "You don't understand."

"Oh, yes, I do," murmured Deborah, while Rebekah went on.

"We both understood and confided in Abraham. We all realised that the younger was to be the heir. But when the boys were born and grew up, and you know how it is—Esau a strong and mighty hunter, a leader of men, and Isaac dotes upon him, and Jacob is quiet and studious, and as a child was not strong.

19

It seems obvious that one is equipped to lead and not the other one."

"But mistress," persisted Deborah, "what do you think yourself? Is Esau fit to follow Abraham? Can you see him going to the holy place to pray, to listen for the Voice? Could he be a priest of the people, as well as the leader? Does he care for the promise? Why did our lord Abraham spend hours teaching and inspiring and instructing Jacob? He knew the promise and, what's more, Esau wouldn't listen. I've seen those two boys sitting with their grandfather, Jacob listening with his whole soul, his eyes, his ears, everything, and Esau throwing pebbles at a passing bird, and wondering when his grandfather would cease his oration."

Rebekah broke out petulantly.

"Have done, Deborah, you know what I think! It is because I love Jacob so much that I am afraid that my love for him makes me want him to be first. He has depended upon me so much during his childish illnesses, and naturally I love him. While Esau has been independent, and so much more his father's boy."

"But you must remember the promise, my mistress," Deborah said, "even if it is presumptuous of me to remind you of it."

Deborah was still in a reminiscent mood.

"I'll never forget the day they were born. I thought the first child would never arrive. It was obvious there was something obstructing him—as if he were being held back. And you weren't like a supple young girl. You'd waited twenty years for a child. It was not easy. And then at last, out he came—a red hairy morsel. And almost on top of him came his brother, and would you believe it, he was grasping his brother's heel! Yes, that's the way he came. Little Jacob the wrestler, we called him. It was as if he were saying, 'Wait for me, brother, I want to be first.'"

"Yes, they were rightly named," said Rebekah. "Hairy and Wrestler—and so they have been ever since. Esau at fifteen is as hairy as a warrior. It is strange that the boys are so different and yet so alike. If you see them in the dusk, you can't tell them apart—the same outline and shape, the same walk. But in the daytime they're as different as light from dark—the one with red complexion and hairy skin and burly build, and the other slight with smooth skin. Esau cares nothing for study or for learning of ancient secrets, the stories of Enoch, Noah and Shem hold for him no interest. But Jacob cannot spend enough time hearing of the ancients and of the promises."

"But how long is it to go on?" said Deborah, who was nothing if not persistent. "You well know Jacob is eating his heart out with desire to be the heir to the promise. It's not greed with him for possessions, but all that his grandfather has told him has taken possession of his imagination."

Rebekah nodded. She remembered years ago finding Jacob, after a long talk with Abraham, sobbing his heart out alone on the hillside. All the child could say to her was, "Why couldn't you have borned me first?"

Deborah's words made Rebekah realise that she must remind Isaac of the promise, and of the injunction that the younger should inherit. But she did not relish the prospect. Isaac was an even-tempered man—she had rarely seen him even irritated—but there was a certain mulish streak in him that exasperated her. If he would only argue or shout or rage. But he just sat and said nothing, grunted, or made some irrelevant observation.

She loved him dearly, but even she realised that he would never be the man that his father had been. Abraham was not only a visionary, but a man of action. She had never realised, until today, that any finer qualities Ishmael had were inherited from Abraham, and those same qualities of spirit and leadership were to be seen in Esau. Abraham too was a man of dedication. Isaac loved his savoury meat, in fact, he was growing more stout than was healthy through over-indulgence. It was her own fault, she thought, she loved to see him happy, and she flattered herself that she could dress a kid in such a way that by her culinary art it was indistinguishable from venison, such as his soul loved. But Abraham was abstemious. He fasted as well as prayed, though he laid no restriction upon his family.

She must act soon. Before long Esau and Jacob would be of marriageable age. Esau's eyeing of the daughters of Ishmael had not escaped his mother's eagle eye. Wives of the highest of the tribe must be chosen, or they might even send to Haran or Nahor for some young woman of their own stock. But time enough for that. After all, the twins were only fifteen.

2

"You really are a fool, Esau," Jacob told his brother, looking at him with affectionate amusement.

"I know I am," said Esau lugubriously, "a big stupid fool. Why didn't I think?"

Jacob reflected wryly that that was the worst of Esau—he always agreed with you so heartily when rebuked. It had ever been the same—anyone in authority had always been completely disarmed by him. Many times in their youth even Eliezer, their grandfather's friend, had tried to take Esau to task about a number of faults—his unruly ways and disobedience. Esau agreed he was thoughtless, he had been wrong, how utterly unworthy he was of such wonderful parents, and would debase himself so much that even Eliezer had perforce just to send him away. At the time Eliezer had reflected how like, and yet how unlike Esau was to Ishmael. Many a time he had had occasion to rebuke his master's bastard son for almost the same faults, but Ishmael would flush, and with eyes flashing would defend himself and would argue, always implying that no one had the right, even the revered Eliezer, to take to task Abraham's heir. It was, of course, Ishmael's mother Hagar who had been at fault, Eliezer reflected. Esau had Rebekah for his mother, and that made all the difference.

How strange it was, thought Eliezer, that although little thought was given to women, many considering them merely as chattels, vessels to bear sons and to minister to their lord's passions, yet the moulding of the soul, the building of the character, were the responsibility of the mother, and a good mother made all the difference. One father could produce an Isaac and an Ishmael. True, in that case one mother was Egyptian and one a Semite, but even if a man married two sisters, he wondered whether their sons might not be widely differing. Then Eliezer had rebuked himself as an old philosopher, and dozed off to sleep.

"You'll have to help me, little brother," urged Esau.

"How can I help you?" said Jacob in exasperation, "and don't call me 'little brother'. I'm exactly as tall as you are, and we're both twenty years of age."

"But I have it on you by at least three minutes," Esau reminded him.

"As if I were likely to forget that," Jacob replied bitterly.

Realising that the subject was not a tactful one, Esau went on, "But you'll have to back me up with our father and think of something. Come on, Jacob, you have all the brains, even if I have the brawn."

Esau flexed his arm and admired the rippling muscles.

"You can stop admiring yourself, and think too. I am not lying to get you out of trouble. You were a fool to join that wild crowd and go to the camp of the Hittites. Our father Isaac told you he was dispensing justice, and that you were to be there as his eldest son to sit with him. All was set in state, and in desperation I was sent for, and I tried to sit there looking as far as possible like my brother Esau."

"I don't suppose they noticed," said Esau. "We're very alike from a distance."

"Yes, but my father wasn't deceived. You must agree we even smell different, and those animal arms of yours bristle like a porcupine of the desert."

Both brothers stood thinking for a while.

"I have it, Jacob, I have it! No one shall say you have all the ideas. We'll pretend I have been out hunting, and we'll say I went to get a special dish of savoury meat to please my father, and I went too far afield to get back in time for the Court of Justice."

"Very clever, very clever indeed, my large brother, but there is one difficulty—where is the venison?"

Esau's face fell.

"I see what you mean, Jacob. I'm not as clever as I thought. I should have realised that. Yes, venison; I wonder if anyone else went hunting, then I could buy the meat from them."

"Well you know that no one went hunting, Esau. Everyone is here on the day of dispensing justice. That's what makes you so conspicuous. Why did you have to be such a fool?"

Jacob was genuinely upset about his brother's dilemma.

As twins from one ovum they were naturally very close to each other. Deborah had always told them that there were two kinds of twins. She had called them joined twins and separate twins. Only a joined twin, she told them, could have clutched his brother's heel at birth. Although widely differing, they had a real affection for each other, but as the years went by their tastes and recreations separated them increasingly.

Esau tried to explain to his brother.

"You have never seen anything like her," he said. "Her name is Judith, the daughter of Beeri the Hittite. The girls here are as insipid as camel's milk beside a heady wine compared with the girls in the camp of the Hittites. I saw her performing one of their tribal dances, clad only in flowers."

Esau continued like one inspired, "The suppleness of her limbs, the way she swayed to the chanting—it was intoxicating."

Jacob spoke angrily to his brother.

"That was a heathen rite you witnessed, Esau. You fool, to allow yourself to see such things. Miram has told me of the shocking bestial rites they perform at the time of the full moon —things I would scorn to speak of, even to you."

Esau wore a mulish expression, which Rebekah would have instantly recognised as being inherited from Isaac.

"Well, all I can say is, it looked very pretty, all those girls swaying and moving around to the music. I liked it."

"I dare say you did, brother," said Jacob dryly, "but it's got you into a sad mess. If my mother knew you have been near the daughters of Heth . . . ."

24

"By our fathers, brother, she must never know. I can placate my father more easily than I can my mother. Promise me you won't say a word," Esau said urgently.

"Have I ever told of your doings, wild though they have been?" asked Jacob.

"No, no, I will say that, brother, you have been very loyal. But where can I get some venison?" he pleaded.

"There is just one thing . . . ." Jacob began.

"What is it?" asked Esau eagerly. He knew his brother Jacob would think of something—he was the clever one. "Come on, out with it, what is it?"

"Our mother can cook and dress a kid so that it tastes like venison."

"Why, yes, she can indeed," replied Esau. "But how can we persuade her to do so? She only does it on very special occasions. She wouldn't do it for me. She'll have heard already that I wasn't at the judgment, so her face will not be towards me. Jacob, you're her favourite, you persuade her—she'll do anything for you."

"It will take some doing. I would have to confide in her."

"Not about the daughters of Heth, you don't. Rather than that I'd face Isaac our father, and persuade him somehow."

"I could make her think that your memory had failed you," Jacob suggested.

"Yes, yes, do that, brother, an admirable scheme. And if I can ever do anything for you, I will."

"There is just one thing," said Jacob, with apparent nonchalance.

"Name it, brother, name it."

"If I asked our mother to prepare meat and arrange it so that our father is completely disarmed and his wrath averted, *will you sell me your birthright?*" Jacob brought out the last words with a rush.

Esau was taken aback.

"Sell you my birthright? For a paltry dish of meat? What a strange maggot you have in your brain, brother. How could you expect such a thing? Why, with the birthright go flocks and herds, the women, the power to dispense justice, the leadership of the tribe . . . .

"And the promise, the promise of the sacred line, the privilege of the priesthood, the coming of SHILOH?"

Esau gave a loud guffaw.

"Oh, that! You're welcome to all that, if it's any pleasure to you."

"The one is tied to the other, Esau, and well you know it. You can't really care. I would promise to give you all the wealth."

Esau seemed to hesitate, and then that mulish obstinacy became uppermost.

"No," he repeated. "No, what stupid ideas you do have! A man doesn't sell his birthright for a thing like this. Forget about it. I'll tell my father I forgot. I won't be beholden to you for your stupid ideas."

Jacob felt very bitter.

"Yes, you'll keep the birthright, and you'll go and witness heathen rites and probably take a wife, and care nothing for the promise, and beget a child and never teach him the sacred things of Abraham."

As Esau turned to go, Jacob flung after him, "It's a pity my father didn't worship Moloch."

"Worship Moloch? Why?" asked Esau.

"If he worshipped Moloch, like some of your friends down in the camp of the Hittites, he would have sacrificed his eldest son. When you were born you would have been offered as a human sacrifice, and flung into the fire and burnt. Then I would have had the birthright automatically."

Instead of angering Esau, this seemed to amuse him enormously, and he went away slapping his knee with amusement. Meanwhile Jacob was anything but amused. Why had he been such a fool as to mention the birthright? It was enough to queer his pitch for the future. He was increasing his flocks, he would sell them to passing merchants, he would acquire shekels and gold and the things that Esau would value, and then he would put it all in order and say, " Brother, this is yours if you will sell me your birthright."

.   .   .   .

Esau got away with it as usual. In the evening as the twins sat with their parents at sundown, eating from the large dish a meal of stewed kid and garlic, Isaac smiled indulgently at his first-born.

"Rebekah," he said, "what are we to do with this son of ours? On the very day of justice, when he should sit by my side, he forgets everything and wanders away over the hills, and arrives back when all is over."

Rebekah gave Esau a shrewd glance, which was not lost on either of the boys. They never quite knew how much she saw and guessed. But she merely replied that his brain seemed to be full of holes, and she hoped that when he found a wife she would think for him.

The meal continued happily. Isaac, whose very name meant ' Laughter', loved joviality, and after the strain of dispensing justice, was prepared to laugh with them over some of the lighter moments that had occurred during the day.

Then he spoke of some who had been guilty of harbouring false gods, and idols had been found in their tents. Jacob had given his brother a sly nudge, and muttered, "Hittites". Esau's mind worked slowly, and during the conversation he suddenly laughed and said, "Oh, father, what do you think—Jacob says he wishes you worshipped Moloch."

Isaac frowned.

"What wickedness is this, Jacob?" he said, turning to the younger son.

But Esau went on to explain, "He says that then you would have had to sacrifice me, and had me burnt alive, so that he'd have had the birthright automatically."

Rebekah looked in consternation at her sons. Isaac's brow had darkened.

"Did you wish such a thing on your brother, Jacob?" he asked. Jacob smiled broadly at his father.

"Does it sound likely that I would wish such a thing, father, when I spend my life keeping Esau out of trouble?"

Isaac looked from one to the other and then laughed—one of his famous belly laughs which resounded all over the camp.

"Me worship Moloch!" he rumbled. "Whatever next!"

3

"I TELL you, Miram, I knew just how it would be. I said from the beginning it was all a mistake."

Miram grunted.

"You always know—afterwards. Ever since I took you to my tent, at the gracious permission of our lady Rebekah, you always knew from the beginning, what it would be from the first. But you never tell me beforehand, do you? You never warn me about anything."

"It's just that I have an instinct. Some women have," his wife Deborah told him.

"You knew from the beginning that those wild beasts would get the lambs if I took them over toward the land of the Philistines, but did you tell me beforehand? No. You knew what I should have done, *afterwards*."

Deborah looked slightly affronted, but deeming attack better than defence, turned on her taciturn spouse and said, "And I told you to take the bodies of the sheep to our lord Isaac, and he would not hold you accountable. But you were too high-minded—you replaced them from your own flock. Yet you knew that the Law exonerates a shepherd who can produce two legs and one ear to prove that a wild beast attacked them."

"Deborah, I have told you—I am no hireling shepherd, I am a master shepherd. To me, to lose a sheep or a lamb is a disgrace of the first magnitude. What if a wild beast does destroy the lambs? Why should I, the shepherd, allow it to stray so far?

No, Deborah, the shepherd never asks pardon, he bears the loss himself. All this I teach our young master Jacob."

Deborah gave a sound of scorn, a mixture of snort and grunt.

"Jacob! What would he want being a shepherd? He'll be the sheik, the priest, the judge of the tribe one day."

Miram shook his head.

"But will he? Our lord Isaac professes to have forgotten the command, and, though Rebekah remembers, what can a woman do?"

They sat together until Miram broke the silence.

"Deborah, my wife, may I, at the risk of causing you again to talk in arrogance, ask you what it *was* that you knew from the beginning?"

Deborah sat up.

"Did I not tell you? Then it was your fault for talking about sheep and wild beasts and distracting me."

"Agreed, it was my fault, but nevertheless, you have my permission to proceed," Miram said graciously.

Deborah inhaled sharply, but allowed the liberty to pass.

"When members of the tribe of Abraham were allowed to go to the market where the Hittites, Jebusites and Canaanites mingle freely, I knew that only trouble would come."

"But Deborah, our master and mistress admitted that we need the merchandise, and we must exchange our flocks and herds for spices, for shekels, and for a variety of foods and wines, and dates that we cannot obtain ourselves. You would be the first to object if robbed of your spices. And if our lord Isaac were denied the herbs for flavouring his savoury meat . . . ."

"Agreed, we need the merchandise. But I said the merchants should come here into our camp, and not run the risk of our people mixing with the heathen, and picking up their habits and learning their ways, and buying their idols. How do you suppose those idols that Hyman was harbouring in his tent got there, if not from the market? How can we keep our people pure if all the time this fraternising goes on?"

Miram could not but agree.

"Did you see those idols?" Deborah continued. "They were

lewd, horrible leering figures of men and women, distorted and vile. That was a beginning, and now this . . . well, I knew. . . ."

"Deborah," said Miram firmly, "I forbid you to say it again this night."

. . . .

Rebekah, clothed in a pure white linen tunic, with a cloak of purple, wearing her golden ornaments, was seated on one of the Egyptian carved chairs which had been purchased from a merchant. When she had occasion to rebuke any member of the tribe, or to speak in judgment, it gave her a sense of authority to be seated in a chair such as Pharaoh himself might have used. The wrongdoers themselves sat on the sandy ground in front of her.

"So it is true," she said. "You have allowed your daughter Lola to be given in marriage to a member of the heathen tribe of the Hittites—a tribe who worship many gods, who perform human sacrifices, and whose licentious cults are obnoxious to any right-minded person."

The woman before her looked sullenly down without answering.

Rebekah went on, "What would you think if your grandson were made to pass through the fire? He might even be actually sacrificed and burnt."

Lola's mother mumbled, and was told by Rebekah to speak more clearly. The other women who had come with Saraph looked on in apprehension.

"He promised he would not expect her to adopt their ways. He said she need not worship Baal or Ashtaroth. He loved Lola, he told us. It isn't as if he had got Lola with child and abandoned her."

"No, indeed," said Rebekah, "your daughter would have short shrift then. The laws of the tribe would have known how to deal with *that*. She met him, I suppose," Rebekah went on, "when the merchants came?"

"Yes," admitted Saraph, "there are many of our maidens who are looked at with admiration by the men of the Hittites, and that is not all. . . ." She stopped suddenly, and looked round anxiously.

"Continue," commanded Rebekah.

Saraph went on with a rush, "Some of our young men cast their eyes on the daughters of Heth."

Rebekah could not understand why this caused a gasp to go round, and why there were embarrassed glances and meaning looks.

"All the more shame to them," she said firmly, and after a brief homily on the necessity of teaching their young people and children in the home, warning them of the dangers, she dismissed the company.

The women went away, and when out of earshot Saraph said defiantly, "If she knew who was the foremost amongst the young men to cast eyes upon the daughters of Heth, she wouldn't be so likely to sit in judgment upon my poor daughter."

"It's surprising someone does not tell her," said another.

But they knew that the tribe would stand together to shield Esau, who was like one of themselves.

.   .   .   .

In spite of prophecies of doom and degradation from Deborah, Isaac and Rebekah continued to allow members of their tribe to visit the merchants in the improvised market, and consort with men and women of other tribes, who gladly took the opportunity of purchasing luxuries and necessities that the traders brought up from Egypt and from Nineveh, Ur and Babylon. There were spices and perfumes, cunningly wrought metalwork, pottery and many images and idols, much in demand by the worshippers of Baal and Ashtaroth and other gods of the Canaanitish people.

The tribe of Abraham, or Hebrews as they were often called, took their herds and flocks to barter and to sell. Jacob, his flocks increasing yearly under the able guidance of Miram, was able to amass things he thought that Esau would value. He watched to see what his brother admired. He noticed his interest in silver neckbands, golden girdles and ornaments, and many of the sheep were exchanged from the merchants who specialised in Egyptian ornaments, necklaces of lapus lazuli, amulets of jasper, bracelets of cornelian and garnets. Jacob's friends jested as they saw his purchases, so that he tried to deal with the merchants privately.

Very soon now he would confront Esau with all that he had amassed. Jacob's whole soul was absorbed in the plan to obtain the birthright on which he had set his heart. Once the birthright was his, his father would be bound, not only by law, but by all that he held sacred, to give him the blessing—that ceremony which, according to the Nuzu Law, was the last will and testament of the sheik, utterly binding and irrevocable.

.   .   .   .

Esau, always with the leader of the young huntsmen, was a prominent figure at the market, laughing and bargaining with the merchants, admiring the young women, buying sweetmeats for the children. It was a gay scene. The merchants had erected booths, better to display their wares. Coniah, the steward, who had succeeded ancient Eliezer of Damascus, together with other servants, sought to spend their shekels wisely—obtaining goatskins of wine, vessels of oil for the lamps, to augment the limited supply the tribe produced themselves.

Coniah was concerned because the wise men had predicted another famine. If a drought came it would be serious for the crops. It was comparatively recently, since the death of Abraham, that the Philistines had stopped up the wells that the old patriarch had laboriously dug—a senseless action, benefiting no one. Coniah spoke with Manuel, who had grown up with the tribe, and served Abraham as one of his men of war, and had himself helped to dig the wells.

"Would to God our master Abraham was with us. The Philistines would think much before interfering with wells dug by a man who freed the king of Sodom from Chedorlaomer."

Coniah nodded. All the older men felt the same, that sense of loss and insecurity. Abraham, their leader, their father, was gone. But Coniah was a loyal servant.

"Maybe our lord Isaac will dig again the wells of his father," he said.

Manuel shook his head doubtfully.

"Our lord Isaac is not a man of action like his father," he said. "He is a man of peace, living quietly in his tent."

"And what of the future, friend Manuel?"

The two men glanced at the group led by Esau, who had eyes for no one but the daughters of Heth. These young women, with newly acquired kohl for making up their eyes, and jewellery from Egypt, were seeking to enchant and fascinate the young Semites. Manuel shook his head.

"What indeed!" he said. "Some say Jacob should be the rightful heir. They say it was foretold."

· · · · · · · · · · · ·

When Jacob returned from the market, he looked to see his brother, but although the other young huntsmen had returned, Esau was not with them. When questioned, they replied evasively. Perhaps the lord Esau was hunting or still at the market, they could not tell. Jacob shrugged his shoulders. He could guess where his brother was spending his time, and he feared for him.

· · · · · · · · · · · ·

Beeri the Hittite with his wife, Amah, had made great preparations. The tent where food was served was garnished with new hangings of goats' hair. An urn holding oil of spikenard, recently purchased from the merchants, was in a place of honour, together with a cedar-wood bench.

"It would be a better fate for Judith than to be the virgin of goddess Ashtaroth," Beeri remarked with apparent irrelevance.

His wife, following his train of thought, countered, "But difficult to bring about. The Hebrews regard us all as wicked heathen, with their talk of one God, Yahweh."

"Yes, indeed," said Beeri. "They gather their garments around them for fear a Hittite's shadow might fall upon them and defile them. Bah!" And he spat through the open tent door.

"Esau is not like that," Amah assured him.

"But Esau's mother, Rebekah, thinks it worse than death for one of their maidens to mate with one of our men, so what of Isaac's heir?"

"It is because he is the heir that we can benefit. Judith, with her beauty, cannot wed *any* mere Hebrew. Better to accept the honour of a priestess, the offerings of gold and silver and fruits of the fertile land—all would be ours if we give our daughter for Ashtaroth."

Beeri nodded, then looked out of the tent at the sound of voices.

"They come," he said. "Have you the shekah and the barley cakes?"

Esau approached, accompanied by several of the young men of the Hittite tribe, together with Judith, Beeri's daughter, and her friend Bashemeth. Elaborate greetings were exchanged, and all sat outside the tent, drinking the proffered shekah and discussing the day's marketing. Beeri brought the urn of spikenard to be admired.

"It was brought all the way from beyond the Sea of the Rising Sun," he told them.

"Tell me, Beeri," asked Bashemeth, "is it settled that Judith shall be Ashtaroth's virgin?"

Beeri looked uneasily at his wife.

"Not definitely decided yet," he said.

"But it is a great honour," persisted Bashemeth. "I had hoped to have been chosen for Anath or Astarte, but it seemed there were many more beautiful than I," and she tossed her head.

Esau looked from one to the other, his cup of shekah poised before his lips.

"What is this you say of Judith?" he asked. "Is there some honour to be bestowed upon her?"

There was a pause, then Amah spoke.

"At the time of the full moon we have a day called Shabbatum, when we worship our god, Baal, lord of the earth, god of fertility. There are many goddesses, chief of whom is Ashtaroth. Beautiful virgins are chosen to represent each goddess in the rites and ceremonies that follow."

34

"What are these rites? Tell me more of them," said Esau.

There were quick glances from one to the other, and by common consent Amah continued vaguely, "Dancing, chanting and er . . . other rites. Then the girls remain as priestesses to serve the priests, and to minister to them."

"Of course, it's wonderful for the family of a goddess virgin," said Bashemeth eagerly. "They receive many offerings of the land, and gold and silver, and they are rich then for ever." Bashemeth sighed with envy. "Just think," she said, "to be able to go to the market and purchase all you wish."

Esau slowly took it all in.

"But if Judith were one of these . . . what do you say . . . virgin goddesses, could she then marry afterwards and bear children?"

"No, she would be only for the priests."

Esau looked puzzled.

"Would you want that for your daughter?" he asked Beeri.

Beeri and Amah looked at each other.

"If Judith could marry a man of wealth," began Beeri, "an eldest son of a sheik, perhaps," continued Amah, "that would be different."

Esau nodded thoughtfully. "I think it sounds a horrible thing to happen to any girl."

"It is a great honour to be chosen," Amah told him sharply.

"Yes, indeed," said Bashemeth in discontent.

"But if a man who was wealthy, who was his father's heir, asked you for Judith, what then?"

"*If* he were his father's heir and had sufficient wealth, it might be worth considering."

Esau became thoughtful. What would his father and mother say about such a union? There was anger enough when some unimportant young maiden married a Hittite, but he was his father's heir, his firstborn. He remembered that with pride and relief.

He was suddenly brought down to earth by a question from one of the young Hittites, Nabhi, who had always resented Esau's interest in Judith.

"But you aren't your father's heir, are you, Esau? I've heard some story, some ancient prophecy that it had to be the younger brother who inherited."

Esau heartily protested.

"What foolish lie is this?" he said. "Some unfounded tale spread by an old crone of my mother's. It still persists. Ask my father who is heir—he will tell you. Can you imagine my studious, weak brother Jacob being the sheik?"

Beeri was obviously satisfied, though Nabhi sat with darkened brow. Rather would he see Judith dancing as Ashtaroth than mated with this arrogant Hebrew.

.   .   , ...

Had Jacob chosen some other time, had he waited until the memory of Beeri's words were not so vivid in Esau's mind, the course of Jacob's whole life might have been altered. But he was ignorant of what had passed in the tents of the Hittites, and the very day after the visit to the market he prepared to buy Esau's birthright. He was anxious to seize the opportunity as the news of the coming drought was serious. Isaac talked of journeying down to Egypt. It was important, therefore, that he should be established as firstborn before his father took the long and hazardous journey.

The stage was set. The merchandise was displayed, the best of his lambs, the pick of his yearlings were assembled. Jacob, having made all the preparations necessary, went to seek for his brother. Esau, realising that something important was afoot, came with him immediately.

"What is it, brother? Is something wrong? Have my parents found out . . . anything?"

"Have no fear, Esau. I want to show you something."

Esau was led to the display, which looked like the merchants' booths in miniature. He exclaimed with surprise, eagerly fingering the jewellery, in his mind placing it round Judith's neck and waist, and putting the golden earrings in her dainty ears.

"Have you become a merchant as well as a shepherd, brother?" he jested.

Jacob paused, to let each of the carefully selected goods weigh fully with his brother, pointing out any particular beauty which had escaped his eye.

At last he spoke. " All this is for you, Esau."

" For me? " asked Esau in surprise. " For me, as a gift, brother? "

" All for you, *in exchange for your birthright.*"

Esau looked at Jacob in incredulous amazement. Then he threw back his head and laughed.

" Oh, brother, your mind revolves on one thing only. I would not sell my birthright for anything you could offer me. Why if I were not the heir, then I could never hope to . . ."

" You could never hope to—what? " Jacob asked.

" Oh, never mind. But cease your foolish strivings. I am the elder, I have the birthright and I will not sell it for gold or silver."

Jacob's bitter disappointment was difficult to bear. He had lived and worked for this day. His desire for the birthright had become an obsession with him. It was with him waking, sleeping and eating, and as he watched the sheep on the hillside under the open heaven.

With bitterness in his spirit, Jacob stowed away the baubles, in which he had no interest, and sought comfort in visiting the tent of ancient Eliezer of Damascus, the old steward of Abraham, who, though weak and emaciated in body, was still active in mind. It was always a surprise to Jacob to find that little escaped the old man's notice and knowledge.

" I have always been an observer, my son, and as such I can see things dispassionately," the old man told him. " But you are sad today, disappointed and bitter. Tell an old man what grieves you."

It all came out, the whole story. The desire for the birthright was not new to Eliezer, only Jacob's latest method of trying to obtain it. At last the old man lay back on his cushions.

" Oh, my son, have patience," he said. " The blessing is to be yours. My lord Abraham knew. The great God has planned it so. Can you not wait His time? "

" But how can I? My father does not recognise the promise. He thinks only of Esau as his heir. It is for me to plan and to scheme, to obtain what everyone else thinks is his by right of birth. Only a few like you and Deborah and Miram think otherwise."

"Jacob, my boy, you believe in the great and all powerful God?"

"I do indeed," said Jacob fervently.

"Then can you not leave it in His hands? Listen, my lord Abraham was promised an heir, it was foretold that his children should be as the stars in the sky and the sands in the sea. His faith was sorely tried, and after all hope was gone, Sarah gave Hagar to Abraham to raise up a son. What misery and sorrow it caused—jealousy, misunderstanding, and who knows in years to come Ishmael's sons may well war and fight with the sons of your father. But in the end God honoured his promise. Will you not be patient? Will you always be an impatient wrestler? May God grant that you may never be worthy of that other meaning of your name—thief and supplanter."

Jacob shuffled uneasily. He must act. It would be no good facing his father with his claims, though Eliezer often told him that would be the right course to follow.

"Eliezer," said Jacob urgently, "will you speak to my father, will you remind him of the promise? He has always listened to you."

Eliezer raised his hand in assent.

"I will, my son Jacob, if only the Patriarch will honour an old man by visiting his tent, for I am too weak to seek audience with him."

With that Jacob had to be satisfied, and changed the subject, saying, "Tell me of the ancients, like my grandfather was wont to do. It makes the promise clearer, when in the market place and with the other men the vision grows dim."

Then Eliezer talked of God's call to Noah.

"The wickedness of the world was great," he said, "and their corruption made them stink in the nostrils of God, who destroyed the world and preserved Noah. You and your father are descended from his son Shem, of whom was born Abraham. Noah cursed his son Ham, of whom the Canaanites are born. Keep

38

yourself from them and from their evil, Jacob. It would be well if your brother Esau did the same."

"Yes, indeed!" burst out Jacob. "What if my brother gets himself a son by a Hittite woman? Will he be heir to the promise?"

"Gently, my boy, you are angry again. We were looking back. Then your grandfather was called out of Ur. His father, Terah, was a maker of idols, which exceedingly angered your grandfather, Abraham, that a Semite should minister to the heathen in their worship. But God called Abraham and promised to make of him a great nation. The God of Glory appeared to Abraham." Eliezer's voice took on a new note of wonder.

Jacob listened, full of interest.

"If God should speak to me," he said, "I would count myself of all men most blessed. If I could meet him face to face, I would say 'Bless me, and give me a blessing'."

"The promise is still made," went on Eliezer. "One day from the loins of one of the descendants of Abraham will come the glory of SHILOH."

"What exactly is the glory of SHILOH?" asked Jacob. "Tell me more of it, Father Eliezer."

"The glory of SHILOH," said Eliezer, lying back on his cushions. "The glory of SHILOH? Jacob, my son, I see the glory of SHILOH now."

He lay back, strangely still. Jacob rushed to his side, and saw on the old man's face an expression of ecstasy and joy, but the eyes that had gazed on SHILOH would never look upon anyone else on earth.

4

ALL plans concerning the departure for Egypt were temporarily in abeyance until the funeral and mourning for Eliezer were accomplished. For Eliezer of Damascus was no mere servant, though he had been purchased as a slave at the market-place in Ur of the Chaldees years ago by Abraham.

Isaac could hardly believe that Eliezer too had left him. There had been something timeless about him. Certain events in the life of an individual are as milestones in experience. The passing of Eliezer was such a milestone to Isaac. He went out again to meditate at eventide, as he had been accustomed to do.

Then it happened.

It was Isaac's first experience. Abraham would have known the signs well. First there was an unearthly stillness, followed by an upsurge of breeze. Isaac found himself trembling. He was in the presence of something far greater than he had ever experienced before. He knew without being told that he was in the presence of the great God, and was about to hear His Voice. Instinctively he put the sandals from off his feet.

Then the Voice spoke.

Isaac was not sure whether he heard it with his ears, or whether it was some inner consciousness, but the Voice spoke clearly and unmistakably.

"Go not down into Egypt. Dwell in the land which I shall tell thee of. Sojourn in this land, and I will be with thee, and I will bless thee. For unto thee and unto thy seed I will give all these countries, and I will perform the oath which I sware unto Abraham thy father; and I will make thy seed to multiply as the stars of heaven, and I will give unto thy seed all these countries; and in thy seed shall all the nations of the earth be blessed; because that Abraham obeyed my voice, and kept my charge, my commandments, my statutes, and my laws."

Isaac stood for some time after the Voice had ceased, and strengthened and full of purpose he went to find Rebekah. She was in the midst of preparations. Deborah was scolding the young slaves for carelessness. They all stopped as Isaac approached and bowed, as became members of the tribe to the Patriarch.

"All is in readiness, my lord," said Coniah. "The camels are watered, the fast dromedaries loaded to advance . . ."

"Enough," Isaac stopped him. "We do not go to Egypt." Surprise on every face caused him to continue. With pride and humility mingling, Isaac spoke to the assembled company. "I have heard the Voice of God, of the great God. He has spoken even to me. We do not go into Egypt. God has other plans for us." Then he turned to his faithful servant. "Coniah," he said, "can you dig?"

"Can I do what, my lord?" asked Coniah.

"Can you dig? What of you, Manuel? We are going into Gerar, land of the Philistines, to dig again the wells of my father Abraham, to wrest from them the wells they have covered, and to find springs of water."

There was immediate rejoicing.

"You'd think it was his own father speaking," said Manuel later to Coniah. "He seems a changed man."

"Yes, indeed," said Coniah, "he takes his place as leader. The men of war will rally if the Patriarch leads."

.   .   .   .

While Isaac was journeying and prospering, the tribe, under the able stewardship of Coniah, moved camp constantly in search of pastureland during the time of famine. Isaac, renewed in youth, health and vigour, travelled from settlement to settlement, dispensing justice as the Patriarch, making sacrifice in the holy places as priest.

It was a busy time for Jacob. Neither he nor Esau had travelled to Gerar with their father. Miram, with his gift of water-divining, was needed for well-digging, and Jacob was now as able as his old instructor to care for the flocks and herds.

Eliezer's death had not only been a milestone in the life of Isaac, but in that of Jacob. The young man had set great hopes on Eliezer's promise to speak with Isaac concerning his position. But Eliezer was dead, his tongue was still and his influence gone, and now who knew of that promise except his mother, old Deborah and Miram? As far as he could tell, the incident was expunged from his father's memory, as though it had never been. Eliezer had exhorted him to patience, faith and trust. "The hearts of all men are in the hands of the Lord," he had told him, but Jacob now determined that anything he was to get in life must be by his own efforts, yes, and by his own guile, cunning and trickery, if need be. He had tried straightforward dealing, without any success. Esau had scorned what had represented years of labour.

Jacob sat on the hillside in the eventide, surveying the parched ground and famine-stricken land, always thinking and scheming. He almost hated Esau, and kept out of his way. The laughing, pleasant face of his brother, which he had once loved, had become an offence to him. He had only ever envied him one thing. As a boy, he had gloried in Esau's strength, and had never wanted to be like him or grudged him any of the praise or even the love his father lavished on him. But year after year envy and jealousy of his right as eldest son was eating into his vitals like a canker. He dreamed wild dreams in his tent at night. . . . Esau was drowning, the water had risen at flood-tide and he was exhausted, crying for help, and he, Jacob, could reach him with the branch of a tree. "Swear to me, if I save you, Esau, that you will give me your birthright," he asked. "Swear to me, Esau, SWEAR, SWEAR. . . ." Jacob woke with a start to find Esau standing over him.

"What ails you, brother? Your voice is heard as far away as the hills, shouting, 'Swear!' What oath would you have me swear?"

Jacob, bemused with the vividness of his dream, gazed stupidly at his brother, and muttered something about a vision in the night. Esau laughed and told him to sleep again, the sleep of one whose conscience was clear, and left him. Esau had nothing but affection for Jacob. He had no cause to envy him. Jacob had always helped him out of trouble. Esau had not been asleep, but had been lying awake thinking of Judith. Maybe, thought Esau, as he went his way back to his own tent, maybe Jacob could think of a way whereby he could marry Judith without displeasing his parents, though he knew they would never give permission. It was unheard of for the eldest son of a Patriarch to marry without his father's consent; indeed, it was surprising that his parents had not chosen a wife for him already. If this should be so, he would have no right to disobey. Their sojourn in Gerar was timely, for at least it was giving him respite. Esau, the eternal optimist, was convinced that something would come about to further his plan.

Jacob slept fitfully again, and in his waking moments day-dreamed of other predicaments in which Esau would find himself —dying of thirst in the desert, being attacked by wild beasts when only Jacob's timely intervention could save him. But these were mere dreams. If only someone were wise enough to show him the way. Eliezer, who would have said to him: 'Enquire of the Lord, the Fount of Wisdom' was dead.

. . . .

A few days later Esau woke early. He had slept the sleep of a man who has little imagination, and neither broods on the past nor fears for the future. He was, in fact, a magnificent animal, with a keen enjoyment of life, material things and the pleasures of the flesh. He was not physically self-indulgent, his father's love of food was not his besetting sin, but he was a man of the earth. The Hereafter, the great God, the Promise, even the desire to propagate his own image and bear sons and found a name for posterity, were a closed book to Esau. He was upright and straightforward, kind in his dealings with the servants, friendly with his fellows. But whereas his brother Jacob was all soul and lived in the unseen world, Esau was a 'profane person', or one to whom any god, be it the God of Abraham or the gods of the Canaanites, meant nothing. He had neither the superstitious fears of the heathen, of curse, evil eyes and tabus, nor fear of his father's God.

It was a magnificent day. In the early morning it was cool, and though by midday the brassy heaven would burn cruelly, the early breeze tempted him to go and hunt, not only for the pleasure of the chase, but for food that was so sorely needed. With his bow and arrow, his dagger and water-bottle, he set off. He would at least be successful in finding some smaller game, and build a fire and eat, rather than overload himself with pro-visions. A mighty hunter such as he would find his own provender.

But his way was not prosperous. Farther and farther he went; more and more barren grew the land. He drank sparingly from his water-bottle. As the sun rose to its height, he sought to find some rock or bush under which to shelter from the blistering heat. The sweat ran down his bearded face, his hairy limbs heavy with sweat felt like lead. Hunger gnawed at his vitals. He searched for some berries or some fruit of the earth to stave off the pangs, but everything was sandy and dry. On he went, led by mirage after mirage; he saw pools of water shimmering in the heat, and that meant animals coming to drink. Then when he topped the hillside the pools had disappeared—they had been only illusions of the vibrating heat of the land.

At last he realised that he had travelled too far to return that night. The sun mercifully hid its face below the horizon, and the cool air was comforting to his glowing body. But nothing satisfied the raging hunger of the hunter. He lay down under a bush of scrub and dreamed of savoury meat, but it only made waking to reality all the harder to bear.

When morning came he rose early, realising that it was mad-ness to try to travel farther. The water in his bottle was nearly spent. He decided to retrace his footsteps and go home empty-handed. He made reasonably good progress in the early morning, though his knee-joints seemed unloosed, and he trembled all over from weakness.

When the midday sun was at its height, Esau was forced to lie down and let the cruel rays beat upon him as he lay in a hollow which provided no shade. I am dying, he thought, I will never live to take Judith the Hittite to wife. I am to be cut off in my prime. But the rest gave him strength, and a sip of the precious water refreshed him. He slowly made his way towards the tents of Isaac. Far away on the skyline he could see them. He was so far spent that he could only see them as through a haze. Each step was like that of an old man. Nearer and nearer came the line of tents. He could see the flocks and then, most

44

wonderful of all—could it be a mirage of smell as well as sight? —an aroma of savoury soup assailed his nostrils. He saw his brother Jacob performing a womanly occupation, sitting over a large pot, in which must be some savoury stew or pottage. He gathered up his failing strength, and with all his will-power he made himself put one foot in front of the other. If he could only get near enough to call, Jacob would bring him food, or he would die within sight of his home.

.　.　.　.　.　.　.　.　.　.　.　.

The shortage of food was really acute. If it grew any worse, Coniah told Jacob, they would all have to go to Gerar and join Isaac in the valley. True, Isaac was sending supplies to them, but they were very scant to feed so many. It was a big decision to make. They had planted vineyards, and the olive crop had bid fair to be really luxuriant before the famine came. It would be unwise to go away if the famine were not to last. The wine-presses were all there, the large stone containers in which the unripe olive berries were placed that the oil might be beaten from them were built, and to strike camp completely meant considerable loss. But it might be necessary to send many of the younger families to join the Patriarch, for messengers had brought news that Isaac was digging another well there.

.　.　.　.　.　.　.　.　.　.　.　.

Jacob often loved to watch his mother preparing savoury meat, and became proficient himself in culinary art. A shepherd may often be away for many days, and has to be able to stew a kid and to make bread and cakes in the glowing embers of a fire. Jacob realised it was no savoury meat he would cook tonight. He had scarcely tasted meat for two moons past. But he would try to cook a mess of red pottage, as his mother had taught him. Jacob was hungry, as everyone was in this time of famine. He stirred the savoury pottage with a bleached stick. It was beginning to look very appetising—red and luscious, and the smell of the herbs with which he had seasoned it hastened the anticipation of the meal.

Then he heard a faint call—the sound of a cry for help. It was getting dusk and he could hardly see. Straining his eyes he looked, and the spurting flame of the fire lit for a moment a staggering figure, lurching, almost falling in its attempt to reach him. Jacob looked again. It could not be true. Was it Esau, empty-handed, spent and falling from exhaustion?

"Is that you, Esau?" he called.

A feeble voice, quite unlike Esau's usual deep tone replied, hoarse with hunger and feeble with fatigue, "Brother Jacob, feed me, I pray you, with some of that red pottage, for I am faint and ready to die."

Jacob suddenly felt as if a clarion call were sounding in his brain.

This was his opportunity.

The chance might never come again. Esau was desperate, he was dying. It was now, or perhaps it might be never.

"Esau," he said, "if I give you of my pottage, will you sell me your birthright?"

This time Esau never even hesitated.

"I am at the point of death," he said. "What profit is the birthright to me? Come, feed me." And he lay back helpless, in hunger and weakness.

Jacob looked round. He must have witnesses. He called to Coniah and several of the servants to hear the words of Esau. They gathered round, amazed at what they saw.

"Swear to me, Esau," said Jacob, "swear by the God of our fathers that you will give me this day your birthright."

Esau raised himself up on his elbow and said, "I swear by the God of Abraham that I give this day my birthright to my brother Jacob."

Jacob breathed a sigh of pure satisfaction.

"Lift him near to the pot," he said, and he sent for wine, that Esau might refresh himself, and bread that he might eat with the red pottage.

Esau ate greedily and drank long draughts of the spiced wine. Soon life returned to his limbs, and strength to his sinews. He felt a new man. Coniah and the servants watched to see what would happen next. Would he turn on his brother in anger for his trickery? Jacob too was anxious. Esau's next reaction could change everything. His brother would be well within his rights to repudiate the oath and say with witnesses that it had been extorted under duress.

But Esau grew jovial, and laughed and jested with Jacob, called him the future Patriarch, and said he himself was well rid of the burden. He ate, he drank, and rose up and went his way, despising the birthright. His thoughts were not on the promises and birthright, but his mind was filled with only one thing. He was consumed with passion for Judith the Hittite. He had thought as he lay dying in the desert that he would never hold her in his arms and possess her in all her glory, but now he was not the heir he could marry as he chose. What matter if he begat sons of a heathen woman? Jacob's was the responsibility to carry on the line. It was Abraham, Isaac and Jacob now, and he wished him joy of it. For himself he was well rid of the restrictions and superstitions of the God of Abraham.

He went without delay to speak with Beeri the Hittite before the news of the sale of the birthright had time to spread through the camp, and into the dwellings of the sons and daughters of Heth.

5

I S A A C watched his servants pitching the tents and preparing for a prolonged stay.

"I feel this place has a very pleasant aspect, Rebekah," he told his wife. "This place shall be our dwelling. The lines are fallen unto us in pleasant places. Maybe we will be able to dig a well, and water our cattle and herds, and send for our sons and kinsmen to remain here with us."

Rebekah nodded, well pleased.

"Your name will go down among your children's children as Isaac the well-digger," she told him.

Isaac walked away to the hilltop above to view the setting sun. These days in Gerar had been good days. He felt well and strong. God had prospered him, and he had not only re-opened the wells of his father, but he had dug many new wells of his own and found springs of water. Tomorrow Miram, who among his other gifts possessed that of water-divining, should take his precious hazel twig and see if there was water here in this place, and if it was so, then he would remain in this pleasant countryside and enjoy the prosperity that had been given him.

.   .   .   .

The next morning Miram was again to use his powers as a diviner and seek for water. The old man was full of importance. Deborah had given him a clean linen tunic to wear, and though she would have died rather than let him know, she was bursting with pride that the God of wisdom had given to *her* husband the power to find water.

Some of the younger lads had never seen a diviner at work, and obtained permission to watch him from the hillside. To the older men, who had watched before, the search still had an un-failing fascination. Miram, looking spruce in his white tunic with cloak of woven goats' hair, clasped the hazel twig in his fingers. He had allowed the boys to look at it first. It was just a twig, such as they would use to make a catapult—a Y-shaped piece of hazel, and with the two arms of the Y lying in his palms and the single twig sticking out before him, Miram, led by the elders of the tribe, started his methodical search. Up and down he walked without a movement from the hazel twig. An hour passed and then another hour, and the boys on the hillside became bored.

"When is something going to happen?" they asked each other.

Then Miram stood still, watching the hazel intently. The elders too watched him enquiringly, but without speaking. They looked at the hazel twig and it was quivering. But Miram shook his head.

48

"It only quivers," he said. "There is water a long way down, but not enough to dig a well."

He started again, slowly traversing each bit of ground, missing not a portion of it, always feeling and watching the hazel.

When the boys on the hillside had almost fallen asleep for weariness, they heard Miram shout, "Here, this is the place! Look at the twig!"

The boys rushed down the hillside, almost knocking each other over in their excitement to see the hazel. There in Miram's hand they saw the hazel twig, which had been pointing straight before, but was now pointing directly down to earth, quivering and shaking in Miram's grasp, as though held down by a powerful magnet.

"Try to straighten the hazel," he said to one of the boys, and the lad had tried with all his strength to force it back into its old shape. "No power on earth can do that," Miram told him, "but see," and as he moved away from that same place the hazel slowly went back to its original form. "This is where we must dig," said Miram, "and we will find much water."

The well was dug, and Isaac called it Shebah, and the city was called Beersheba even unto this day.

.   .   .   .

It was with great anticipation that Isaac and Rebekah awaited the coming of the tribe with Esau and Jacob. They had often talked of who should be chosen to be their wives. There were many fine young women of the tribe, but no one seemed worthy.

Isaac said at last to his wife, "We look too high. Where could we hope to find a Sarah or a Rebekah?"

Then his wife told him of her great desire to send to Padan-aram to find wives for her sons from her own family, so that it would not be a servant or daughter of a slave, but a descendant of Nahor, Abraham's brother, who would one day take her place. Parents can dream and plan, but there was a rude awakening awaiting Isaac and Rebekah.

.   .   .   .

Isaac was a mild-tempered man. Rebekah had rarely seen him

even ruffled or angry, but the night that Esau arrived with his Hittite wives would long stand out in her memory. Esau himself was certainly apprehensive. For him all had gone according to plan. After he had sold his birthright he went to Beeri the Hittite, who had readily given his daughter to Esau. The tokens had been exchanged, and several flocks of sheep had been driven over to Esau's father-in-law. Esau had taken Judith to his tent, and after some months had taken another wife, Bashemeth, daughter of Elon the Hittite, who had spent much time in his wife's company. Judith showed no jealousy in his taking a second wife; indeed, it was at her instigation. She found life among the Hebrew women insupportable. They were unfriendly and, instead of treating her with the honour and respect that she had expected, she heard herself called 'the Canaanitish woman' or 'the heathen'. She would have had more position, she reflected, had she become a priestess of Ashtaroth. What was worst of all was that she had discovered, after dwelling among the tribe for some time, that no one considered Esau to be his father's heir. There was some absurd story about Esau having sold his birthright to his younger brother for a mess of pottage. She had visualised much pomp and ceremony as she was welcomed as wife of the future Patriarch, but she felt alone and unwanted. It was therefore a comfort to her to have Bashemeth, who could never rival her in beauty, but who could share with many of the Hittite ideas, which were a closed book to these Hebrews.

Esau found that the daughters of Heth were not docile women, like his mother and her people. Judith would sulk and rage and ask him how he dared to deceive her, and why was she not given due honour? In vain he pleaded with her to wait. When he could present her to the sheik, his father, things would be different, he told her. She still raged and was so temperamental that Esau had perforce to beat some sense into her, and found it was the only way she understood. She became docile and loving, and gloried in his strength.

He had promised that his parents would welcome his wives, but he felt this was a forlorn hope. He discussed the problem with Jacob. There was no ill-feeling between them now. It was strange, thought Jacob, that Esau never held it against him that he had tricked him of his birthright. Rather he seemed to admire his cunning, and feel relieved of the burden.

"My parents must first be told of the sale of the birthright," he said, "then the way will be prepared for me to present Judith and Bashemeth."

"Esau, you fool!" Jacob told him. "It is not only because of the birthright that my parents will have a grief, but for any Hebrew to marry a Hittite is to them a forbidden thing."

"I know, brother, I know well the difficulty, but they will soon see things my way. My father loves me not merely because I am his eldest son, but for my own sake. But go before me, tell them of the birthright, and I will come later."

More than dubious, Jacob agreed. It was true, his parents must be told about his changed position. It was very important that his father should fully understand. He would take Coniah the steward with him to bear this out.

.   .   .   .

Isaac and Rebekah were waiting outside their tent at Beersheba.

"Can you see him coming?" Isaac kept asking. "Has my son Esau arrived?"

Rebekah too was looking. It was a long time since she had clasped Jacob in her arms, and her love for him was greater than ever. She loved Esau too and longed to see him.

"He comes at last," said Isaac, as Jacob and a small group approached. Then a sigh of disappointment escaped him when he saw that it was only Jacob. "Greetings, my son," said Isaac, and he bid Jacob rise from his knees to greet his mother with a kiss. "But where is thy brother?"

"He comes," said Jacob, "but he bade me come first with tidings of considerable importance." Isaac kept looking up the road from whence Jacob had come, hopefully, with longing, for his beloved firstborn. "My father," began Jacob, "hear my words, for they mean much to us all," and then he went on, speaking in measured tones. "Before my brother and I were born, I have been told by many, especially by Eliezer of Damascus, that the Lord God promised that the younger of thy sons should be the child of promise, and the elder should serve the younger. Is this not so?"

Isaac frowned and shifted about in his seat.

"That old story," he said, "I had well-nigh forgotten it. It is some tale that Deborah often repeats. We have not regarded it. Esau, my firstborn, is more fit to lead the tribe than you, Jacob, and well you know it."

"My father, Esau cares nothing for the promise. He cares nothing for the God of his fathers. He cares only for the things of the present—to hunt, and to enjoy the fruits of the earth. Esau cares so little for his birthright, my father, that he sold it to me for a mess of pottage, and has sworn it before witnesses. Coniah, your steward, is here to bear out my words."

Isaac looked from one to the other.

"What madness is this?" he said. "Some tale about a mess of pottage. Esau jested with you, my son. He was ever one for boyish pranks. I will not listen. Esau is my firstborn, who will follow in my steps. I will find him a wife of the daughters of Nahor to raise up seed, to fulfil the promise of the God of Abraham, Isaac and Esau."

Jacob looked with compassion at his father, and then he told him, "Esau has already taken to him two wives, Judith, the daughter of Beeri the Hittite, and Bashemeth, the daughter of Elon."

There was a deathly silence, broken only by a gasp from Rebekah. "Our son has married one of the daughters of Heth, the heathen worshippers of idols?" she asked. "How can we hold up our heads among our people? Well that he had sold his birthright first."

At that Isaac spoke, his voice hoarse with anger. "How dared he do such a thing? My firstborn to marry an idolatrous woman!"

Jacob tried to explain. "For years Esau has yearned to take Judith to wife. His passion for her has well-nigh consumed him, but it was not until he had sold the birthright that he went and took her to his tent."

But this did little to placate the angry father. In a manner quite unlike the placid Isaac, he raged and spoke aloud his hopes and disappointments. He refused to see his son and his wives when they arrived.

He became quiet at last, realising that he must accept the situation. He laid his hand on Jacob's shoulder.

"You have purchased the birthright, my son," he said, "though it was strangely done. But had Esau valued it, he would have died rather than sell it for a mess of pottage. It would seem that he sold it not only for that, but for a heathen woman. In you will the promise be fulfilled. We must find you a wife who will be worthy."

.   .   .   .

Although Isaac ignored the existence of Esau's wives, it was not easy for Rebekah to do so. She was aware of the curious glances of Saraph and the other wives whose sons and daughters had strayed into the camp of the Hittites. They remembered her proud words and stern denunciation. Yet here, to her daily shame, were the heathen wives of her firstborn son. She tried to bear it as best she could, and determined that Judith and Bashemeth should be treated no differently from the other women. Without compunction, she sent Judith back to her tent with instructions to clothe herself decently when she found she was parading herself, scantily clad, swaying her hips voluptuously, earrings jangling, wearing anklets and bracelets in profusion.

She heard much that grieved her. It was said that Judith and Bashemeth had idols in their tents—lewd figurines that were horrible to look upon, and some told tales of dancing at the time of full moon in a grove that they had made, and how that Esau's two wives had been watched by the sons and daughters of the tribe as they had sported themselves almost naked, dancing suggestive measures, and behaving in such a way that could only be told in whispers in the secret of the tents. How could she rule the tribe as wife of the Patriarch with such an example always before them? It made her rebukes just idle words, and lowered the sheik and his wife before them all.

6

TIME heals not only wounds, but family misunderstandings.
Isaac was unable to be estranged from his much-loved son for
long. A few days after their arrival, in the cool of the evening
when Isaac was alone, Esau presented himself before his father
with downcast face and great humility. Isaac could not contain
his great joy at seeing him, and embraced him tenderly. Esau
endured the parental rebuke, but after that came constantly to
be with his father, mother and brother, though he never presumed to bring his wives near the Patriarch. To their great anger,
they were treated more like concubines than wives, and had
neither place nor position.

As the years went by, Jacob often wondered if the fact that
he had purchased the birthright had penetrated his father's mind.
Isaac sometimes fondly called Esau his 'firstborn', but that might
have been force of habit. Jacob discussed the matter with his
mother, to whom he told all his thoughts.

"Your father is failing rapidly," she told Jacob. "His eyes
fail, and the world is growing dim to him, and I often wonder
if his memory is affected too."

"But does he remember that I am the child of promise, the
one to whom he must one day give his blessing?" Jacob asked
urgently.

"I cannot tell," said Rebekah. "Memory is a strange thing—
it can forget those things it would not wish to remember, and
pleasant happy things come to the forefront of the mind. It is
perhaps God's kindness to us that it is this way. But never fear,"
she went on, "before the Patriarch blesses he will do as his
father did and go and pray in the holy place and fast for at least
three days."

Jacob was comforted. He had been so happy since he knew
that he was the child of promise. He went sometimes to the
holy place himself, but God had never spoken to him yet.

Rebekah was worried about Isaac, and Deborah noticed it.

"You can't fool me, my mistress," said the old nurse, "You're worried—that's what you are. And little wonder with these daughters of Heth disporting themselves as large as life, *if* not larger. You should have seen Judith yesterday. I was ashamed for the young men of the tribe to see such a display. They do say that she and Bashemeth went off to the feast of the god Dagon, down there in the valley where the Philistines are encamped. The lord Esau knew how to deal with them when he heard about it. He knows the only way to subdue the heathen women," said Deborah with some satisfaction.

Rebekah knitted her brows in distress, while Deborah continued, "Didn't I say it was all a mistake letting our people go to the market?" she asked smugly, and went on, "but Jacob got his birthright. Really clever he was. And they do say Esau never even hesitated. 'Take the birthright,' he said, 'You're welcome.' That just goes to show he wasn't fit to have had it."

Rebekah sat and listened. Deborah was like a babbling brook—nothing would stop her once she started. "It's to be hoped that our lord Isaac realises that the birthright has been sold. Sometimes I think he forgets. I see him just laughing in his old way with Esau, as though nothing had happened."

"It pleases me to see him happy," said Rebekah. "Sometimes his health seems so poor. How do you think he prospers?"

"He is not the man he was," said Deborah with emphasis, "that's easy to see. Why, when he was digging the wells he was like a man half his age. But since he heard about the wives of Esau he's gone down the hill steadily. A man gets it into his head that he's growing old. I know how it is with Miram. Why, only yesterday he was talking about where he wanted to be buried. I told him that would not be my worry, that I would be called to my fathers long before he was. But these men, they only have to have a pain in their vital parts and they're planning their own funeral rites. Mind you," she went on, "I think our lord Isaac is just as bad. He was saying to Miram only yesterday that it was fifteen years since his brother Ishmael had died, and that he was that same age now—as if he thought the sons of Abraham could only live a like number of years."

"He seems to fail and his strength greatly decreases. He rarely goes even to the holy place now," Rebekah said sadly.

Deborah thought Rebekah had been depressed enough. "My lord Isaac will do well," she said easily. "There's one thing about him," she chuckled, "there's nothing wrong with his appetite—he enjoys his food like a lad, especially Esau's venison."

Rebekah took heart at Deborah's words. If Isaac were really ill, he would be unable to eat. It was his dim sight that made him seem so old. He could recognise her outline, but was often unable to tell whether Jacob or Esau approached, until he could feel their skin. Though this was not surprising, she reflected. In the dim light she herself could hardly tell them apart.

"It's time you sent to Haran to get a wife for Jacob," said Deborah, changing the subject.

Rebekah sighed. "Yes, true, but whom could I send? There was only one Eliezer of Damascus. Whom could I trust? And if I send Jacob himself he might never return. Even Abraham would not consider sending Isaac to find a bride for himself."

"It's quite time you had your children's children around you —pure-bred children, pure Semites, not half-bred heathen idolaters," concluded Deborah in her downright manner.

.   .   .   .

Isaac lived in a world of shadows. It was strange only to see vague shapes and outlines. He had difficulty in getting about unless he was led by someone. He found himself happy just sitting meditating, remembering happier days, thinking of his beautiful mother Sarah, and of his father Abraham. There was not much left for an old man but his memories, and he was an old man. Ishmael was just my age when he died, he reflected. True, his father had lived longer, and Terah, his grandfather, had lived longer still, and as for his forbears, Shem, Noah and Methuselah, their longevity was a byword. Men did not live to such great ages now. There was one pleasure not denied to him, thank God—he had a good digestion and an enjoyment of the meats of the table. As he sat, he longed for a dish of savoury meat, the venison his son Esau obtained from his hunting. It was a long time since Esau had brought his father any venison. He did not see so much of him now. It was those heathen wives of his that kept him away. But Esau was his son—his eldest son. The old man dozed and thought, and suddenly Esau stood before him. Isaac had only two thoughts in his mind as he was aroused from his doze. One was a strong desire for a dish of savoury meat, and the other was that this was his eldest son. Was there not something one did for an elder son? Yes, he remembered, his father Abraham had reached the time when he was soon to be called to his fathers, and had given him a blessing. It had been a solemn moment. He must do that for Esau. He pulled himself together. He would compose himself for this patriarchal exercise.

"Esau, my son," he said, "I am old. I do not know the day of my death. I crave a dish of the savoury meat, such as my soul loveth. Take thy quiver and bow and go out into the field, and see if the Lord will prosper you. Bring it to me that I might eat." The old man paused and added, almost by way of parenthesis, "then I will bless thee before I die."

Esau could hardly believe his ears. He would gladly get his father some venison; he had felt guilty that he had not done so before, knowing his father's love of it, but Isaac had said he would bless *him*—he, who had sold his birthright, and had further forfeited a place in his father's good opinion by marrying idolatrous women. If this blessing could be his, Judith would cease her complaints, it would reinstate him as head of the tribe, and with the blessing came great prosperity, riches and power. It was a thing to be coveted. It did come into his mind that his father's failing memory was possibly responsible, so it would be well not to delay, and to gain the blessing in secrecy, not demanding the public ceremony that had been accorded to his father by Abraham.

.   .   .   .

Those who live in tents cannot expect their secrets to be unheard. Rebekah was filled with anger and wrath when she heard the words of Isaac. He had asked Esau to bring venison, and said he would bless him. Where were the traditions of his fathers, to perform so solemn a ceremony as the Blessing, without fasting, prayer and preparation, but merely after the animal gratification of a meal? Moreover, he had forgotten that Esau was no longer entitled to it. She narrowly restrained herself from going to her spouse and pouring out her wrath to him. But no, she must use cunning, just as Jacob had used guile to gain the birthright. She must think quickly now. She did not feel that it was deliberate on Isaac's part, purposely favouring his favourite son, it was just that he had forgotten. If she went and reminded him, he would agree, but he might forget again, and next time she might not be so conveniently placed behind the tent to hear the conversation.

She sent quickly for Jacob, and told him what had taken place. His horror was equal to her own, and he too wished to confront his father face to face with his claim. His mother restrained him and explained the danger.

"This only proves," she said, "that we can never trust either of them. Esau is much at fault to try to take this blessing, but Isaac forgets, and he could forget again. We must make a plan." She held her head in her hands. An idea was coming which would take skill, cunning and speed. "I have it," she said at last, speaking rapidly. "You know that I can dress a kid so that even Isaac cannot tell it from venison? I have a supply of the herbs put by. Go to the flock, and fetch two good kids of the goats, young and tender, and I will prepare the savoury meat, and he shall bless *thee*."

Jacob was aghast at such a plan. "But, my mother, Esau is a hairy man. My father would know at once that I had deceived him. He always feels our skins to find out which of us is which. He would know that I had deceived him, and it is a curse that I might get, instead of a blessing."

Rebekah would hear no objections. "I will think further as I work."

While Jacob fetched the kids, Rebekah remembered with joy that she had a goodly raiment actually belonging to Esau that she had not allowed him to take to the tent of his wives. They were sluts, those women of his, and knew nothing of how to care for fine material. They perfumed themselves rather than washing, and Esau's clothes were a shame to him. This garment actually smelt of the fields.

The kids were soon being prepared, and Jacob watched, fascinated, as his mother prepared the skin of the goats to fit over his hands, chest and arms—anywhere where the questing fingers of the old man might touch to find out his identity. Jacob was shaking with fear and apprehension. The masquerade seemed terrible to him, such a travesty after what he had expected. He had looked forward to receiving the blessing as an outstanding day in his life. He still remembered, when only a lad, seeing Abraham bless his father. It was one of the factors in making him desire to be in the line of promise, and in the day that he was to receive the blessing it was to be by trickery and deceit. His heart failed him.

"Mother, I cannot do it," he said. "Let me go to my father and ask him to bless me now, tell him who I am and proclaim my right."

But Rebekah would have none of it. "This is our chance," she said. "You seized at the opportunity of buying the birthright, and now we must be brave and seize the opportunity of obtaining the blessing. Come, my wrestler, nothing comes easily to you."

The dish was prepared, appetising and savoury, with bread to dip into the rich broth, and wine to refresh the old man as he ate. All this Jacob carried on a lordly dish, with beating heart into his father's tent. His father smelt the savoury aroma and saw before him a shadowy form. He could not believe that Esau had returned so soon.

"Here I am, my father," said Jacob, trying to imitate Esau's lower gruff voice.

"Who is that?" asked Isaac incredulously.

"Esau, thy firstborn," said Jacob. "Sit and eat, I pray thee, of the venison, that thou mayest bless me."

Isaac asked, "How is it that thou hast found it so soon?"

Jacob, ashamed of himself, but realising that the deceit must go on, said, "The Lord God brought it to me."

Isaac shifted uneasily. He was not convinced.

"Come near, my son," he said, "that I may feel thee, whether thou be my very son Esau," and trembling with fear, Jacob drew near, and his father felt his arms, his hands and his chest. Even the smell of his clothes was there, and his outline against the light was certainly that of Esau. Still a little puzzled, Isaac put out his hands again, and said, "It is the voice of Jacob, but the hands are those of Esau."

Then the smell of the savoury meat, hot and fragrant, rose to his nostrils, and put all doubts out of his mind. Only Esau could hunt for venison and prepare it like this. He ate ravenously, throwing the bones of the kid away from him as he sucked them dry of the tender meat. Then Jacob brought wine—heady spiced wine, that he might drink and feel mellow and unsuspicious.

His father seemed to spend an age over his eating, although in actual fact the time was comparatively short. Jacob dreaded the arrival of Esau before the promised blessing was his. Once the blessing had been given he cared nothing. It was irrevocable and binding. Isaac sat back, replete. Jacob removed the dish from him. Isaac felt at peace with all the world, and full of love for his son.

"Come near unto me, my son, and kiss me." Jacob came. Isaac was further reassured by the smell of Esau's garment. "The smell of my son is as the smell of the field that the Lord hath blessed. Kneel now," he said, "and receive my blessing."

Jacob knelt, and as he listened to his father's words, he forgot the deception, he forgot everything except the words he heard for these were not spoken in the voice of a feeble old man. As Isaac spoke, the spirit of the Lord came upon him, and, in spite of his self-indulgence, in spite of the unworthy way in which Jacob had obtained the blessing, it was obvious that this was the blessing of God Almighty for the child of promise.

"Therefore God give thee of the dew of heaven, and the fatness of the earth, and plenty of corn and wine; Let the people serve thee, and nations bow down to thee: be lord over thy brethren, and let thy mother's sons bow down to thee; cursed be everyone that curseth thee, and blessed be he that blesseth thee."

Jacob stayed on his knees for a few moments after Isaac had finished speaking. He was carried away with the glory of the words. Isaac had surprised himself. He had known that the spirit of the great God had come upon him; the words that he had spoken were not his. He had been inspired by an unseen force. He sat back, spent and yet uplifted. A strong desire came upon him to go again to the holy place.

How long he sat meditating, with that sense of communing with the Unseen, he did not know, but as he awakened from his dream, it was as though a scene were being enacted again before him. A tall young man stood there, bearing a dish of savoury meat.

"Who art thou?" asked Isaac, in a tone of amazement. Could he have dreamt all that had gone before?

"I am Esau, thy firstborn. Eat of the venison," he said, "and bless me."

Isaac trembled exceedingly. "Who was he that hath brought me venison, and whom I have already blessed?" he asked. But well he knew who it was. "I have blessed him," he said, and added with emphasis, "Yes, and he shall be blessed." They had been no empty words he had uttered, and Isaac knew it.

Esau gave an exceeding bitter cry. He took the dish of savoury meat and threw it out of the tent, and came and knelt before his father.

"Bless me, oh bless me also, my father. Hath thou not a blessing for me too?"

Isaac was silent. He was to blame. He had so recently been in touch with the Infinite that he knew Jacob was the child of promise, though he had blinded his eyes to it all those years. He should have remembered not only the sale of the birthright, but the promise before the conception that the blessing was Jacob's by right.

Esau's words of denunciation of Jacob fell on deaf ears. Isaac said no word against the son whom he had blessed. Esau raged, "Is he not rightly named Jacob, thief and supplanter? Has he not supplanted me these two times, tricked me of the birthright and stolen my blessing?"

Esau waited for Isaac to rise in wrath and send for Jacob to denounce him, but they both knew that the blessing was Jacob's. Isaac was ashamed that a dish of savoury meat had blinded his eyes, and Esau cursed the day when he had despised his birthright, and sold it for a mess of red pottage. He ceased to argue and vilify, continuing only to plead.

"Hast thou not reserved a blessing for me?" he asked at last. Isaac said sadly,

"Behold, I have made him thy lord, and all his brethren have I given to him for servants; and with corn and wine have I sustained him: and what shall I do now unto thee, my son?"

Esau continued to plead with his father. "Hast thou but one blessing, my father? Bless even me also, my father." And Esau, usually so stolid and unmoved, lifted up his voice and wept. He knelt before his father, and Isaac put his hand upon his head and said,

"Behold, thy dwelling shall be the fatness of the earth, and of the dew of heaven from above; and by thy sword shalt thou live, and shalt serve thy brother; and it shall come to pass when thou shalt have the dominion, that thou shalt break his yoke from off thy neck."

It was not much of a blessing compared with the one given to Jacob, but with it Esau had to be content. He was to serve his brother. He had never realised the possibility until now. He had subconsciously thought that some day, somehow, his father would revoke the cunning sale of the birthright, which, though it gave him his wives, had robbed him of his position. He cared nothing for the promise, but to be subservient to his brother, to lose face with his wives and the tribe was most bitter. For the first time in his life, Esau hated Jacob and breathed murderous words against him. He went to the tents of his wives to lick his wounds in privacy.

Rebekah had anxiously awaited the outcome of the incident, and was prepared for a scene and to do battle on Jacob's behalf. She cared nothing now that the blessing was assured to him. She would speak bravely with Isaac to his face, telling him what she thought of his ineptitude and lack of reverence for tradition. But no one could be more surprised than she, going to find her husband, to find Isaac sitting peacefully outside his tent.

"Rebekah," he said, "I have spoken the words of the Lord God this day. I have blessed Jacob, yea, and he shall be blessed. The Lord God gave me the words to speak. The promise is for him, and from his seed shall come the Deliverer."

Rebekah was silent with astonishment. After some time Isaac put out his hand on to hers.

"Lead me by my hand, Rebekah, my wife," he said, "I would go up to the holy place tonight."

.   .   .   .

If there was one thing that angered Esau even more than the theft of the blessing, it was the fact that for the first time Isaac treated Jacob as his heir, and gave him both place and honour. It was Jacob who sat beside his father at the dispensing of justice; indeed, it was Jacob, with the help of Coniah, who made the decisions, Isaac often being unable to understand the issue. Not one word of blame or reproof had been spoken to Jacob, in spite of his dastardly action and deceit. Isaac smiled upon him, and gave him respect and place. Esau raged and threatened, incited by his wives, with a crowd of his cronies to bear witness to his angry ravings.

"Yes," he shouted, "let that thief and supplanter watch out. My father is not long for this world, and when he is gathered to his fathers, and the days of his mourning are over, I will kill Jacob with my own hands, as I would a small animal. I will break him in pieces, and let us see whether Jacob the supplanter will be any match for the strength of Esau."

His wives applauded, and urged him not even to wait so long. And the young men agreed that no one could match the strength of great Esau, the hunter. These words were passed from mouth to mouth throughout the camp, and Deborah sought her mistress.

"Esau is threatening to kill Jacob," she told her. "Just as I thought." Rebekah looked up. "Shouting his head off for all the tribe to hear," Deborah went on. "'When the days of mourning for my father are over,' he says, 'I'll kill that brother of mine rather than serve him'. And those wives of his are urging him on."

Rebekah was filled with foreboding.

"Mind, I doubt whether he would carry out his threat," Deborah continued. "No, Esau's no Ishmael. It's just his rage and humiliation before his friends. But you never know what might happen with those women to urge him on."

"But this is indeed terrible," said Rebekah, "I would lose both my sons in one day, for if Esau killed Jacob, the law would demand his life, and who could stay the hand of the avenger? I must send Jacob away."

"But what reason can you give?" asked Deborah. "The heir cannot go away without the Patriarch's permission, and you must have a good reason to send him away. Isaac smiles upon him now. He cannot just be banished."

Rebekah was not listening. She had acquired the art, through long practice, of allowing Deborah to talk without having to hear. At last she spoke.

"I have it," she said. "I will send him away to my brother, Laban. I will tell Isaac that he must seek a wife. I will make him realise the urgency. Nothing must be said of Esau's threats. It must not seem that the next Patriarch flies in terror from his brother's threats."

For Rebekah to make a decision was to act. Jacob was told of the plan.

"Esau's anger will not last long," his mother told him. "Even as a child Esau could never hold a grudge. But go to my brother,

Laban. Stay until the month of Kharsidi, and then I will send for you when your brother's anger has cooled. Seek a wife as Eliezer sought for me."

Jacob allowed himself to be persuaded. After all, it was only for a short time. Esau's threats were making life most unpleasant, and it was time that he took a wife—someone like his mother, and not like Judith the Hittite.

Parched corn was prepared for the journey. It was sustaining, and took up very little room in the traveller's pouch. Jacob also took with him some of the jewellery he had bought from the merchants. His mother had told him the story of how Eliezer had given her bracelets. He would do no less.

Rebekah still had to make Isaac agree. Her husband might be old and blind, but he was still the Patriarch and had absolute power over his sons and the members of the tribe. She came and sat beside him and sighed deeply.

"What makes my Rebekah sigh?" asked her husband.

"Oh, I am weary," she said, "weary of the behaviour of those daughters of Heth. Why should I be plagued with such women? They are quarrelsome, dirty and lazy. It is difficult to put them to any work. If I put them to help in the olive groves, they leave all the impurities in the oil and are too lazy to decant it carefully. They are too idle to weave goats' hair, and as for their idolatrous ways, they are past bearing. If Jacob takes a wife of the daughters of Heth, I might as well die here and now, for my life will not be worth living."

"My poor Rebekah," said Isaac, in a comforting voice. "You have had a bad day. But what can we do? Where can we find a wife worthy? It is certainly time that Jacob was begetting sons."

"Where, indeed?" asked Rebekah. She was not going to suggest anything definite; the idea must come from Isaac, but she could put it into his head. "If we could send someone to my brother Laban," she said tentatively, "he may have daughters, and you remember how many sons Milcah bore to Abraham's brother, Nahor. There must be many descendants of Terah that would be of our own blood. But whom could we send?" asked Rebekah again. "Only a man can choose a wife for himself."

"I was fortunate," said Isaac. "There was only one Eliezer, and there was only one Rebekah." Then he continued, "Would it grieve you, my wife, if we sent Jacob himself to Padan-aram, that he might see and choose a wife suitable to follow you? Would you feel deprived of him and yearn for his presence?"

Rebekah allowed herself to consider. At last she said, "My lord Isaac, your wisdom is profound. You have indeed received inspiration from above. Jacob shall go to my brother, and not many moons hence will return. Speak to thy son Jacob, my lord, and send him on his way."

Well pleased with her work, Rebekah withdrew. It is always well, she thought, to let the husband be the one to have the plan. Had it been my idea, he might have opposed it.

Jacob was sent for by his father.

"The Patriarch would give an audience to my lord Jacob," the servant told him, so he knew that it was more than a family conference that inspired the order.

Isaac was standing.

"Kneel before me, my son," he said, "and listen well.

"Thou shalt not take a wife of the daughters of Canaan. Arise, and go to Padan-aram, to the house of Bethuel, thy mother's father, and take thee a wife from thence of the daughters of Laban thy mother's brother. And God Almighty bless thee, and make thee fruitful, and multiply thee, that thou mayest be a multitude of people; and give thee the blessing of Abraham, to thee, and to thy seed with thee; that thou mayest inherit the land wherein thou art a stranger, which God gave unto Abraham."

Jacob went his way. Rebekah watched him go, unshed tears in her eyes. They would be shed only when she was alone in her tent. When would she see Jacob again? Why was it that there seemed to be some streak of fratricide in the family since the day Cain had killed his brother Abel? Ishmael had tried to kill Isaac, and now Esau was threatening to be the murderer of his own twin.

66

"God of our fathers watch over him," she murmured, "and bring him safely back."

Rebekah imagined that Isaac's decease was at hand, and that Jacob, as the next Patriarch, would return with a wife, and she would watch his children grow up. She did not know that she would be in her grave long before Jacob's return, and Isaac, who gave an old man's dying blessing, would still be alive.

.   .   .   .

It is well that the future is hidden from us. Rebekah sat down to wait for Jacob, happy to see Esau's anger subsiding just as she had thought it would. He seemed anxious to regain his parents' favour, and often sat and talked with his mother as Jacob had done. He was like a boy in some ways. He had quite forgotten his anger against Jacob, and often said to his mother, "It will be a great day when Jacob returns. We will go out to meet him, and make merry with him and his bride." Then he was silent. "Mother," he asked, "if I had sought a bride of our kinsmen, would you and my father have smiled upon me?"

"Indeed we would," said Rebekah, "but you have brought into the camp heathen Canaanitish women."

Esau nodded. He did not need his mother to tell him what a mistake that had been. He rued the day when he had been for a wife into the tents of the Hittites.

"I cannot seem to please my father," he said. "Even my savoury meat does not now seem to gain me his favour. Maybe if I could seek a wife, some kinsman of ours, and bring her home like Jacob, I too might be in favour like he is."

Rebekah smiled. He was so like a child, wanting approval, yet without understanding how greatly he had erred.

"You have made your bed, and you must lie on it," she told him, "but see if you can keep those women of yours from teaching the ways of Ashtaroth to our young women."

Esau lumbered off.

It was a few days later that Esau, with beaming smile and great pride, made his way to Rebekah's tent.

"My mother," he said, "smile upon me and approve. I have

taken a new wife, one from our own kinsmen, closer even than the daughters of Laban."

Rebekah waited anxiously. What had Esau done?

"I went to the tents of our uncle Ishmael, and asked for his daughter, Mahalath. She was only a child when I first saw her, and I have taken her to my tent. May I bring her to see you and my father?"

Rebekah wrung her hands, appalled at what he had done.

"Esau, oh Esau! Brain of a flea! To bring here a daughter of Ishmael, who hates your father and tried to murder him, and has always been at enmity with him. How can you expect your father to be pleased and rejoice to have a daughter of *Ishmael* in his tents?"

Esau's face fell like that of a child wrongfully reproved.

"What has my uncle Ishmael done? I thought he was a very fine fellow when I saw him at my grandfather's funeral. He spoke with me kindly."

Rebekah rubbed her brow with her hand in weariness.

"See that your father is not plagued by seeing her," she said. "I must tell him gently when a suitable time arises. At least she's not a heathen, but remember that she is the daughter and granddaughter of Egyptian women, and see that she brings no further false gods into the camp. The Egyptians have more than two thousand deities, I am told."

Esau shambled off, despondent. He had hoped that he would come into favour, and it seemed he had done the wrong thing again. How was it that he always made a mess of things? He shrugged his shoulders. Never mind, Mahalath was beautiful, she was waiting for him in his tent, and who cared anyway?

Rebekah laughed a rueful laugh. Her firstborn was indeed a fool. To think to find favour by bringing a daughter of Ishmael and the Egyptian wife his mother had chosen for him into the camp, the daughter of Isaac's bastard brother. May Jehovah grant that Jacob may choose more wisely, and soon come home to gladden my eyes, she prayed.

7

T H E short eastern twilight was over, and darkness fell like a sudden blanket. There was no moon in the sky, and the stars gave little light to the weary traveller as he journeyed through the eerie darkness. The hoot of an owl, the bark of a jackal, and constant murmurs of the crickets were the only sounds that broke the heavy stillness. Jacob was conscious of weariness of body and deep depression of mind. He had felt uplifted, as he set off with his father's blessing, but he shared with his mother the pain of parting.

As the night grew darker, so darker grew the inner recesses of his mind. A thousand doubts and fears assailed him. He had never known such heaviness before. He was well accustomed to being alone—it was part of a shepherd's lot—but this loneliness was something of the soul. It was as though all he believed and held dear was slipping from him. He must not give way to it.

He stumbled on a loose stone, and decided that some refreshment of body might lift the blackness of his mind. He sat on a long boulder, and drew from one of the capacious pockets in his cloak some bread baked freshly that morning. He munched silently, and looked at the stars above. Little wild creatures, lizards and cockroaches, scuttled at his feet as he was wrapped in meditation. In the wilderness a man can see himself as he really is, thought Jacob. What he saw gave him no pleasure. Whereas he had deemed himself a fine fellow, crafty and clever, gaining his ends by his own will and determination, now under the open heaven he saw himself rather as something mean and grasping. Eliezer had said, " Wait God's time, and the blessing will be yours." But he had not been content to wait. He had thought himself master of his own fate, and reckoned that only *he* could work God's will in a contrary world. He had determined to have the blessing, he had determined to be the child of promise, and had stooped to trickery and fraud to gain his ends.

Then a thousand horrible doubts crowded into his mind. What

if there were no blessing? What if there were no promise, and what if. . . . ? He looked up, and as he thought, his whole body broke into a sweat. What if there were no God? Might He not be a figment of his imagination? What if he had been chasing a shadow? But he encouraged himself as he remembered Abraham and Eliezer. They had spoken with such conviction, and the God of glory had appeared to Abraham. Yes, there was no doubt about it—there must be a great God above all, the Almighty Jehovah.

But then greater doubts assailed him. There must be a God, can He have any use for such as I am? Have I not forfeited my right to His favour, been presumptuous and grasping? If only I could hear His Voice, yet the heavens have been closed to me when I have visited the holy place. How happy would be the man who had heard God's Voice, and knew himself to be the object of the promise!

Jacob tortured himself with his thoughts. In his loneliness he reminded himself that he was not a fugitive, he had not been banished from his father's presence; he had been sent away with his full approval and blessing to find a wife, to beget sons of promise. If I but knew that God was with me, he groaned to himself, I would strive and search to find a wife worthy, and then to beget a son fit to be the progenitor of the Deliverer, to be the vessel through whom SHILOH will come.

Exhausted with his self-castigation, doubts and fears, he fell asleep, using the stone which had been his resting place as a pillow.

Suddenly the desert place was brilliantly lit, and a blinding light shone in Jacob's eyes. Before him was a ladder, stretching from the desert around beside him, right into heaven itself. Heavenly beings were ascending and descending as though they had some business on earth, and were returning for further orders, and others as though they were messengers to carry out a heavenly behest.

Then Jacob, the wrestler, heard for the first time the Voice that had spoken to Abraham and Isaac. Jacob heard,

"I am the Lord God of Abraham thy father, and the God of Isaac: the land whereon thou liest, to thee will I give it, and to thy seed. And thy seed shall be as the dust of the earth, and thou shalt spread abroad to the west, and to the east, and to the north, and to the south. And in thee and in thy seed shall all the families of the earth be blessed."

Jacob listened exultantly. There it was! That was the promise, the promise of SHILOH. Then the Voice of God continued with words of quiet love and understanding:

"And behold, I am with thee, and will keep thee in all places whither thou goest, and will bring thee again into this land, for I will not leave thee, until I have done that which I have spoken to thee of."

The very words told Jacob many things. It was as though God knew and understood. It was almost as though God had said, 'Jacob have I loved', as though the Lord knew him through and through for what he was, but valued above everything his faith and desire for the promise. 'Whithersoever thou goest', Jacob told himself in ecstasy.

Then came the awakening. The vision had gone, the chill of the night made him shudder, and Jacob rubbed his eyes, still dazed. It was then that the fear that had not touched him during the vision came upon him.

"The Lord is in this place," he said, "and I knew it not. How awful is this place!"

But the fear he felt was not the craven fear of one who cowers and flees, but the fear of one who reverences and worships.

"I must build an altar unto the Lord," he said, "for this will be my holy place."

He took the stone which had been his pillow and set it up on end, for it was long in shape, and made a pillar. He had no beast to sacrifice, but poured some of his precious oil upon it, and named the place, not Luz, as formerly, but Bethel, House of God.

God had spoken to him, and now he would dare to speak to God, and swear a solemn oath.

"Seeing God has promised to be with me," he vowed, "and help me, and give me bread and raiment, and bring me again to my father's house, so will I serve Him, and of all that He gives me, I will surely give a tenth to Him."

Jacob remembered that Abraham had given tithes of all that he possessed to Melchizedek the priest, and God had confirmed to him that Abraham's God was his God, and he would learn and seek to follow in the ways of his great ancestor.

8

RACHEL sat for a moment's rest on a small crag, to ease the pain of her aching back. She wondered if anyone felt as weary as she did. The care of so large a flock of sheep was exhausting. Many said it was a man's job, but her father, Laban, would not listen to such talk. A man required wages, but a daughter worked for nothing. Any suggestion that the work was heavy was dismissed without consideration. Rebekah, his sister, had been a genius with sheep, he told her. She cared for the flocks, milked the goats, and he rued the day when he had let her go to marry her cousin Isaac.

Rachel's health was poor, and she was not strong like Leah, who cared for the household and worked from dawn till dusk overseeing the work in the vineyards, making butter and cheese, baking bread, roasting and stewing, weaving and performing a thousand household tasks. But they seemed as nothing to her. Laban was proud of such a strong daughter, and said she had equal strength to a man.

Rachel changed her position for greater ease. Maybe if her mother had not died at her birth it might have been different, she thought. But no one had patience with all the many small ailments and weaknesses that Rachel tried to bear without complaint. If her father had taken another wife and had sons, *they* could have cared for the sheep and lightened her load. She put her hand to her brow. The sun was making her head ache, but she must take the sheep to be watered.

She loved animals, and if it had not been such hard work, she would have chosen to look after sheep. If only there were not so many of them and so much disease. They needed care, and some of the ointments and balms the merchants sold. But Laban would spend no shekels on what he considered unnecessary. She had to manage as best she could with the little help of old Cobah, the shepherd, who was long past his work and little better than useless.

. . . .

Leah was making cheese. The sour milk had been beaten and poured into a goatskin, while she moved it rhythmically to and fro until it should become solid, and could be placed in the wooden bowls to set in a cool place away from the glare of the sun.

Laban, her father, was not a dweller in tents, though many of their serving people camped round about the spacious house, fine as anything to be found in the city of Haran. The work was hard, but Leah was strong. Often as she laboured on day by day she wondered—would she live and die a virgin in her father's house? She was a woman, with a woman's instincts, and could not stifle the feeling of desire that came to her to fulfil her womanhood, to go to a man and bear his children.

But she knew her father for what he was. True, she was his favourite daughter; he did not look at the pink-lidded eyes which marred her beauty, but saw only the strength of her arms and her fine physique. He knew that no other woman could work as she did—keep his house, rule his servants, and make him so comfortable, with no wages but the food she ate, and the cloth she herself could spin and weave.

" I was made to bear sons," she told herself, and felt her broad hips, realising that child-bearing would be easy and natural to her. But how could such a thing come about? A miracle had happened for her aunt Rebekah, who had worked like a slave, they said, as little Rachel did now with the sheep, until the day when, with a blaze of glory, she set off covered with gold earrings and bracelets and riding on a lordly camel, to be the wife of the Patriarch, Isaac. Her father had always regretted her loss, and was unlikely to fall into another such error, even should Isaac send an embassy to fetch a bride for his sons—if, indeed, he had any.

That had always been Leah's daydream. She had lived it over and over again. A tall handsome man, with regal bearing, would one day present himself before them. A man who would make the men of Padan-aram seem like pygmies and slaves. He would look at her and see in her a wife to raise his sons, and would take her far from this place, where all her days were spent in household chores and spinning flax and goats' hair, and scolding sluts and idle menservants. It was a foolish idea, for, even if such a man came, Laban would chase him from the door.

Leah finished the cheese and laid it to cool on a stone slab, and allowed herself the luxury of standing idle in the doorway, looking down the road towards the well.

She looked again.

Was her dream materialising before her eyes? Walking towards her, led by little Rachel, among the bleating sheep, was the man of whom she had dreamed. He was tall and slender. He was speaking courteously to her little sister, not with the rude tones which were her father's only mode of address. He was tanned with the sun, but his skin was smooth, not hairy. His deepset eyes looked kind and penetrating. Leah's heart beat faster. Who was he—this man to whom her whole body and soul responded? Could it be that her dream was indeed coming true?

.   .   .   .

Unlike her sister, Rachel had not indulged in daydreams of princely men coming to rescue her. Her favourite dream was of someone coming, who would say to her father, " I will care for the sheep, and allow Rachel to rest."

74

To Rachel's great relief, she found the stone had already been rolled away from the well. Several others were there before her, talking to a stranger. She only looked with enquiry at this stranger, who was regarding her with such interest.

Jacob had never tired of hearing the story of how Eliezer sat dreaming at the well, and when awakening, saw Rebekah walking towards him, and realised that she was the wife for Isaac. It seemed to Jacob, as he stood questioning the shepherd, that history was repeating itself. Was he too to find his wife at the well? For the slight girl who led the sheep to quench their thirst had about her that promise of beauty—even in her present immaturity—as great as that of his mother. There was something about the way she moved her head, and when she turned her large eyes, like those of a trusting animal, upon him, Jacob's heart turned to water within him, and he experienced for the first time in his life the love that a man has for a woman. Not the lust of desire, but the outgoing of love to one who will be a helpmeet and companion when all passion is spent.

Jacob told her simply that he was Rebekah's son, and wished to see her father, Laban. With the simplicity of a child, Rachel lifted her face to his for a kiss of greeting, and led him with natural grace and hospitality to her father's dwelling.

.   .   .   .

There was feasting that night in the house of Laban. In the very room where the table had been loaded with provender to welcome Eliezer when he sought for a bride for Isaac, his son Jacob was royally entertained. Leah put her heart and soul into her preparations. Servants were sent scuttling to see if there were not a fat ram from the herd that could be killed. Fruit and wine were brought out in abundance, and the choicest vessels and bowls of pottery kept for feast days only were produced.

Leah's heart sang as she baked the fresh bread on the heated stones, and rejoiced that her father was pleased to be gracious to his guest and welcome him as bone of his bone and flesh of his flesh. The welcome had been very affecting and Leah, knowing her father, wondered what was going on in his mind to make him so affable. He was not given to hospitality, and rarely showed kindness unless he expected to reap a hundredfold. There was a gaiety and happiness that night not often known in the household of Laban. His moods and tempers set the temperature of the atmosphere, and often Rachel trembled when she heard his harsh voice as he approached, knowing that a cloud would descend upon them all until he had changed his mood.

But tonight they talked of happy, far-off things. Jacob told them of Rebekah and his father and brother. He made no boast of being his father's heir, being content to be thought a younger son. Laban led him on to talk of his chief interest and occupation —the care of his father's flocks. Jacob spoke with enthusiasm of the many things Miram had taught him, and as he told of the health and prosperity of the flocks, Laban's little piggy eyes gleamed, and Leah began to understand. The only indication Laban gave of what was passing through his mind was his suggestion that Jacob might be gracious enough to look over his flock the following day, and advise him out of his store of wisdom.

.   .   .   .

Even out of courtesy to his host, Jacob was unable to disguise his poor opinion of Laban's flocks.

"But who is your shepherd?" he asked at last, as he looked over the thin, worm-diseased sheep, seeking desperately to find sustenance on land that they had cropped and cropped again.

Laban grunted. "An old man, one Cobah, well stricken in years," he told his nephew. "His eyes are dim, and he prefers to keep the sheep near to the homestead, instead of taking them farther afield in search of green pastures. Rachel, my younger daughter, helps him." Laban, seeking to justify himself, started to vent his spleen on her. "A weakly creature she is, who should care better for them and take them farther afield herself. They're a lazy pair, not worthy of the meat they eat."

Jacob's brow darkened, and his heart was filled with anger against his uncle. He was amazed at the depth of his feeling at hearing any word spoken about Rachel so adversely.

76

"To care for the flock, except to take them to the well for water, is no work for a woman, especially a child like Rachel."

He spoke with heat, and Laban saw that he had made a mistake in laying blame on his daughter. He shifted the responsibility higher and laid it on the Almighty. He shrugged and looked up piously to the sky.

"Great Jehovah has not seen fit to bless me with sons," he said. "Had healthy sons been vouchsafed to me they could have cared for the flocks, as you do for your father's. But," he continued, laying his hand on Jacob's shoulder, "Jacob, son of my beloved sister Rebekah, will you not stay and care for your uncle's flocks?" He watched Jacob anxiously.

Jacob had no wish to jeopardise his chances by making a precipitate claim on Rachel, so he promised to stay until another moon had waxed and waned, and then he would have to consider.

Laban wanted time to consider as well. According to the law, he could adopt a young man as his heir, and if this son married one of his daughters, he would be really bound to him at Padan-aram. For an adopted son, although he can claim equal inheritance with natural sons, should they subsequently be born, may not take his daughter away, but is bound by his adopted father. Laban considered it deeply. Jacob was a younger son, and it seemed logical that, as he, Laban, was without a son, he should be looking into the future to raise up heirs. Jacob seemed eminently suitable, having inherited his mother Rebekah's gift for caring for the flock.

The month passed by on wings. Jacob had not been idle. It would soon be time for the ewes to be served. Many of them, toothless and weak, were not fit to breed from—if, indeed, any ram could get them in lamb. There was hardly a ram fit to sire a fine flock. Jacob realised that it would take time and selection, but he told Laban he was confident that, with patience and faithful shepherding, he could double his flocks in a year, and after that there was no limit to what success might attend their labours, if the God of heaven saw fit to prosper them. The land where they were now pastured was sheep-sick, parasite-ridden, and if the ewes were to produce fine lambs they must be led to other pastures and to the farther water-holes.

There was nothing gladdened Laban's heart so well as to hear of prosperity and prospective wealth, provided it was to be his at little cost to himself. Jacob's skill and knowledge astounded him, and he was anxious to keep him at all costs. He was even prepared to make a small sacrifice to gain his ends. He clapped Jacob on the back, telling him that he was a fine fellow, and that he was proud of his sister's son, "but, nephew Jacob," he said expansively, pausing as they walked—he must stand to develop his theme, he needed to watch Jacob carefully to see his reactions, and assess how far he need go—"just because I am your uncle, it is not meet that you should serve me for nought. Tell me, what shall thy wages be?"

The time had come, and Jacob boldly made his request. "I will serve you for your younger daughter, Rachel, if I may have her for my wife.'

Laban was taken aback. This was a new development. He must think quickly. He had thought of Leah, but not Rachel.

"She is a mere child," he said. "Had it been Leah, a woman grown . . . ."

"Rachel may seem young, but she too is a woman grown," said Jacob, "and it is Rachel to whom my heart is knit, and it is for Rachel that I would serve you." And Jacob added impulsively, "I would wait, yea, I would serve you seven years for Rachel."

Seven years! Laban's heart lifted. In seven years his flocks would increase beyond all knowledge in the care of such a master-shepherd. Seven years—and then who knows? Jacob was obviously deeply attached to Rachel, and willing to wait, and this started another plan evolving in Laban's crooked mind.

"You will serve seven years for my daughter," he said, "It shall be. Serve me seven years, and she shall be your wages."

Jacob was a little taken aback. He mentioned seven years as a figure of speech. Seven years was the time of service as an apprentice, and he was no mere apprentice. But so great was his desire to possess Rachel that he agreed. A witness was called, and the oath was sworn. Jacob would serve seven years for Laban's daughter. Jacob's joy at the promise of Rachel was so great that he did not notice that in swearing to give him his daughter as wages, Laban did not specify which one.

Laban, well pleased with his bargain, went on his way. He had feared that Jacob might have wanted shekels or a share of the flock. There would be time enough after seven years to think about different wages. Laban smiled to himself. If his plan succeeded, Jacob was not bound to him for seven years only, but by the love he bore Rachel, it would be twice seven years before anything more tangible in the way of wages need pass between them.

9

THEN followed the seven happiest years of Jacob's life. He greatly desired to go home to see his mother, but sent messages with merchants that he was to stay with Laban seven years, and then he would bring his bride home in triumph.

Jacob put his heart and soul into caring for Laban's flock. He took them far afield after the rains had come and found them green pasture. There was no danger of wild beasts to the young lambs, for he slept out under the open heaven, protecting them himself. He neither spared himself at lambing time, nor denied Laban's flocks any of his skill and knowledge of breeding and selection.

To Leah it was a time of mingled ecstasy and despair. When Jacob went away over the hills for weeks together, the house seemed like a tomb, but after his return her whole life was changed, and she found herself tingling with the love that she bore him. Both she and Rachel were amazed at the changed aspect of life when there was a man in the house to care for, as well as their father; a man who was courteous and thanked them for their care of him, and one who laughed and made merry with them, and even helped them to bear their father's moods and rages.

"The sky is lowering today, cold winds from the north are upon us," he would say, as Laban glowered and raged. Leah and Rachel stifled gales of unbidden laughter, knowing well that it was not of the weather that Jacob spoke, for the sun shone brilliantly and no breeze stirred.

When Jacob pastured the flock near the household, Rachel helped him. No one knew what Jacob's coming meant to her. Her health improved beyond all believing. Gone were the aches and pains caused by carrying loads too heavy for her slender arms. Jacob was always at hand to take the heavy pitcher of water from her, and to forbid her to exert herself beyond her strength. Rachel sat by the well, thinking of the wonder of the past months. She stretched out her slender arm in the sun. It was wonderful to feel well and strong, and to have that continued fear of her father removed. Since Jacob had come, Laban looked at his younger daughter differently, with a certain calculating glance that she had often seen as he looked at one of his cows which he hoped to sell for a good price. He never shouted at her when Jacob was near, and even when his nephew was away with the flocks he stayed his tongue.

Everyone knew that Laban had promised Jacob one of his daughters in marriage. Though Jacob sometimes spoke to her as if she were to be his bride, Leah told her forcibly that no one would want to marry a child, who was not strong enough to do a day's work, let alone bear children. At first she had not thought of Jacob as anything but a strong and kind brother, one who made life easy and protected her from parental wrath. But recently extraordinary thoughts had entered her mind, and she had experienced strange feelings and ideas. Were these the feelings a woman had for a man she loved? She had never talked to anyone but Leah of these things, and the chatter of the servant girls had never interested her. They were given to husbands by Laban, and they bore children, but no one told her of these delicious and exciting feelings that came unbidden to her when she heard Jacob's voice, or heard him speaking with authority to the servants, like the lord of a tribe rather than head shepherd.

He walked towards her now, and her heart leapt at the sight of him, tall and tanned with the sun, his eyes full of joy at the sight of her. He sat beside her, and gently touched her hand.

"Oh, Rachel, well are you so named, 'Little ewe'. You look like one of the best of my flock."

Rachel looked up and said, "Don't tell me my eyes are like those of a sheep, Jacob."

"No, not a sheep," said Jacob thoughtfully, "more like a gazelle of the mountains, wondering and unawakened. But you will awake some time, for me. Only a few more years to wait, and you will be mine."

Rachel listened, but said nothing. The thought of belonging to Jacob was strangely exciting, of being with him all the time, pitching their tent together and not having to say goodbye when he went far away over the hills. They dreamed happily together, and the years passed by on wings. They seemed to Jacob as a few days for the love that he bore to her.

.   .   .   .

The crisis was approaching. The seven years' waiting was nearly fulfilled. Jacob spoke constantly with evident eagerness of the day when he would claim his bride. Laban had secretly marvelled at Jacob's chastity and patience, knowing that his love for Rachel was deep, and that desire often burned within him. Laban was well aware that it had been a mere figure of speech Jacob had used in promising to serve for seven years, but he had seized upon it, and reaped the benefit by the prosperity of his livestock. He had confidently expected Jacob to confront him long before this, asking to be given his wife before his full term of service had expired. He was prepared to accede to this only if the seven years had been subsequently completed.

Laban was unaccustomed to dealing with men of Jacob's calibre, who never robbed him from the flock, and who neither spared his strength nor skill in caring for the sheep. A man who thought nothing of the frost, and would allow himself to be consumed by drought if need be, he thought, must have some ulterior motive. Laban was quite convinced that when Jacob's time of service was over he would change his tactics, and either insist on taking his bride away to Beersheba, or stay demanding the highest of wages, and in return feather his own nest with Laban's goods. It was impossible to keep a check on anyone who had such a free hand, and Jacob would have ample opportunity for acquiring quite legitimate perquisites.

·   ·   ·   ·   ·   ·   ·   ·   ·   ·   ·   ·

Laban was having his domestic troubles. Jacob made it quite clear that it was Rachel who was the object of his affections, and though Laban had paved the way by swearing only to give a daughter to wife, not mentioning her by name, no one living in the house of Laban could be under any misapprehension as to which daughter Jacob had determined to marry. Leah, Laban's favourite daughter, who had cared for his home, ruled his servants, and dealt prudently in the purchase of merchandise, was behaving in a manner quite out of keeping with her usual sensible manner of life. She constantly upbraided him for not seeking a husband for her—she who was in every way fitted to be a wife and mother. Did he think to marry his younger daughter before his elder? And Leah was flung into a mood of utter despondency, and neglected both the care of the house and the work in the fields.

In desperation Laban talked of finding some man who, in his turn, might come and live at Padan-aram and serve for Leah as Jacob was doing for Rachel. He was not minded to lose Leah and all her skill to some other chieftain. But it became obvious that it was not *any* man whom Leah desired, but that she had set her heart on Jacob, and him alone. Laban considered how this might be turned to good account. At last he shared his plan with Leah.

" Jacob is not familiar with our laws and customs, and has so much respect for tradition that I have only to say to him, 'It is against our custom', and he will bow to it."

Then he went on to explain his plan to marry Jacob to Leah instead of Rachel, then securing his service for yet another seven years while he waited for the younger daughter. It would be difficult to arrange the substitution, but having taken her veiled, with his senses befuddled by wine, he would abide by his oath and live with Leah. Of this Laban had no doubt.

Leah was uncertain. What if Jacob took her to his tent, and then repudiated her in anger? How could she support it if she were almost in his arms, and then the cup of joy was dashed from her lips?

Laban reassured her. "No bridegroom after feasting ever goes to his bride except his senses are slightly bemused," he told her. "It will be my task to lace the wine with special spices and drugs, so that he is only fit to take his bride, but not to distinguish her from any other woman."

Leah considered. It was a tempting proposition. She would have Jacob to herself for seven long years. Surely in that time she could win his love, give him sons, and knit his heart to hers so strongly that Rachel, if not completely forgotten, would take a very secondary place.

One stipulation she made; Jacob was not to be told of her part in the plot, she must appear to be the helpless victim of custom, marrying by her father's decree, as became a docile daughter.

.   .   .   .

Jacob set off with the herd, taking them over the 'midbar', that semi-desert where cattle are driven over sparse pasture to the green grass beyond. He went alone for the last time. Soon he would be with his Rachel, and together they would care for the sheep and minister to the tender lambs.

Laban had promised to arrange the wedding feast on the very day of his return. Jacob had waited seven years, but each one of these last days felt like a year, and on his return he wished not to wait for as long as seven hours before claiming his bride.

Laban had told him of the customs. There would be feasting, and all the men of the district would be invited to celebrate, but Jacob would not see his bride until, heavily veiled, she was presented to him, and together they were taken to the marriage tent, which was woven of the finest goatskin and hung with embroidered awnings.

.   .   .   .

Rachel watched Jacob disappearing over the skyline. Before another moon passed he would return and claim her for his own. The love that at first was unawakened within her had steadily grown until it was deep and enduring and would, Rachel felt, at Jacob's touch rise to an ecstasy of fulfilment.

That evening she spoke with quiet joy to Leah of the coming ceremony, and asked questions concerning wedding garments. Rachel was staggered by the shock Leah's words gave her.

"I have my special robes and veiling all ready for my wedding to our lord Jacob. See, sister, here they are," Leah told her.

"For *your* wedding to Jacob?" gasped Rachel. "What of me?"

Leah looked at Rachel with a mixture of well-assumed pity and scorn. "My dear Rachel, you must know that a younger sister cannot marry before her elder. Did you think it was for you that Jacob served?"

"But it *was* for me," Rachel told her. "Everyone knows it to be so. Jacob agreed to serve my father for full seven years, and then to wed me."

"And then to wed his *daughter*," Leah corrected. "Any of the witnesses will tell you that. However, little sister, take heart—Jacob is to serve another seven years, then he will wed you."

"But he spoke as if he wanted me and as if he loved me," said Rachel in bewilderment.

"Indeed, he does love you, as one loves a little child. Why, he said himself to our father that you are far too young. Do you think that you, Rachel, you who have been feeble and ailing from a child will be able to give a man sons, and to work for him as I can? Jacob has seen the work I do, and he who knows so much of breeding cannot but realise who is the better fitted to bear his children. Not for nothing have I been named Leah, 'wild cow'."

"Are you trying to say that Jacob does not want me?" Rachel asked, still unconvinced.

"Say rather that he desires me more. Full many a time when you have been with the flock he has talked with me here of many things, and told me of his hopes and fears. Many men take a second wife, and if Jacob will serve another seven years, then perchance you too shall be given to him."

Rachel rushed out of the house, away towards the well where she had first met Jacob. She could not believe what she had heard. Jacob had talked constantly of the day when they would be one, but it seemed he had also talked so to Leah. Could she have been mistaken? It was true that she had not often been alone with Jacob—it was against the custom—but their moments together had been very precious. Could she have been so deceived? Had she to wait another seven long years, and then only be a second and less-loved wife? Leah was right, she had never been strong, though of late her health had improved beyond all believing. Leah was more gifted and fitted in every way to be the wife of a patriarch and mother of his sons. But Jacob had spoken of taking her to see his mother and father, and showing her off to the tribe. And now none of this was to be, and Rachel laid her head on the cool stone that covered the well and wept until there was no strength left in her.

. . . .

As the preparations for the wedding drew on apace, Leah told Rachel it would be better if she were not one of the ten young girls who attended her at the wedding. These young virgins, chosen on account of their beauty, from among the tribe, were expected to dress the bride and attend her to the ceremony, when the sons of the bride-chamber came in a body, carrying the bridegroom, to demand the presence of the bride. Rachel agreed only too eagerly. The agony of seeing Jacob married to another would be too great to be borne. She would go right away and care for the sheep, and not attend the feast at all. This suited Laban and Leah well, and they took care to see that this was so.

. . . .

Jacob returned, impatient and ardent, to find tremendous pre-parations on hand. He was taken in charge by the sons of the bride-chamber, dressed in gorgeously embroidered apparel, and the feasting began. It was the custom for the men to feast together in the men's quarters, while the women and girls had their own separate feasting, until the culmination of the day came when the bride's presence would be demanded by the attendants of the bridegroom.

Jacob noticed that his uncle was ill at ease, and he who should have been the expansive and genial host was distraught and anxious. However, the bridegroom could not complain of neglect, for he was constantly supplied with special wine, which, Laban told him, was of the choicest and for the bridegroom alone. Jacob could carry his wine as well as any man, and had never to his knowledge drunk to excess, but this wine of Laban's was cer-tainly stronger and more potent than anything the vineyards of Isaac had produced. Laban seemed deeply offended when Jacob had tried to refuse, and talked of the custom, and hinted that his son-in-law must be weak indeed if he could not hold his wine.

The moment came for the bridegroom's procession to move towards the women's quarters. Then the bridegroom was lifted on to the shoulders of the attendants, and dizzily Jacob sat in this uplifted position, while musicians provided music with lutes and harps. There was singing and much rejoicing. At first the women made the usual show of refusing to accede to the bride-groom's request, and of keeping the bride from the sons of the bride-chamber. But at last the bride, heavily veiled, was carried out to meet the bridegroom. Leah had been anointed with spices by the attendant virgins, and Zilpah, the handmaiden, given to her by Laban on her marriage, had dressed her hair with great skill.

Both Laban and Leah knew that the next few moments were the most dangerous of all. Although it was towards evening, the light was still strong. Jacob would see the outline of his bride, even though her face was veiled. Laban had foreseen the danger, and prepared to meet the problem. It was the custom for the bridegroom to put his cloak over the bride, claiming her for his own, and then for one of the attendants to throw over her a man's cloak, saying the words of ritual, "None shall uncover thee but Jacob." Laban decreed that the ceremony of the bridegroom and the cloak should be dispensed with, but that the throwing of the man's cloak over the bride should take place before Jacob had time to gaze upon his bride.

It happened as Laban decreed. The bride was thankfully enveloped in the cloak, which hid the largeness of her form. Jacob, by now, was more than weary of the ceremony. The music was sounding strangely in his ears. He wanted to have done with all the mummery, and claim his bride. Laban was more than cooperative, insisting only that he should finish the vessel of prepared wine.

"It is the custom," he said again.

And the bride and bridegroom were carried ceremoniously to the marriage tent, and left to consummate the marriage.

.   .   .   .

Jacob stirred uneasily as the morning rays of sunshine penetrated the slit in the goats' hair of his tent. He moved his head, and felt as though a thousand knives were penetrating his brain. He groaned and sank back into a fitful sleep. He dreamt he had married Rachel. She was with him now in his arms in the tent. And then the dream acquired nightmare proportions, and he dreamt it was not Rachel with whom he had been bedded, but his bride had turned into an enormous cow. He shook himself to throw off the fantastic imaginings of his subconscious mind. He opened his bloodshot eyes, the sun's rays causing him acute pain. It must be true he had married Rachel. There was indeed a woman lying with him. But then he shrank back in horror, not sure if he were still in his nightmare. This was not Rachel, his tiny ewe-lamb, whose dainty form he had dreamed of holding. He lifted the flap of the tent that the merciless glare of daylight might shine upon the bride, and blinking at the sudden onrush of light were not the gazelle-like eyes of Rachel, but the little pink-lidded eyes of . . . Leah.

Jacob sprang up, his swimming head forgotten, an over-mastering rage possessing him.

"What infamy is this?" he said, "that I should be given a 'wild cow' for my bride?"

Girding on his tunic, and not staying for his cloak, he strode off, breathing imprecations as he went to confront his perfidious father-in-law.

Laban was expecting him. He had prepared many speeches. He must remember his promise to Leah, to absolve her of all complicity. Laban could hear Jacob approaching long before he arrived. His nephew was quite shaken out of his usual calm. Laban reflected that a lion robbed of its whelps would be easier to face than his new son-in-law.

"What hast thou done? What trickery is this? Did I not serve you these seven years for Rachel? Did you not swear to me? Have you no fear of a curse falling upon you as you break the oath that you swore by the God of our fathers?"

Laban allowed Jacob to spend himself. He had already made up his mind that it would be useless to expect Jacob to wait another seven years for Rachel. He would have to make the best of it now. When Jacob paused for breath, Laban talked soothingly with placating tones, ignoring the constant interruptions and interjections of Jacob.

"True, I swore to give you a daughter, but you are new to our customs and laws, you are ignorant of them, Jacob. As a loving father and head of a family, I could not so go against custom as to give the younger daughter before her elder sister." As he spoke, Laban allowed himself to look staggered and shocked at the mere suggestion. "I have gone farther than you asked. See, I will give you *both* my daughters. As for Leah, fulfil her week, it is all the law demands, and then in seven days you shall take Rachel. We of Nahor and Haran often take two or three wives to bear our sons. Leah will be fruitful, and Rachel shall gladden your heart. Turn not your countenance from me in anger, son Jacob, I only acted as befits a father."

Jacob was silent, only half convinced. He felt himself cheated and tricked.

Laban, anxious to make further amends, felt it was the time to bring out an idea which he was keeping in abeyance for the furtherance of his ends: while Jacob was silent, his anger a little appeased but not wholly spent, Laban told him that it had been his desire for some time to adopt him as his heir.

"Now that you have married my daughter, this is the time to proclaim you as my dear son, who will share everything that I possess, my herds and flocks, my wealth, my manservants and my maidservants."

Jacob sat on a wooden bench to ponder. He would then not only inherit his portions from Isaac, but from Laban as well. He would eventually be even richer than his father Isaac. Such an offer was not to be despised, though material things were never to be the chiefest of Jacob's desires. Now his overwhelming desire was for Rachel. He only vaguely heard Laban explaining the laws of adoption.

"If I should take another wife and have sons, they would share equally with you, Jacob. You would then be free to go out and take your wives with you. But you will still serve another seven years for Rachel.'

Jacob cared nothing for that, if only he could have Rachel now. He signified his agreement, and Laban, anxious to cover up the unfortunate incident of yesterday's deception, made a great show of proclaiming Jacob as his adopted son and heir to his possessions. Jacob stood silently passive during the ceremony, until the point when Laban handed to him a number of images as a token. Jacob recoiled, and pushed them from him.

"Idols! Idolatrous images!" he said. "I did not think to find these in the house of Laban, kinsman of Abraham."

Laban spoke to him patiently, as one does to a fractious child. "Again, Jacob my son, you are ignorant of our laws and customs. These images are no more than tokens of your right as my heir. All families have their images. True, these represent the moon goddess, and some may be of Nanna of Ur, the god of the sun, but we do not bow the knee to them or worship them, but worship the God of Abraham, and the God of Noah and Shem."

Jacob fingered the images gingerly, and decided that he would not take them to his tent. He had seen too many such objects in the tents of his brother Esau. True, they were not sensual and lewd like the images of Ashtaroth, but he would leave them in their place in Laban's house, to be produced in years to come should need arise.

Laban was at pains to assure Jacob that Leah was not to blame for the deception. She had to obey her father. All daughters under the ancient law were bound to do so, Laban told him. It was for a father to give his daughter in marriage, even to take her life if he so desired.

"Fulfil her week," Laban urged again, "and then you shall have Rachel."

. . . .

It had all been a mental shock to Jacob—the joyful anticipation, the excitement of the feasting, the overdose of heavy wine, and then the horror of finding himself deceived. He tried to think rationally. Leah was not to blame. Maybe it had been as great an ordeal for her as for him, though daughters expected to be given in marriage, and he was no stranger. Then he thought, wryly, who was he to rage about a masquerade when he himself, only seven years ago, had played the leading part in just such a deception in another tent many miles away? Was it the judgment of God upon him? he wondered. Does a man reap what he sows? He would be good to Leah. Men did take two wives; his brother Esau had certainly done so, within a very short time of each other. Both he and Leah were victims of Laban's guile, but he would be aware of his uncle's malice and greed, and not be so easily deceived a second time.

. . . .

Leah waited in the tent, watching Jacob's angry departure. What would happen, and would Jacob hate her and rail against her, repudiate her? Would she never again lie in his arms and feel his face against hers? If he would only come to her willingly, not in drunken ignorance, but knowingly, even if not lovingly, she would know sheer ecstasy.

She sent her maid, Zilpah, to enquire what was happening. Zilpah, a past-master at listening to conversations and gaining information, returned to tell Leah all that had transpired. Leah applauded her father's wisdom in performing the ceremony of adoption at once, and was relieved to know that Jacob's wrath had cooled. Zilpah was unable to give her mistress any further information concerning his feelings to his bride of yesterday. Leah dared not go to the house, but stayed in her tent, and in the cool of the evening walked on the hillside in an agony of apprehension and desire.

It was there that Jacob found her. They stood facing each other. Jacob was tall, but Leah was almost his equal in stature.

"Jacob," she said in a low voice, "I am sorry."

He took her hand in his.

"Fear not, Leah," he said, "we were both victims of your father's duplicity. It must be hard for you to marry a man for whom you may not feel any love."

Leah looked at him in amazement.

"Are you so blind, Jacob? A man I do not love!"

Jacob looked at her in the fading light.

"You love me, Leah?" he asked.

"With my whole body and soul," she said, hardly able to restrain herself from casting herself into his arms. She went on quickly, words falling over each other, knowing her pride should restrain her, but caring nothing. "I loved you when you first came from the well. My whole being yearns for you. Jacob," she said eagerly, "I can give you sons. Forget Rachel, and live only for me."

At the mention of Rachel, Jacob withdrew from her embrace, saying, "Rachel is the one I love, and I can never forget her. It is Rachel for whom I have served seven years, but I have promised to fulfil your week, and then your father will give me Rachel."

Leah let her hands fall to her sides.

"A week! You are to give me a week?" she demanded incredulously, "and then go to Rachel?"

"That is what your father has decreed. I am to serve another seven years for Rachel."

So Laban had got his way, she thought bitterly, but this time he's not making you wait.

"And I have you for a paltry week," she stated. "And when it is over, do you leave me and never return?"

Jacob answered evasively. He would have to go away with Rachel. It was the season for travelling with the sheep, and when he came back—who knew? He would come again to her tent.

Leah stifled a torrent of bitter words of disappointment that rose to her lips. She must keep a grip on herself, and not sicken and alienate him with her overwhelming passion. She mastered her voice and spoke quietly.

"But we have this week together. You will come to my tent again this night, my husband Jacob?"

Jacob said he would, and with that she was well content. Zilpah was busily occupied bringing fresh spices to anoint Leah for her lord. She would live in the present, and savour each day of this week that was hers. Each day she would prepare meals of surpassing savour and succulence, and at night she would lie in his arms, and wish only to die when the week would be over.

.   .   .   .

Although, as a bridegroom, Jacob was exempt from work with the flocks, he was no time-server, and rose early, leaving Leah in the tent, to see that all was well with the sheep. Over the hill he went in the cool of the morning, and as he rounded the bluff on the hillside, he came upon the flock, and sitting with them, gazing into the distance with unseeing eyes, was Rachel. Unable to contain himself for the joy the sight of her produced, Jacob ran to her and covered her with kisses in a way he had never permitted himself to do when years of continence awaited him.

"Rachel, my little ewe, my beloved," he repeated again and again.

Rachel gave herself up to the joy of the moment, then firmly pushed him away from her.

"Jacob," she said, "how can you deal so with me, when you have chosen Leah, and will not take me for another seven years?"

Then Jacob saw that Rachel too had been deceived, and told her that although he was to serve for another seven years for her, he need not wait so long.

"Only a week, my love, and you shall be mine. We have all been wrongfully and shamefully treated."

Rachel was comforted. It was galling to feel that she had been forestalled, but although she realised that Leah must have her week, she knew that she had Jacob's love, and they would go away over the fields and beyond the hills together, never to be parted again.

10

IT was the first time that Rachel had been away from the tyranny of her father, Laban, and away from the authority of her sister Leah, and the work that clamoured daily to be done. She was free, away in the open country with Jacob. To her, it was complete and utter bliss. There was no one to make her afraid, no cloud to mar the glory of her happiness.

About one thing Rachel showed deep concern, much to Jacob's surprise.

"You should not have left those images in my father's house," she told him. "He will trick you. I know him far better than you do."

"I think I know him a little better myself now," Jacob told her. "But Rachel, my love, we cannot have images in our tent. We are the worshippers of Jehovah, the one unseen God," and he told her again the story of her great-grandfather, Haran, who perished in the flames trying to rescue his idols. He told her a little of the horrors of Baal worship, and the idols he had seen in Esau's tent. "These things are an abomination unto the Lord, Rachel," he told her.

She listened and learned much, but concerning the images she was not convinced.

"If they had been clay tablets or merely carved stone," Jacob told her, "it would have been different, but my whole soul revolts to see such things."

.   .   .   .

During the seven years of waiting and the months of marriage, Rachel learned more and more of Jacob's God. In some ways, He became more real to her than He was to Jacob. Her husband was often surprised at her naïve way of speaking of the One Whom he feared and worshipped afar off.

"When I have a son," she said, "I will teach him that all that is good is of God, to be kind and not selfish, not to seek his own, to be tender like you, Jacob, are with the little lambs. I will teach him that wherever he is, in accord with the promise God made to you at Bethel, God will be with him."

"Do you feel He is with you, Rachel?" Jacob asked curiously.

Rachel looked away into the dark blue of the night sky.

"I do," she said. "I sometimes feel very near to Him."

Jacob shivered. He often sensed that Rachel was almost too near the unseen world; a premonition came to him that he might lose her.

"Let us hope that before those ewes bring forth their lambs, you will tell me that our son, the son of promise, is to be born."

.   .   .   .

The happy months of seclusion were over. It was time to bring the flocks back to the homestead, and Rachel felt a sense of foreboding as they led the sheep towards the familiar settlement.

Laban was well pleased with Jacob's success. The flock had multiplied as if by magic. Laban, with his empty piety, assured Jacob that the Lord had prospered him. Laban preferred to give

Jehovah the credit rather than Jacob. His son-in-law soon discovered that Laban treated him very differently now that he was bound to him, both by adoption and marriage, and there was no likelihood of his returning to Beersheba. It was not Laban's way to praise his servants. They might think themselves worth higher wages. And it was as a servant that Jacob now found himself treated—a servant to be rebuked and questioned, not even treated with the respect accorded to a master-shepherd. Laban counted the flock suspiciously, and demanded of Jacob whether any had been torn by wild beasts, but there was never a word of praise, only pious thankfulness for divine intervention and no acknowledgment of the unremitting care lavished on the flock by Jacob.

.   .   .   .

To Leah, the return of Jacob was like life coming back to her. Her whole being longed for him, and it was all she could do to restrain herself from falling upon him and weeping with joy to see him. Rachel was a little bewildered and puzzled as to how to share her husband, having had him to herself for so long. Jacob too felt he owed Leah a duty, but longed to be with Rachel. It was Rachel who urged Jacob to go to her sister, and the fact that Leah realised this made her all the more bitter. She would have liked to have told Jacob not to come to her at all, if it were only as a duty, and by the gracious permission of her miserable, ailing little sister. But her need of him was so great that she tried to dissemble and hide from him her feelings, showing only the extravagance of her love. But when alone with Rachel, Leah showed no such restraint, and there was no taunt too bitter or malicious suggestion too unkind to make, provided Jacob was well out of hearing.

And now Leah had a rod with which to beat Rachel. She, Jacob's first wife, was with child, while Rachel had as yet no sign. Leah flaunted herself, secretly hugging the thought: If I bear a son, Jacob will love me. Jacob was glad to hear of his approaching fatherhood. Leah was the cause of some embarrassment and anxiety to him, constantly waylaying him as he went about his business, demanding that he spend time with her, that he visit her tent. Now she would soon have a child to occupy her, and they said that motherhood took much of the passion from women like Leah.

.   .   .   .

Leah lay back in her tent, exhausted but happy. Zilpah held up the tiny morsel of humanity for her to see, screwing up his face as he gave a healthy cry.

" See, a son," she said.

" That is what we will call him," said Leah, " for that is what the name Reuben means." Tears of joy and weakness rolled down the young mother's cheeks. " Send for my lord Jacob," she said. " The Lord has looked upon me in my affliction, and seeing that I have borne him a son, peradventure my husband will love me."

But even though she bore him another son, Simeon, and then another, Levi, though he was pleased at her fruitfulness, his heart was still knit to Rachel, and Leah hoped in vain that she would take the first place. Only her maid Zilpah knew the extent of her mistress's suffering and misery. Her unrequited passion became like a disease with her, her feelings for her sister became hatred, and even the birth of a fourth son, Judah, did nothing to compensate for the love of Jacob, which she had so ardently desired from the moment she had seen him coming from the well.

.   .   .   .

Judah sat by the tent door, whittling a stick to fashion a whistle. He could hear the sound of women's voices—his mother's high-pitched and scolding, and another voice low and indistinguishable. They were always quarrelling, his mother and aunt Rachel —at least, it wasn't exactly quarrelling, Mother shouted and scolded, and aunt Rachel just answered meekly. She was weak; Judah despised weak things. He was strong. He could throw any of the other boys in wrestling, and he could make them obey his commands. Reuben was weak too; he was the firstborn, but that didn't make him important. Oh, no, his father Jacob had made

96

it quite clear to them all that being born first was just an accident, and he was going to choose the one to be his heir.

Judah had the feeling that his father would choose him. He had heard him raging angrily at Reuben and saying he was unstable—unstable as water, his father had said. As for Simeon and Levi, his father's anger was kindled against them when he saw the cruel way they treated the livestock. His father had found them tormenting a ewe by keeping her lambs from her, and to their father it was even worse to ill-treat a dumb animal than a human being. Simeon and Levi were certainly mean and cruel. Reuben was not cruel; he was kind, but he could not prevent Simeon and Levi bullying the other little boys, from twisting their arms and taking away their treasures, unless Judah came and helped to make short work of them and their cruel, mean practices. Yes, he, Judah, was strong, and one day his father would call everyone together and give him the coat of many colours, which meant so much, which proclaimed him to be lord over his brothers, and heir to his father.

It was quite a good life here at Padan-aram. His father was only the adopted son of grandfather Laban, but he was heir to his own father Isaac, a great and wealthy sheik. Jacob had often spoken to him of the day when they would all set off to Beersheba to take up his inheritance. But he had warned Judah not to speak of this before Laban, as his grandfather would do all he could to prevent their going. Jacob was too skilled a shepherd and herdsman to be easily spared, and his mother Leah ordered the household in such a way as to make her indispensable. True, his grandfather Laban had taken another wife, and she had borne him two sons, but she was younger in years than his mother Leah, and knew little of the overseeing of the winepresses, olive groves, and care of the dairy, and was content to leave it to his mother, which was as well, thought Judah to himself, for his mother would not easily have been deposed.

Leah had some rooted bitterness against her sister Rachel, though it seemed she had been the first to marry. Yet it was plain for anyone to see that to his father Jacob there was only one wife—Rachel. That she was barren counted for nothing in the eyes of his father, whose love for her was as a fountain or a deep well of water.

．　　．　　．　　．　　．　　．　　．　　．　　．　　．　　．　　．

Jacob's continued love and devotion was very satisfying to Rachel. Many a husband might have reproached her for her lack of fruitfulness, but he cared only for her, and of course he had his sons. Leah had never let her forget that; hourly she was taunted with her barrenness. If they could only all have lived together peaceably. She tried to persuade Jacob to go to Leah from time to time, but her sister's appetite seemed insatiable— ravenous, rapacious, unsatisfied with anything but his exclusive love and constant attention.

Rachel would have rejoiced with her sister in her sons. She had loved little Reuben, and when he was only a few months old, had fondled him in her arms, and felt his downy head leaning against her breast, and dreamt of the day when she would hold Jacob's son born of her own flesh. But Leah had found her, and snatched away her son angrily from Rachel, and exclaimed bitterly, "Give Jacob a son of your own, and don't drool over mine. The gods know you have opportunity enough to conceive, but any fool could have seen you would never bear children. You are just a useless ornament, a plaything of a wife." And Leah had marched away, with one son in her arms and another in her womb, trying vainly to pretend that the joys of motherhood compensated for the lack of a husband's love.

As Reuben grew up, he liked to sit with Rachel. She didn't shout like his mother, or rave in anger like his grandfather. Even his father Jacob seemed to find little pleasure in his firstborn. But his aunt Rachel told him stories, and taught him to play games with stones. Rachel enjoyed her games with Reuben, but took care that Leah was away among the olive groves before she called him to her. She had no wish to play with Leah's other sons, Simeon and Levi. She had been revolted by their cruel ways; killing frogs by taking them to pieces limb by limb, and torturing small animals, and even bullying the other children.

Judah was not like that. He tended to be arrogant—Leah had

taught him to be so—and it was little wonder that he treated his aunt with scant respect, even flinging her childless condition in her face. Such remarks and treatment had been applauded by his mother ever since babyhood. But there were times when he was different. He would come and sit and talk with her, asking of his forefathers, of Isaac and Abraham, and this mysterious promise of a Deliverer called SHILOH, which his father seemed to deem more important than flocks and herds, and to be prized above riches. Rachel told him all she could, and wondered whether Judah's name would go down in history as a father of the mighty Deliverer.

These sons of Terah were a strange mixture, she thought; there was so much to admire, and so much that seemed wild and ruthless. Her grandmother, Milcah, had told her of Terah's sons. Haran, Milcah's own father, who had married her to his brother, Nahor, had founded the tribe and built a city—the tribe from which her father Laban had come. Haran was concerned only with material things, to make money from fashioning idols and images. But Abraham had deemed the promise of God of such value that the joys and comforts of the city life in Ur of the Chaldees were things well lost to win the promise and God's approval.

There had never seemed to be a gleam of spiritual desire in her father Laban, though he could talk with pious unctuousness of the god of his fathers, especially if it were to make an impression or to gain some end. Judah seemed to be a mixture of the two family traits. He was not weak like Reuben, or grasping like his grandfather. He was strong, and could be ruthless. If anyone got in his way, he would not be needlessly cruel like Simeon and Levi, but he would ride rough-shod over them. He was concerned about the promise, and Rachel hoped that Jacob would choose him as his successor, and one day give him the Patriarchal Blessing.

.   .   .   .

Jacob was not the happy man he had been during those seven golden years when he had served for Rachel. They had passed like a weaver's shuttle, and now he was a man who found himself constantly in the midst of domestic strife. He was treated by his adopted father as a servant to be brow-beaten and accused. It was not in Jacob's nature to do his work in a slipshod manner. The welfare of the sheep was always his first concern. Had he been dishonest and not a conscientious man, he could have cheated his father-in-law, and made himself a fortune. But the ewes had lambed and the herds increased so greatly that Laban hardly knew the extent of his flock, and praised his Maker ostentatiously for such prosperity. Had Jacob been crafty, he could have constantly traded droves of sheep to passing merchants, and laid up for himself shekel upon shekel. But until his second seven years of service were over, he would have scorned to take an ounce of wool or a tiny lamb for himself.

His father-in-law's suspicion of him and attempts to check his actions angered him.

"My name may be Jacob, the wrestler, but I am no thief," he said, "though Laban, judging others by his own mean mind, thinks me so."

He was not, however, prepared to serve Laban for nothing, and now that the years of service were over, the time had come to agree concerning wages, and Jacob would need to rise early in the morning to guard his interests, and those of his family, if Laban were not to trick him again. He had his sons to think about.

He grieved with Rachel that she had not been able to give him sons, but her grief was far greater than his. If Leah provided him with sons, then Rachel gave him of her love, and satisfied his. He had told her only yesterday that she was his whole love, and had asked her if she were equally satisfied with the love he gave her. Then it seemed as if a well were opened, and his quiet little Rachel sobbed out her misery and desire.

"Give me children, or I die," she had said.

He was angry at first. No blame could be attached to him, no one could call him, father of four fine sons, impotent. Did she think he was God, Who had withheld the fruit from her womb? He was well accustomed to Leah flinging herself at him and saying, "Give me your love, or I will kill myself and your sons with me," but gentle Rachel had been a comfort and a haven after the storm. But it now became apparent that she too had a pent-up well of desire within her. Being a man, he could not understand the emotional need for a child, for Rachel did not seem to want a child so that she could have rank and position. She did not even seem concerned to breed him an heir. She only kept talking of empty arms, and a heart yearning to hold a little one to her breast.

He had told her of his mother, and of her waiting twenty years before he had been born. He had tried to cheer her by lightening the conversation with tales of Deborah and her astringent tongue and blunt manner, and her claim to have cured Rebekah's barrenness by finding mandrakes for her. But Rebekah always said it was the goodness of God. Rachel sat up from their cushioned bed, and caught hold of his arm.

"Mandrakes, Jacob? Tell me, what of them?"

"They are often called love-apples, and some say they can cure a woman of her barrenness and make her fertile."

Rachel still sat tense.

"I have heard of mandrakes as something used by witches to brew love potions, but never of this."

"You have no need of love potions," he said, drawing her to him. "Your husband's love is yours, all yours."

He had promised her, however, that according to the custom, as she seemed to be barren, he would go in unto her maid, Bilhah, and seek to beget a child by her. Not that he wanted another child, but Bilhah's child would by law belong to Rachel, and she could fondle and love the child, and comfort herself with this second-best.

Rachel did make one other request, and he must try to remember it—to seek in the wheat fields for mandrakes, and bring them to her without fail.

11

L E A H had grown stout with much child-bearing. Her little eyes, so like her father's, with their greedy self-seeking expression, looked out of the pink lids, which seemed more unsightly as the years went by. Jacob's hope that bearing children would decrease her passionate desires and make her more content had been a vain one. She was still eaten up with longing for him, and at certain times of the moon, she would have flung herself down a well to forget her misery, and sought oblivion in spiced wine, drugging herself into forgetfulness. She had ceased bearing for a time, and as Jacob came so rarely to her tent, it was little wonder so much time had passed since she herself had been with child.

Rachel had become mother by proxy, and Leah had laughed at her little sister when Zilpah had brought her the news that Jacob had been seen going into Bilhah's tent. When Dan and then Naphtali had been born to Rachel's maid, Zilpah looked with anxiety at her mistress.

"It is some years now, my mistress, since you have borne your lord a son."

Leah had no secrets from Zilpah.

"Had I my sister's opportunity," she said, "I would have been with child as often as my lord Jacob's ewes are with lamb. But you know what little opportunity I have had, and an older woman does not conceive as easily as a bride."

"Our lord Jacob came more often when your sons were young," and there was still a note of suggestion and interrogation in Zilpah's tones.

Then Leah understood. Slaves such as Zilpah and Bilhah could not marry or have children unless their mistress proved barren. Then they could bear a child who, although it was the slave who bore them, was her mistress's property. Such a son was Ishmael, born of Hagar the Egyptian to Abraham, when Sarah proved barren. Zilpah had instincts and desires even as her mistress, and she was well able to sympathise with Leah, for the feelings she herself had for Jacob were such that she was careful to hide them from her mistress.

Leah gave a short laugh.

"So you want my lord Jacob to lie with you," she said. " Is that what you're after? "

Zilpah protested. "It is to bear a son, seeing you yourself have ceased bearing," she said meekly. "It will bring our lord Jacob to our tents, and may cause him to come to you again."

Leah sighed deeply.

"If only I could think of a way to gain his love . . . ." Leah had made this statement so many times over the years that Zilpah hardly heard her. She went on, "Tell me, Zilpah, you often hear of the strange ways of witches and heathen women; is there some rite, some potion they can brew to cause a lover to turn to them, or to gain their husbands' love? "

Zilpah paused. She had learnt just such a secret, but she did not part with such information without due reward.

"I could perchance seek out one of the wise women of the heathen, and see if there is some such secret," she said tentatively. "I would be willing to take the risk of my lord Jacob hearing I had consorted with the heathen if . . . ."

"If, if . . . so you presume to bargain with me, you, my slave, over whom I have the power of life and death, to sell and to keep, and you say to me 'If, if . . .'"

Zilpah remained silent. She knew the reason for her mistress's impotent wrath.

"Yes," said Leah at last, "it shall be done. Prepare yourself, anoint yourself with spices and perfume, even as I did during that one week when Jacob was mine alone. Go now to your tent and prepare, before I change my mind."

So Jacob went to Zilpah at Leah's request, while the unloved wife writhed in her tent to think that Jacob was so near, and yet not in her arms.

* * * * * * * * * * *

Zilpah was fruitful and bore Jacob two sons, Gad and Asher, and Leah's interest was taken up for a time with them, even forgetting to taunt her sister, who was assuaging her maternal instincts by lavishing her love on her two sons by proxy, Dan and Naphtali.

But it was only for a time that Leah's mating instincts were in abeyance. As middle life approached, her desire burst out afresh.

"Zilpah," she said to her maid one day, "do you remember that you were to seek the secrets of the heathen women concerning a love potion? Were you successful?"

Zilpah laid her fat little son Asher on the sandy ground to play. She was emotionally at rest. Her sons had satisfied her, and Leah had been a kinder mistress to her than she had expected, assisting the midwives at the birth of her sons, and naming them herself.

Zilpah had been waiting for this piece of information to be requested, and slowly she told her mistress, "There is a love philtre, they say, which has many strange ingredients, the main one of which is the love-apple or mandrake. But these are hard to find. The others can be obtained quite easily, consisting of spices and drugs. But mandrakes present more of a difficulty."

Leah saw a miracle happening. The heathen were very skilled, and from Egypt came extraordinary tales of magic spells. She would speak to her firstborn, Reuben, who wandered far afield with the sheep, and also worked in the harvest field where the strange plants might be found. Reuben was always willing to do his mother's bidding, and day after day he searched the hedges and fields for the strange fleshy plant with its orange berries.

.   .   .   .

Rachel sometimes felt that she herself was the mother of Dan and Naphtali. She delighted to point out to Jacob the wisdom of Dan and the clever sayings of Naphtali. Jacob was indulgent, and said that one day Dan would be a judge with his tribe, his wisdom was so great, and of Naphtali, that his goodly words had such a flow that he was like a hind let loose. Rachel thought that such words of praise were only fitting for these wonderful children. Jacob was delighted to see his Rachel looking so much more plump and happy. It might even be, he thought, that she might yet conceive. A barren woman who looks after another woman's child as her own would sometimes be blessed with children. It was one of the ways of the great God, Whom no one could understand. Jacob was more familiar with the way of a ram with a ewe than the workings of the human body, and did not voice this thought to Rachel, as she seemed now so well content.

. . . .

Reuben had been out since sunrise in the harvest-field, and as the heat of the sun grew high, he was returning to the tents for the time of siesta. But as the sun beat down upon him, instead of the heat retarding his progress, he walked with a spring in his step, for his mother would be pleased with him. While working in the harvest-field he had come upon some strange plant with small yellow berries. It had dawned on him that these were the much coveted mandrakes. There was not only one plant but several, and with his knife he dug deep into the soil and started to pull the roots from the ground. The noise it made was as though a soul in torment protested at each pull. The sound was hardly human, it had a positively unearthly sound, and almost frightened Reuben as he pulled. But he chided himself for his foolishness, and went to work with a will. At last with his arms full of both root and berry, he made his way home in triumph.

As he reached the tents, he saw the slight figure of his aunt Rachel standing, holding the hand of little Naphtali. Full of pride at his achievement, he showed her his find.

"Look," he said, "I have found mandrakes. My mother bid me search for them and bring them again to her."

"*Mandrakes!*" said Rachel, breathing deeply, and letting go of little Naphtali's hand, and seizing Reuben's arm with both of hers. "Reuben, give me of your mandrakes, just one little plant. You have so many. Nephew, for the love you bear me, give me of your mandrakes," Rachel urged.

But Reuben was too afraid of his mother to risk her wrath in parting with the mandrakes, by which she evidently set such store. Naphtali had now run away and joined his brother, while Rachel followed Reuben to Leah's tent, putting aside her pride in her desire to have a share. Leah applauded Reuben with all the enthusiasm he had hoped, and he began to feel quite puffed up with his own cleverness, as words of praise were showered upon him. Then Leah saw Rachel standing by. She looked at her sister with hostile eyes.

"And why does the wife of my lord Jacob condescend to visit me?" she asked.

Without further ceremony, Rachel requested, "Give me of your son's mandrakes, only one little plant, for he has many. Please, sister Leah, grant my request."

Leah looked at her with calculating eyes from between their red lids.

"And why should you be so anxious for mandrakes?" she asked. "You have no need to make a . . . ." and then she remembered that Zilpah had said something of the other properties this extraordinary plant was said to possess. She gave a loud coarse laugh that grated on Rachel. It was humiliating enough to have to plead like this, without having the cause of her request published round the camp, and find herself a laughing-stock. It was all very well for Leah—she had no need to seek a cure for barrenness, her quiver was full. Leah went on, "Is it not enough that you have taken my husband, and now you must take my son's mandrakes?" she demanded. "He who came first to my tent has not been here these many years, but you have kept him from me, denied me my right, robbed me of my husband."

Leah's voice was beginning to grow hysterical. Zilpah knew the signs, and Reuben was standing by in an agony of embarrassment. Rachel knew what to say. It had come to her like a flash.

"Give me of your son's mandrakes, and Jacob shall be with you tonight."

Leah stared at her sister, torn between pride and desire. She wanted above everything to have Jacob come to her, but it was humiliating indeed to have him do so at the suggestion of her sister. At last desire triumphed. Leah threw a mandrake plant at her sister.

"With this I hire your husband," she said scornfully. "See that you keep your bargain."

.   .   .   .

All day long Leah alternately hoped and raged. One moment as she mixed her potion her heart was filled with joy and anticipation, but then she was overcome with impotent rage that she should be so humiliated. She was angry not only with Rachel, but with Jacob. The love she had for him almost turned to hatred.

She was standing by the path when Jacob came in from the fields. One part of her longed to say the loving words that were not far from the surface, but as she saw him, the years of misery he had caused rose in her mind, and she lifted her chin, saying, "You must come in to my tent tonight. I have hired you with my son's mandrakes."

As Jacob hesitated, a little mystified, she continued, "Go, enquire of Rachel if it is not so." Then, ashamed of her outburst, she said, "Come early and sup with me, Jacob, my dear lord. I'll prepare a savoury feast, and a special wine for you to drink." For she had prepared the potion to be taken in the best wine the vineyards could produce.

.   .   .   .

That night when Jacob went to Leah, hired by his son's mandrakes, he found Leah very different from her usual passionate self. She had felt ashamed of her bitterness, and determined not to alienate Jacob on this first visit to her for some long time. They sat by the tent, eating from one dish, and talking of their sons, for this was the one thing they had in common, and which she was able to share with him alone. Jacob drank the wine, and if he detected an unusual flavour, he attributed this to special spicing.

As Leah lay supinely in his arms, showing none of her usual passion, Jacob thought that if she had always been so docile, they might have been happier together. Leah found herself content.

It was as though the potion which had been prepared to rouse Jacob's desire and passion had assuaged hers. How foolish she had often been! It was easy now, as increasing years moderated the keen desires of youth, to see that she had acted unwisely. Man ever wants to be the hunter—not the hunted, and she had made it obvious that her need of Jacob was far greater than his for her, and had hunted, and even hounded him, with her insatiable sexual appetite.

That night was the beginning of a happier relationship. When her fifth son was born, she called him Issachar, 'hired', but not in bitterness. When her sixth son, Zebulun, was born, and then her daughter, Dinah, Leah felt that she had given her husband a goodly dowry, and earned the right to have him dwell with her.

Then something happened which changed the status of many people, and Jacob, from being a man content to be a shepherd in his father-in-law's house—a master-shepherd without wages or recognition—overnight took on the dignity of a chieftain who longs to be head of his own tribe.

.   .   .   .

The astonishing news went round the tents that Rachel was with child. The reactions were varied. Leah was openly scornful. If Rachel could indeed be brought to bed with child, it would be too weak to survive; probably she would die in child-birth, and they would be rid of them both. Judah was filled with a certain apprehension, having been told that there was never any likelihood of a son being born to Rachel. He was reassured by his mother's scornful prophecies, and dismissed any possibility of a rival from his mind. Jacob was alternately filled with joy and anxiety. He was more experienced with ewes than women, but he knew that Rachel was not strong, and it was not so easy to have a child after many years of waiting as it was for a bride.

When the time came that Rachel was brought to bed, it was evident that Jacob's fears and Leah's scornful prophecies were by no means unfounded. Hour after hour Rachel lay in pain, her face bathed in sweat and grey with agony. All the skilled midwives were brought to the house of Laban, for it was there, in the greater comfort, that Rachel was to bring forth her son. Laban himself was more concerned than Jacob expected, and sought relief in trying to blame Jacob for the situation.

At last the ordeal was over, and Bilhah brought a tiny baby to Jacob. As he looked at the perfect little specimen of humanity, there stirred in Jacob something that none of his other sons had aroused. Here is my son, thought Jacob, and the future Patriarch. Here is my successor. What am I doing as a hired servant in my father-in-law's house? I must go, I must go to my own country, and establish my position as Isaac's heir, and live as becomes a chieftain.

How Jacob longed to show the perfect child to his mother, Rebekah, but merchants had brought word some time before of her death, and Jacob had mourned her many months. It was this one factor which made him content to remain, and not to seek to return as soon as his time of servitude was over. His father Isaac still lived, they told him, dim of sight, but still able to interest himself in the tribe's affairs. He was sorely mourning the death of his beloved wife, while Deborah, still living, cared for him as she had done for Rebekah.

Rachel herself, after her ordeal, felt strangely uplifted. Her maid Bilhah, who was a devoted slave and friend, repeatedly told her that this son, Joseph, must be her only one. She must not risk her life in a repetition of such an ordeal. Rachel refused to agree, but insisted that she would have one more son.

"You forget, my mistress," protested Bilhah, "now that all the agony and pain is over, it has gone from your mind. But at the time when the travail was upon you, you would have agreed then."

Rachel shook her head.

"Why do you think I called him Joseph?" she asked.

Bilhah knew that the name meant 'adding', but imagined that her mistress thought of adding joy to her already happy life.

"No, it was not that," said Rachel. "I called him 'adding' because God will add to me another son."

12

E V E R Y O N E knew that there had been a great scene, and that Laban and his adopted son had bandied many words together. Laban's meek little wife had run from the house; the sound of her husband's voice raised in anger always terrified her. Her sons curiously tried to listen, not fearing when they themselves were not the object of parental wrath. At such a crisis Leah and Rachel forgot their differences in siding vehemently with Jacob, and like enemy kings, were drawn together by a common foe. They listened from the dairy to the raised voices, as Jacob demanded the right to take his wives and go to his own country. His time of servitude was over; indeed, it was long overdue. No one could say that in any small point he had defrauded his adopted father.

"When I came to Padan-aram, can you remember the flock? Wormy, emaciated, dying, ewes losing their lambs, goats and cattle a shame to behold. But now look at your possessions," and through the open door Jacob pointed to the healthy sheep grazing, and to the goats on the hillside. "There they are, healthy, multiplied hundreds and hundreds of times. When I kept my father's herd, he let me make up my own flock. Have I one speckled lamb to call my own? All that I have tended is yours."

Leah whispered to Rachel that it was indeed a scandal. Jacob's honesty in dealing was such that Laban could not bring himself to believe in it.

"Indeed, anyone else would have made himself rich beyond believing," Rachel agreed, and Leah told her in whispers of other shepherds whose masters were impoverished by their dishonesty.

Then they heard Jacob's voice continuing, "I must provide for my family. I must receive payment, and go again to my father's house. Would you have me go empty-handed and say 'thus and thus has Laban the Syrian dealt with me'?"

It was obvious that Jacob's departure would be a calamity of the first magnitude to Laban. To give him some sheep and goats would be agony enough, to allow his daughters to go would be a wrench, but to lose a shepherd of Jacob's skill, honesty and reliability was not to be contemplated. It was obvious that some sacrifice would have to be made. Laban was prepared to go a long way. Words cost nothing, and he excelled himself in fulsome speeches. He still attributed the blessing he had received to Almighty intervention, rather than to Jacob's conscientious shepherding, but he was gracious enough to say, "The Lord hath blessed me for your sake," and humbly asked Jacob to tarry with him if he found favour in his eyes. As Laban had by no means found favour in Jacob's eyes, this was a forlorn hope, but Laban brought himself to utter words which were like drawing blood from a stone.

"Appoint me thy wages," he said. "I will submit. Let us try to reach agreement."

Jacob prepared to negotiate. He would have liked to have set off there and then into his own country, but it would be humiliating to return after so many years with only sons for his hire. He must wait a few more years and try to build a flock of sheep and goats and cattle so quickly that he might then return home prosperous and wealthy to Beersheba.

· · · · · · · · · · ·

The two men surveyed the healthy flocks. Some were pure white, some were black, and a few were speckled and ringstraked. Laban, always expecting dishonesty, and unable to believe that everyone with whom he dealt had not an ulterior motive, considered the problem of how Jacob's flocks could be chosen with the minimum loss to himself. Laban felt he must devise a scheme whereby Jacob could not take the choicest and healthiest for himself. At first he had considered whether Jacob should have all the black sheep, but looking at them Laban saw a problem—Jacob would be able to breed healthy black sheep by his clever knowledge concerning selection. The question of the white lambs arose, but the same difficulty applied there.

At last, in exasperation, Jacob said, "Let me have the speckled ones, those poor spotted ringstraked goats and sheep. Let me take them. Give me but something for my hire."

Laban smiled blandly. It was a way out. No one living could find a way to breed sheep and goats speckled and spotted. They were the freaks of the flock, and he could see before him that they were the poorest and weakest. That idea commended itself to him, and in high good humour Laban returned to the household, and surprised his daughter and his wife with his joviality.

. . . .

Laban had not been as clever as he thought, and had not bargained for the ancient lore and secrets passed on by Miram, the master-shepherd, to his erstwhile pupil, Jacob. When Laban had given his son-in-law permission to have the ringstraked sheep and goats, there was not a man or woman of the tribe who did not think this grasping and mean, and wondered at Jacob for accepting such a scurvy offer. Shekels in plenty and the pick of the flock would have been small wages for all that Jacob had done. But to everyone's surprise, Jacob seemed content, and carried on with his work, driving the few ringstraked sheep from their fellows and giving them to Reuben and Judah to care for, sending them three miles journey apart from the rest of the flock. He then spent many hours under the open heaven thinking, remembering and trying to work out a plan. When the time would come for the ewes to be served, then his ideas would be put into operation.

Laban did not understand all the intricacies of breeding, but was pleased to note that Jacob seemed to give little attention to the few spotted sheep which were his portion, but spent a great deal of time and thought on the main flock. Indeed, day by day he could see him going through the flock, selecting and choosing. His hand ran over the flank of a ram. Was it too fat? he wondered. It must have a good girth round the heart, and strong loins. A big coarse head would breed lambs difficult to deliver. The muzzle must be fine, eyes docile, back level.

As he made his selection, with a little purple dye purchased from the traders, each of the finer rams was marked. Jacob had reared many rams, and refused to allow them to be killed for the table. No ram should be expected to serve too many ewes if perfection in breeding was to be achieved, and all through his years of service Jacob had aimed at perfection, even though another man was to benefit. Now at last there was an added incentive to all his care. He was to benefit himself, and provide a portion for his sons, especially that dark-eyed child who was already the joy of his heart.

Then the ewes were eagerly scrutinised. Those that had rotten teeth or any form of disease or infection of the udder were discarded, and soon the purple mark—Jacob's secret sign of perfection—was to be seen on the pick of the flock.

With rising excitement, Jacob went forward with his experiments. He would allow no one to come near, demanding complete privacy. This caused no undue suspicion. Jacob was known to be no casual shepherd, allowing breeding to be haphazard. He had often known shepherds who had expected one ram to serve over a thousand sheep. Such shepherds often found that many ewes had not been served at all, and were merely a liability on the land, instead of producing lambs. It was Jacob who had conceived a plan over the years to prevent this happening. The chest of the ram was constantly smeared with a composition of charcoal and oil, and an examination of the ewe's rumps made it plain which had been served. By this method Jacob was able to see that maximum lambing was achieved. But his new secret processes needed even more concentrated care than the use of charcoal and oil.

.   .   .   .

Anyone watching Jacob might have wondered at his preparations—armfuls of hazel rods, green poplars, and chestnuts were laid in the gutters and ditches, and "pilled" white stakes were placed between them. Anyone might have wondered to see certain ewes, those only of the purple marking, released to drink at the gutters, their short-sighted eyes looking directly into the poplars and hazel rods, with the light of the white strakes reflected between. Then the purple-marked rams were let loose, and their instincts drove them unerringly to the ewes ready to be served. Nature took its course. The ewes conceived while gazing at the rods, and the next day the operation was repeated until all the selected ewes were in lamb.

Then Jacob had to wait. Was the ancient secret, so carefully entrusted to him by Miram, just an old wives' tale? He had thought little of it when Miram had first divulged his secret under the stars. "Why," he asked, "would anyone wish to breed speckled and spotted sheep?" As a perfectionist, he gloried in the pure white and pure black, thinking anything ringstraked only fit for killing for its flesh. But Miram had nodded sagely, and told him to store it up in his mind and tell no one, but one day it might be useful. Time alone would tell whether this would be so. Jacob prayed to the God of his fathers to make his way prosperous, and of all that he was given, according to his promise made at Bethel, he would give a tenth to Jehovah. Strange, he thought, that now for the first time he would have possessions of his own to give. He only had his eleven sons, but one was Joseph, that special son, who should be set apart for God and for the tribe.

·　·　·　·　·　·　·　·　·　·　·　·

Lambing time for the shepherd is always the most exacting and weary of seasons. True, by Jacob's method of marking the ewes served by the ram, he had been able to stagger the season so that all the ewes did not lamb at the same time. Over the years he had worked to a programme, and with his sons to help, he was able to give himself unstintingly to the task. Reuben and Judah were trustworthy, and had all the makings of good shepherds. Jacob imparted much of his knowledge to them. They knew how to place the skin of a dead lamb over an orphan lamb, so that the ewe whose lamb had died would accept the orphan as her own. They knew how to assist Jacob at difficult deliveries, and showed all their father's love of the flock.

This lambing season was different. Jacob's sons, knowing that every speckled lamb was one for their own flock, waited and wondered. They did not know of Jacob's secret experiments, but only knew that he hoped God would prosper him and send him many ringstraked lambs and kids for their own herd.

It was fantastic! Day after day Jacob and his sons returned jubilant to the homestead, where Laban sourly enquired how many lambs had been born spotted that day. When the figure was beyond believing, he sent his sons secretly to join with their cousins, ostensibly to help, but actually to see whether Jacob had some device or markings that he put upon them. They could find nothing, and only brought back the depressing news that not only were the ringstraked lambs and kids like grasshoppers for number, but they were all the strongest and finest of the flock.

And so it was, season after season, that Laban and his sons impotently raged, while Jacob's flocks and herds increased a hundredfold, and his sheep and goats were the finest and strongest ever seen. Shepherds and tribesmen from as far away as Haran and Nahor came to see the flocks, and comment on the quality and fruitfulness of Jacob's breeding. His popularity became great, and people admired his skill. He was able to purchase man-servants and maid-servants, and raised a flock of which any patriarch could be proud.

13

THERE was news of a group of traders coming towards Haran, following the trade routes through to Nineveh. Jacob thought this would be a good time to barter some of Laban's flocks for merchandise. He intended taking some of his own speckled and ringstraked sheep, which, in spite of their markings, and because of their excellence, always commanded a good price. It was a source of continual humiliation to Jacob that Laban never trusted him to visit the traders alone, imagining that he would keep back part of the price, or make some private deal to his own advantage. He was now on his way to see Laban before going to his own tents, to suggest dealing with these traders.

Deep in thought, he had entered the room before seeing that Laban was entertaining important guests. The sons of Laban, attired like princes, made Jacob conscious of his soiled tunic and tattered shepherd's cloak. Laban stared at him, and the sniggers of Laban's sons did nothing to put Jacob at his ease. He would have instantly withdrawn, but Laban asked in his unpleasant, bullying tone, "Well, fellow, what brings you here in that attire? Has some mischief come to the flock, or have you by your carelessness permitted the lambs to be torn by wild beasts?"

Jacob flinched, as he ever did at this particular tone, and said, "It was to discuss bartering some of the flock with the traders that I came. I purposed taking some of my own sheep to obtain produce for my wives."

"And were no doubt wondering whether you could try to get a better price for your poor ringstraked sheep than for my fine flock. Well, Jacob, I'll talk about it later," and Laban would have dismissed him like a lacquey, had not one of the merchants enquired, "Did you say 'Jacob'? Surely he is your kinsman, of whom we have heard? His fame as a skilled shepherd is told around every fireside in these parts."

Jacob pulled himself up, and tried to forget his soiled raiment. It was when he met his own kind, such as these, that he realised what servitude in Laban's household had done to him, how it had taken from him his self-respect, and almost made him forget how to speak to a man of substance, such as his father Isaac.

"Surely," continued Laban's guest, "this is one of the sons of Isaac, the seed of Abraham, the great Patriarch."

Jacob held up his head. "Indeed, I am Isaac's son, and I am his heir, to whom he has given his blessing."

This was too much for Laban, who growled, "In the meantime, you are my servant, and it would be well if you went back to the flocks and ceased neglecting them."

Jacob went out with what dignity he could muster, the mocking laughter of Laban's objectionable sons following him, as he made his way towards the encampment where his wives, concubines and sons, together with the members of the tribe, had their dwelling. It was only here that Jacob was treated as the chieftain. Every contact with Laban and his two sons spelt humiliation for him. Jacob felt he could not go on He sat on a smooth stone, where he and Rachel had often rested during those first happy years.

He searched his heart, asking himself what it was that made it so easy for Laban to browbeat and bully him. Why did he not take his father-in-law by the throat and make him choke back the words he spoke? It would serve him right if he *had* cheated him, lost his lambs, undersold him at the market, but Jacob knew he could never do that. The day he lost his integrity, he would lose everything. That counted to him far more than riches.

It was not often that Jacob let his mind dwell on the past. Now he felt he must ask himself why he—Isaac's heir by promise, purchase and blessing, Laban's adopted son by all the ceremony of Nuzu Law—should not be able to hold up his head, and throw back proud words into the face of his tormentor. Twenty years' hard labour! It was a long time to be treated as an inferior servant, subjected to suspicion and constant accusation. Before that, even since he was a child, he had never known that certainty and unconscious lordship experienced by those who, from birth, are given first place.

All through childhood he had been overshadowed by Esau. To his father, he had been 'only Jacob'. He had longed to be the child of promise, and even after the purchase of the birthright, had no satisfaction in the position. His father ignored it, and never acknowledged him until the day when he had blessed him. Jacob bowed his head at the thought. He could never forgive himself for yielding to his mother's entreaty in being party to that masquerade. He should have boldly faced his father and demanded the blessing. I believe, if I had done that, he would have given it to me, Jacob mused, for the Spirit of God came upon him, and he blessed me, even me. I should have been bold and faced Esau, with his attempted perfidy. It was he who tried to steal my blessing, yet I was made to feel the guilty party. But it was by that very action that his father accorded to him his true position. Had he remained longer with his father, all the respect of the tribe and his father's loving approval might have developed that regal bearing and innate sense of the right to command that had evaded him.

He had been weak with his father-in-law. His love for Rachel had made him particularly vulnerable. But when he had found himself defrauded after seven years, he should have insisted upon taking both Leah and Rachel, and going back to his own kindred. He felt he could never forgive himself for not being at his mother's death-bed, and of robbing her of the satisfaction of seeing him happily married and the father of sons, before she died. He should face his father-in-law now, and demand his flocks, back payment due, and the right to take his wives and go into his own country. But he was weak and cowardly, and he knew it. Once Laban started to shout at him, he was like a beaten child who fears further punishment.

He put his head in his hands. What a man he was! How could he command such love from his wives and sons, he often wondered. Yet through it all, he knew that the God of his fathers loved him, and had promised to be with him. He wished he knew if God would have him stay here in Padan-aram, or take his courage in both hands and dare to go.

He sat thus, quietly musing within himself, and then it was that he was conscious of the Voice, speaking, not from heaven, but from his inner consciousness. It was just a brief sentence, but it was all that Jacob required.

"Return to the land of thy fathers, and to thy kindred, and I will be with thee."

The reiteration of that promise of God's presence with him was a balm to Jacob's soul, and an encouragement to him in the big decision that he had to make. Jacob rose, a new man, refreshed and renewed. He must make a plan, and acquaint his wives with all that had to be done.

.   .   .   .

Since Leah had passed the age when ardent desire had been so strong, she and Rachel had been drawn together, and experienced again something of the old relationship that was theirs before

Jacob had ever arrived in Padan-aram. In those days their lives had been dominated by Laban and his moods, and though this was not so much the case as far as they were personally concerned now, they were drawn together by a common hatred and distrust of the way in which their much-loved husband was treated, and anger at the way in which he had been defrauded. As is the way with those dominated by a tyrant, all conversation seemed inevitably to return to the subject of the dominant one's evils and sins.

Together they recounted Jacob's virtues, his patience, skill, and utter honesty, and contrasted it with the greed and craftiness of their father Laban. Every degradation heaped upon Jacob was resented, and Laban's sons, with their arrogant ways and lordly bearing, were compared unfavourably with all the sons of the tribe of Jacob, whether by lawful wives or by concubine.

It was thus deep in conversation that Jacob found them, and his heart leapt again for gladness to see the better relationship that existed between them.

"I have much to say to you, my wives," he said, "but there is no privacy here beside the tents. We must go into the fields, where I can speak freely, for what I have to say is for your ears alone."

The fields were deserted and empty of workers. As the slanting rays of the sun painted the tents with golden light, Jacob delivered his soul to his eagerly listening audience. He did not need to tell them that their father's face was not towards them as before.

"You know well I have served him with all my power." Rachel and Leah nodded, while Jacob went on, "Your father has deceived me, defrauded me, and yet the God of my fathers has prospered me." Jacob reminded them of his success in breeding the sheep, attributing this not so much to the ancient secret, but to the blessing of the Almighty. "I have obtained by this means many of my father-in-law's sheep and cattle, but was it not my right?"

His wives, both speaking at once, vied with each other to agree.

"Now I have something of the greatest possible importance

to say. I have told you before how God spoke to me in Bethel, and promised to be with me and to prosper me, and now God has called me to return again to my own country, to the land of my kindred. Now tell me," said Jacob, leaning forward, and looking from one to the other, "do I go alone, do you remain in your father's house? I have no right to insist that you leave with me, for by doing so, we all forfeit any inheritance that we are entitled to—yours by birth, and mine by adoption."

Rachel and Leah listened intently, and then both answered. "Is there any portion for us in our father's house?" Rachel asked, and Leah went on, "Are we not counted strangers?"

Laban had made it clear that he resented Jacob's success, and counted every lamb born in the flock of Jacob as stolen from him, though it was only rightful shepherd's wages.

"Shall I go bravely to your father, tell him of my plan, and bid him farewell as a man and not as a craven fugitive?"

Both Leah and Rachel were adamant against such a suggestion. "He has the mind of a fox, and subtlety of a serpent," they said. "He will devise some means to make you serve another twenty years to suit his own ends. He will stick at no trickery or violence for the furtherance of his purpose, and his sons have minds as crooked as his own."

Jacob's experience had taught him that this was so. He would send his eldest sons ahead with the flocks. This would cause no suspicion. Then overnight every preparation would be made for secret flight.

.   .   .   .

Jacob may not, as a child, have shown the qualities of leadership that were evident in Esau, and although before Laban he might have felt a sense of inferiority, as he had grown to man's estate he had developed that ability to inspire love in those who counted themselves as members of his tribe. He had acquired manservants and maidservants, and with his eleven sons, wives and concubines, there was not a more loyal body of people who listened to the instructions their leader had to give. Jacob's treatment at the hand of Laban had been a favourite subject of discussion round the camp fires, and one and all longed to redress his wrongs. Absolute secrecy was enjoined upon them all. If the lord Laban knew what was afoot, there would be serious hostility.

Murmurs of agreement broke out among them while Jacob continued, " I am not taking you out as my forefather, Abraham, did, not knowing whither he went. I take you to our own kindred where, on my father Isaac's death, I will be the chieftain of all his tribe. His wealth in flocks and herds, wells and pastures, is far greater than that of Laban. My father is no mere son of an eighth child, as Laban is, but great Abraham's son, and I am his accredited heir."

All the tribe looked at him with love and pride. Now they did not see him as the poor relation, brow-beaten and treated as an underling; this was their undoubted chieftain.

Then Jacob looked at them sternly.

" Listen to me, each man, woman and child among our ranks. I may have been treated scurvily here in Padan-aram, but I am a servant of Jehovah, in Whose sight I seek to find favour. He it is Who in a vision of the night, has sent me to my kindred. We do not take one shoe-latchet from Laban or his tribe that is not our own. I swear by the God of our fathers that anyone who disobeys me will die the death."

Anyone who had been contemplating a little petty larceny soon disabused his mind of such a thing, as Jacob's eyes, those deep-set eyes of the thinker, searched every face. Only Rachel's eyes dropped, for her conscience was not perfectly clear. Jacob had said that nothing was to be taken that did not *belong* to them, that was not theirs by *right*, but no one could deny that the images given to Jacob at the ceremony of adoption were his. Rachel, with a courage born of anger at her husband's wrongful treatment, had sought her moment carefully, and had crept into her father's house while he and his sons were out shearing the sheep, and had taken from the place of honour the images which had belonged to Jacob for thirteen years, but which he had refused to claim. These images would be valid in any dispensation of Nuzu law. In years to come one of Jacob's sons might want to come back and claim his share of the inheritance.

Mounted on their camels, the wives and younger sons of Jacob set off. Hidden in the saddle-bags of the camel on which Rachel rode were the images. If these were discovered, Rachel did not fear the sentence of death that Jacob had threatened, for every man and woman in the camp would uphold her, saying these were Jacob's and his sons by right.

· · · · · · · · · · · ·

The shearing of the sheep was a time of great activity. This part of the work was the responsibility of Laban and his sons, and if they had perforce to admire the quality of the wool the sheep produced, no word of acknowledgment was ever given to Jacob.

Laban mopped the sweat from his brow.

"It is a fine crop of wool—even more so than last year's, is it not, my father?" asked his eldest son.

"Yes, indeed," said Laban, and added loudly for the benefit of the servants, "It has pleased Jehovah to bless and reward me by such fine fleeces."

Then as Laban continued working with a will, he became conscious that his younger son was not doing his share of the work. Laban turned with an oath to rebuke him, and was surprised to see his son, looking a little shaken, walking towards him.

"What is it, you idle dolt, leaving your brother to work alone? What ails you? Speak up!" he shouted, seeing his son looking astonished.

"Zerug says they've all gone, clear away, three days' journey."

"Who have gone? Speak plainly," said his father impatiently.

"Jacob; he has taken his sons, his wives, and all his servants, and the flocks and herds, and where their tents have been is just waste ground. Not a hoof or piece of goatskin has been left behind, Zerug says."

"And I dare say he has taken the pick of my flock and herds, the cheat and thief. I will make him pay for this."

With scant explanation, Laban threw down the shearing knife, and with his sons went to count the sheep, and check the herds, and see how much had been taken. Then he planned to travel on fast dromedaries to chase Jacob, and make him pay for his perfidy, bringing him back in disgrace.

Laban's sons insisted upon accompanying their father. It would indeed be a scene not to be missed. Their father was able to make proud Jacob cringe, they had seen him do so many a time; Jacob, who thought himself so important, yet who could be humiliated by their father.

.   .   .   .

There is something about the relaxation from routine and restriction that gives a gaiety and joyousness to those so released. Jacob and his tribe had become accustomed to working every waking hour. Suddenly there was a sense of release and holiday, as the vast cavalcade moved first stealthily and then gaily towards Mount Gilead. The many maidens sang songs, Jacob joked with his handsome sons, perched little Joseph up on his own camel, and thought with what pride he would show this prince among his sons to Isaac, Esau and the tribe.

During those seven days of travel, care fell from Jacob. Men were sent ahead on the fast dromedaries to prepare the camping place for the night, and to find a well of water. Reuben and Judah drove the flocks, and kept a sharp eye on Simeon and Levi, for their father had straightly charged them that the direst of punishment would fall on any who drove the ewes in lamb at too great a speed. Colour came to Rachel's pale cheeks as she journeyed, and Leah looked the picture of a contented matron.

Jacob began to wonder why it was he had ever felt any fear of Laban. Here he was a man and a sheik. He would owe no man anything, and could look the whole world in the face. At last Mount Gilead was reached, the exhausting days of travel were over, and Jacob had promised that here they would rest for several days.

Then word came that men on dromedaries were seen throwing up the dust on the skyline.

"It will be our grandfather, Laban," Reuben told Jacob in a frightened voice, while Judah scowled and clenched his fists.

All looked at Jacob to see what he would say. Would he show

craven fear? Jacob's face was impassive as a mask. It was strange, even to him, that Laban's coming inspired in him no fear. It only brought back to him the misery of the last twenty years, which during that past week had gone from him in merciful oblivion.

Jacob bade the tribe set themselves in array; some were to prepare food, and all must treat the pursuers as honoured guests. His sons stood by, these fine young men, with all the handsome bearing of descendants of Terah. Tradition said that this old patriarch's sons were all outstandingly handsome men, and that all his daughters were beautiful. This had certainly been the case with Sarah, Rebekah and Rachel, and Jacob's only daughter, Dinah, child though she was, by her beauty caused many a head to turn in her direction.

* * * * * ' * * * * * *

Laban's wrath against Jacob made him almost demented. The fact that none of the sheep were missing from the flock, instead of appeasing him, made him even more angry. He stood in his house, shouting to his wife to make ready for their journey, and then he stopped short. Conspicuous among the array of images in the place of honour were the spaces where, until three days ago, the images of Jacob's adoption had stood. Laban snarled with rage, but also with a certain sense of glee that Jacob had not been so scrupulous as he had thought. So that was the villain's game! The images he had professed to despise he had taken. He thought to come and stake his claim to the inheritance with his sons of the blood; the double-dyed knave! The fact that Jacob had a perfect right to do so made Laban all the angrier. He wanted Jacob back to tend the sheep, but more than anything he wanted to reclaim those images and destroy Jacob's right to any share of his inheritance. His sons were equally anxious to obtain these tokens, for they were shrewd enough to know that any court of law would uphold the claim.

Taking with him his strongest and most warlike servants, Laban set off, never doubting that before long he would have Jacob beaten to his knees.

* * * * * * * * * *

During the first three days of travel, as Laban pursued hotly after Jacob, his anger increased and was fanned into flame, as he and his sons whiled away the journey recounting their grievances, real and imagined. Every occasion when Jacob had shown arrogance, every time Jacob had received the glory for the excellence of Laban's herds, was remembered and dwelt upon.

As Laban sat by the rudely constructed fire, satisfying his hunger with strips of dried mutton after the long journey, he comforted himself by dwelling on the vengeance he would take when Jacob was again in his power. But that night, as he slept, a terror came upon him. In his dreams he heard a Voice say, "I am the God of Abraham, Isaac and Jacob. Do him no harm." The terror that seized Pharaoh in Egypt years ago, causing him to shake with fear, and stay his hand from harming Abraham and Sarah, the terror that had smitten Abimelech of Gerar in a dream, when he thought to take Sarah for his wife, now came upon Laban. This fear was so real that when he awoke it was still with him. During the next days as they journeyed, his sons found him strangely silent and unresponsive when they breathed out their imprecations against Jacob.

* * * * * * * * * * * *

The impressive group on Mount Gilead, waiting to receive Laban, watched the approaching riders with mixed feelings. Reuben felt fear, Leah and Rachel anger, not unmixed with apprehension. Jacob was only conscious of a great calm. Laban no longer had power to hurt him. Laban's sons watched eagerly to see how their father would proceed. Would he burst into a torrent of words, or be deceptively calm, making the explosion all the more devastating when it came? Laban approached his son-in-law with a bland and genial expression.

"Well, Jacob, my son," he said, "What have you done? Why did you flee away in secrecy? I knew you wished to visit your own people, and longed for your father's house. You forestalled me. I had it in my heart to suggest that very thing. But, Jacob, I had planned to send you away with merriment, with songs, with the tabret and harp."

Such a salutation caused a gasp to go round the assembled group. Judah muttered to his brother, "The double-faced liar! When has he ever given us a kid to make merry, or thought of calling his musicians to brighten one of *our* feasts?"

Laban's sons were hugging themselves with glee. What a clever way to prepare the way for the great denunciation that was to follow! Their father, in his craftiness, was a past-master at disarming his enemy with soothing words, and then baring his teeth with rage that sent them rocking back on their heels.

Laban went on, as Jacob was quite bereft of words at such an uncharacteristic approach, every word of which rang false. "And all my dear grandchildren, and my dear daughters." Laban's voice assumed a convincing quaver. "You would give me no opportunity to kiss them farewell. Was it kindly done, son Jacob?"

"The old hypocrite!" hissed Simeon to Levi. "When has he even shown that he knew we existed?" and Leah and Rachel could scarce forbear to smile at such a bare-faced change of attitude.

"I could by law have dealt hardly with you, Jacob," went on Laban mildly. "It was in my heart to do so, but the God of your father spoke to me last night and forbade me to do you any harm."

Jacob noticed that Laban spoke of the 'God of *your* father', though he was glib enough to speak of Jehovah in familiar terms if it was to take credit for his own blessing and prosperity. Jacob was relaxing. It was evident that from the way Laban spoke of 'the God of your father', there was fear upon him that was certainly restraining him.

Then Laban turned and bared his teeth. He had one thing of which to accuse Jacob. Even Jehovah could not uphold him in this villainy.

"It is not to be wondered at that you longed to be gone after your father, but," then his voice changed, "*wherefore hast thou taken my gods, those images upon which you know I set such great value?*"

Jacob recoiled, and his heart sank within him. He had felt so safe and certain in his complete integrity. But this accusation seemed to stab him to the heart, and brought back all his fear and sense of inferiority.

He started in just his old manner to excuse himself. "I was afraid that thou wouldst take my wives from me by force." And then his new-found strength returned, and he looked round upon the tribe in anger, raking the group with his eyes. "But as for the idols—search and look. Whosoever hath stolen them shall surely die." For Jacob, as a chieftain, had the power of life and death.

So great was his wrath at the disobedience to his implicit commands, that all could see that this was no empty threat or figure of speech. The tribesmen trembled before him, and eagerly opened their packs and bundles, so that Laban and his men could see that all they had brought were only their lawful possessions.

Only Rachel sat on her camel and trembled. Never had she heard Jacob speak in such a manner, and she knew that if the idols were found she was under the sentence of death, beloved wife though she might be. Laban and his men searched each tent, particularly the dwellings of Jacob and his wives. Leah had dismounted, and was assisting in the search. Rachel remained mounted on the camel. As Laban approached, her heart beat wildly. She hardly recognised her voice as her own, as she tried desperately to smile and sound at ease.

"Let it not displease my father," she said, "that I cannot rise and give the honour due to him, but the custom of women is upon me."

Laban shrugged his shoulders. Rachel was ever a martyr to female ailments. The wonder was she had ever borne a living son. And without further thought, he searched on and found nothing.

Jacob's relief was so great that it restored to him, not only the self-respect he had lost, but a new sense of power came to him, and all the indignity of years of servitude rose before him. The tribe gathered round, and their leader spoke to Laban in a way no living man had ever before presumed to do.

"What is my trespass?" he asked in ringing tones. "What

is my sin that you dare to pursue after me so hotly? I call upon your men here to judge betwixt us. What have they found among our possessions that is not rightfully our own? Twenty years— the best years of my manhood—have I served you. Ask yourself, during that time have your ewes cast their young, have I ever taken of your fat rams, and eaten them, as any hireling shepherd would have deemed it only his right to do? Has it ever been known for a shepherd, when lambs have been torn by wild beasts, *not* to bring their legs and ears and claim exemption from blame? How many times have I done that, in these last twenty years? Try to think of one instance. You know well that I have borne the loss myself. Have I spared myself? Would another shepherd have slept outside in the frost, caring for the ewes? Would he not have sought shelter in the homestead, and never told you of the ewes and lambs that died through lack of care? Did I spare myself in the drought and heat of the day? By trickery you made me serve fourteen years for my wives. You deemed it an honour to send Rebekah your sister to marry great Abraham's son, yet you expected me to serve without payment of wages for Leah and Rachel. And now during these last six years I have toiled and laboured that I need not return to my people penniless at your hand." Then Jacob continued with pride and dignity, "But the God of my fathers saw my affliction, and has made me to prosper, and honoured the labour of my hands."

Then Jacob pointed an accusing hand at Laban.

"And yesternight Jehovah rebuked you, God Himself spoke to you in anger."

Laban's sons listened with astonishment. Never had they heard their father so addressed. Yet even Laban's servants standing by could not but agree with every word that was spoken. Jacob's life had been to them all an open book, and no man through all those twenty years had ever been able to point a finger at him in accusation.

Laban blustered a little, trying to say that his daughters and their sons were part of his tribe, and Jacob and his possessions too belonged to him. Jacob himself was bound by the laws of adoption. But Jacob would have none of it. Laban could not try to do Jacob out of his inheritance, and yet claim his privileges, for if that were not his plan, why the anxiety to reclaim the images? Jacob too was a chieftain, not a mere vassal of Laban, and he was going, not as a returned fugitive, but as an heir to claim his inheritance.

Laban became meek, and anxious to make the best of the matter. Jacob thought grimly that this was the way he should have treated Laban all these years. A bully only responds to such treatment. Had he valued himself more, and not been so conscious of a sense of inferiority, if his early training had not made him so vulnerable, he might have been able to hold his own with Laban.

They all sat round together for a meal. Laban became the genial father and grandfather that he might have been. He made a covenant with Jacob, and a heap of stones was raised to mark the occasion. With tears in his eyes, he besought Jacob to treat his daughters well, and not to afflict them, and forbade him to take other wives from among the Canaanites. Jacob had no intention of afflicting the wives to whom he had always shown love and consideration, and recoiled in horror from the idea of taking Canaanitish wives. He agreed amicably to all Laban's injunctions.

In his desire to forget the past, Laban piously invoked the God, not only of Abraham, but that of his own grandfather Nahor, ignoring the fact that Nahor had never worshipped Jehovah, but presented himself annually at the Ziggurat of the sun-god in Ur. However, Jacob was not going to quibble, but took care to swear only by the God of his father Isaac.

Laban further excelled himself by calling the beacon where they had met 'Mizpah'—'the Lord watch between me and thee when we are absent one from another'—and the name 'Mizpah' has become a saying for many generations among those who are separated from each other.

14

W H E N Laban had taken ceremonious farewells of his daughters and grandsons, Jacob moved on his journey towards Ramoth-Gilead and the brook Jabbok. His heart was singing within him, and he felt at last that he was a chieftain in his own right, and that God was with him. Even as he went, he was conscious of angels, 'God's host', as he called them when telling Leah and Rachel of their presence, though they themselves had not eyes to see them.

It seemed inevitable that whenever Jacob was particularly uplifted, something happened to cut the ground from under his feet. He had felt able to face Laban; then the accusation about the idols had temporarily stunned him, and made his heart turn to water. And so it was that as he journeyed, full of confidence in God, and enjoyment of his new-found liberty, that a message came saying, "Esau comes, bringing with him four hundred men."

Jacob's confidence collapsed. That which he had greatly feared had come to pass. Esau, his warlike brother, had heard of his impending arrival, and had summoned the men of war to go out against him. Jacob was caught in a trap. His men were peaceful shepherds, not trained for battle, and what made him completely vulnerable was the presence of his wives and children. Had it not been for them, he would have been able to muster some of the strongest of his servants and make a stand. But with women and children as hostages, his position was precarious.

Jacob, in an agony of mind, went out to meditate on what he had heard, and sought the comfort that had sustained him often in the past unhappy years. He prayed,

> "O God of my father Abraham, and God of my father Isaac, the Lord which saidst unto me, Return unto thy country, and to thy kindred, and I will deal well with thee."

He began praying thus, and then his sense of his own unworthiness overcame him:

> "I am not worthy of the least of all the mercies, and of all the truth, which thou hast shewed unto thy servant. . . . Deliver me, I pray thee, from the hand of my brother, from the hand of Esau; for I fear him, lest he will come and smite me, and the mothers with the children."

He returned strengthened from his meditation, and tried to imagine the workings of Esau's mind. Then he reflected, Esau did not grudge the promise; Esau had no desire for spiritual blessing, but it might be that he still held it against his brother that Isaac had promised him prosperity; indeed, that promise had come true, Jacob thought, mentally counting the milch camels, the she-asses, the bulls, the sheep and the goats that he possessed. Esau should share these with him. He would send gifts now to placate him and stay his wrath.

Jacob called his servants together, and put the plan in operation, sending them off with droves of asses, camels, sheep and goats, to arrive in relays, instructing each man to say to his brother Esau, "These are a present from 'thy servant Jacob'." Jacob's most precious possessions were not the flocks and herds, but his wives and children. He still feared for them above everything else. As a precaution, he took them over the brook, feeling that, with water between his family and the approaching host of Esau, he would be able to sleep with greater peace of mind.

But Jacob could not sleep. What sort of man was he, he thought, to be so cast into a state of fear? God had promised to bless him; Isaac had blessed him, saying, "Yea, and he shall be blessed,' in such a tone that all who heard it were filled with awe. If I could see God face to face, he thought, as he had once told Eliezer, I would say, 'Give me a blessing, bless even me, Jacob though I am—Jacob, the wrestler, the hireling, the masquerader.'

Then Jacob found himself wrestling with a man. He was not sure if his opponent was part of a dream, if he saw a vision, or if it indeed was reality. At first he thought an enemy had crept up on him—a thief, perhaps, or even one of Esau's host. But then he knew his opponent for what he was, and he knew that he wrestled with an angel of the Lord. Indeed, it was as though he wrestled with God Himself, and he found himself pleading, "Bless me, oh my God, and give me a blessing." The angel tried repeatedly to break loose, but Jacob, in an agony of spiritual desire, held on with an ever more tenacious grip, saying through clenched teeth, as he felt his strength ebbing, "I-will-not-let-thee-go-except-thou-bless-me."

On went the struggle.

Jacob suddenly felt a burning pain in his thigh, as though a sinew had contracted. His leg was useless, but he still held on with his arms. At last the man with whom he fought spoke to him, and Jacob loosed his grip.

"What is thy name?" asked his opponent.

The answer came from the exhausted wrestler, "Jacob."

The angel loosed his hold on Jacob and spoke to him, and the words he spoke were in the Voice he had come to know so well.

> "Thy name shall be called no more Jacob, but ISRAEL; for as a prince hast thou power with God and with men, and hast prevailed."

And the Man of God gave Jacob a blessing.

This, thought Jacob, is the greatest moment in my life. He called the place 'Peniel', "for," he said exultantly, "I have seen God face to face, and still live." He was to be called 'ISRAEL', 'prince with God'. He felt unworthy of such an honour, a mixture of both humility and pride mingling as he realised that his name would go down through posterity, not as Jacob, the wrestler, the supplanter, but as ISRAEL, prince with God.

The next morning, with the reflection of his celestial experience still on him, Jacob called his people together, and told them that on the authority of God Himself, Who had appeared again to him, he was to be called ISRAEL. All the tribe rejoiced, knowing that this was indeed an honour, for ISRAEL is the male counterpart of Sarah, the name given to the wife of great Abraham. As they journeyed on, if men should ask, "Are you the children of Jacob?" they would proudly answer, "Nay, rather say we are the children of ISRAEL."

. . . .

How differently we view things we dread when morning comes! So thought Jacob when, with new-found strength, he set out to meet Esau. The horror of the night was over. After the experience of Peniel, Jacob would never be quite the same; for the rest of his life he would limp, but his faith had been immeasurably strengthened. It was to be one of his life's milestones.

The moment must be faced. He was in no position to fight, but must submit himself to Esau, who, if the gifts had not placated him, might listen to reason. Bravely, at the head of his tribe, Jacob, on his camel, went forward. Then he saw Esau, and on his face was no anger, only joy, and in his hand was no sword. Esau ran towards his brother, and Jacob, forgetting his anxiety, dismounted and ran too. The brothers fell upon each other's necks, the past forgotten as though it had never been. They looked into each other's eyes, and the years rolled from them. It was as though they were boys again, calling each other 'Hairy' and 'Wrestler', no cloud to mar their fellowship.

"I heard of your arrival, brother Jacob," Esau told him, "and I sent word throughout the tribe, telling men to leave their work, for they must go in a body to welcome the future Patriarch, and do homage to the one who will one day rule the tribe."

Jacob looked at his brother incredulously. He might have known better than to worry. Esau could never hold a grudge for a few hours, and certainly not for twenty years.

"Now that you are come, my father will allow me to journey to Mount Seir," Esau told him. "I greatly desire to dwell there, but our father has had me stay with him these many years. 'When thy brother returns, you can have my leave to depart' he has said constantly, 'but until then I need you with me'." Esau laughed. "I had to obey; the Patriarch had spoken. You remember how it has always been."

"Well, nearly always," said Jacob.

Esau gave a rumbling laugh, so reminiscent of his father, and slapped his brother on the back with a huge hand.

"Yes, indeed, brother," he said, "there were times when I did not always please the Patriarch. But who are these—your wives and children?"

With pride Jacob presented his sons, one after another, and then he brought Rachel with Joseph. Esau exclaimed to see a woman so like his mother Rebekah, with all her beauty, and noticed the pride with which Jacob brought forth his youngest son, Joseph.

Esau laughed, asking, "Is this the child of promise?" for it was plain to see where his brother's heart was anchored.

"But tell me," said Esau after a time, "what mean these droves of sheep and camels, asses and goats?"

Jacob bowed himself down to his brother and said, "They are a present for my lord Esau," saying nothing of his fears, which now seemed meaningless and foolish.

Esau, full of enthusiasm at being with Jacob again, urged him to travel with him, but Jacob knew Esau of old, and the way he rode ruthlessly, thinking only of himself. Jacob looked at the faces of his wives and small sons. Joseph could hardly keep his eyes open, while Rachel's face was drawn with fatigue. Jacob's tender heart was touched to see their exhaustion, and he bade Esau go on alone.

"The children are tender," he said, "and I must not overdrive the ewes with young."

Esau shrugged. Jacob always was womanish. Imagine any man hanging back because of women and children. He himself would have ridden on, and left them to fend for themselves. With a fond farewell, he rode off, with promises of a meeting again soon.

. . . .

There was great rejoicing at Jacob's return. Deborah, who had lamented the death of Rebekah and her own husband, Miram, left Mamre to be with Jacob, and when she saw Rachel, her heart yearned toward her.

" If ever I saw anyone like my mistress, Rebekah, it is my lord Jacob's wife, Rachel," Deborah told him, but what she did not tell him was that though her husband's eyes might be blind, anyone with any sense at all could see that Rachel would not live many more years.

.   .   .   .

Esau stayed with Jacob for a while after his return, but so numerous were their joint flocks and herds that Esau deemed the time had come to make his way to Mount Seir, as he had longed to do. Here his many children and children's children were called the Edomites, for that name 'Edom' (red) had clung to Esau ever since he sold his birthright for a mess of red pottage.

It was strange to Jacob to find Isaac still alive. The blessing he had thought his father's dying bequest was now twenty years old. But the old Patriarch still lived, and was glad indeed to hand over the reins of judgment to Jacob, so that he, with his blindness of eye and feebleness of body, could end his days in Mamre, near Hebron, where he and his greatly mourned Rebekah had enjoyed each other and their love.

.   .   .   .

If Jacob was ignorant of the state of his wife's health, Rachel herself suffered no such illusion. She knew that her years were numbered. It might please God to leave her with Jacob and Joseph for a few years more, but she knew she would never see Joseph grow up to full manhood. She had accepted this fact and was able to live with it, savouring each day as a precious gift. Her urgent concern was the training of her son Joseph. He loved her with a complete devotion, but she tried never to cling to him, to make his loss all the greater when the time came.

She taught him of his father's God, told him everything she had ever heard of the ways of God with men, stressing the importance of honesty, purity and uprightness. She ever held before him the example of his father, who in spite of provocation never stooped to anything that was not right, bore the insults heaped upon him with dignity, and had a clear conscience before God and men.

She was well aware of all that Joseph had to put up with from his brothers. When Joseph was only a baby lying on a cushion outside her tent, she had seen Judah's eyes looking at his little brother—Judah, who so longed to be his father's chosen heir. She could almost read his mind: This little bit of life, to stand between me and leadership of the tribe. It was to me my father would have given the coat of many colours, had you not been born. If I put my finger on your windpipe, no one would see, but you would just cease to exist. Then Judah had seen his aunt Rachel looking at him with smouldering eyes. "If you touch that child, or hurt him in any way," she told him, "I will kill you with these hands of mine." Judah had slunk away, and wondered why he had ever thought that his aunt Rachel was weak. He veritably believed that, had he hurt her child, she would have carried out her threat and killed him, and strangely, he never doubted that she had the strength. Well, he excused himself, I never meant him any harm. It was just a passing thought.

Rachel had spoken often with Reuben, who still came and talked with her, liking not only her company, but that of her maid, Bilhah.

"Reuben," she said urgently, "promise me that you will protect Joseph from his brothers."

Reuben had said easily that Joseph would be all right, she need not be concerned.

But Rachel went on, "I have a feeling, a premonition and a sense of evil. Judah is not cruel like Simeon and Levi; they will try to bully and vent their spite on Joseph in a way that Judah would scorn to do—he would never bully the weak—but if his ambitions were threatened, he might be dangerous."

Reuben looked a little surprised at the intensity of her tone, but assured her that he would do his best.

Rachel had thought of the strange streak that ran through the family, where brother had seemed from generation to generation to have murderous thoughts against his brother. God keep my little Joseph from harm, she breathed.

Rachel warned Joseph not to antagonise his brothers by taking any advantage of his position as his father's favourite. She did not implant in him a desire to be the child of promise, from whom would come SHILOH. Joseph was not imbued with the great sense of destiny that had eaten into his father's vitals. Rachel was much more concerned that Joseph's service of Jehovah should be in purity, honesty and kindness.

"The followers of Jehovah," she told him, "do not give themselves to women before marriage, but value truth and integrity above everything. For seven years your father yearned to take me," she said to Joseph, as he grew older, "and many would have excused his doing so, but he kept himself pure."

The children of her sister Leah were not so instructed. From being tiny children they had heard their mother speak slighting words to Rachel. They were taught to avenge themselves of any slight, to behave arrogantly in the tribe; they were never checked for cruelty, except occasionally by their father, they were taught to think a lie something to be used to gain one's ends. It would have been well had Jacob been aware of where his sons were going, and had he taken more responsibility for their instruction and reproof, the course of their history might have been very different. The lack of teaching in honesty and purity was reflected in the subsequent behaviour of Jacob's sons, and his daughter.

15

HAMOR the Hivite sat in his house situated on a hillside in Shalem. Servants had been dispatched to bring him wine and sweet cakes. On a small carved table beside him were a number of pieces of silver, one hundred in all.

"You seem to have prospered, my father. In what way have the gods smiled upon you?"

Hamor looked up to see Shechem his son, prince of the country and his heir. Hamor smiled his welcome. The sight of his son, in all the glory of his manhood, never failed to rejoice him. Never had a man fathered so handsome a son, thought Hamor.

"Sit down, my son, and hear how we of Shalem are to be honoured. No less a person than Jacob, son of Isaac, has deigned to buy from me a parcel of land on which to build a house, booths for his cattle, and ground where his tribe may pitch their tents. We shall have distinguished neighbours." Hamor spoke with considerable irony.

Shechem was interested. Ever since great Abraham had penetrated the land of Canaan from far-off Ur of the Chaldees, the stories of his doings and those of his tribe had been a source of interest and conjecture.

"But I thought they gathered their skirts around them, and feared to pollute themselves by contact with the corrupt dwellers of the land."

"Oh, think not that he would seek to dwell *in* Shalem. His parcel of ground is outside the city. But he is wealthy, even beyond the wealth of Abraham and Isaac, and has flocks and herds and camels and asses, and fine sons."

Shechem was interested.

His father continued, watching his son closely to see his reactions, "He also has a very beautiful daughter."

Shechem made an impatient gesture.

"So Jacob has deigned to buy of our land?" he asked. "I thought that Abraham would take nothing of us at all. Is there not some story that when the king of Sodom would have loaded him with gifts, he said not one thread or shoe-latchet would he take?"

"True, he would take nothing as a gift, but even he bought the cave of Machpelah from the sons of Heth, in which to bury his dead."

"So Jacob follows in his steps, but buys land to house the living?"

"He does, my son, and mayhap we will benefit. His sons might find wives of our people, and our men might make marriages with their maidens. It might even be. . . ."

"We will leave it at that, my father," said Shechem firmly. "Make no plans for me to wed with strange women. I will seek a bride for myself when my heart is so disposed."

. . . .

To live in a house again, after being a tent-dweller since her marriage, was for Rachel like returning to her childhood. But Jacob's house near Shalem was finer than anything Laban had owned. There were rooms for Leah and her sons, a place for Rachel and Joseph, where Jacob himself chiefly dwelt, and in the centre of it all there was a court where Jacob loved to sit with his sons, wives and daughter Dinah around him at the time of siesta, or in the cool of the evening.

Since he had bought the land and built his house, Jacob felt in very truth a patriarch, away from the frustrations and anxieties of servitude, and he sought to be a fair master, a wise father, and just ruler of his tribe.

The cattle were housed in booths, crops were sown in the fields, and everyone, even little Joseph, had learned to help in the corn-fields, gathering the sheaves.

Rachel had not been altogether happy at Jacob's choice of a dwelling place. It was too near the city of Shalem, with its temptations.

"Their ways are not our ways, Jacob," she told him. "They worship strange gods and have different customs and ideals."

Jacob easily quieted her forebodings.

"We will warn the people, and keep our children from going among the Shechemites, and as for their idolatrous ways—I will build an altar unto the Lord. I plan to call it El-elohe-Israel, for God is the God of Israel."

. . . .

Jacob was in his element. The Patriarch sat in the family court, surrounded by his sons and wives and Dinah, his beautiful daughter. Next to Joseph, she was his favourite child. She was a well-developed girl, who, though she had only reached maturity, was more like a woman of a much greater age. She had all her mother's splendour of form, without the pink-lidded eyes to mar her beauty.

The sons of Jacob sat talking together in groups. Simeon and Levi jested with Dinah. The only good thing about them, thought their father, was their love for Dinah. They might be unkind to the sons of Zilpah and Bilhah, but never to Dinah. Judah, as usual, sat aloof, not responding to Reuben's attempts at conversation. As if by common consent, the sons of the concubines sat in a less conspicuous place. Dan, Naphtali, Gad and Asher never presumed to push themselves when Judah, Simeon and Levi were in evidence. Issachar and Zebulun, Leah's younger sons, played together—a game with stones that their aunt Rachel had taught them, as she had their brother Reuben, when he was a child.

Joseph sat between his parents, day-dreaming happily. He was mercifully endowed with a happy disposition, and he lived in a world of fantasy of his own making. This make-believe world was a great comfort to him. When his parents were not present, his older brothers did all in their power to make life a misery for him. Simeon and Levi were past-masters at hurting small boys without being found out. Joseph cared less for this than for the quiet scorn of Judah, who tried to make him feel as though he were of less importance than the lizards and small reptiles that darted about in the undergrowth. Joseph's favourite dream was that one day he would be very important, and even proud Judah with all his brothers would have to bend the knee to him. He never sought to harm them, only that they should treat him with reverence. Even his father's love and regard could not compensate for Judah's scorn. Strange to say, Joseph was drawn to Judah in unwilling admiration. While he cordially disliked Simeon and Levi, he admired though feared Judah.

Jacob's eyes rested with admiration upon the comely form of his daughter, who, by her quick wit, was holding her own with her brothers, who were jesting with her concerning some of the young men of the tribe who had eyed Dinah with no little admiration. Simeon and Levi noticed that Dinah was by no means indifferent to their glances, indeed, it was because she had looked so boldly at them that Simeon was teasing his sister, saying she yearned after them. Dinah hotly denied the accusation, and Leah did nothing to check the frivolous conversation, any more than Jacob did. Jacob was blind to the fact that the overwhelming desire that had been so embarrassing to him in Leah was manifesting itself early in his daughter. He only saw her beauty, and was unable to deny her slightest wish, when she twined her graceful arms around his neck and pleaded for her desires.

A servant entered with melons and pomegranates, for the day was hot. He went to his master and bowed, saying, " Certain maidens of the city of Shalem ask that my lord's daughter Dinah go with them, that they may show her their dwellings."

Dinah, hearing her name mentioned, came over to Jacob.

" My father," she said, " it is Ira and Shalma, daughters of Hamor. I met them in the fields, and they told me of their country, and asked me to tell them of our journeyings. They promised to seek leave for me to visit them. Please say I may go."

Jacob considered, glancing over at Leah. Dinah's mother only shrugged. " Let the child go, if she has a mind to. It is dull for a girl to be among so many brothers, and having no maidens to talk with."

Jacob was doubtful, but Dinah was holding his hand and stroking it, and looking up at him with pleading eyes. Jacob allowed her to go at length, with strict instructions to stay with the maidens, and not to linger.

.   .   .   .

After living with a crowd of brothers, Dinah found it a refreshing experience to be with a group of girls, to chatter with them of trivialities, and exchange confidences and jest together. They took her into their home, where Hamor lived like a king, and showed the treasures which had been purchased from merchants —little models of cows, a carved monkey, and bears, all made out of alabaster, and some carved from wood, little pots of kohl for painting the eyelids like the Egyptian women, jars containing perfume and oil of spikenard.

Ira and Shalma were very kind, and sent their maids to bring wine and date cakes sweetened with honey, that they might refresh themselves, sitting in the wide court under the climbing plants which scented the air. All the maidens smiled at Dinah and admired her beauty, except one—a girl with a deformed back and one shoulder raised higher than the other. She rarely spoke, but looked at Dinah with deep smouldering eyes, as if her beauty gave her no pleasure.

Sitting in the courtyard, trying on one of the necklaces of cornelians, Dinah made a picture of great beauty. Her long dark hair, black as a raven's wing, hung round her like a cloud. So it was that Shechem, son of Hamor, saw her as he entered the court of his sisters. It was as though he saw a vision. He stopped under the shade of one of the arches and gazed at her, his eyes held by what he saw. So intent was his gaze that Dinah looked up and saw him, tall and manly, standing clad in his embroidered cloak, a jewelled dagger in his belt. He was as handsome as Judah, she thought, but with a much kinder expression in his eyes. With parted lips she too sat and stared, unconscious of those around her.

Zotaph, the crooked maiden, followed Dinah's gaze and saw Shechem standing transfixed. Her brow darkened with anger. So that was it! Shechem had never before looked at any maiden like that. They said he was impervious to women, and had a stone instead of a heart. This had pleased her well, for her whole heart was given to this prince, she, who was too crooked to be desirable to any man. But someone had pierced his armour at last, and it had to be one of these Hebrew women.

The other girls looked where Dinah's and Zotaph's eyes were riveted, and Ira and Shalma gave cries of welcome. Shechem gladly joined his sisters in taking refreshment, and in making much of their visitor. Dinah's heart was beating very fast. Never had any man of those who had looked upon her in admiration awakened such a response in her.

At last it was time for Dinah to go, and Shechem joined the party to escort her out of Shalem to her father's house. Promising to come again, Dinah bade them farewell, and went to her room to think over all that she had experienced, determined to say nothing concerning Shechem. But as she talked of all the maidens had shown her, of the jewellery and the treasures, Leah thought with inward amusement that a girl who has eyes like stars and displays that inner radiance has not only seen jewels and maidens, or even daughter of a prince.

When they were alone, Leah asked in her deep lazy voice, "Tell me all about him, Dinah."

Dinah looked at her mother, startled. "About *him*, mother? How did you know?"

Leah laughed. "Wear a veil, my daughter, if you would keep your secret."

"Do you think they all know?" asked Dinah anxiously.

Leah laughed again, saying easily, "No, it takes a woman who has loved to understand."

Dinah looked in unbelief at her mother, and wondered that anyone with her gross form and unsightly red-rimmed eyes could possibly understand this feeling of inner excitement and delicious uncertainty.

"Come, tell me," Leah invited, and Dinah, feeling that if she did not speak of Shechem she would burst, told her mother of the son of Hamor, of his pleasing countenance and manly bearing.

Leah was as enthusiastic an audience as Dinah could have wished, and showed more understanding than Dinah could have credited. Leah herself was enjoying it all, living again her own love-life. Happy Dinah, if she could love and be loved. What matter if Shechem was a heathen? He was a prince, his father was rich, and best of all—he loved Dinah. Leah shut her eyes. What greater bliss could the earth hold than to love a man and be his only love, to dwell with him and enjoy that love without let or hindrance, not always longing and starving for that love which, when it came, made the lack of it later seem all the more acute. She would do all in her power to help Dinah achieve this greatest of all joys.

Each time Dinah returned, she had more stories to tell of Shechem, of his obvious love for her.

"He told me, mother," she told Leah, "that his father would

come and ask my father to give me to Shechem." She looked doubtful. "Will he consent?"

Leah was not sure. Jacob was devoted to Dinah, but that very devotion might make him adamant against a heathen marriage.

"I will do my best, dear daughter," Leah told her.

"I feel if I cannot go to Shechem, I will die," Dinah told her. "You cannot believe the pain and the ache I have here," and she placed her hand on her heart.

"It is because I know that pain so well that I will do all in my power to help you," her mother assured her.

.   .   .   .

Shechem had been very discreet. He knew that the Hebrews were strict concerning the chastity of both their young men and maidens, and that the Hivite custom of taking a girl and then if she pleased you marrying her was not allowed to them. Their marriages were often arranged by the parents, without the young people being consulted at all. He was determined to act circum-spectly, to ask his father to wait on Jacob, and to do all with ceremony and decorum.

It was a hot day. Many of the maidens were sitting almost asleep at siesta time. Dinah and Shechem talked in low tones of many things. They cared not of what they spoke if they could only hear each other's voices. Shechem yearned to have her for himself. He would be discreet. But to be with Dinah, away from prying eyes, would be bliss indeed. He was always conscious of Zotaph, his sister's crook-backed maid. She seemed to see each tentative caress he would have lavished upon Dinah. In a low tone he asked if she would come with him to the balcony to see the view of his father's vineyards. Silently Dinah nodded, and they both rose with one consent, and walked slowly together round the side of the court, climbing the stairs to the balcony, where there was a view right across the valley.

It was so seldom that Shechem could speak to Dinah alone. He burst into speech, telling her again of his love. "My father will wait upon your father Jacob, and ask him to give you to me in marriage."

Dinah became weak and yielding in his arms. It was no un-awakened child he held, and her obvious response took from him all his caution, and sense of decorum. Forgetting everything except his desire to possess her, and sensing in her a passion equal to his own, he took her, thrusting aside the awning to his own apartment, and possessed her.

Zotaph had watched the entire scene from a vantage point of her own. The passionate embrace and the withdrawal could only mean one thing, and she cursed the day that the gods had given her a crooked body, and left her with a woman's heart and feelings. She would keep her own counsel at present, and make what use of it she thought best.

.   .   .   .

To obliterate from her mind the scene she had witnessed, Zotaph went to the well outside Shalem. It was cool there, and she could drink of the water and be alone. But she was not to be alone for long. As she sat there, two young men came, with an arrogant overbearing manner, saying, "Move, crooked woman, and let us water our sheep." And with rough hands, not regarding her infirmity, indeed, it seemed because of it, they removed her from their path.

This roused her spirit, and caused her to say, "Who are you to ill-treat one of the daughters of the Shechemites?"

Simeon and Levi arrogantly replied, "We are the elder sons of ISRAEL, the great sheik."

Zotaph gave a mirthless laugh, and looked at them with scorn. "So great a sheik, to have cruel and discourteous men for sons, and a harlot for a daughter!"

Simeon and Levi turned in a rage upon her.

"How dare you utter such a lie?" they asked.

"It is no lie," said Zotaph. "With my own eyes I saw Shechem take your sister—take her to his dwelling, as he would any harlot." And she walked quickly away, leaving them too dumbfounded to do her any further injury.

Dinah went home that night filled with fear and apprehension. It must have been madness that came upon us both to lose control in such a way, she thought. Shechem had promised that the very next day his father would meet with Jacob, but they must try to keep their own counsel about what had happened. Having already taken her only increased his desire for her a thousand-fold, and to lose her now, he told her, would be anguish indeed.

Leah did not need to hear from Dinah's own lips what had happened. Her white-faced daughter had lost her look of innocence and virginity. The bloom had gone, though her beauty remained.

"What will my father say?" was all that Dinah could utter.

Leah, though deeply concerned at what had taken place, promised that she would speak to Jacob, only hoping that Dinah's brothers would hear nothing of this until after the marriage had been arranged. They might rise up in a body and seek revenge upon Shechem.

Leah decided to tell Jacob everything. She had expected an outburst of rage, but found him strangely silent. He would say nothing, he told her, until he could consult with his sons. This was a family matter.

In reality he was stunned. He remembered the havoc Esau had made in his marriages with heathen women, whose morals and standards were so different from their own. The fact that Shechem had already defiled Dinah showed him the man for what he was worth, and how little respect he had for Jacob's daughter. He would not trust himself to say more, but wanted to see the kind of man who would do this thing to Dinah.

The next day he had to receive Hamor and Shechem without the support of his sons, for they were still with the cattle. He thought they were still in ignorance of what had happened, and knew nothing of the plotting and schemes that were being hatched in the minds of Simeon and Levi.

As Jacob looked at Shechem standing by his father with humility and dignity, he was more than surprised. This was no libertine, who would treat his daughter as a harlot, and then lightly disregard her. Hamor pleaded his son's cause, and Shechem himself told of his deep love for Dinah, promising to keep her and treat her with great honour.

Jacob, impressed in spite of himself, gave no definite answer, but asked Hamor to return the following day at the same time, when he would have been able to consult with his sons, who had come to man's estate and in whose judgment he trusted. Hamor and Shechem went their way, watched through the window by Leah and Rachel.

When Dinah heard that her brothers were to be consulted, she was filled with apprehension and foreboding. She knew what the outcome would be, and told her mother that as she was already the wife of Shechem in fact, she intended to slip away and join him before her brothers could show their intolerance towards him, for they would not be as mild as Jacob had been.

There was a great uproar among the sons of Leah when the news of Dinah's defilement was heard. Jacob, in a vain attempt to be fair, told them of the honourable proposals made to him by Hamor on behalf of his son, and of the rich dowry that he promised. He himself was grieved that a heathen marriage should be contemplated, but he blamed himself for bringing his family so near to the dwellings of the Shechemites. What a father sows, his family reap, he thought in sorrow. Simeon and Levi said little in the discussion, for they had their own plans. Reuben and Judah agreed to wait until Hamor and Shechem came the following noon for further parley.

. . . .

When Hamor and Shechem received the message inviting them to come to Jacob's dwelling at an earlier hour, and to meet at the well, midway betwixt their dwellings, they felt no surprise. They were met only by Simeon and Levi. These two, gorgeously attired, waited for their guests.

"We are to talk with you on our father's behalf," they told them. "He has appointed us as his elder sons to act for him."

Hamor bowed and explained again his son's desire to marry Dinah, going into further detail concerning the dowry of gold and silver and treasures, which would be paid over on her behalf, and renewed again the promises that Dinah should receive the very best of treatment.

Simeon and Levi dismissed anything so paltry as a dowry as beneath their notice, and spoke in measured tones. "Your gold and silver are of little account to a man so wealthy as our father Jacob, but we have a rite which marks our tribe from the nations round about, and for any daughter of our tribe to marry a man who has not submitted to the rite of circumcision is a reproach to our family name. We are willing for the sons and daughters of the tribe to intermarry with your tribe and dwell with you, but for this one thing. It is a rite of our God, and it cannot be that our tribe can ignore it."

Hamor and Shechem considered. It would be of great mutual advantage, Hamor agreed, if intermarriage could take place. But was there only this one difficulty in the way?

Simeon assured them that this was the only obstacle that separated them. No mention was made of idolatry or heathen rites.

Shechem himself cared nothing for the intermarriage of their peoples, if only he could have his Dinah. He would agree to anything his father decreed. And each party went their way.

.   .   .   .

"We need new blood. Their young men and maidens are of fine physique, their cattle and herds are renowned for excellence, the fame of Jacob and his stock runs from one end of the land to the other," Hamor told the men of Shechem. "I have seen their milch camels and their she-asses. All this substance of theirs can gradually become ours. We know how to acquire it by peaceful means. Once they dwell with us, and our people have inter-married with theirs, it can be part of our own possession. Have we not done just the same thing before with the tribe of Jabok? It is a little thing to ask. Let us consent with them; we have so much to gain."

Hamor pleaded and persuaded, speaking all the more easily as Shechem his son, who was more honourable than he, had left him to parley with the men alone. At last every man of the city agreed, and Hamor went his way.

.   .   .   .

Jacob had been more relieved than otherwise when Simeon and Levi brought the message that Hamor and his son Shechem were not coming for an audience that day. Very properly, with a desire to win Jacob's approval, his sons told him, they were causing the men of Shechem to submit to circumcision, so that Dinah might not be expected to dwell with an uncircumcised people. Jacob was impressed with this evidence of sincerity on Hamor's part, and was content to leave the matter until approached again.

But if he was content, Leah and Dinah were not.

"I am convinced that Simeon and Levi have done something dastardly," Dinah told her mother. "Their faces have that evil expression on them that I have seen when they have been torturing some helpless animal. They mean no good by Shechem. I feel sure they have some plan to harm him." And then she told her mother, "I go this night to join my husband, and will not wait for all their discussions."

Leah had not the heart to prevent her.

.   .   .   .

The men of Shechem lay in their tents and dwellings, some with a fever and all weak, on the third day after circumcision. Simeon and Levi, having ascertained from spies that all had gone according to plan, came at dead of night. In base treachery they went through the camp and slew each male with the sword, silently and swiftly, not sparing the greatest or the least.

Hamor and Shechem were the last to be put to the sword, and only when Dinah gave a cry of agony and terror to see her husband slain before her eyes did Simeon and Levi pause in the blood-lust that was driving them on, as though drunk with wine, their eyes gleaming, and their faces and arms bespattered with blood.

Dinah fled, shrieking, to her mother's house, up the hill, past the well, her eyes staring out of her head at what she had witnessed. Not content with blood-shedding, Simeon and Levi sent for their brothers and looted the city, taking the flocks and herds and wealth, justifying themselves that their cause was righteous because their sister had been defiled.

.   .   .   .

When Jacob heard what had been done, his anger was greater than ever before in his life. He assembled the whole tribe and vilified his sons.

"You have made my name to stink in the nostrils of the people of the land, the Canaanites and the Perizzites. We are but few in number. What if they seek to avenge the men of Shechem? What shall we do? We shall be destroyed in our house."

Simeon and Levi tried to save their faces by saying, "Should they have treated our sister as a harlot?" but even in their own brethren there was no sign of approval, and Jacob ceased to treat them as any sons of his, and it was many days before the bitterness that overwhelmed him at the infamy of his sons was abated.

.   .   .   .

There is a balm and a solace. Man cannot always hang down his head in shame. After a while Jacob sought to atone for the wrong of his sons by caring for the widows and children of the men of Shechem, and going himself to dwell there, making Shechem one of the cities of Jacob, rather than of the heathen. But first there was to be a great purge. Every idol, false god and image was to be brought to one place.

"Put away your false gods, and cleanse your garments of uncleanness," Jacob commanded.

From every tent or dwelling came some image or idol. Jacob reflected wearily that there was so much evil under the surface, it was little wonder that trouble had come upon them. This was Rachel's opportunity to rid herself of the images she had taken from Laban's house. She mentally renounced his claim to her father's wealth. Jacob had enough of his own, and these idols, though only to be regarded by her as tokens, were better destroyed with the rest. A huge pit was dug under the oak at

Shechem, and every idolatrous thing was put away, and the camp of Jacob was purged clean again.

.   .   .   .

Jacob, at the command of God, went on a pilgrimage to Bethel, where he had made his first vows to God. It was here he renewed his vision, and heard God's Voice again. As he poured oil upon that pillar of stone, he was quite transported as he realised again, in spite of his failings as a Patriarch and a father, Jehovah the great God loved him—even Jacob.

God told him again, "Thy name shall be no more Jacob, but ISRAEL," and renewed His promises to him.

Jacob's heart was full of thankfulness for this strengthening of his faith. It seemed that, each time he failed, God met him again and reiterated the promise, which might have become unreal to him had this not been so.

Jacob went, taking only Rachel, Joseph and Deborah with him, and a few of the servants, and he dwelt at Bethel, and while Jacob remembered his vision, he regained his confidence that even after many years could be shattered. The memory of the evil and shame his sons had brought upon him faded, and he felt himself rejuvenated. The years fell from him as he and Rachel dwelt together in tents, as they had done on the hills of Haran. He found himself desiring her again, as he had done in those happy days. He had time to talk to Joseph, and tell him of God's Voice speaking to him at Bethel.

Deborah grew weaker, and soon her indomitable spirit failed, and she gave up the ghost. They buried her under the oak tree at Bethel, calling the place Allon-bachuth, 'place of weeping'. As Rachel laid the old nurse to rest, she knew, as though she too had heard the Voice of God, that Deborah would not long precede her, for by now she realised that she was again with child, and she had a positive premonition that although the child would live, she herself would not.

16

JOSEPH sat down on an empty earthenware pitcher. He ached all over from the rough treatment he had received. His brothers had always been cruel to him, but yesterday had brought matters to a head. His father had sought to honour him and show his love, but Joseph had known it would only bring him trouble, and the vengeance of his jealous brothers.

There was a saying among the old wives that deaths never came singly, but in threes. It had certainly been so in this case. First Deborah had been laid under the oak of weeping, so named by his father to commemorate one who was so much more than a servant. Then there was his beloved mother, Rachel. She had been taken from them in Bethlehem, as she brought into the world little Benjamin. And now grandfather Isaac had been gathered to his fathers, and uncle Esau and his father Jacob, or ISRAEL, as he was called on state occasions, laid him to rest in the family cave of burial at Machpelah.

All Jacob's sons had been summoned from Shechem to join their father, who had come up from his pilgrimage in Bethel. It had been a solemn occasion, and no doubt it was with a sense of destiny, now that he was the Patriarch, that had made his father consider who would follow in the line of Abraham, Isaac and Jacob.

Reuben, his firstborn, was the obvious choice by reason of his birth, but Jacob had never held a high opinion of this vacillating eldest of Leah's sons. And then of course Reuben's latest indiscretion had robbed him of any chance he might have had, for Reuben had lain with Bilhah, his father's concubine. Such behaviour was horrifying to Jacob, to whom any moral irregularity was an anathema. Reuben had been weak rather than vicious, Joseph reflected. He had comforted Bilhah, who was mourning the loss of her mistress, had been tempted and had fallen. But though he, Joseph, had known what was happening, it had not been he who had told Jacob of Reuben's behaviour. There were many tongues ready to bear tales. Rachel, his mother, had reproved him for tale-bearing on the only occasion when he had brought to his father an evil report. She had warned him of the many sins of the flesh that boys and men might fall into, and when with the sons of the two concubines, Bilhah and Zilpah, he had known of their evil deeds, he had told his father in horror of what he had seen.

"Never be the one to bring tales to your father of his sons' conduct. He will find them out for what they are all too soon," Rachel had told him. And though the name 'tale-bearer' had been added to the many used by his brothers to vilify him, he had never again told his father of the petty cruelties and spite that were daily his portion.

He had sometimes complained to his mother in a torrent of words of the bitterness of his lot. Why should he have to suffer so? Why should he put up with it all? She had told him in her gentle way that if a boy complained against his circumstances, he complained against his God, for God planned all his life, and it was a terrible thing to complain against Jehovah.

Joseph found it difficult to accept this, but he had to believe what his mother said was true. "If you can keep your spirit and control your rage and rule yourself, you will be able to rule others."

"But I have no desire to rule others," he had told her. "I am but my father's eleventh son. Why do you talk to me of ruling?"

Rachel had said little then, but during the time when she was carrying Benjamin it seemed as though a curtain between now and the Hereafter were lifted, and that the division between the present and future were no more. She could look into the future, not in the way that Miram the water-diviner told the future by the stars, but as though her eyes, soon to see the celestial light, were given a touch of that supernatural vision now.

"You will rule, Joseph," she said, "not as a patriarch—that

is not for you—but I see you ruling almost as a king, all bowing down to you. You are not only for one tribe, but to bring blessing to many peoples. You are like a branch that climbs over the wall; you cannot be enclosed here, but you will bring blessing to many. Prepare yourself, rule your spirit, suffer and avenge not, endure without complaint. Always remember, God will be with you."

Joseph treasured every word he could remember of those last months. As for ruling, maybe his mother was wandering in her mind, remembering the foolish dreams of his childhood. Joseph smiled in remembrance of the tactless little boy he had been. He could see the scene clearly, although it was years ago. Jacob and Rachel had been sitting in the courtyard at siesta time, Leah and her sons reclining, conversing in low tones.

"My father," he had piped up in his clear childish voice, "I had a dream last night."

Judah had murmured audibly to his brothers, "Listen, my brothers; let no dog bark. The young princeling had a dream."

Jacob had smiled indulgently at his younger son. "Let us hear your dream," he said.

"I dreamt we were all in the corn-field binding sheaves."

"'Tis well they say dreams go by opposites. Listen, brothers, our little lord was actually *working*, even as his low-born brothers," Simeon commented.

But this was quite lost upon Joseph, who had continued his tactless recital, "And lo, my sheaf stood straight up in the middle, and all my brothers' sheaves made obeisance to mine. Was it not strange?"

Jacob laughed aloud, and looked at the lowering countenances of his sons.

"You see, my sons," he said, "a vision from on high, telling my son Joseph that you will all bow to him. What say you to that?"

The brothers had plenty to say, and grew angry and wild in their replies, so that Rachel had perforce to chide them for even listening to the foolish babblings of such a child.

What a silly child I was! Joseph thought. I wouldn't learn. For the very next day his father, still chuckling, asked, "Have you had any more dreams in the night, my son Joseph?"

And he had piped up again, "Father, I had an even more extraordinary dream than before. Before sleeping, I was gazing at the heavens and looking at the stars. Then, before I knew, I must have been dreaming, for the sun and the moon and eleven stars made obeisance to me."

What a storm this utterance had caused!

"There is no bearing with the arrogant child. Shalt thou indeed reign over us?" they said. "And will you have dominion over us?"

Even Jacob had rebuked him mildly, saying, "You go to far, my son. Think you that thy mother and I too would bow to you?"

But though his brothers were angry, and filled with hatred and imprecations against him, Joseph never knew how deeply Jacob pondered over the dreams, wondering if these were indeed a message from on high, concerning who should be heir to follow in the patriarchal line.

That was a long time ago, thought Joseph, as he changed his position on the earthenware pitcher, and flexed his aching arms. Last night had been the climax of many things, and had focused the hatred of his brothers upon him. For Jacob had called together all the sons of Leah and the concubines, and before them all had put on Joseph the coat of many colours. He had made little comment, but no one who saw could mistake what the action meant. That coat marked out the wearer as being lord of his brethren, and the one on whom the birthright was to be bestowed.

It was perhaps his way of giving a public rebuke to Reuben for his incestuous behaviour, and a public slight to Simeon and Levi, whose treachery Jacob would never forgive. But what of Judah? Joseph had longed to say. Why pass him over? Judah had many qualities of leadership needed in the head of a tribe. If only Judah had been the recipient of Rachel's teaching and constant instruction, he could have been very different, for there was good material in Judah. Joseph could sense it, and unwillingly admired the brother whose unspoken threats often made him tremble.

Perhaps it was the memory of Joseph's dreams that turned the scales in his favour. God spoke often through dreams, Jacob maintained. But his brothers had used the name 'dreamer' as a term of contempt these many years.

Ever since last night Joseph had been on the watch for an attack from behind, or some evidence of petty spite. It had been in one of the booths that Simeon and Levi had caught him, and practised every trick they knew for inflicting pain without leaving any mark. Simeon had twisted his arms until Joseph had shrieked with pain, and Levi had warned his brother to leave off before breaking a limb. Every joint had been maltreated, and his tormentors only desisted when Judah appeared, hearing Joseph's cries of agony. It was not for consideration of Joseph that Judah interfered.

"Do not soil your hands on him," Judah had said, "Wait until the day comes when we will put him out of the way altogether. Do not think you will live to wear that coat and lord it over us," Judah told him, and Levi gave him another wrench, and called him 'bastard son of a weak woman'. For this Judah struck his brother on the mouth. Not even to degrade Joseph would Judah allow his aunt Rachel's name to be lightly used.

Joseph felt that surge of feeling arise in him that Judah often caused—that feeling that, as a child, had been hero-worship, that emotion no other brother had aroused in him.

"Would to God I could give you this coat, Judah," he muttered.

Judah looked at Joseph strangely. There was sincerity in the lad's words. . . . But he steeled himself. "Fear not, Joseph the dreamer, that coat will be mine, but not by your gift. Fear for yourself and the day when you fall into our hands. Our sheaves will never bow to yours."

Then they left him. They had neither forgotten nor forgiven him for his dream, and the constant reminder that the coat of many colours brought did nothing to make his lot lighter. This gift, by which his father had thought to honour him, might even have signed his death warrant. Joseph hoped he would never find himself alone in his brothers' power.

.   .   .   .

Joseph cheered himself with the good news that he had heard. On the following day his brothers were to go with the flocks to Shechem. He and Jacob would be left in peace, with only baby Benjamin for company. Joseph regarded Benjamin as a precious legacy from his mother. He played with his little brother and, although the baby was unable to understand, Joseph told him constantly that he would never suffer at the hands of his cruel brothers.

"Let them try to hurt a hair of that tiny head of yours, and see what comes to them," Joseph told Benjamin, and if Judah had seen him then, he would have been reminded of Rachel, who had threatened to defend Joseph with just such a spirit.

.   .   .   .

At quite an early age Joseph had been forced to admit to his father the terrible truth that he really had no interest whatever in sheep! That, to his father, was almost bordering on blasphemy, but Jacob soon realised that Joseph had other gifts. Coniah said that never before had he met anyone with such a gift for coping with the household stores, bestowing the merchandise and planning the commissariat. In Joseph's care, at the age of seventeen, were placed the stores of oil, flax, dates and goatskins full of wine, and these were all kept in perfect order. He had learned to write on clay with a stylo, to keep a note of all their possessions.

"Well it is," said Jacob at last, "that one of my sons is not anxious to keep the sheep, but can act as my steward," for Jacob knew how easily a man can be robbed by unscrupulous servants, who can reduce a man to penury if he deals with a slack hand. "You, my son Joseph," he said, "have inherited that flair for business and trading which from time to time is seen in our ancestors. Terah, your great-grandsire, and his son Haran were great men of business and commerce. I am told their eyes gleamed at the sight of shekels to be earned, and Lot, son of Haran, could write on clay even as you do. They loved nothing more than to increase their prosperity, though their business of idol-making was not a worthy one."

Abraham had often told Jacob that all the Semites had a dual personality; part of them worshipped the God of their fathers, and another part had a desire for gain. Either one or the other could prevail. The very gift for trading could become greed, and even crowd out the worship of Jehovah, as it had done with Terah. This too had been seen, Jacob told Joseph, in his grandfather Laban. Greed had eaten him up, and all that was left of the other side of his nature were empty words and hollow piety.

"Seek to keep a balance between these two, my son. Despise not the gift of organisation and planning that God has given you, but never let the desire for material things crowd out the knowledge of God and the desire for His blessing."

Jacob, even while he spoke these words, realised that he himself was a complex character. He could say with sincerity that material things had not held an ascendancy over him, for until six years before leaving Laban, he had possessed very little. But he had failed in many ways. Jacob was never one to be filled with pride and self-confidence. I must have failed, he thought, to have such evil sons.

So mused Jacob as he watched his ten sons set off for Shechem. They were fine to look at, but on the faces of some were the small mean eyes of Laban, their grandfather, and as he looked at them, they brought him very little pleasure. Then he turned his eyes and they rested upon Joseph. What he saw there caused a glow to come into his heart, and it removed from his mind the sorrow his unsatisfactory sons caused him. Joseph at seventeen years resembled closely his grandfather Isaac at that age. He was just a year older than his grandfather had been when, full of the laughter which had given him his name, he had set out for Mount Moriah—that expedition which was to prove not only Abraham's fervent love for his God, but Isaac's complete obedience and subjection to his father. Whereas Isaac's face had a peculiar quality of sweetness, Joseph's face, similar in beauty,

had a firmness and purpose [...] either in Isaac's
face or in his character.

Joseph had been a chil[...] [a]nd laughter, but much
of the gaiety of life had [...] by the oppression of his
brothers, and latterly [...] crushing loss of his beloved
mother. He was as t[...] himself had been at that age,
but without the co[...] [o]f character that had marked his
father. At seventee[n ...] had been eaten up with frustration
and desire, but Jos[...] learnt to accept what life had in store
for him, to endur[...] to find solace in hard work. Jacob thanked
the God of his [...]ers that He had given him such a son as
Joseph to gladden his old age and maintain the family tradition.

17

JOSEPH and Coniah were stacking away provender in the improvised store.

"Would our master had barns and storehouses, as he had in
Shechem," Coniah remarked, trying vainly to balance dates and
nuts beside the strips of dried mutton.

Joseph whistled while he worked. He felt like a bird let loose
when his brothers were away. There was no one to mock him if
he sang or whistled, no one to scorn him, call him 'dreamer', or
snatch at his coloured coat and seek to trip him if he carried
baskets of bread on his head from the baking house.

"We are better here, Coniah," he said. "Shechem has many
unpleasant associations for my father."

Coniah nodded in compassion. "And for poor Dinah too,"
he added. "She stays by her mother, and they say she has never
really recovered her senses."

"It was a dastardly deed," Joseph said, "for though we know
it is not according to our code of rules to wed with a heathen,
Dinah had loved Shechem, and surely such a base act as that

perpetrated by my brothers was no way of setting right the wrong."

"Your father Jacob is happier living here in his tent, as his father did before him. Houses are for city dwellers, people in Ur and Nineveh."

"Or Egypt," said Joseph.

"Or Egypt," agreed Coniah. "Now there you would see some fine houses—houses with courtyards, with all manner of sweet-smelling plants growing up the walls, painted frescos, and carved furniture."

"It must be a wonderful place," said Joseph.

"I thought to see it one day," Coniah told him. "In time of famine my lord Isaac planned to seek refuge there, but later stayed in Gerar. It was better so. But there is always corn in plenty to be found in Egypt, though all the world may starve."

"Why is it? Does God smile on them more than on the rest of the world?"

"God?" Coniah laughed. "The Egyptians have two thousand gods. I am told that they worship one, Sobk, the crocodile god, Apet, the hippopotamus goddess, Bes the god of music, singing and dancing. Then they have a cat goddess, Bubastis, they say, and Horus, the hawk-headed god, and many others. But no, it is not the gods that are responsible for their prosperity. It is the River Nile—that river that rarely dries up, and comes down in a flood, watering the land. They have wise men in Egypt who can tell the rising and falling of the Nile, who can watch the future and tell the stars, and know when famine comes, and when there will be a time of plenty. They are men of great wisdom and great learning."

Joseph was silent, as he neatly arranged the earthenware pitchers of oil and smaller jars of wild honey.

"Yet with all their two thousand gods, not one is as wise and knows all things like the one great God Whom we serve."

Coniah nodded. "Happy is the man," he said, "to whom God reveals His secrets."

Coniah had served Isaac faithfully ever since he was just a lad, and Eliezer of Damascus had chosen him to act as his bodyguard. And this was no empty office, for Hagar, eaten up with jealousy, had sought many opportunities of disposing of the one whom she imagined had usurped her son's position as Abraham's prospective heir. Keturah, in whose care Isaac had been placed, discovered him about to eat some poison berries that Hagar had given him. And there were other incidents. The final one was when Ishmael had promised to teach Isaac to swim and, had not Coniah dived into the deep pool where Isaac was floundering, Hagar might indeed have had her way.

Coniah's loyalty to the tribe was great. Gladly would he have given his life for a son of Abraham, and Joseph in his many-coloured coat, denoting his position, was a son worth dying for, and worthy of his life-long service.

.   .   .   .

When the days passed into weeks with no sign of Joseph's brethren returning, Jacob became concerned. To Joseph, of course, each day without them was like a day given to him to enjoy, but Jacob feared for his sons' safety, and that of the herd.

"Maybe some of the Hivites and Perizzites might seek to avenge themselves on my sons for the death of Hamor and Shechem," he said. "Little wonder if they should," he added bitterly. "But I fear for them."

Joseph reassured him. "Had there been any to avenge, they would have fallen upon them when we were at Bethel. Time cools the avenger's anger and clouds the memory."

At last, when they still tarried, Jacob came to a decision.

"Joseph, my son," he called.

"Here am I, my father."

"I am filled with concern for thy brothers. I would send you now to Shechem to see if all is well with them, and then to come back and bring me word."

Joseph listened to his father's order with a sinking heart.

"Shall I go alone among my brethren, my father?" he asked.

"Why, certainly, Joseph, my son. Take food and water for your journey, and if all is well with them, bring me back word."

Joseph considered. Should he tell his father of all the threats his brothers had uttered? Never, saving only that one time, had he ever brought any evil report, and the fact that Jacob could contemplate sending him out defenceless was a proof of his ignorance of all that Joseph had suffered, and all the black hatred that was in the hearts of his sons to the one he had honoured with the many-coloured coat.

"But if I go among them, my father, they might seek to. . . ." began Joseph. No, his mother had told him never to speak evil of his brothers, but to endure and to trust in his God. He would go. His father had commanded it, and his mother's God would protect him.

He prepared himself, then he went to bid farewell to Benjamin, that little brother who was his delight.

"Oh, baby brother," he said, "what if I never return? Who will teach you all the things my mother taught me?" Impulsively he turned to Bilhah, who cared for Benjamin. "Bilhah," he said, "you often listened to what my mother taught me. If anything should happen to me, and I come not again. . . ."

"But Joseph, speak not such foolishness. Whatever could befall you?"

Joseph was silent for a while, and then he said, "A wild beast might set upon me, or thieves. Teach Benjamin the things my mother taught me," he said simply, and seizing Benjamin in his arms, he kissed him, and almost had to tear himself away, so great was his fear and premonition of evil that he would never see his brother again.

Joseph said farewell to his father. I wonder what he would say if he realised that he might be sending me to my death, Joseph said to himself as Jacob blessed him, and quite light-heartedly wished him farewell and bade him speed back with word.

"I do not think you need fear the Canaanites. They have no quarrel with you," his father told him, as Joseph went. It was with a great fear in his heart, but not of what the Canaanites or any heathen people would do to him, that he set off. It was with fear of treachery from those in his own father's house.

. . . .

162

On he journeyed. It was several days before he reached the outskirts of Shechem. The freshly roasted parched corn, dried mutton and dates he had brought with him were nearly gone, and he had refilled his water-bottle constantly at the many waterholes which were landmarks on the journey. It was a sparsely populated countryside through which he went, but the shepherds and travellers he met were friendly.

He had perforce to admit to himself that when he reached Shechem and found no trace of his brethren, he was more than relieved. He wandered in a field, lost in thought. It was almost as if he were reprieved. Thus must Isaac have felt when he faced certain death, and then the knife was stayed.

"Hello there," shouted a voice. "What do you seek, all alone and wandering in the field?"

Joseph looked up, and saw a man watching him curiously.

"I seek my brothers—ten men," he said, "caring for their flock of sheep. Have you seen them? Can you tell me which way they went?"

"Yes, they did not linger here, but seemed anxious to be gone, and went over towards Dothan."

Joseph thanked him, but his heart was heavy. It was as though the knife, temporarily sheathed, had been taken out again and was pointing towards him. Maybe Judah's threats were idle, he told himself. Perhaps they would not actually kill him. It was a terrible thing to take the life of one of your father's sons in cold blood, but even if they did not take his life, they would certainly deal hardly with him, and without the restraint of his father's proximity, and that of his servants, Simeon and Levi would vent their spite on him in no gentle way.

He went on, setting his face flint-like for what was coming. He need only find out their whereabouts, he told himself, to see that they were well and prosperous, and return again to his father.

He plodded on up the hill. The summit would give him a vantage point, and from there he could survey the whole panorama, and find out whereabouts they lay. He topped the hill, and there in a hollow, not a hundred yards from where he stood, were his ten brothers. He stood outlined against the sky. Escape was impossible. The sight of him had caused a shout to go up.

"Look who we have here! Behold, the dreamer cometh!" were the words that welcomed Joseph.

Reuben cursed under his breath that Joseph should be so foolish as to come alone. "Had you no more sense than to come here?" he murmured to Joseph, who replied, "It was my father's command."

All vied in mocking the brother who stood before them in his many-coloured coat. The sons of the concubines had never forgiven him for carrying the evil report of their doings to Jacob, though that was years ago. Judah saw only the obstacle to his overwhelming ambition standing defenceless and in his power. Simeon and Levi gloated only at the chance to hurt someone who was not in a position to hurt them in return.

Joseph was tied hand and foot and thrown into a ditch, while his brothers took counsel about what they should do with him.

"We must make an end of him, that is certain," said Judah. "It has come about most propitiously. Just a quick thrust of a knife under his ribs, and all will be over in a second, and the vultures can have his carcass."

Simeon and Levi felt that was too easy a death. They would like to indulge in a little playful torture first. But Judah scorned their suggestion, and said that what had to be done should be done with rapid dispatch.

Reuben was horrified. This blood-lust which devoured his brothers was obnoxious in the extreme to him. Unbidden to his mind came the words of Rachel, 'Swear to me, Reuben, you will protect my son Joseph from his brothers.' He had sworn. He braced himself; he was the eldest; he had been weak, and he was discounted because of his sin, but he would not stand by and see Joseph killed ruthlessly in cold blood. Desperately he sought a way out. When the lust for blood has seized a group of men, they will not only kill the object of their hatred, but will often kill anyone who tries to prevent them. But he would speak out.

"Listen, my brothers," he said, "we cannot go again to our father with blood on our hands. We must rid ourselves of him," he said in subtlety, and they listened well, for Reuben feigned to be with them in their desire to dispose of Joseph, and, they reflected, who had a greater right to hate Joseph than Reuben, who should by right of birth be wearing the coat of many colours? "Let us put him into a pit and leave him tied and helpless, and as we move away, we can forget his very existence. Then we can in sincerity tell our father that we know not what has befallen his precious son. But we will have clean hands, and no blood guilt."

The saying pleased Reuben's brethren, and before they could change their minds, Reuben went over to where Joseph was lying, wondering how long it would be before he felt the knife that he feared. Reuben pretended to lift him harshly, but murmured, "Fear not, Joseph, I have persuaded them to put you in a pit, but I will come again and will surely deliver you to our father Jacob."

The words were music in Joseph's ears. Again, he felt like Isaac when God had said, "Slay not thy son. See . . . a ram."

He was taken roughly, his many-coloured coat stripped from him, and his tormentors, Simeon and Levi, lowered him into the pit. He looked up at the cruel faces, jeering and mocking. He saw Judah, and he looked with pleading at this brother of his, who as a child had called out his hero-worship, and even as a man had aroused his unwilling admiration. He said nothing, but that look would haunt Judah night and day for many years to come.

Then they went away and left Joseph, Simeon gloating over his coat, and Levi reflecting that death by thirst, with vultures overhead, was a more satisfying memory than the quick thrust of a knife. With utter callousness they sat down to eat bread, and only Reuben was absent from them, caring for some of the flock that had strayed.

. . . .

Joseph thanked God that Reuben had been minded to save him. It was dry in the pit, and the cords cut into his wrists, but soon Reuben would come and rescue him. He had a burning thirst, and had not eaten for many hours, but when death has seemed inevitable, any form of life is sweet. He lay on the hard ground fitfully dozing, as the harsh glare of the sun moved from the pit, and its steep sides gave him a little shade.

He was awakened by a commotion at the pit-head. It must be Reuben coming for me, he thought, but he had expected him to come by stealth. He looked up. No, it was not Reuben he saw, but a number of merchants. He could see the shadows of camels, and hear the voices of his brothers talking loudly, apparently bargaining with them, but of Reuben there was not a sign.

.   .   .   .

Judah had not enjoyed his meal. That look of Joseph's had haunted him. To leave him there to die was rather a terrible thing to contemplate. If there could only be some other way of getting rid of him, without shedding his blood, he would grasp it. Then they looked at the skyline, and behold, a company of merchants approached.

"Let us trade with them," said the men. "Maybe they have come from Gilead, and have some of the balms we need for our sores and wounds."

Then Judah saw a way out.

"I wonder if they would like to purchase something from us," he said.

"But we have nothing to sell, save maybe a kid from the flock."

Judah looked inscrutable.

"I wonder," he went on, "if they would like to buy a strong lad as a slave, and take him down to Egypt."

At first his brothers did not understand, then pandemonium broke out.

"An excellent idea, brother," they applauded. "Silver for us, and we'll be rid of this encumbrance."

"And all without the shedding of a brother's blood. For after all," said Judah with irony, "he is our own flesh and blood."

And the deal was done. Twenty pieces of silver were exchanged, two for each brother, and Joseph was bound and mounted on the back of one of the camels, the brothers watching him disappear into the distance on the road that led through the desert of Gaza, and on to the mysterious and fascinating land of Egypt.

"That," said Judah with satisfaction, "is the last we shall see of him. So much for his dreams of domination and rule."

.   .   .   .

Reuben crept back to the pit, bringing with him a stout rope. It was nearly dark. He called Joseph's name, but there was no answer. He called it again more insistently. He looked desperately to see if his brother had fainted, but even though the light was faint, it was enough for Reuben to see that the pit was empty. In a frenzy he ran to his brothers and accused them, his fear overborne by his anxiety.

"What have you done with Joseph?" he panted. "Have you indeed killed the child?"

Judah pacified him. "We have sold him to Ishmaelites, who journey into Egypt. Our hands are now clean, and here, brother, is your share—two pieces of silver."

"Hands clean! I think not!" exclaimed Reuben, and with great daring, he flung the shekels in Judah's face. "What can we say to our father?" And he ran away almost demented. "What shall I do, and where shall I go?' he said, dissociating himself from the crime of his brothers.

Judah and his confederates, having not balked at what was virtually murder, did not hesitate to commit deceit and lying. Joseph's coat, that had so enraged them, was to be the proof of Joseph's death. It was dipped in the blood of a kid, wrapped carefully, and together, with mixed feelings, the brothers slowly retraced their footsteps to Hebron.

Judah shared his thoughts with no one. It took great resolution on his part not to turn and follow hard after the Ishmaelites and to bring back his brother, but he knew he could not if he would. He had no mount, and they had fast camels. Simeon and Levi were only afraid for their own skins. They had no remorse, only concern that Jacob might not believe the lie they had planned to tell.

.   .   .   .

Jacob was alone at last. His family had sought to comfort him. Dinah, forgetting her own grief, or perhaps because of it, sought to help her father. But no one could do anything for him. He sat, his mind full of desolation and bitterness that he dared not contemplate.

He had been filled with anxiety all the time Joseph had been away. Coniah had done nothing to relieve his anxiety by reproaching his master for allowing Joseph to go alone.

"I protected your father against his one brother, and yet you have sent your son among ten who hate him with as great a hatred as Ishmael ever had for Isaac."

Jacob had scanned the horizon daily, and at last he had seen the group coming slowly over the hilltop, walking as men who attend a burial.

"Count them, Coniah," he had said hoarsely. "See, are there ten men, or is it eleven who come?"

Coniah had counted, and counted again. At last he had to say, "I can only see ten, my lord Jacob."

Then they had come nearer, carrying in their hands a blood-stained coat. . . .

All his hopes had been centred on Joseph. His lovely Rachel had been taken from him, and now Joseph in all his youth and beauty had been cut off, perished in the jaws of wild beasts. Or had he? A terrible suspicion kept coming into his mind. But no, it *was* a wild beast that had killed Joseph. He must not believe what he suspected, or he would lose his reason.

18

I T was at the feast of the god, Nilus, that Hamat, the steward of Potiphar, first noticed Joseph the Hebrew. Usually to him slaves were all alike and quite indistinguishable. He left their purchase and their ordering to Pharez, the slave-master, who could be relied upon to beat or cajole, threaten or bribe them, so that on a great occasion such as this, their master Potiphar, Captain of Pharaoh's guard, had no cause for complaint.

It was common knowledge that Potiphar's great ambition was for preferment to the priesthood. It was for that reason that he was meticulous in observing the feasts of the gods. Had he not been on a pilgrimage recently to No-Amun, or Thebes as it later was called, earning for himself the right to have the words, 'This is a good house' over the door of his magnificent mansion? There was much more life and excitement as Captain of Pharaoh's guard, but as a priest the life would be more peaceful and hold more honour. Priests were exempt from taxes, had a special allowance of corn and land, places of honour in the processions at festivals, and the privilege of carrying the Hydria, or holy vase, which only Pharaoh, besides themselves, might bear. But all wondered how Potiphar's wife, Zadia, might endure the quieter life, should such a preferment come his way. Potiphar was in the middle of his years, but his wife was gay and beautiful, and Potiphar's jealousy of her was a by-word.

Hamat himself was growing old. He found his task onerous. The care of the household stores, wines and trading brought much responsibility, which fell heavily upon one who felt the grass-hopper to be a burden. Another festival such as this, thought Hamat, might well be too much for him. He doubted whether he would see another month of Tobi, that month when the inundation of the Nile began, and the feast was made for the god Nilus, and prayers for 'a good Nile' were offered. He did not doubt that Potiphar would wish to hold a feast of thanksgiving in the month of Paoni, the festival of tanks of water, when the successful harvest had been assured. The thought of all the extra work and planning that this would entail made his brain reel.

He was suddenly conscious of Pharez standing beside him, watching the slaves running to and fro at his behest, as he stood, whip in hand, ready to punish any slackness, and correct any fault in the service.

"I'll get him this time," Pharez said. "By the god Horus, I'll find out how he does it."

Hamat asked for an explanation.

"That young Hebrew slave—there—the one that carries the jar of mareolis to the ladies. . . ." He broke off. "Here, fellow, what have you in that jar?"

The young slave, tall, dark and well-proportioned, stood still with the heavy jar on his shoulder.

"Mareolis, as directed," he replied.

"Well for you it is,' said Pharez. "That young fool Jabez gave the ladies ecbolada by mistake last festival."

Hamat expressed his horror, for that particular wine was known to be only for men, and had a peculiar effect upon them, indeed, it was forbidden to be drunk by newly married brides.

The young Hebrew went on his way. Hamat observed that this young man did not look like a slave, and asked his name and from whence he had come.

Pharez dismissed this with a word. "Joseph he's called. I purchased him in the slave market, as I did all the rest. He works well, and as he has a good appearance, I gave him the task of dispensing the wine. Any crook-backed or one-eyed slave can work the foot-bellows on the spit, or knead the dough with his feet, but a slave who is to be a cup-bearer must have a pleasing countenance."

"And what have you against this slave? It would seem to me that you are fortunate in him."

"Where does he hide it? That's what I mean to find out."

Hamat waited for an explanation.

"I have been a slave-master these twenty years, and never have I known any slave who did not rob his master, especially after a feast. They slink away, wearing their large flowing garments, and each time—although I cannot search them all—I take a few to one side, and out of those garments fall cooked geese, ducks, all manner of breads and pieces of beef. But every time I search Joseph, he never has anything concealed. I hate to be outwitted by a slave. He must conceal it in some remote place, and return for it later. I have taxed him with it openly, and all he says is, 'I do not steal my master's goods'."

"Has it not occurred to you, Pharez, that he might be speaking the truth?"

Pharez made a sound of scorn.

"Whoever heard of a slave who did not rob his master?" he asked.

Hamat continued to watch the young Hebrew thoughtfully. He could well understand why Pharez had chosen him for his present task. With infinite grace he transferred the wine to the small vase, and poured it into the cups for the women, and into the one-handled goblets for the men. He never forgot the ritual words he must utter each time, 'May it benefit you', and never omitted to hand them a napkin with which to wipe their mouths after drinking. The other servants seemed clumsy beside him, almost falling over the feet of those who reclined. He seemed to know which guests preferred wine from wineskins, and which had acquired a taste for that wine which had been stored in jars lined with resin.

This new custom complicated matters for a feast, thought Hamat wearily, but wine was more easily stored in these jars, and many were coming to like it as well as the wine from the animal skins. Storage space was a headache to any steward of a household the size of Potiphar's. He would find out more about this Hebrew slave, who held himself like a prince, and dispensed the wine, not with servility, but with the courtesy of a host entertaining in his own house.

.   .   .   .

Joseph's back ached. Soon there would be a moment's grace when he could lean against a pillar for support, while Potiphar made his speech. It was always the same one. The slaves knew it by heart, and those far enough away from Pharez would repeat it under their breath with their master as he made it.

Since early morning the preparations had been set in hand. According to the custom, meat and poultry must be freshly killed on the day required. First the butchers had arrived and slain the vast bulls, cutting off their heads, which no Egyptian would eat, except the slaves, whose portion it was, and the carcass was scientifically cut up and jointed and borne away by the chefs—some to roast on the spits, and some to boil in the cauldrons. As it was a feast, a few sheep were included in the menu. These were so prized for their wool that, for fear of depleting the stock, they were seldom slain, except on a great occasion, beef and geese being the staple diet. Egyptians were not clever with sheep like his father Jacob, thought Joseph. With his skill they would need to fear no dearth. It was a pity that the Egyptians held shepherds as an abomination. Only in Goshen were they regarded as better than scum. Joseph had often laughed to himself when he first heard this, thinking of his proud brothers, and longing to see their faces if he told them how a shepherd was regarded in Egypt.

Joseph had often asked why this was—why there was this abomination for shepherds. Some said it was because the shepherd kings from the north had come down and conquered Egypt years ago, and oppressed them—though one must speak softly of this, for Pharaoh himself was of Semitic stock. The two races had mingled now, and although they lived peaceably together, the Egyptians were proud to be so called and, like Potiphar the Egyptian, made it known that they were no shepherd stock from the north.

"It is for those of Semite extraction that we kill the sheep," the slaves had told him. "There are always some at the feasts, some of Pharaoh's party. They will even eat the head of the animal, which no pure Egyptian will do."

The preparations had continued without a break throughout the day. Pharez shouted and threatened while the duck, teal, quail and geese were prepared, and in the bakehouse, after the slaves had kneaded the dough in the huge trough with their feet, the master-bakers had formed it into fancy shapes—a crocodile's head, a recumbent ox, and other fancies, all covered with seeds, not only of cummin and caraway, of which Joseph knew, but many strange new flavours—nigella, kamoon and simsim.

There were many things new to him in this strange life into which he had been sold. The years had accustomed him to the grandeur of the house, the lavish display at the festival time, and the constant unremitting work of a slave from the first moment of waking, to the time when he flung himself exhaustedly onto his miserable couch at night. He could have borne it better but for Pharez, who, though he willingly promoted Joseph to a place of honour on account of his ability, seemed determined to trip him up, to find him in some fault or dishonesty.

He certainly had been subject to temptation. Joseph often wondered whether a man was called upon to be strictly honest when he had been stolen, sold and then flung into a life where slaves were considered as little better than beasts, underfed and overworked. It was considered the right thing for slaves at feast-times, when the kitchens abounded with food, and supervision was impossible, to take what they could, and feast on it later. Then Joseph remembered his mother's words, and his father's example.

"Your father was oppressed," she had told him. "He could have made himself rich, and none would have blamed him. For fourteen years he served without so much as a lamb or a shekel for wages, only his wives. But because he served Jehovah, he scorned to take a skin or a hoof that was Laban's."

Joseph would do the same, he determined. And each time he resisted the temptation he felt a certainty, as though he had tangible proof, that 'God was with him'. He was a servant of Jehovah, and would keep himself from the abominations of his fellow slaves, who, to forget their wretched lot, spent their time in wenching or worse abuses, and stole and pilfered as though it were an achievement, vying with each other to what extent they could rob their master.

Joseph concentrated his mind on the task of the present. He was now to pour some wine for his mistress, the wife of Potiphar. Not for her the wilder mareolis. Joseph knew that her taste was for sebennytic, a rare wine made from three different grapes, and only served at festivals. He only saw his mistress occasionally, though all the slaves talked of her beauty.

Today, clad in a loose robe fastened at the neck, with a rich sash of glorious colours, she looked magnificent. Her luxuriant black hair was plaited into eight coils, and dressed to stand out like the wigs the older women wore, whose hair was no longer luxuriant. In her ears she wore large gold earrings, single loops, some formed into the shape of an asp. He saw her dainty feet were clad in sandals of painted leather of rare craftmanship, embroidered and interlaced.

He remembered, as he knelt, many of the stories the slaves told of Potiphar's jealousy of this young wife of his, on whom subordinate officers cast their eyes. There were bawdy stories too, saying that their mistress was not above casting her beautiful painted eyes back at them. And who could blame her, they said, married to a man old enough to be her father?

Zadia stretched out her hand languidly to take the wine. A pet monkey was tied to one leg of her fauteuil, a massive armchair with legs carved in the shape of a recumbent lion. Sitting leaning against the other leg was Potiphar's little daughter, Asenath. It was considered an ornament at feast-days to have pets and small children sitting at the feet of the great ones.

Joseph poured out the wine with a steady hand, but was very conscious of the close scrutiny of his mistress.

Then the child, Asenath, whispered, " Joseph, look at me, I'm wearing a new head-dress. Is it not fine? "

Joseph turned and smiled at little Asenath. She sometimes sought him out, for she had heard he was famous as a story-teller, and sat enthralled as he cleaned the brass vessels, and told tales of far-off Canaan.

Without embarrassment, Joseph said, "It is indeed of great beauty, mistress Asenath," and turning to his mistress he said the words, "May it benefit you," and turned swiftly away.

"Asenath," said her mother sharply, "how dare you speak to a slave!"

Asenath raised surprised eyes to her mother. "Oh, Joseph isn't a real slave. He's not like the others. I think," she said confidentially, "he's a prince in disguise."

Zadia looked startled. Strange to say, she had received the impression that it was no slave offering her wine, but he served her as a trusted friend or officer of her husband's guard might have done, not as though it were a duty.

She merely said, "I cannot have you consorting with the lower orders. Whatever next!" But she did not actually forbid her, thought Asenath thankfully.

The time had come for the speech. The signal for this was the passing from hand to hand of a carved wooden image of the god Osiris, lying in a bier, to remind them all that they were but mortal. Then Potiphar arose and stood under the canopy fashioned of red and blue silken hangings, for these were the colours of the god Nilus, representing the shades of Nile waters at the two seasons of the year. Potiphar was very meticulous in all his observance of religious rites. He was well versed in matters concerning gods, and at this festival of Nilus, or Niloa as some called it, offered invocations for blessing on the Nile, at the beginning of the inundation. At a time like this, Potiphar felt, there might be among the guests those who had the ear of Pharaoh, and would bring his piety to the notice of the king, that he might be promoted.

Then he made his celebrated speech. To Joseph, standing by a pillar covered with frescos, the sound of the chanting slaves in the background made the speech, which he had heard many times before, exceedingly amusing.

Potiphar hoped they had all observed the figure of Osiris in the bier, and he solemnly told them, "Men ought to love one another, and to avoid those evils which made them consider life too long, when in reality it is short. Bear in mind that your existence is precarious, and that death must eventually close your earthly career."

The speech came to an end, some of the slaves claiming that

he had left out half a sentence this time, and the bit about 'the perils by day and dangers by night' was the best part.

This speech was the signal for more feasting. Joseph observed with not a little amusement that, rather than curbing the excesses of most, the reminder of their precarious existence seemed to stimulate a desire for a further outburst of gluttony and drinking, as though they deemed it wise to feast while it was yet today!

Then the entertainment began. Wrestlers vied with one another, acrobats and tumblers swung each other round by the hand, and stood on each other's shoulders in pyramids. Jugglers threw many-coloured balls in the air. Each sought to be chosen as the best performer, the winner receiving necklaces and jewellery from the hand of Potiphar's wife.

It was during the entertainment that most of the pilfering was done, under the guise of clearing the debris and restoring the kitchen from the appearance of a shambles to its normal cleanliness. Pharez, with eagle eye, watched the slaves, but he could not be everywhere at once. When it was all over, and the exhausted slaves were making their way to their own quarters, Pharez stopped one after another, demanding to be shown what they had stolen. When Joseph, clad only in his tunic, would have passed by, Pharez gripped him by the shoulder.

"Look at him," snarled Pharez, "not even wearing a cloak to disguise his wickedness," and taking Joseph by the throat, he shouted, "What have you done with it? Where have you hidden it? You shall tell me."

Joseph stood looking at Pharez, a long considering glance. What could he say to this brainless, bullying man, not fit to be an under-shepherd, hardly fit even to act as a swine-herd?

He said patiently, as one talking to a child or an imbecile, "I have taken nothing. True, I have eaten the extra portion, as is the custom on feast-days. But to take what is not mine by right would be to lower my estate and to degrade me."

"Degrade a slave! What is this estate of yours to be lowered?"

"I serve the great God, Jehovah—the greatest service I know."

Pharez stared, his bullock-like face reflecting a mind unable to comprehend such a thing. But there was something in the face of Joseph that compelled his fear. He was in the presence of something beyond him.

He let Joseph go, and wondered, did Joseph serve some evil god who taught him to use supernatural powers? Maybe he could spirit away the geese and beef joints without even hiding them. Worse still, he might have the power of an evil eye, and cause the slave-master to suffer from an inward canker, or strike his children with blindness. He would take care to avoid contact with the proud Hebrew, who served some strange god.

.   .   .   .

Hamat sat in his storehouse writing accounts on a piece of papyrus. His hieroglyphics noted the amount of grain, wine and oil recently purchased, and all the extra stores that were needed since the feast to replenish the stock. The guests of Potiphar are like a cloud of locusts, thought Hamat, ruefully regarding the denuded shelves. He would have to go to the market and order further supplies. Then the thought of such an effort made him groan. He was feeling more than his age. In Egypt a man who has lived a good life is said to live a hundred and ten years, but he would never see that many. He must rest his hand, for it was tired. He liked the office of a scribe least of his many duties. A cup of wine would refresh him. He clapped his hands, and a tall young slave entered. When had he seen this slave recently? thought Hamat: of course, serving at the feast. A Hebrew, and Pharez had spoken of his ability to steal without being found out.

"I would have a drink of wine, slave," he said. "Bring me of the thebaid in my own silver cup. Bear it yourself, for I would speak with you."

Joseph went to the wine store and found the pitcher of thebaid. This was a wholesome wine, and light, so that invalids were partial to it, thinking it had some healing quality. He wondered if Hamat was sick, for he usually preferred thasian, that wine excelling all others in sweetness.

"May it benefit you," said Joseph, handing the silver cup to Hamat.

"I hope it may indeed. I need benefit," said the old man.

Joseph looked with compassion at Hamat, and could see that he was old and fatigued, and forgot that he was so great a personage, but felt as he would have done had his father Jacob sat thus, weary and discouraged.

"My lord, you are in great weariness. May I not help you in some way?"

Hamat looked with considering eye at Joseph. He did not speak like a slave, with the craven fear that he was wont to arouse in slaves, but more as a son to his father.

"What is your name?" he asked.

"Joseph, son of Israel the Patriarch," he replied proudly.

"You, the son of a patriarch! How came you to be a slave serving here?" asked the steward.

"I was stolen, purchased by passing traders, and sold in the market-place as a common slave."

Hamat made no comment, but continued asking questions. "They tell me you are adept at stealing without being found out."

Joseph drew himself up. "Then they tell you lies, sir. I have never knowingly taken anything of my master, save only the extra meat granted to slaves at feast times."

"But I am told that all slaves steal and pilfer and rob their masters."

"That may be true of slaves, my lord Hamat. I was free-born, son of one who owns many slaves, menservants and maidservants, and flocks and herds in great abundance." Even to speak of it caused such a yearning in the heart of Joseph that he could not continue.

"But why is it that you do not take what comes to your hand? If what you say is true, you have been grievously used, and might well feel yourself justified in improving your miserable estate."

Joseph looked at Hamat and saw that here was no Pharez, but one who might understand.

"My lord Hamat," he said, "I worship the one great God, Jehovah, the all-powerful God of Abraham. I am His servant, and there are many things which those who serve Jehovah think forbidden to them."

Hamat nodded. He could understand this more easily. If there were rites and tabus concerning his god, then this was explicable.

"Many of you Egyptians will not eat the head of an animal. On the ninth day of Thoth you must all eat fried fish outside your doors. You may eat fish such as kishr and benni, but you may not eat of phagrus or lepidoth."

Hamat nodded, while Joseph continued, "My God, Jehovah, is not concerned with such prohibitions and tabus, but to worship Him is to follow what is good. To take possession of another man's goods is not worthy of a follower of Jehovah."

Hamat was silent in sheer amazement.

"Joseph," he said, "never have I met a slave like you. But such ideas commend themselves to me. Tell me, what do you think of Egypt? How does our way of life differ from yours in Canaan? Talk with me; I am fatigued, and would be entertained."

Joseph talked for a long time to Hamat, who was surprised at his words. Hamat asked his opinion of the way the vast store-rooms in which he worked were organised. Joseph hesitated, but was told to say on. Then the Hebrew slave astounded the old steward by the suggestions he made for improvement. The wines, Joseph declared, were stored in quite the worst possible place, so that any slave who was commanded to bring a drink had to pass through two large rooms of dry goods, and through the baking house where chefs were constantly working. The wine could as easily be stored in the place of the dry goods, which were not needed so suddenly.

A list of all the stores contained should be kept in each room and a note made when the stores were withdrawn. Endless trouble and frustration were caused to the cooks when the supply of spices ran low, and had not been renewed at the market.

Warming to his task, Joseph told Hamat how he would re-organise the entire storehouse, re-arrange his system of marketing and the distribution of the goods to the household, planning ahead with more foresight for times of festival.

Then he paused, overcome with his temerity. "Have I so

forgotten my position as to utter such things?" he said in humility.

But the old man was full of wonder at what he had heard. Joseph had no idea how his heart lifted to hear those plans, which to his experienced ear made such infinite sense and showed such wisdom.

"You have indeed the wisdom of the gods, or perhaps it is of your own God, Who in making men honest and pure, also makes them wise. But you do not realise this fact—only I can scribe. To write the contents of the stores on papyrus would require my constant presence, and I am old and infirm."

"Then why not call upon me to help you with the writing?" asked Joseph eagerly.

Hamat stared at him. "You mean, wonder slave, that you can write?"

"I had always kept my father's stores, and learnt to write on clay with a stylus. It is our custom. Here you have papyrus, and it is easier for records to be kept. I have learned your characters, and could help you to keep the stores. I have learned to reckon and calculate from my father Jacob, who had it from his grandfather Abraham. He was skilled in reckoning, and those who learnt in Ur of the Chaldees of arithmetic and astrology have a knowledge even as great as that of the Egyptians."

Hamat lost his fatigue. His exhaustion went from him as though it had never been. To have this young man as an assistant would make it possible for him to continue serving Potiphar for many years to come. Joseph would take from his shoulders the great responsibility, and do much of the work, re-plan the stores, and Hamat would get all the credit. Not that he would exploit Joseph, for he too had his integrity, though his loyalty was to Horus, the hawk-headed god. Joseph should be well-housed, and should eat with the upper servants, and be given a portion like that of the soldiers in Potiphar's army, that portion which everyone knew was five minae of bread, two of beef, and four arusters of wine daily.

.   .   .   .

Hamat's renewed health enabled him to carry out many of Joseph's suggestions. To be able to lie on a comfortable couch at the time of siesta, knowing that Joseph was grappling with the accounts, going to market, checking the stores, rejuvenated the old man, and caused him to reward Joseph with many gifts and honours, which brought him the respect of his fellow slaves. Pharez was thankful to have Joseph removed from his jurisdiction. He had never overcome the fear of the evil eye. Joseph's fellow-slaves were at first inclined to jealousy at his preferment, but when he came to their quarters as before, and sat with them, sharing much of the bounty that he now received, they thought him a fine fellow, and begged him to entertain them again with stories and tales of far-off lands.

Potiphar's little daughter Asenath found Joseph was now more accessible than before, and many times when she could escape from the supervision of her maidens, she crept into the storehouse and asked Joseph for a story, pleading as she did for just one more honey date. Joseph teased her gently. It was always the same request. When he saw her, he often forestalled her request, saying, "*Please*, Joseph, give me just *one* honey date," imitating her childish voice. "It is always just one more," he said, "yet before my story is done, I know the jar will be empty, and Hamat will probably beat me."

But Asenath shook her head. "No one will beat you, Joseph," she said. "You aren't a real slave, are you? You're only pretending. I think someone has put a spell on you, and said that you will not be free until you have married a princess, like the old tales say."

"And now we'll have to find a princess," Joseph told her.

"I wish I were old and could marry you. I will, if you like, when I'm grown up; but then I'm not a princess," Asenath said plaintively.

"What terrible utterance is this?" said Joseph, pretending to be shocked. "If anyone should hear my lady Asenath speaking so to one of her father's slaves, I should be bound and thrust into the inner prison."

Asenath just laughed. She thought Joseph was the most wonderful person in all the world.

At last he said, "It is time you went back to your play, and left me to check my stores."

"*Please*, Joseph . . ." began Asenath, and Joseph finished it for her, ". . . give me just one honey date. And that," he said, popping it into her mouth, "will be the sixth you have devoured. May it make you sick, so that your stomach will loathe them."

Off she ran, laughing. Joseph watched her go. He loved all children, thinking with a yearning he could hardly contain of his brother Benjamin. He wondered how he fared; if his brothers were kind to him, or if they meted out the treatment he had received from them as a child. And he wondered with deep longing if he would ever see his father again. It was years since that terrible day when he had journeyed with the traders, sons of Ishmael and Midian, his kinsmen as sons of Abraham, into this land of Egypt. Yet it was his own brothers, his own flesh and blood who had callously sold him into a life of slavery.

It had been a wretched existence at first. Egypt was an extraordinary country, though as a slave he saw little of it, except as he entered the land. Then he had come to the city, with its teeming mass of people rushing hither and thither, all centred round the Nile. Far away he had seen the pyramids, the most recent of which had been built six hundred years before. They stood out as the only high ground on this flat green belt of land, which like a serpent wound itself around the life-giving Nile.

It had been humiliating to stand shackled in the market-place, to be assessed like livestock, pushed and prodded by would-be purchasers. All the blood of a free people and descendants of patriarchal race had risen in Joseph. Pharez had felt his muscles, looked him up and down, and finally paid the price asked for him; he had been driven to his new home, assisted by blows, and received treatment never even meted out to the animals of his father's flocks, and set amongst the slaves in Potiphar's house.

Joseph found it best to submit and stifle his pride, though the habits, conversation and mentality of his fellow-slaves sickened him. He was determined that, with the help of his God, he would not sink to their level, or debase himself by their example.

That had been some time ago. Now that Hamat had promoted him, life was very different. Joseph had again that consciousness that 'God was with him'. His mother had said that a man who complains against his circumstances complains against his God. He had many a time been tempted to complain against his lot, and to feel that God had forsaken him, and he might as well go to the bad with the companions of his slavery. Then he told himself that a man must not be subservient to his circumstances —that was the action of a weakling, who worshipped nothing but gods of wood and stone, like the Egyptians. He would make something of his life, keep his mind active, and his body pure and healthy. And when the time came that by some miracle he would be restored to his father's house, he would go with head held high and no shame to hide.

19

POTIPHAR was pacing up and down his palatial apartment in a frenzy.

"It *cannot be*!" he shouted. "At such a time as this! Hamat must be brought, however ill he is. Send for the physicians to give him a potion. I cannot manage without his help."

The Nubian eunuch, who had charge of the court of women, listened impassively, and told him, "Hamat is in a deep coma, my Lord. They say his face has about it the look of death. Should he regain consciousness, he would still be quite unable to join you in council."

Potiphar wrung his hands. For Hamat to be ill now of all times was beyond bearing. Hamat, who had recently shown such wisdom, that never had Potiphar prospered so greatly. The new plans for the household, trading and marketing had shown Hamat to have the mind of a genius, even though it had only manifested itself in all its brilliance these last months.

The Grand Vizier of all Egypt was calling together the nomarchs from the kingdom for a council, accompanied by great feasting. Men were coming from the upper Nile, from nearer places on the fringe of the green belt, Abydris, Anthribis and Tentyris, and beyond the great pyramids. As Captain of Pharaoh's guard, Potiphar's chief duty was that of quarter-master—some called him 'Pharaoh's chief cook' instead of Captain. In time of political gathering it was Potiphar's opportunity to excel, and to bring himself to the notice of Pharaoh and the princes, so that when an appointment as a priest became vacant, his name would figure high on the list.

Pharaoh's chamberlain, one Sebbeku, was Potiphar's chief rival. He had the closest contact with Pharaoh, and though he did not aspire to the priesthood, for that promotion came only to men from the army, he always sought to outshine Potiphar in any way that he could. It was necessary that they should arrange the details of the feast at the palace together, and Potiphar guarded his right to organise the catering, co-operating with Sebbeku's men, but not giving place to them.

Then tragedy had struck.

Sebbeku was coming with his crafty assistant to discuss the plans and organisation, and Potiphar's lack of knowledge and experience would be exposed to all. He had ever been one to leave his affairs in the hands of others. It was for this reason that he desired so earnestly to rise to the priesthood, and have done with responsibility. He had put everything into Hamat's hands, and at such councils as these he remained aloof, and pretended to be so great a personage that the ordering of beef and grain was beneath his notice, instead of beyond his ken.

"I am undone," said Potiphar at last. "Sebbeku will see the nakedness of my mind, and will gain complete ascendancy."

The Nubian begged leave to speak. "Hamat has a wise young slave, who acts as his scribe, and knows much of his business."

Potiphar waved an impatient hand. "What use is an ignorant slave to me? Doubtless he lifts and carries for Hamat, and performs menial tasks. I need a man of wisdom, of infinite cunning, to match Sebbeku."

The Nubian would not be gainsaid. "This Hebrew young man is no ordinary slave. They say the new plans and ideas of Hamat originated in the mind of the Hebrew."

Potiphar considered. "But can he write, and use his brain? Sebbeku and his wily confederate can calculate in their minds when others are still fumbling."

"They say the Hebrew is learned in all the arts of calculation and scribing equal to any in Egypt."

Potiphar thought the Nubian was exaggerating in order to pacify him, and he fell to wondering if he might not feign illness himself, when he heard the approaching chariot wheels. The chamberlain was arriving in style. There was no way out.

"Send this Hebrew to me," he said, and called for his flabellists to keep the air cool. Potiphar, to preserve the dignity of his position, seated himself in a throne-like chair in state, with slaves fanning him and servants seated nearby trying to look very wise.

Only the hastiest explanation was given to Joseph. Before entering the presence of Potiphar, he merely slung about his shoulders an embroidered cloak over his tunic. He sensed that this was a great occasion, and he would try to do his master honour and take Hamat's place. Papyrus in hand, Joseph entered the room calmly, with even tread. Potiphar's guests were being given wine and sweetmeats. Joseph merely bowed and took his place near to Potiphar, as though it were the usual thing for him to be seated with the great ones.

. . . .

The discussion began, the chamberlain taking it upon himself to outline the plans, the number of guests expected and the extent of the feasting. When he had finished his explanation, Potiphar experienced a feeling of utter helplessness. What should he say now?

But he had no need for concern. Joseph requested his permission to speak. Potiphar nodded. Anything to keep the truth at bay, when his lack of knowledge would be exposed. Joseph asked searching questions, making notes constantly, such questions that showed a complete inside knowledge of customs, tabus and differing tastes. The men from upper Egypt, he said, would, of course, only drink a certain kind of wine, would not touch mutton, would expect the fish silbeth to be served as a delicacy, whereas the Semite Egyptians would consider mutton a necessity and refuse fish. What proportion of each would be expected? And many more questions, so that the chamberlain found himself answering obediently, sometimes floundering, sometimes trying vainly to cover up his lack of knowledge. Potiphar could almost have laughed aloud when Joseph gently put Sebbeku right on some point of custom with which the chamberlain should have been familiar—a matter which Joseph took as a matter of course.

It was Joseph eventually who took charge of the proceedings, who said from which granary they should order the corn, firmly refusing to patronise the one suggested by Sebbeku. He told him that this particular granary gave underweight. The sacks he had last ordered had not been measured by the approved wooden measures, but by an unauthorised one of their own design.

"Go to them, if you will, for your own catering, my lord chamberlain, but I cannot advise my master, Potiphar, to give them his custom on an occasion like this. You know, I am sure, that my lord's standards for these occasions are of the highest."

Potiphar could have embraced Joseph to see the discomfited expression on the face of Sebbeku, and the ill-concealed smiles on those of the Nubian and the other slaves.

At last it was decided. Joseph assured the chamberlain he could leave everything in his hands. He would order the supplies, but the chamberlain's help in arranging the seating of the guests, and the order of precedence, would be greatly valued. He could safely leave the catering in the hands of Potiphar, Captain of Pharaoh's guard.

.   .   .   .

Potiphar dismissed his flabellists, with their massive fans. It was cool now, and this room enjoyed the comfort of a mulkef, those wooden wind-sails which were fitted to upper-storey terraces facing the prevailing north-west winds. He felt mellow, and in such good humour that he sent for vessels of thasian to refresh his guests for their journey.

"That is a remarkable young steward you have, Potiphar," remarked Sebbeku. "I thought Hamat was still with you."

Potiphar waved his hand. "I have the best of servants," he said. "Hamat is indisposed today, but this man . . ." With horror Potiphar realised that he did not even know Joseph's name. But the omnipresent Nubian murmured, "Joseph."

". . . er, Joseph," went on Potiphar, "is equally skilled in management."

"More skilled, I should say," said Sebbeku, who was coveting Joseph for service at the palace, and wondering how large a bribe would be needed to prise him away from Potiphar, not realising that Joseph was a slave, and as such could only be bought with the consent of his master.

.   .   .   .

Potiphar's wife, Zadia, was reclining on her couch. It had been made to her own specification, with its end raised, receding in a graceful curve. Its comfort made siesta time a pleasure. Her head was resting on a wooden head stool, for her hair was newly dressed in the latest fashion, standing up from her head at least two hands' breadth.

Potiphar had entered. He was fresh from his interview with the chamberlain, and she dreaded the fully expected outburst of temper that was the invariable result of an interview with Sebbeku. The obvious person on whom to vent his ill-humour was, of course, his young wife. But she would not mind. She would make her mind a blank and think of other things. Let him grumble and complain as he would. But Potiphar seemed in rare good humour, sending a slave with instructions to summon one, Joseph. Potiphar's wife vaguely remembered having heard that name.

"And who is Joseph?" she asked.

"A Hebrew slave," was the reply her husband gave.

She exhaled a breath with impatience. Some slave who had

spilt wine or committed some fault, and Potiphar was no doubt going to vent his temper on him. Well, better on some slave than on his wife.

When Joseph, still wearing his embroidered robe, entered the room, Potiphar's wife thought there had been a mistake. But Potiphar welcomed him genially, and gave him permission to be seated. Zadiah thought she could not have heard aright, for no slave would be asked to sit in his master's presence.

" Joseph," began Potiphar, " I understand that you are Hamat's helper, and yet you seem to be his brain and mind as well. I am told these ideas that have transformed my household are yours and not his. Is this so? "

Joseph would not allow this to be believed. " My lord Hamat has consulted me, and treated me very well. I have been permitted to make suggestions, some of which he has adopted."

Potiphar nodded. The young man was modest, and he would not press the matter. He liked his loyalty to Hamat. Potiphar commended Joseph for his conduct in the conference with Sebbeku, and praised his wisdom.

Then Potiphar asked him, " Have you other ideas you would put into operation, if you should ever rise to be steward in Hamat's place? "

Joseph considered, then spoke boldly. " I have indeed, my lord, many changes."

" Tell me of them," said Potiphar.

Joseph, emboldened by Potiphar's interest, said, " I would have the conditions of the slaves improved," and then speaking as though to an equal, Joseph warmed to his subject, and forgot his position. " We must treat our slaves and servants well, if we expect service and honour from them. We must feed and house them, not as beasts of the field, but as servants whose work is honourable. Then will our slaves give us the service we desire."

Potiphar was astounded.

" But am I mistaken," he said, " or are you not yourself a slave? "

Joseph had been so enthusiastic in outlining his ideas, that he had talked as with an equal, and just as he had with Hamat, he apologised for his boldness. "I forget myself, my lord Potiphar, but in truth I was not always a slave, but was born free. Some years ago, when travelling in Canaan, I was set upon and sold into captivity." For Joseph never betrayed the treachery of his brothers, seeking to hide it even from his own mind.

"You speak of 'our' servants as if you yourself were a master."

"My father has many more servants and slaves than even you have here, my lord, though his home is not so magnificent as yours. My duty was to keep his stores, and to fulfil something of the office that I do here, though not on so great a scale." Joseph said nothing of his father's gift as a shepherd, for he would not allow his father's occupation to be held in contempt.

"Tell me how your slaves were treated, and why you would alter our ways."

Joseph told him that every slave had sufficient food, every under-shepherd was allowed a proportion of the lambs to make his own little flock, to feed his family, and that all men were treated as God's creatures, and not as animals, as was so often the case in Egypt.

Potiphar listened in amazement.

"Are all Canaanites equally careful in the treatment of servants?" he asked.

Joseph, thinking of the treatment his father had received from Laban, said this was not always so. But when men truly worshipped Jehovah, they were merciful and kind.

"I have heard of Yahweh, the God of the Hebrews. Is it because you worship this God that you have the gift of wisdom?"

"All the wisdom I have is His gift," said Joseph humbly.

Potiphar encouraged Joseph to tell him more, and while he spoke of his aged father and his brothers, and spoke longingly of Benjamin, Potiphar felt deep stirrings of pity. I ought to set him free, and send him to his father's house, he thought. But how could he just now, when the Grand Vizier's Council was upon him, and Hamat was almost giving up the ghost? Potiphar put away the generous thought, and spoke to Joseph, who was looking through the window, unshed tears of anguish in his eyes, as his whole being longed for the valley of Succoth and the hills of Hebron.

Potiphar's wife listened to the conversation enthralled. Her eyes feasted on the handsome countenance of the young slave who behaved like a king. This was surely the slave whom Asenath had told her was not really a slave, but a prince. A childish fancy she had thought then, but one could weave such fancies round a man like this. His bearing was only equalled by the sheer beauty of his countenance. His chin denoted purpose and determination. Here was a man who could not easily be moved. His eyes were kind, belying the almost grim expression of his mouth. Potiphar must appoint him as a steward, she thought. Hamat was ill, and unlikely to recover. And who knew—perhaps she might interest herself more in household matters, the wines and stores, and the mysteries of catering.

.   .   .   .

Hamat died and was laid in the tomb he had been preparing all his life. Only foolish men did not prepare themselves an eternal habitation, he had often told Joseph. The cave, hollowed out in the valley, was filled with furniture to rest him, dice and counters to amuse him, and papyrus on which he could write. And as his embalmed body was laid to rest, food and drink were placed beside him for sustenance on his long journey into the valley of the dead.

Joseph was appointed steward, and Potiphar called him into his presence, giving him a free hand to make any changes he was minded to: to trade, to purchase, to oversee the crops and flocks. Potiphar only wanted to eat and drink, and be left in ignorance of everything else. He had complete confidence in Joseph.

The first change the new steward made was to dismiss Pharez as keeper of the slaves. One holding such a position must be fitted to rule, Joseph thought, and one who could use authority without abusing it, and need not carry a whip to enforce his orders.

It was not easy to make changes, but when the slaves found that the food they ate not only increased in quantity, but that it did not consist only of boiled vegetables and beef once a week, but that their rations were almost equal to that of the soldiers, they could not believe their good fortune. After a feast, each one had a share in all that was left over, but Joseph warned them that theft would be punished unmercifully, and the worst punishment that he could devise was not the well-known bastinado, the punishment usually meted out to both male and female slaves, but that they should be taken to the market-place and sold to another master. This fate was feared above everything, for where else would slaves sleep on clean rushes and have adequate food and a share of the feasts, and two arusters of wine daily, and not go to rest with backs covered with weals of the whiplash?

Asenath was not the only member of the household who sought out Joseph in his steward's office. Potiphar's wife consulted him about the arrangements for her many social engagements, and, when it was the festival of some goddess, all her women friends would be invited and entertained. She felt it only right, she told him, that she should know more about the various kinds of wine, grain and meat that were in the storehouse. Joseph felt honoured with her attention. Zadia was indeed very beautiful, and it was as though a goddess had condescended to him, so gracious was her manner, and so kindly were her favours. She liked to listen as he gave orders to the slaves at the time of feast preparation. It gave her a thrill to note the way they rushed to do his bidding, leapt to attention as he approached. Yet he never raised his voice, and rarely spoke in anger. All the servants, from the greatest to the least, treated him with wholesome fear and great regard.

Zadia often listened while Joseph told Asenath stories, though he always stopped if he saw her mother approach. She hid herself to listen, not so much for the interest of the story, but for the sheer joy it gave her to hear his voice.

.   .   .   .

For some years Zadia was content to live each day for the anticipation of her contact with Joseph, satisfied with the pleasure of consulting him, seeing him listen respectfully to her orders. She even occasionally rebuked him or tried to cross him, but he listened with such impassivity and respect that she gave it up. It was obvious that to so perfect a servant a rebuke was undeserved and there was not much amusement in crossing someone who refused to show a spark of emotion or anger.

To a woman with an ageing husband, and possessing a woman's natural emotions, one who was in her prime of desire, the mere presence of a servant of Joseph's calibre was not enough. Potiphar's wife lived in a dream where she and Joseph reigned together in a palace, where Joseph ruled her and she was not the mistress, but willingly subjugated herself to his stronger will, and together they satisfied their love. For she was convinced that it was impossible that her love for Joseph could not be returned. Naturally, she could not expect him to show it by look or sign until she made the first move. He was not like Potiphar's young officers, who tried to flirt with her when her husband was not by. His subservient position made it impossible for him.

But one day she would declare herself, and she could imagine the joy he would manifest when he knew of her love, and that he need no longer hide his. They would plan a life together. Potiphar was an old man, and he knew little of what went on around him. He dreamed his dreams of the priesthood, and left his wife very much to her own devices. The young officers with whom she had dallied had ceased to be an anxiety to him, and he thought his wife was reaching years of discretion, and had relaxed his vigilance.

·   ·   ·   ·   ·   ·   ·   ·   ·   ·   ·   ·

It was in the month of Mesore, the last month of the year, that Potiphar and his wife were invited to a feast in thanksgiving for another good Nile. Potiphar was a little put out that Sebbeku had forestalled him in planning this feast. The chamberlain knew well that Pharaoh's Captain of the guard always gave feasts at any festival to do with the Nile. Sebbeku was welcome to plan festivities for the nomarchs, or even to plan a festival to the goddess of the moon, but Potiphar always felt that the Nile was his peculiar prerogative, almost as though he himself arranged its rise and fall by the very regularity with which he prayed to Nilus for his blessing.

With bad grace he prepared himself for the festival. He could not absent himself—this would cause comment, so he would have to listen piously while Sebbeku made the speech, which he always enjoyed making himself.

Joseph felt nothing but relief that the feast was to be held at some other residence. Potiphar never realised the work and planning that these vast assemblies demanded, upsetting the routine, causing discontent and exhaustion. While Potiphar was away, with many of his other servants attending him, Joseph decided he would seize the opportunity to check the stores and to plan a new granary. Sometimes he was bidden to attend his master at the feasts, and recently, to his surprise, he was required to act as an escort, travelling with Potiphar and his wife in their own chariot. But this time Potiphar had acceded to his request to let him stay at home to work on his plans.

Zadia, her hair dressed in an amazing erection on the top of her head, wearing her choicest necklaces of cornelian and faience, green jasper and lapis lazuli, sat waiting in her room for Potiphar. She knew he was out of temper, but what did that matter? On these occasions she had managed to insist that Joseph, as steward and chief of all the servants, should travel with them in the chariot, acting as escort.

"Confound that son of a jackal for arranging this feast," muttered Potiphar. "Joseph could arrange it far better than Sebbeku's steward. Everyone says our festivals outshine even Pharaoh's."

The mention of Joseph's name made his wife turn her head sharply. "Is Joseph ready to attend us?" she asked.

Potiphar grunted. "He's not coming. He wants to plan his new granary. There's no stopping the fellow—works in his sleep, I declare! Suits me. I don't know what I'm worth these days. I reckon it's doubled from what it was in the days of Hamat. Very fortunate we are indeed. Glad I didn't send him back to Canaan."

"Send him back to Canaan? Whatever for?"

"Oh, my dear love, just a little thought I had. Felt I ought to free him and send him home."

Zadia drew a breath of anguish at the mere thought. "I should hope you would not do such a thing. How would you ever hope to manage the household without him, cope with Sebbeku, and hold on to your present position, let alone hope for promotion?"

"Calm yourself, my dear. You are getting yourself quite unnecessarily upset. I did not say I was going to send him away."

"It is not that," said Zadia, feeling she had shown her hand too obviously. "It's just that I feel . . . rather ill. I must have eaten something that disagreed with me. Perhaps it was the fish."

"Fish? That was all right; I ate the fish," said Potiphar, fussing round her.

"Then it is just that I am feeling a little faint." She lay back, only taking care not to damage her enormous head-dress.

At last she said desperately, "Potiphar, my lord, I fear I am too ill to accompany you. Will you make my excuses? Say that I have a fever, or some respectable sounding malady. But I fear my head feels too heavy to lift."

"It's that confounded beehive you've got on your head," Potiphar said disagreeably. He liked his wife to have her hair dressed simply, as it had been when, as a young girl, he had taken her as his wife.

Zadia shut her eyes wearily. All husbands liked their wives to dress their hair as they had done as brides, she thought; they had no regard for fashion. She merely shut her eyes and waited.

"Send my maid to me," she said eventually, "and leave me, and soon I will recover."

Potiphar stamped out of the room, irritated that not only had he to attend this detestable feast, but he had to go alone. He liked to take his wife with him, and see the glances of envy that the young officers cast upon him for owning such a woman. And if his wife was not with him, who was there to grumble to? For a man may not give way before his own servants.

. . . .

194

As soon as the house was deserted, Potiphar's wife recovered marvellously. Her maid had hidden her disappointment at being called back, for she had been given permission to go to the bazaar while her mistress was away. Zadia was aware of this, and endeared herself to her astonished maid by saying, "There, Fatma, I am recovered. Go your way. You have been helpful. Take with you this silver piece, and buy yourself a trinket at the bazaar."

In delight Fatma skipped away, leaving her mistress full of delicious anticipation, and to make careful plans. First of all, she anointed herself with many spices and perfume of spikenard, as a bride would for her wedding. Then, putting on a diaphanous robe, she took the fearsome erection from her head, and brushed her hair into sleek coils, so that it hung down naturally like a black veil.

The servants were all at the feast or at the bazaar. Joseph was insistent that they should be given a certain amount of liberty when the work was slack. It was well for her, she thought, that he had such revolutionary ideas.

She prolonged the time of anticipation so that Joseph could attend to his business. Her whole being tingled with anticipation. She felt like a young girl waiting for the bridegroom of her dreams. Potiphar at forty had seemed old to his young bride of not yet twenty years, and as a bride she had never felt like this.

She could hear Joseph's firm tread as he paced the floor below, measuring the distance with his stride, designing his new granary, and writing the notes on his papyrus. At last he stopped walking about and, looking over the gallery to the courtyard below, Zadia saw him in the fading light. At first she allowed herself just to look. Was ever a man more desirable??

"Joseph," she called softly.

He looked up, startled. He had imagined himself alone. Unable to see, he called, "Is it Asenath?" doubtfully.

"No," she said, with a ripple of laughter, "it is Asenath's mother."

"But, my lady, why are you not at the feast? I thought you had been gone these three hours."

"I was faint and unable to go," she told him. "At the last moment I stayed behind."

"I hope your maid had brought you everything you need?" he asked.

"I sent Fatma to the bazaar. How often have you told us that we must treat our slaves more humanely!"

Then Joseph had a sudden premonition of evil, as though he were caught in a trap. Why he should sense danger, he did not know, but it certainly was not right that he should be alone in the house with his master's wife.

"Please, Joseph, bring me a cup of thasian," she asked him. "I am feeling faint again. Bring a cup for yourself as well; I like to drink in company."

Her voice saying, 'Please, Joseph' was so like that of little Asenath that he felt that his foolish fears were unfounded. All the same, he put on his most formal manner as he bent to give her the wine with the words, "May it benefit you", not looking at her diaphanous robe, or her unbound hair. He stood motionless, like a soldier on parade, while she drank, looking at him with provocative eyes over the rim of the cup.

"Where is your cup, Joseph?" she asked.

"I do not wish to drink," he said coldly.

"But I commanded you to do so. You are my slave, you should obey me," she said.

Joseph was becoming more and more uneasy. His mistress's manner was strange. She seemed to have forgotten her dignity, and was behaving like one who had taken too much wine. Had her maid brought her some undiluted teniotic? That could have had a disastrous effect.

Zadia put down the cup on the carved table near her hand, not into Joseph's outstretched hand, waiting to receive it.

"Joseph," she said, "lie with me."

Joseph stiffened. His mistress must be drunk. He reached for the cup, and would have left her without a word, pretending he had not heard her softly spoken words. But she sensed his intention, and held on to him.

"Joseph," she said urgently, "we love each other. We could

196

satisfy our love. My husband is aged, and he need know nothing of our actions. We are young, and full of life and love. Why should we deny ourselves?"

Joseph loosened her hand from his, and said sternly, "My mistress, you forget yourself, and what is due to your high estate. I am a slave, and my master has done me the highest honour—he has raised me above all the other servants in his house. There is not one higher than I. He trusts me utterly with his possessions, and such trust requires complete integrity on my part."

"But he need never know. I know that you would not rob him of his possessions, but . . ."

"What greater possession can a man have than his wife? I had sooner take my master's goods, than take his wife."

She stood still, clinging to his arm and pleading, seeking to seduce him with every feminine wile at her command.

Seeing that she regarded not her high estate or her duty to her husband, Joseph said with anger, "I am no adulterer, to sin in this way against my master, and more than all I would refrain from doing this great wickedness against my God." And he tried to leave her, but in an agony to hold him she caught his loose garment and held on to it, as if to force him to lie with her by any means possible. Joseph, rather than stay any longer in so compromising a position, knowing that at any moment the servants, if not his master, would be returning, wrenched himself free, leaving his garment in her hands.

There is no fury greater than that of a woman who has offered herself and her love, and been spurned. All Zadia's love turned instantly to hatred, and in her frustrated desire, she sought only to injure the one whom she had thought the object of her love.

Heavy steps were heard from the returning servants. She called to the Nubian eunuch. He came quickly to her side, and she told him to bring the other men with him. She was panting with rage.

"Look," she said, holding out Joseph's coat, "that Hebrew whom my husband has brought into the house and exalted, has tried to seduce me. He would have forced me, but I heard your steps returning. See, as he fled he left his coat with me."

The Nubian, with the other servants, was horrified and, rushing down to the steward's room, set about Joseph and bound him, to await Potiphar's return.

While Zadia's anger was cooling, in place of frustrated rage, came fear. She had been a fool to call the Nubian. She surely could have bribed Joseph to keep silence, but now that she had shown his garment, there was nothing she could do but accuse him. Joseph must not be allowed to speak and tell his story before she had told Potiphar her own version. She gave orders that she was to know as soon as her husband returned.

Potiphar was in the worst of tempers when he was confronted with his wife's accusations against the steward. Tearfully, she told of Joseph's attempt. Defenceless and alone, he had set upon her, and only the return of the servants had saved her from degradation and shame. Potiphar's old jealousy for his wife flared into a flame. What cared he if Joseph was the best steward he had ever had? He took no thought for the future, but in a rage, ordered Joseph to be taken to that worst of all places of detention —the King's prison. He refused to see him, or to allow him to utter a word in his own defence. A man who would so take advantage of his position as to seek to commit adultery with his master's wife was capable of anything. So Joseph was led away.

That night, his feet bound, his limbs aching from the buffeting and blows he had received, he was at the lowest ebb of all his misery. Was he fated to be so treated? The last time he had been stripped of his robe, it had been the coat of many colours given to him by his father, and now the coloured robe of his steward's office had been taken from him, and he was cast into captivity. It seemed this time that God had forsaken him. He could never expect to rise above this degradation.

Potiphar's wife cried herself to sleep in rage and frustration, and also with an agony of desire. She must keep up the lie to save her own skin. Many a wife had had her nose cut off for less than the crime that she had tried to commit. But her future without Joseph was bleak indeed. So sorry was she for herself, that she never thought of what she had done to the man who had valued his honour, chastity and integrity above his freedom.

Potiphar, his anger cooling fast, wondered how he would cope with the next annual visit from the Vizier. Sebbeku would triumph, for he would never find a steward like Joseph. Confound all women and chamberlains, was his last waking thought.

20

J O S E P H sat at a long wooden table, sheets of papyrus spread before him. Laboriously he copied down the stocks of prison requirements, and noted the number of arusters of bouza consumed. This was the prisoners' only drink. Not for them were the wines he had served in Potiphar's house. This bouza was made from barley bread crumbled, mixed with water, and left to ferment, and was the usual drink for Nile boatmen and the lower orders, including prisoners.

Joseph selected a new reed with which to write, reflecting how different were the entries he made on this papyrus from those in the house of Potiphar. Yet the work was similar. He dipped the reed in water, and rubbed it on the solid cake of red ochre, which served for him as ink. No longer was he to write orders for duck, teal and quail, or the refreshing melons and cucumbers. But he had grown accustomed to it, and with that patience that characterised him, he accepted his present occupation, reflecting that his lot here as prisoner, with so understanding a governor as Rahmet, was preferable to the first unhappy years in Potiphar's house, under the eye of Pharez, and under the lash of his hippopotamus whip.

" Joseph, leave that scribing, and sit with me. I am weary and filled with boredom. Not only is this the first time in ten years of governorship that I have had a scribe for a prisoner, but I have never had a man like-minded, with whom I can talk. Come," said Rahmet, " I command you to amuse me. Philosophise, tell me of your people and your God, and I will tell you of our gods and our battles long ago."

Joseph flexed his fingers. He was glad to leave off writing, for the light was getting dim. He sat down on his stool beside the governor.

"You are good to me, Rahmet," he said. "You give my life here purpose. The days do not crawl so when one occupies the mind and hand with work."

"You are a strange fellow, Joseph," said the governor. "It is my work to assess men's characters, and to judge which person will give trouble, which prisoners are best and safest alone, who can be trusted to perform menial tasks without trying to escape. I soon found out your ability, and consequently I have given everything into your hand. You could have fled from the prison, you could have stolen my goods, and yet my trust in you has been vindicated."

Joseph was silent, lost in thought. At first when he had been flung into the prison by Potiphar's infuriated servants, his lot had been hard. He had expected some sort of a trial, and it was the request to the prison governor for papyrus and ink, with which to prepare his defence, that first revealed his ability to write. Rahmet had given him the papyrus, but quickly disabused his mind of any thought of a trial. "This is the King's prison," he was told. "It is used by Pharaoh and his officers." And Joseph realised that he had no redress, and could only be released by the command of Potiphar or Pharaoh himself.

The realisation of this had been hard to bear. He cried aloud to his God, asking had he not borne enough. His brothers had beaten and sold him, he had endured the degradation of slavery, and his good name, which he had guarded so closely, was sullied by an unprincipled woman. He might rot and eventually die in this stinking place.

Then in his captivity it was almost as if he saw a vision. He realised that he was not alone, but that God—the God of his fathers—was still with him. He knew that ecstasy of communion with the Divine; his prison became a place of glory, and the governor of the prison, who visited him the next day, was amazed. He had expected bitterness, anger, even to be subjected to abuse, but this man had about him a radiance as though he had spoken with the gods.

Rahmet soon found that Joseph was more than willing to act as his scribe, and though at first the papyrus was brought to Joseph in his cell, after a while Rahmet gave him the freedom of the prison. The only curtailment of his liberty was confinement to the prison premises. He took the meals to his fellow prisoners, who soon looked for his daily appearance as the bright part of a tedious routine. He kept the stores and checked supplies, and soon it was said that 'whatsoever they did there, he was the doer of it'.

Rahmet soon found that not only was Joseph an accomplished scribe, and a brilliant storekeeper, but an amusing companion. He learned of Joseph's sad story, and burned with indignation at the treatment he had received.

"Potiphar has deliberately blinded his eyes to the truth," he said. "There have been many stories of the intrigues of his wife, and the only wonder is that her nose has not been cut off before now, because of her adulteries."

As they sat together in conversation, Rahmet remarked, with apparent irrelevance, that if only Pharaoh knew of his cause, he was likely to side with Joseph rather than Potiphar, for Pharaoh favoured any Semite when he was in opposition to an Egyptian.

Joseph asked, "Tell me more of this. I heard little or nothing of your peoples when with Potiphar. How say you Pharaoh would favour a Semite, when surely he is the ruler of all Egypt?"

"You must have heard," said Rahmet, "that the shepherd peoples from the north moved peacefully into the delta of the Nile. They found our pastureland desirable, they increased in numbers, more and more of them poured down from Syria, and it was not until they were greater in number than the Egyptians that anyone realised what this might mean. They were still under Egyptian rule, but one day they arose and, in a barbarous manner, threw off the yoke of the Egyptian kings, and set up a ruler for themselves. They made one Salatis king, and he became great, and received tribute from both upper and lower Egypt. He built a capital, calling it Avaris, as it is to this day. That, of course, was many years ago. The people have intermarried and almost become one, but some men are still proud of their Egyptian ancestry, like Potiphar, and many like Pharaoh Apepi still acknowledge their ancestry from the shepherd kings, or Rulers of the Upland, as they prefer to call them."

"What are the differences between these two peoples?" asked Joseph. "Is there much to choose between their way of life and religious outlook?"

"At first, of course, there was a great deal. The way of the Semites, who had held contact with the desert, was to cling to tradition and resist innovation. They preferred purity and simplicity of life. The Egyptians are more inclined to accept innovations and incorporate them with their own thoughts. Apepi, the present Pharaoh, is a strange mixture. He has very progressive ideas, he despises many of the Egyptian gods, and refers on state occasions to one God, as though there were only one he worships, though no one knows which god this is. Many think he worships the sun-god. The Ruler of the Uplands brought into Egypt a deity whom they called Sut, or Sutkeh, who is identified with the sun."

"The dwellers of Ur and Nineveh worship the sun-god," said Joseph, "and the moon-goddess. It may have had some connection with this."

"That may be so," said Rahmet, "but Apepi has built a temple at Tanis to Sutkeh—a great monument of granite blocks, with fourteen obelisks and many sphinxes."

Joseph listened with interest, occasionally interrupting and questioning. He was always anxious to learn, to increase his knowledge, and this strange country in which he found himself a prisoner held a great fascination for him.

"All men know that Potiphar wishes for promotion to the priesthood," Rahmet said, "but he has little hope of such a thing, being so aggressively an Egyptian. Pharaoh always seeks to promote his own party and descendants of the Asiatics to any high position."

"If only I could get the ear of someone near Pharaoh who would speak for me," said Joseph with longing.

"Hope on, Joseph," Rahmet told him. "You trust in your great God; maybe He will deliver you."

Joseph's eyes glowed. He had learned many things in prison, and reflected that, had he not been incarcerated, he might not have this great inner joy that any mention of his God brought to him.

"Apepi makes a great feast today to Sutkeh. There will be much feasting and revelry."

"I can imagine it all," said Joseph. "How many such festivals have I arranged in the house of Potiphar! The wines, the breads, the meats, training the slaves to work like machines, with every detail perfect." And Joseph in his turn told the prison governor of his experiences in the house of Potiphar.

Then they heard the sound of tramping feet outside, gruff voices raised, and a loud knock that echoed round the thick stone walls of the King's prison. Calling Joseph to follow, Rahmet opened the massive door, and saw members of Pharaoh's guard, the King's Followers, as they were called, bringing in two men bound with fetters.

"These two are to be imprisoned at Pharaoh's pleasure," said the chief officer, "accused of a conspiracy to assassinate Pharaoh. Take them and put them in the ward: very dangerous men."

Rahmet handed the prisoners over to Joseph's charge, while he took all the details from the soldiers. Joseph led them into the cell in the inner prison. These 'very dangerous men' looked more bewildered than violent. Joseph wondered how they had offended Pharaoh, or if, like him, the men had been falsely accused, for they had not the air of assassins. The two men seemed terrified, and shrank from Joseph as if expecting a blow. They were relieved, however, when he merely showed them the cell, removed their fetters, and later returned bringing them bouza to drink. He never forgot his own first night in prison, when he had been flung there, bruised and shaken, suffering from a raging thirst.

Finding someone unexpectedly kind, both men burst into speech.

"It's all a lie, I tell you," said the taller of the two men. "I am Pharaoh's cup-bearer, the chief butler. For years I have been privileged to hand him his wine, and would not stoop to anything which would bring him harm. I have been falsely accused by others, who would shift the blame on to my shoulders."

Joseph looked at the man, and realised by some inner wisdom that every word he said was true.

The other prisoner, a short, fat little man, spoke in sulky resentment. "I have baked my bread in Pharaoh's kitchen these three years, and for the feast I excelled myself. For Pharaoh himself I fashioned a model of his crown, that of lower Egypt and upper Egypt, with the serpent decorated with cummin and caraway. But the assassins sought for a scapegoat, and I was their choice." And he cursed and swore by all the gods, and spared not Pharaoh, his followers, the prison or even Joseph himself.

Later Rahmet asked Joseph about the prisoners.

"The chief butler is peaceful enough," he told him, "and had an air of sincerity about him. However, I am not quite so sure concerning the chief baker."

"You cannot tell though," said Rahmet. "Some of the most innocent-seeming are the greatest liars, and can deceive you by their very ability to act. And some of the most sullen and unruly are only so because they know of their innocence, and are frustrated by their helplessness."

Joseph agreed that this might be so, but still held to his former opinion. His daily contact with the men only confirmed his first impression.

.   .   .   .

The two prisoners settled down to sleep. The butler, accustomed to every luxury, made the best of the lack of comfort. He had been amazed to find that Joseph, whom he had at first regarded as the chief governor of the prison on account of his dignified bearing, was only a prisoner like himself. He had, it seemed, been shamefully treated; to be sold as a slave and then betrayed by false accusation must be galling indeed to a man of his calibre. The chief butler was well accustomed to employing slaves and servants to do his bidding, and he knew a man from the ruling classes when he saw one. He knew too what it was like to be falsely accused.

He lived over again the day of the feast. He had prepared the wine for Pharaoh—that favourite of Apepi's, sebennic. He had taken it himself from the wine jar, and waited while Pharaoh finished making a speech, and then he had proceeded to hand it to his lord. Some time during that speech his attention must have been distracted, for when he took the wine to Pharaoh, according to the custom, Apepi, wishing to favour a visiting dignitary from upper Egypt in whose honour the feast had been made, signed for the butler to pour a little into his guest's cup, and let him drink first.

Then there had been a terrible scene. The guest had taken a sip of the wine, looked up in horror at Pharaoh, and asked in a trembling tone, "My lord Pharaoh, have I offended you, that you seek to poison me? This wine tastes of bitterness." Then he had doubled up, and appeared to be in great pain, and was carried out.

The butler had not heard whether he had died or not, but of course everyone had seized on the man who had proffered the drink. He was the obvious suspect, and had been borne away in fetters to the prison. Could he hope for justice, or would he hear the tramp of feet coming to bear him away to his execution?

He began to doze, and thinking of wine, he saw a vine with three branches, first blossoming and then bearing fruit. Soon he was deep in sleep.

.   .   .   .

Will Semat tell all? wondered the chief baker. No doubt there would be a thorough investigation, torture and questioning. Why had he been such a fool as to enter into the conspiracy of Kemah, the Egyptian? The money that had been promised was tempting. He could leave the palace, travel to No-Amun, where he had been born, and live a life of ease on the proceeds. Or if he preferred it, they told him, when Apepi was killed and the Egyptian party seized the throne, he could have a high appointment at the palace.

The chief baker wondered how much of the intrigue was written on papyrus, and if the conspirators had been able to destroy the evidence. It had been easy to knead the poison into the dough for the special bakemeat. Even if Pharaoh had only eaten a little it would be fatal, for the poison was kneaded into every portion. The baker was anxious to know what had led up to the discovery of the poisoned bread. It must have been that everything exclusively for Pharaoh was inspected. It might have been that a piece of the special bakemeat was flung to an animal, and it would prove instantly fatal.

Naturally, he would come under suspicion. However, he was determined to deny everything, and to try to assume the look of outraged innocence that the chief butler wore. Poor fool! Everyone knew how devoted he was to Apepi, and would have cut off his right arm before he would have handed poison to his lord. The cursing and sullenness had been a mistake. He must be mild and a little grieved. This Joseph seemed to be a man of some importance, and he must make a good impression on him; for it was only to the butler that Joseph had told his sad story.

The baker dozed. Bakemeats, special bakemeats all in white baskets rose before his mind. He breathed deeply and snored a little. Then his mind was in a whirl of horror as he dreamt of terrifying birds swooping down upon the baskets, pecking at the seeds of nigella and camoon from the bread. He was frightened. He cried out, and awoke covered with sweat.

· · · · · · · · · · · ·

Joseph entered the cell occupied by the officers of Pharaoh. Recently they had greeted him cheerily, in spite of their state, but today they were sitting lost in anxious contemplation. The baker had his face in his hands, and the butler's face wore a worried and fearful expression.

"Come," said Joseph, "here is food and drink. What ails you?"

The men looked up.

The butler drew a breath and said, "We have both of us dreamed dreams. Indeed, so vivid have our dreams been, that we think it must have been a vision from the gods. I felt so strangely after I awoke, I felt as if I were still in that dream, and found the chief baker too crying out with fear, and bathed in a cold sweat, saying he had been terribly affrighted. We are here in prison, and have no access to the interpreters. Had we been at the palace, we would have called in the magicians and wise men of Pharaoh to interpret our dreams, but here there is no one to help us, and we have no wisdom of our own."

Joseph felt himself moved by an inner power.

"Do not interpretations belong to God?" he said. "Tell me of the dream."

The butler looked sharply at Joseph. Yes, there was something strange about this man. He looked like one of the wise men who could see into the future. He could but try and see if Joseph, as well as his other gifts, could tell the meanings of dreams.

"I lay thinking of my later occupation," he said,

> "and behold, a vine was before me; and on the vine were three branches, and it was as though it budded, and her blossoms shot forth; and the clusters thereof brought forth ripe grapes; and Pharaoh's cup was in my hand, and I took the grapes, and pressed them into Pharaoh's cup; and I gave the cup into Pharaoh's hand."

There was triumph in the voice of the butler, as he thought back on his former greatness.

Joseph lifted up his heart to God, Who alone can reveal secrets, and saw as plainly as though he read the meaning upon a papyrus scroll. He rejoiced that he had good news for his friend, the chief butler.

"This is the interpretation," he said to the butler, not saying "I think", or "maybe", but speaking with authority:

> "The three branches are three days; yet within three days shall Pharaoh lift up thine head, and restore thee unto thy place; and thou shalt deliver Pharaoh's cup into his hand, after the former manner when thou wast his butler."

As the butler listened, he had no doubt that the words of Joseph were just and true. He had an inner conviction as he thought upon his dream that this was what it was meant to convey to his mind. He grasped Joseph's hand.

"How can I thank you, Joseph," he said, "for what you have done for me? I can never repay you."

Joseph looked at the butler, and thought of him, so soon to be restored to his former glory, soon to leave this place of captivity, the place where he, Joseph, had been for so long, and was like to remain.

"You can indeed help me," said Joseph eagerly, for he saw that here was one who was going back, right into the palace itself, and would have Pharaoh's ear, and Pharaoh was the only man who could bring about his release. "Think on me when it shall be well with thee, and show kindness to me, I pray thee, and make mention of me unto Pharaoh, and bring me out of this house, for, as I have told you, I was stolen away out of the land of the Hebrews, and here also I have done nothing for which they should put me into the dungeon."

The butler promised that to secure Joseph's release would be his first thought on returning to Pharaoh's palace. Joseph allowed the butler to pass into the outer prison, to apprise Rahmet of the good news of his imminent release.

The baker was left with Joseph, who looked with enquiry at him. Encouraged by such a favourable interpretation given to his colleague, he in his turn told his dream.

"Behold," he said, "I had three white baskets on my head, and in the uppermost basket there were all manner of bakemeats for Pharaoh; and the birds did eat them out of the basket upon my head."

Joseph was silent. He now had no wish to speak, but even as he knew the interpretation of the dream, he saw the heart of the baker for what it was. He saw greed and treachery, he saw naked guilt in his eyes.

"Can you not tell me the interpretation of my dream?" demanded the baker. "You had good news for my friend. Give me some cheerful intelligence."

Joseph spoke briefly, but again with such authority that the baker knew each word was true.

> "This is the interpretation thereof," Joseph told him. "The three baskets are three days; in three days shall Pharaoh lift up thy head from off thee, and shall hang thee on a tree; and the birds shall eat thy flesh from off thee."

Joseph made no comment, but passed swiftly from the cell, only hearing the curses that followed him from the baker, as he vilified those who must have betrayed him, and revealed his complicity in the plot.

. . . .

It was three days later. Joseph and Rahmet had bidden the butler godspeed, as with great ceremony he was taken from the prison, and led back to the palace in time for Pharaoh's birthday, to hand his lord the special cup at this, the greatest of all Apepi's celebrations. The tramp of feet taking away the baker to be hanged had only just died away.

"Sit down, Joseph," said Rahmet, looking at him with curiosity. "You are a strange man. You never cease to amaze me. Not only are you the most gifted of scribes and brilliant of organisers, a man of integrity and piety, one who can amuse me and laugh with me, and play instruments of music, but now it seems, you have become a revealer of secrets. Even Pharaoh's magicians would be hard put to it, to divine the meaning of those dreams. I might have thought that some news had reached you from without, but the officers of Pharaoh's guard tell me that only last night a papyrus was found revealing the whole plot, naming among the conspirators the chief baker, but plainly vindicating the butler, and absolving him from all guilt. And yet you revealed that secret three days ago. What kind of a man are you, Joseph?"

"I cannot tell," replied Joseph simply, "except that any wisdom I have is given to me by God—the God Whom I serve. It

209

is nothing to Him Who has all knowledge to reveal secrets, but to reveal them to such as I, and to use me as His mouthpiece makes me feel humble indeed."

Rahmet continued to look in curious speculation at Joseph. He would not describe him as exactly a humble man, except, as he said, before his God. He never seemed to be cowed or humbled by his station as a slave or prisoner. He was the kind of man who could rise to great heights, had he the opportunity.

"Maybe the chief butler will tell Pharaoh all about you, and you will soon be given a position as chief of all his wise men and diviners."

"I would not care to fill such a role," said Joseph. "I only seek to have my liberty, to return to the land of my fathers."

Rahmet continued in the same strain, "When the butler speaks for you, and Pharaoh raises you to a great position, think of me. I have served as keeper of this prison these ten years, and I had hoped for a very different life after my years of training."

"Tell me of your life and training," Joseph asked. "I believe all Egyptian boys may go to school if they so desire. We had no such opportunities in Canaan."

"Yes," said Rahmet, "any boy with the necessary application may go to school and learn to read and write. I studied many things. Such a schooling brings certainty of a public appointment, either in the central government, or as a representative of one of the various nomes of Egypt. I could have become a scribe, or one of Pharaoh's wise men."

"Did that particular aspect of learning appeal to you?" asked Joseph.

"Oh, no," said Rahmet, laughing. "I was not studious enough. My schoolmaster did his best with me. He had a saying, 'The ear of a boy is in his back—he hearkeneth only when he is beaten'. He certainly tried to open my ears with the rod of correction. It takes great learning to be a wise man. They are not merely soothsayers and frauds. They have to learn all about the human body. They are Pharaoh's physicians, and excel in everything to do with healing. They can sew up a wound as neatly as a woman can sew cloth. They invent cures and balms, and as well as studying the stars, they know all about the future prosperity of the land by a close study of the vagaries of our sacred river Nile."

"Yours is a wonderful land," said Joseph. "It is strange that I have lived here these eleven years, yet have seen so little. I would like to know more of it from all that I have heard."

"You would like far better to be free to journey up to the land of your fathers," Rahmet told him.

Joseph agreed. "My heart is there," he said.

But he had grown accustomed to the life that was his lot, and the ability to prove himself as trustworthy had always been rewarded.

Joseph, like his father, was to spend nearly fourteen years in servitude. True, Jacob had not been a slave, though servitude had made a greater impression upon his mind than it had upon the mind of his son. Joseph had experienced greater degradation, and yet there was something in his make-up that made it possible for him to rise above his circumstances. It may have been that early childhood leaves a lasting impression upon the mind. Jacob, never his father's favourite, must have nursed in his subconscious mind a sense of inferiority, making him a victim to the dominant bully. Joseph, though ill-treated by his brothers, from earliest infancy had known himself to be foremost in his father's eyes, and had been given a coat of many colours. He had developed the inner dignity of a ruler that his father had only acquired since returning to the land of his fathers, when with his new title of ISRAEL, he had shed the memory of his servitude. Jacob, when confronted with Laban's important guests, had forgotten that he himself was of their kind. Joseph was able to speak as an equal with anyone, be it Hamat or Potiphar, and had no sense of inferiority or undue humility.

Rahmet was right in thinking that Joseph could rise to great heights, but immediate exaltation or release was not for Joseph. For, to his everlasting shame, the chief butler, in the joy of restoration to Pharaoh's favour, and the excitement of Pharaoh's birthday feast, forgot his promise to Joseph. The experience of prison and everything connected with it were not things he wished to keep in remembrance, and together with the fetters and indignity of captivity, the chief butler forgot the one who had shown him kindness. Each day for two long years Joseph waited hopefully for the sound of the feet of those men who would come to announce his release.

'Hope deferred makes the heart sick' says the proverb, and whereas formerly, when the sound of Pharaoh's guard coming to the prison made him leap up with eager anticipation and beating heart, after a while he hardly heard it, and schooled himself to live in the present, for to live in anticipation, when the hope is not realised, plunges the one who hopes into a deeper abyss of depression.

21

JUDAH was sitting alone on the plains by Mamre. His sheep were grazing on the new pastureland to which he had led them. Like his father before him, he never spared himself in seeking new land whereon to feed his sheep. When he was alone, Judah could not control his thoughts. He had tried to forget, and to rid himself of the burning remorse that consumed him day and night.

There had been a time when he could no longer bear to look at his father's sorrow, and left his brethren for a while to sojourn with an Adullamite named Hirah. Any company was better than that which reminded him of his base act of treachery. Often tearless sobs would shake his vast frame, and he would reflect that it was not only his brother that he had sold for twenty pieces of silver, but his peace of mind and ease of conscience.

He had returned to his brethren now, ashamed of his unchaste behaviour. Sitting alone, with only his thoughts for company, he reflected that he was little better than his great-great uncle Lot, who had fathered his own grandsons, Moab and

Ammon, deceived by his incestuous daughters. Well, he had been deceived by his own daughter-in-law, Tamar, who had played the harlot, and the result had been his twin sons, Pharez and Zarah.

But ashamed though this conduct made him, nothing weighed upon his conscience like the thought of Joseph as a slave in Egypt. Judah wondered if he had been treated reasonably well. Had he been beaten, ill-treated, was he hungry, was he . . . dead? If some magical power could have come to earth and said to Judah, "You may have one day of your life to live over again' he would have cried out, 'Give me that day at Dothan; only wipe out that day from my life'. He would have offered the magical one all he possessed, his ambitions, his hopes of his father's blessing—all were nothing compared with this. If only he could see Joseph beside him, well and unharmed. He could still remember Joseph's pleading eyes looking up at him from that pit. He could hear his voice saying softly on a former occasion, 'Judah, would I could give you this coat', and he had meant it. Judah shut his eyes, but his mind could not forget Joseph's last look.

He opened his eyes and gave a start, for Joseph's eyes were looking at him with that long considering expression that he knew so well. Then he cursed himself for an imaginative fool, for, of course, the eyes were those of Benjamin, Joseph's young brother, who was standing looking at Judah.

"Well, young man, what are you doing here?" asked Judah.

Benjamin hesitated, then asked, "Can I stay with you for a little while, Judah?"

Somewhat taken aback, Judah assured him that of course he could. But then he saw that Benjamin was trembling, and looking furtively around as though afraid.

"You are frightened, little brother," said Judah. "Was it some wild jackal that made you fearful, or some snake in the grass?"

"No," said Benjamin, hesitating, and then Judah saw two men approaching. Benjamin put his hand instinctively into Judah's, and his big brother closed his hand protectively over his small brother's. Then he recognised Simeon and Levi. He let out a long breath.

"I see what it is," he said. "So they have been ill-using you. Is that it, Benjamin?"

Benjamin said nothing, but pressed closer to Judah. Simeon and Levi walked boldly up to where Judah was seated.

"Oh, there you are, Benjamin," they said. "You're to come and help us drive the sheep into new pastures."

Judah could feel Benjamin trembling. He rose to his feet and looked at his brothers. They were older than he was, but Judah's massive frame towered over them, dwarfing them.

"He will not come near you now, or ever again," he said in a voice of anger, "and listen to me, you craven-hearted snakes, if ever you lay a finger on this child, or ill-treat him in any way, God do so to me, and more also, if one bone of your mean despicable bodies is left unbroken. Go, before I avenge some of the wrongs you have already inflicted."

The two brothers slunk away without argument, knowing themselves to be in the wrong. It was a brave person who dared defy anyone of Judah's dimensions and reputation.

"So you've had a hard time with those two?" asked Judah.

Benjamin nodded. "Sometimes when I'm alone they catch me. I try to stay with the others when I can. If my own brother Joseph had not been killed, he would have protected me," Benjamin said. "Bilhah says I mustn't talk about him, for my father Jacob grieves if I do."

Judah said nothing, but went on listening.

"Dinah is kind. She doesn't like Simeon and Levi at all. She says the most dreadful things to them sometimes."

Judah nodded, thinking grimly that she had reason. Dinah, after being mentally deranged for a while, had married the son of Jacob's head shepherd, and though she would never again recapture that ecstasy of love she knew with Shechem, she was quietly happy, and proud to be the mother of sons.

Judah put his hand on Benjamin's shoulder, and looked into those eyes which conjured up such memories.

"Listen to me, young Benjamin," he said, "if anyone ill-treats you or ill-uses you, he will have me to reckon with. I command you to tell me of it, and by the God of my fathers I swear that it shall go ill with them."

Benjamin was well content, and felt a new sense of security. In happy companionship the two brothers walked back to the tents.

.   .   .   .

Jacob in his old age had become famed for his wisdom. He had always been given to learning, and was a deep thinker. He still lived in his tent, and he and Leah had arrived at an age of understanding and companionship. She would never be a Rachel, and had not that extra understanding of the deeper things of God, but she made him very comfortable, and cared for his sons.

He liked to talk with Naphtali, who was a great conversationalist. He also found great comfort in his youngest son Benjamin. He was not to Jacob what Joseph had been, but he constantly sought to teach Benjamin the things that Rachel had taught Joseph. He instructed him concerning the God of his fathers, and of God's purpose for his race. The old man sometimes looked back with regret, realising that had he instructed, inspired and chastised his sons as he should, there would be much more in them to admire.

Judah was now his right hand. He knew there had been shameful things in his life, but Judah was home again, and seemed very different—less arrogant and ruthless, and he showed an almost fatherly interest in his younger brother Benjamin, as well as in his own twin sons. The loss of his two oldest sons, Er and Onan, had been a grief to him, but from what Jacob had heard, they were hardly sons to be proud of.

Oh, Joseph, Joseph, mourned Jacob to himself. Would to God I had never sent you to Shechem to seek for your brethren. If you had but lived to gladden my old age. You, who had so much of my beloved Rachel in you, and were so worthy to be a son of Abraham, Isaac and Israel. Jacob pulled himself together. He must forget his memories. The sorrow which had been so acute had now settled down into a dull pain, and though it sometimes surged forward into the front of his mind, it must of necessity be put away from his present thinking.

He had promised to give Issachar and Zebulun some advice about special sheep-breeding. He knew himself to be still as skilled a shepherd as any of his sons, and they acknowledged it. He had prospered abundantly, indeed, the spring rains had fallen in abundance these last two seasons, with every promise of continuing, so the prophets foretold that prosperity was almost inevitable. Strange, the famines that at one time had disorganised life and caused such anxiety were little heard of nowadays. Perhaps these were things of the past. Former and latter rains now came with such regularity that the people of the land had become accustomed to prosperity.

Jacob rose to his feet with great agility, considering his age, and calling Benjamin to accompany him, walked over to where Issachar and Zebulun, Leah's two youngest sons, were watering their flocks.

22

I T was Pharaoh's birthday. Not that such festivals made much difference to Joseph. The feasts of all the gods passed by, and in the prison Joseph knew little, except what prisoners told him, of life beyond the thick prison walls. But Pharaoh's birthday caused him to realise that two long years had passed since the chief butler had returned in time to hand the cup to his master, and be restored into even greater favour than before.

The next month Tobi would see another year's Nile inundation, when the inhabitants would bring the cattle into shelter, sometimes having to rescue them by boat if the Nile rose too excessively. Joseph had not seen the open landscape now for more than three years, and thought with longing not only of the flooded land of Egypt, with sycamore trees and palms rising out of the water, but of the wells of Beersheba, the hillside of Hebron with its famous vineyards. Was this captivity never to end? Would the God of his fathers never deliver him, he wondered. Perhaps, he thought, Pharaoh's birthday would bring his name to the mind of the chief butler, for Joseph could never imagine that the butler deliberately refrained from mentioning his name to Pharaoh, according to his promise.

Rahmet stretched himself. The prisoners had been taken their food, and it was about midday. The hour of siesta was at hand, and that would give him an opportunity to rest. Joseph could be left to deal with any prisoners who might be brought in. After Pharaoh's birthday there was often someone who had offended, and by some act of omission or commission made himself liable to imprisonment. Rahmet had great compassion for many of the men under his care. The common thieves and murderers were sent to the people's prison, and though many place-seekers and conspirators, like the chief baker, were sent to the King's prison, often there were others whose only fault was the jealousy they aroused in the hearts of men in high places.

" I go to my couch, Joseph," he shouted. " Call me if the need arise."

Then they heard the tramp of feet.

" 'Tis well I had not gone—this sounds like a mighty host. Make ready, Joseph, it seems we are to entertain a legion. Perhaps we are to celebrate the aftermath of Apepi's birthday."

The doors were opened, and the officers of the guard enquired, " Is there one Joseph here? " Without waiting for a reply, the officer went on, " Pharaoh requires his presence. He is to interpret his dreams."

Joseph came forward, his passive countenance giving no evidence of the fast beating of his heart.

"Prepare yourself," said the officer. " Find him raiment."

Joseph went to shave himself, after the manner of the Egyptians, and Rahmet, full of excitement, produced fine raiment of linen cloth and a cloak of rich embroidery. So it was that Joseph was led by the soldiers into the presence of Pharaoh, looking like a prince of the blood, and not like a slave or prisoner.

.　　.　　.　　.　　.　　.　　.　　.　　.　　.　　.　　.

Pharaoh was sitting in state, his wise men and magicians assembled, all wearing expressions of deep concern, and not a little anxiety. Standing beside Pharaoh was the chief butler.

"Tell me more of this fellow. How is it I have not heard of one whose wisdom would seem to exceed that of my accredited magicians?"

The butler was wringing his hands. He was genuinely filled with remorse that in his prosperity he had forgotten Joseph.

"I do remember my faults this day," he repeated, as he had already done many times, and told Pharaoh all he had heard of Joseph—of his Hebrew birth (which fact predisposed Pharaoh in his favour), and of all that he had heard of his skilled service in great houses. The butler did not know where, but so great were Joseph's gifts, he said, that both in his former employ and in the prison had he become chief overseer. Whatever was done there, he was the doer of it. And prisoner though he was, the butler told Pharaoh, no one would have known of it to see him carrying out his duties with wisdom and dignity. And as an interpreter of dreams, was not the fact that Joseph had foretold his release and the chief baker's execution three days before the event sufficient proof of his wisdom?

"Why should I be surrounded by such fools?" demanded Pharaoh. "Did I not straightly charge my people that any man of wisdom and understanding should be brought to my notice? Yet this man of such wisdom and intelligence is left to moulder in my prison, and no one tells me of it."

"I do remember my faults this day . . ." began the butler, but Pharaoh told him to be silent. The King of Egypt was not in a mood to suffer fools gladly, and he had suffered many things in a dream last night. His inept magicians could only invent meanings, which had no ring of truth in them. He could tell they based their interpretations on nothing but their foolish imaginings. They sought to find wisdom by calling upon their gods, and sought Pharaoh's favour as they bowed in his presence, saying to him, "Thy Majesty is the great god, the great god, the sun-god. I live from the breath which thou givest." And they raised their arms in adoration to him, as though he were a god. The implication being, thought Pharaoh with curling lip, that if I am a god, I should be able to interpret my own dreams.

They tried to invoke the cat-god, the crocodile-god, and all the thousands of gods in their pantheon, but he could see that their minds were darkened. If the brilliant young man of whom his butler spoke in such glowing terms were indeed able to reveal secrets, Pharaoh had it in his mind to exalt him above all these men who wearied him with their fawning and ineffective prognostications. If, of course, the butler was lying, then he might find himself in the prison again, or even sharing the fate of the chief baker.

Pharaoh was tired of being surrounded by Egyptians. The fact that Joseph was a Hebrew commended him to Pharaoh. His last Grand Vizier had been deposed, deprived of his office after the attempted assassination of two years before. Nothing had been proved against him, but he was a weary old man, and Pharaoh was waiting until his sons were old enough to take office, for it was usual for such a high position to be filled only by a kinsman of Pharaoh.

The court waited, some hoping that this young Hebrew who had been sent for would be successful, many of the magicians fearing that he might be. It was not often that the great Apepi dreamed a dream, thought these magicians, and why when he did so he could not accept their interpretation they could not tell.

. . . .

Joseph felt strangely that he was fulfilling a great destiny as he walked through corridors, through open foyers with tall decorated pillars of such magnificence that Potiphar's house seemed but a boatman's dwelling in comparison. Joseph bore himself well. On his face there were new lines, but an even greater sign of purpose and character was there than in his youth. He had been good to look upon when he had won the heart of Potiphar's wife, but as the massive doors opened and the heralds sounded the trumpets, many who sat about Pharaoh thought that the man who came slowly forward to bow down before Pharaoh looked more like a god than a man.

Pharaoh was even more accustomed to summing up his fellows than Rahmet, and in the few seconds before Joseph bowed, the King of Egypt made up his mind that this was his man, a man he could trust. It was the man he had been waiting for. He never varied from this decision in the many years of their association, and Joseph never gave him reason. The young Hebrew bowed before Pharaoh, waiting to hear what the great King Apepi had to say.

Without preamble Pharaoh told Joseph, "I have dreamed a dream, and there is none who can interpret it. I have heard tell of thee, that thou canst understand a dream to interpret it."

Joseph bowed. "It is not in me to interpret dreams," he replied, but added, "God shall give Pharaoh an answer of peace."

The King was a little surprised that this young Hebrew did not say, 'My God' or 'Your God', or even 'The God of the Hebrews', or one of the gods of the Egyptians, but just 'God', as though there were no question about there being only one God. The tone in which he spoke gave Pharaoh a conviction that he had some hidden store of wisdom.

Then Pharaoh proceeded to tell him of his dream, saying, "In my dream behold I stood on the bank of the river, and there came up out of the river seven kine, fat-fleshed and well-favoured, and they fed in a meadow, and behold seven other kine came up after them, poor and ill-favoured and lean-fleshed, such as I never saw in all the land of Egypt for badness. And the lean and ill-favoured kine did eat up the first seven fat kine. And when they had eaten them up, it could not be known that they had eaten them, for they were still ill-favoured as at the beginning. So I awoke. And then I saw in my dream, and behold seven ears came up in one stalk full and good, and behold seven ears, withered, thin and blasted with the east wind, sprung up after them, and the thin ears devoured the good ears. And I told this unto the magicians, but there was none that could declare it unto me. And now," said Pharaoh, when he had done, "would you desire to go and call upon your God, or make an offering or an invocation, that He may give you the interpretation?"

Joseph looked in surprise at Pharaoh, and said, "No, my lord Pharaoh, the meaning is plain to see. The dream that Pharaoh had is one dream, and God hath shown Pharaoh what he is about to do. The seven good kine are seven years, and the seven good ears are seven years, and the dream is one. The seven thin and ill-favoured kine that came up after them are seven years, and the seven empty ears, blasted with the east wind, shall be seven years of famine. This is the thing which I have spoken unto Pharaoh. What God is about to do, He showeth unto Pharaoh. Behold, there come seven years of great plenty throughout all the land of Egypt, and there shall arise after them seven years of famine, and all the plenty shall be forgotten in the land of Egypt, and the famine shall consume the land. And the plenty shall not be known in the land by reason of the famine following, for it shall be very grievous. And for that, the dream was doubled unto Pharaoh twice; it is because the thing is established by God, and God will shortly bring it to pass."

And Pharaoh knew for a certainty, as the butler and baker had known before, that this was the true interpretation. Indeed, it was so clear that he even wondered that he had needed an interpreter. Pharaoh could see that Joseph had received some further revelation.

"Your God has more to say?" he asked enquiringly.

Joseph spoke again, his eyes looking out into the coming years as though the veil of time were lifted and he could see beyond. He was speaking as God's mouthpiece, not as a slave presuming to advise the monarch.

"Let Pharaoh look out a man discreet and wise, and set him over the land of Egypt. Let Pharaoh do this, and let him appoint officers over the land." Here Joseph paused, considering, as one giving advice from a store of wisdom. Then he went on, "Let him take up a fifth part of the land of Egypt in the seven plenteous years."

And he went on, impervious to the feelings he was causing around him, for men were holding their breath at one having

221

the presumption to tell Pharaoh what he should do, as though he were a god who had all knowledge. True, this man sounded as though he was no ordinary man, almost commanding Pharaoh, certainly telling him what he must do. They rubbed their eyes, and tried to believe that he was newly released from prison, and was nothing but a slave.

"Let them gather all the food of these good years that come," went on Joseph, "and lay up corn under the hand of Pharaoh. And let them keep food in the cities, and that food shall be for a store for the land against the seven years of famine that shall be in the land of Egypt, that the land perish not through famine."

It was as though the Spirit of the Lord had come upon Joseph, and after he had spoken, he became himself again, and bowed low to Pharaoh, wondering at himself for being so bold.

Pharaoh was dumbfounded. What man is this, he thought, who could speak with such power, wisdom and understanding? All the chief butler had said to him was true; indeed, the half was not told. The thing was good in his eyes. He could see, as he looked round upon his servants, that they too were impressed.

"Do we need to look further?" he said. "Can we find such a one as this man, in whom the Spirit of God dwells?" And turning to Joseph, Pharaoh, without further consideration or consultation, said, "Forasmuch as God hath showed thee all this, there is none so discreet and wise as thou art. Thou shalt be over my house, and according to thy word shall all my people be ruled. Only in the throne will I be greater than thou."

When he said these words, everyone knew that Joseph was to be the new Grand Vizier, that position second only in Egypt to Pharaoh. They felt that this was right, and it must have been fate that prompted Pharaoh to leave the appointment vacant for such a man, for all agreed that no one had ever shown such wisdom, or looked better fitted to grace the great position.

Then Pharaoh took the ring off his finger and put it on Joseph's hand, and put a gold chain about his neck, and called for even more gorgeous raiment to be brought, and attired him as befitted his new position of splendour. And a decree was written, and criers were sent out to proclaim throughout the land, that Joseph was to be the Grand Vizier, second only to Pharaoh, and to ride in the chariot next to the King in all the great processions.

Pharaoh turned to Joseph and said, "I am Pharaoh, and without thee shall no man lift up his hand or foot in all this land of Egypt. I shall no longer call you Joseph," he said, "but Zaphnath-paaneah," for that name meant 'revealer of secret things'.

23

COULD it really have happened, or had he been dreaming? Would he turn over on his hard bed, and find himself shut in by the thick walls of the prison, to spend another day with Rahmet on tedious routine? But no, everything was real. He was housed in the heart of the royal palace, in an apartment specially given to him. Through the massive doors made of moulded bronze, the shape of a lion with outstretched wings, came a slave bearing refreshment, and pouring it out into his cup, saying the words, "May it benefit you," just as he had done in Potiphar's house.

Overnight his life had changed. Many a man might have shrunk from all that faced him, but to Joseph the work, planning and organisation acted upon him as a challenge. Already in his mind he was building granaries, arranging for the wholesale purchase of supplies, building reservoirs against the coming lack of Nile water, and arranging so many things that he almost ignored the messenger of Pharaoh summoning him to the royal presence. He started to walk briskly to the door, but realised that etiquette demanded that his fan-bearer should precede him, and his servant should walk with him, so that all in his path should make obeisance to him, Joseph, Grand Vizier of Egypt.

Pharaoh awaited this interview with his newly appointed Grand Vizier with interest. He sent his servants away, keeping only his confidential scribe and his wife, Queen Nebyret. She had not been present when Joseph had interpreted the dream, and she was anxious that he should be presented to her. She wondered that Pharaoh had appointed a Grand Vizier so precipitately. A queen in Egypt was no mere consort. As succession in Egypt always went through the female line, she had been the daughter of the last Pharaoh, and she was Queen by right of birth, while Apepi was King only by right of marriage with her. Many sons of the Pharaoh, in their desire to rule, married their sisters, but Nebyret had not done so. Apepi was well fitted to rule, and she had the utmost confidence in him, approving of his progressive ideas, and admiring his ability to put them into operation. All the same, to take a Hebrew slave out of prison overnight, and exalt him to the highest office in the land, usually held by the sons of Pharaoh, was indeed going beyond the bounds of discretion.

"When you meet and talk with him, you will think as I do," Pharaoh had told her, but she was not convinced, and steeled herself to meet this arrogant young Hebrew who, she had been told, actually gave Pharaoh orders, speaking as though he himself were a god.

She looked with interest towards the door as Joseph was ushered in. She would not expect a slave newly out of prison to have court manners, but she supposed he could soon learn. Joseph came towards them and made obeisance, first to Pharaoh and then to the Queen. Nebyret had to admit to herself that here was no raw slave. He had the bearing of a prince, and the manners of a courtier. He neither showed uncouth embarrassment at the august company in which he found himself, nor the undue familiarity of ignorance.

Pharaoh presented Joseph to Nebyret, and made it easy for him to converse with her. Joseph conducted himself modestly, not speaking of the past, but plunging straight into his ideas concerning the future. Pharaoh listened with absorbed interest as Joseph proceeded to tell them both of the ideas that had come to him overnight.

"But surely you have had no time for reflection?" Pharaoh said, almost laughing at the speed with which Joseph made his plans. "Many men would have spent the time planning their apartments and arranging for their comfort, and yet you have already conceived plans to send messengers throughout the land to collect the grain, to build storehouses and reservoirs."

Joseph bowed his head.

"My lord Pharaoh," he said, "my life has been strange, and the only way in which I have kept my reason and sustained myself has been in planning and ordering. From being a boy in my father's house I was gifted as a storekeeper, and I think God was preparing me for the position to which you have exalted me," he concluded simply.

Nebyret decided suddenly that she liked him. He did not seem to be unduly awed by either of them, and included her in the recital of his plans, turning to her with a charming smile, assuming that she was as interested and well informed as her husband. He had a gift of making her feel wise and learned, and any remark she contributed to the conversation was so well received by him, that she was encouraged to say more. Here was a man, she thought, who would not only be servant to her husband, but a friend. Here was one who would help to lift his burdens, and not merely work for him, but with him.

Pharaoh watched Joseph making a conquest of his wife with inward amusement.

"Did I not tell you he was a man of wisdom upon whom the Spirit of God dwells?" he asked his wife with a smile.

Nebyret said, "Frankly I admit, my lord, that all you said of him was true, but I fear he is such an indefatigable worker and planner, that rather than relieving you of your burdens, he will only encourage you to further activity."

Joseph turned to her and said, "I will seek, O Queen, to carry out my lord Pharaoh's behests and spare him anxiety." Then turning to Pharaoh, he said, "I shall need helpers with this large project, my lord."

"Indeed you will," said Pharaoh. "And I was forgetting, you are so concerned with my plans that I overlooked the fact that you are newly become Grand Vizier. A man appointed to a great position seeks first to avenge his enemies, and then to exalt his friends. Say on, Joseph. Those that caused you to be put in prison shall be sent there themselves in fetters, and those whom you would desire to honour shall be exalted."

"I would have no one put in fetters on my behalf," said Joseph, "but there are two requests that I would seek to make."

"Say on," said Pharaoh.

"There is a public appointment of supervisor of grain and harvest, I am told. A man who oversees the granaries, and who would, under my direction, help to arrange our many projects, pull down your barns and build greater. I know just the man for this position. His name is Rahmet. He is a keeper of the King's prison, but he had had all the education needed for such a public appointment. He showed me no little kindness, and manifested the gifts necessary for this task."

"It shall be done," said Pharaoh. "We will send for him."

Joseph pictured mentally Rahmet's excitement at the royal summons.

"You still have one more request, Joseph," said the Queen. "Is it something for yourself?"

"No, it concerns a man who showed me kindness once. He has a great ambition to become a priest."

"It shall be," declared Pharaoh. "Only say his name."

"His name is Potiphar, the Captain of your own guard."

"Old Potiphar, the Egyptian," Pharaoh frowned. "How many times that old bore has wearied me with his requests. You say you know this fellow?"

Queen Nebyret was looking at Joseph in amazement.

"But I heard a rumour—I think my maid told me when she dressed my hair—that it was Potiphar in whose house you laboured, and who had you put in prison."

Pharaoh frowned. "If that is true, he shall himself be put in prison."

Joseph looked Pharaoh full in the face and said, "My lord Pharaoh, you promised to grant my request. Potiphar was in no way to blame. I was misrepresented to him; a false accusation was made by one in whom he had perforce to believe. No blame could attach to him."

"He has a notorious wife," said the Queen. "One wonders how she will take to being the wife of a priest. They have to renounce their life of gaiety and live in seclusion."

"Then that will be as well for all concerned," said Joseph firmly.

Nebyret, with her woman's intuition, suddenly knew who it was who had accused Joseph, and reflected that she was not surprised, for Joseph would make a considerable stir when introduced to the ladies of the court at the next festival. Neither of these thoughts did she share with her husband.

.   .   .   .

To say that Potiphar feared when summoned to the presence of Pharaoh, was to understate his feelings. His horror when the intelligence reached him that Joseph, his erstwhile slave and overseer, whom he had flung into prison, was made overnight Grand Vizier, filled him with panic. He now knew from bitter experience that if anyone had been to blame for the incident with his wife, it was not Joseph. It was only to save his face that he had not put his wife away these many times. Now Joseph was exalted, and as was usual the enemies of the newly appointed Grand Vizier would be laid low, and who better than himself to be debased? Imprisonment, if not death, awaited him.

With sinking heart and filled with dread, Potiphar was ushered into Pharaoh's presence. He made obeisance not only to his sovereigns, but to Joseph. Pharaoh went straight to the point.

"I have good news for you, Potiphar," he said. "Joseph, our new Grand Vizier, tells me that you have shown him kindness in times past, and he wishes to reward you. I am therefore appointing you as priest of On. You will take up your new appointment immediately. The honourable insignia and robes will be supplied. You have my permission to proceed with the necessary arrangements, though you hold your appointment by Joseph's wish."

Potiphar turned to Joseph and bowed to him.

"How can I thank you, when it was I . . ."

" . . . who treated me with such kindness," said Joseph firmly. "It is in my power to fulfil your great ambition."

Potiphar would have made further speeches, but Pharaoh motioned to his servants to show him out, saying to Joseph, "I am grateful to you for removing him from my court. He is wearisome in the extreme, and loves nothing more than to make speeches and invocations to the gods. He can spend the rest of his life in such exercises," and turning to his scribe, he dictated a few details concerning the new appointment.

Queen Nebyret, under cover of this conversation, looked at Joseph with twinkling eyes.

"Joseph," she said softly, "think you that Potiphar's wife will enjoy the life of seclusion to which she is now condemned? Tell me, did you really wish to reward Potiphar, or to punish his wife?"

Joseph's eyes creased with amusement.

"Maybe, O Queen," he said, "it was a little of each, but I would not speak of Potiphar's wife."

The Queen nodded. "I will never speak of her again," she promised.

.   .   .   .

"This is a change of position," Joseph told Rahmet, who knelt before him. "Rise, Rahmet, and prepare to work harder for me than ever I worked for you in the prison."

Rahmet, still a little dazed at his unexpected exaltation, said, "I cannot rightly express my thanks to you, my lord Joseph, for bringing me from the prison, and raising me to such a position."

Joseph stopped him. "We are alone, Rahmet," he said, "Let us dispense with the 'my lord Joseph' and all this obeisance. I confess I cannot move without falling over people bowing to me, and I find my progress sadly impeded. Did you not say that if I should be exalted that I should think on you?"

"Well for me that you had not a memory as short as that of the chief butler."

Joseph laughed. "I will have to send him back to prison if he does not cease wringing his hands and saying, 'I do remember my faults this day'. When we are alone, let us have done with ceremony. You never treated me as an inferior prisoner, when you might have kicked me around at your will. You made me your friend. I need you as my friend now to work with me. Listen, here is what I plan to do, and what you must do immediately."

Rahmet listened, dazed at first, but following closely all the instructions and ideas that he was given. At last he drew a breath.

"Well may you say that I will have to work hard. I only hope that I shall give you satisfaction, and not find myself deposed and sent into the inner prison."

"For your sake, I hope not," said Joseph, "for I would not be there to bring you your bouza and interpret your dreams."

24

THE years of prosperity were bringing joy to all Egypt. The Nile had risen to sixteen cubits, and those who studied the Nileometer and forecast the extent of the inundation were in ecstasies, for, they told Joseph, who was absorbingly interested in such matters, that if the Nile only rose to twelve cubits or less it spelt famine. Fourteen caused security, fifteen joy, but sixteen delight. The harvest was so plentiful that the people were careless of the corn, and Joseph, together with Rahmet and other representatives, had no difficulty in buying the surplus from the farms. Indeed, the growers were relieved to get a price for it. At times of glut they had often been obliged to cast it into the Nile, having neither granaries nor barns in which to store it.

Joseph supervised all that concerned the harvest. The wheat was ready for reaping five months after sowing, and the barley in four. The wheat, he saw, was cropped just below the ears with a tooth sickle, carried to the threshing floor in wicker panniers upon asses or in rope nets. It was placed on the threshing floor, and animals trod on the grain, walking around in a circle. Then it was winnowed with a shovel, and taken to the granaries in sacks, each containing a fixed quantity determined by a wooden measure.

The people seemed happy as they worked. Joseph liked to hear them sing the same song, many times:

> "Thresh for yourselves, thresh for yourselves,
> O oxen, thresh for yourselves, for yourselves,
> Bushels for yourselves, bushels for your masters."

He liked to see the ox and the ass unmuzzled, enjoying their portion.

Joseph would have spent his entire day in work, but Queen Nebyret, with the full support of Pharaoh Apepi, insisted that he must relax sometimes. The King had invited him to join him and his Queen on a trip up the Nile hunting crocodile. The Queen had issued a further invitation to Joseph to attend a special festival she was arranging in honour of the moon-goddess. Joseph protested that festivals and parties were not occasions which he enjoyed. He had been willing enough to organise and cater when he had been a slave, but merely to sit at ease and listen to the conversation of others was not a role that suited him. The Queen told him that he must not absent himself entirely from all social events; he must obey her in this, she told him firmly, and he smilingly told her with a bow that to hear was to obey. He would not only help to catch the crocodile, but would attend the special festival arranged by the Queen.

. . . .

Although the relaxation offered to Joseph by Pharaoh and the Queen was to be informal and private, there was of necessity great formality, as they made their way from the palace in Tanis to the Nile where the royal barge was waiting. This would convey them to the upper reaches of the Nile, and then ceremony would be dispensed with and the hunt begin.

Pharaoh sat in state in his chariot with his Queen by his side as they drove through the main street, teeming with life. The workers, traders and children all stopped in their tracks as the cries went up from the four runners, ordering obeisance and clearing the way. Joseph followed in the second chariot, finding it all very novel still, as he looked about with avid curiosity and interest. The small craft on the river darted about like brightly coloured insects, and the stately gilded craft of Pharaoh and his nobles made a majestic contrast to the barges, freighted with stone blocks for temples and palaces.

Soon they were seated in the royal barge, with striped awnings above them, slaves fanning the air to keep it cool for the royal party. The sailors stood with ropes in their hands, ready to loose the vessel at the word of command. Joseph had already travelled about the land, both by means of the Nile, and in his own chariot. He not only received reports from the district officers, but insisted on visiting provincial boundaries, to see for himself all that was being done.

As the journey proceeded through a rather dull panorama of cotton fields, mud-brick villages and palm trees, with the pyramids dominating the sky-line, and caravans of camels proudly stepping on the nearer horizon, they came to a branch of the Nile, and the wind dropped. Taking the smaller tributary, the rowers pulled on their oars, for now they had no help from the sails. They had to work hard to bring the barge to the upper reaches, where the crocodile hunt would begin. Queen Nebyret dismissed the servants, dispensing with ceremony. Refreshments were brought, and Joseph was alone with Apepi and Nebyret.

Observing the tremendous state which surrounded them, and indeed surrounded him too, and the artificial existence which inevitably was theirs, Joseph never ceased to marvel that these two were just mortals like himself. The people sought to deify the monarch, and to exalt him as a being apart. But Joseph knew them as friendly people, whom he dared to look upon as his friends. The Queen described to Joseph the many places of interest through which they were passing, and told him stories and legends of the Nile. Joseph in his turn was fascinated by it all, and his active mind became full of plans.

"Joseph," he heard the Queen say, "I do not believe you have heard one word of what I have been saying these last few minutes."

Joseph had the grace to look a little ashamed.

"I do remember my faults this day . . ." he began, but Pharaoh implored him not to continue. "If you say that again," he said, "I will have both you and the chief butler sent back to the King's prison to await my pleasure," for the genuine grief of the chief butler in forgetting Joseph, and his constant expression of regret, had now become a cause of amusement between them.

"You see, my lord Pharaoh, his face acknowledges his guilt. Admit, Grand Vizier, was not your mind planning some mighty scheme for our granaries? Come on, own your guilt."

"It was not granaries that I planned, O Queen. In that I am guiltless, but . . ."

Pharaoh looked at him in considerable amusement. The dynamic personality of his Grand Vizier never failed to stimulate and interest him.

"Come, Joseph, on what was your great mind soaring when my Queen would instruct you in Egyptian folk-lore?"

Joseph told Pharaoh with enthusiasm, "Look over there, my lord Pharaoh. Imagine and see, is it not just the place for a vast reservoir to be built, equal in size to that built by your forbear, Amenhat—the lake Moeris? I am told he found just such a depression in the land a little south of Memphis, and built there a vast reserve of water to guard against a poor Nile. He dug a canal by El-lahoun, and by a system of canals and sluice-gates retained perfect control of the water, and by that, could control the inundation at his will. We spend our energies on storing grain, but what of the water?"

Pharaoh was greatly inspired by the suggestion, and prepared to make plans at once, but as he was in the very act of sending for a scribe to note their plans, Queen Nebyret rose magnificently and stopped them.

"My lord Pharaoh," she said, in a voice at which even her royal husband took note, "remember our reason for coming on this expedition. I forbid either of you to mention grain or reservoirs or court affairs once again this day."

Pharaoh laughed, and looked with a face of comical amusement at Joseph.

"You, a Hebrew," he said, "would not understand that Egypt is a woman's country. Men here have to obey their wives, unlike the slavery in which the Hebrew keeps his womenfolk."

Joseph smiled back. "Her Majesty the Queen is right," he said, "I am discourteous to turn a day's excursion, to which she has so graciously invited me, to a consultation of so unimportant a matter as the welfare of Egypt."

The way in which he uttered those words was so droll that the Queen forgave them both.

"But I think your Majesty paints a picture too black and too white. In Egypt, where I have travelled, I see that the wives have a far greater position of importance than among our race, especially in royal and noble families. But they seem to me, from my brief observation of them, to own their husbands as their lords. But with my people, wives are not slaves. My mother Rachel," and Apepi and Nebyret could not but note the tenderness in his voice, "was treated like a queen by my father Jacob. It is only in the Canaanitish races, who do not worship the great God, that women are treated as beasts of the field, merely regarded as bearers of children at their lord's pleasure."

"I have been thinking for some time, Joseph," Nebyret told him severely. "It is time you took unto yourself a wife. I fear the jealousy of all the nobles in Egypt when their wives start sighing over you, and their maidens languish for you."

Joseph refused to listen to such a suggestion.

"Since I have been in Egypt these many years," he said, "I have given no thought to women."

"Then it is time that as well as having a mind filled with granaries and reservoirs, you thought about the woman to take to wife. Listen to the advice of one of our wise men, Ptah-hotep. Many years ago he gave our people this instruction:

'If thou art a man of note, found for thyself an household, and love thy wife at home as it beseemeth. Fill her belly, clothe her back. Gladden her heart as long as she lives, for she is a goodly field for her lord'."

"Your wise men have some lovely sayings," said Joseph.

"Yes, indeed," the Queen told him. "Another wise man, a great sage called Eney, gave instruction to sons, though I do not think you yourself need such instruction, for I can tell that you loved your mother well. He said:

'Never forget what thy mother hath done for thee. She bear thee and nourished thee in all manner of ways. If thou forgettest her, she might blame thee, she might lift up her arms to God, and He would hear her complaint. After the appointed months she bear thee, and nursed thee for three years, she brought thee up, and thou didst enter the school, and wast instructed in the writings'."

Joseph was so moved as he thought of all that Rachel had done for him, and the way in which she had taught and instructed him, that his whole being yearned in a way he had thought he had long since overcome. The Queen, seeing she had caused him sorrow, returned again to the subject which started the discussion.

"Have you seen no maiden in Egypt that has aroused your interest and desire, or shall I seek out maidens for you?" she persisted.

Joseph considered. The vision rose unbidden to his mind of a little girl sitting among the goatskins, eating honey dates, and of that same child, her long black hair falling round her shoulders like a cloud, growing older, but never too old to listen to his stories and pester him to tell tales of his own country.

"There was a maiden," he said meditatively, "who promised me her hand in marriage."

"She offered herself to you?" said Queen Nebyret, rather shocked. "Had you asked her to wed with you? Was she some maiden of the court, or some . . ."

"She was only seven years old," said Joseph softly, and the Queen laughed.

"Just a child," she said, dismissing the matter.

It was strange how this conversation had dismissed the thought of corn and inundations from Joseph's mind more effectively than the Queen's express command. Joseph was back again in Potiphar's house, working year after year with Hamat, then as a steward over all the household. As he looked back, he remembered how he would often see Potiphar's daughter Asenath stealing through the corridors to talk with him when she knew he would be alone.

. . . .

Then the excitement started, Joseph was intrigued that such a sport should entertain the Queen, but he remembered that the blood of many Pharaohs ran in her veins, the blood of the fighting Hyksos, Rulers of the Uplands. The object of the chase, Joseph found, was not to kill the crocodile, but to bring it back alive, to swim about in the vast ornamental lake in one of the palace gardens. This object, of course, made it important that the sportsmen should not spear the crocodile at some point where the head joins the spine, as they would have done normally, but they must use more subtle methods.

They took a hook and baited it with a joint of pork, and threw it in the water at a point where the current would carry it out into midstream. Then they took a live pig to the riverside and belaboured it well with a stick, until it set up a squeal familiar to most ears. Any crocodile within hearing was sure to come to the sound, and coming across the pork on the way would instantly swallow it down. Upon this, the hunters hauled at the rope to which the hook was attached, and in spite of the struggles of the crocodile, drew him to shore. Then he was carried home in triumph, to end his days in the ornamental lake in Pharaoh's palace.

. . . .

It was only a few days after the crocodile hunt that Joseph

attended the Queen's festival. It was ostensibly for the feast of Nin-gal, the moon-goddess, but was in actual fact a social occasion rather than a religious feast. There were no invocations, no speeches such as Potiphar delighted in. The guests arrived gorgeously attired, the women wearing the most fantastic head-dresses, that Joseph secretly deplored, rich robes, embroidered girdles and all manner of necklaces, amulets and anklets of torquoise, worked together on silver with lapus lazuli and cornelians, huge gold and silver earrings in their ears, their eyes painted with kohl to look at least twice their normal size.

As it was a feast given by the Queen to the goddess, there were of necessity not only matrons with their husbands, but many beautiful maidens. Each one was handed a lotus flower on arrival, to proclaim to the world her virginity. Just as Joseph had seen, indeed, organised on so many occasions, wine was brought by slaves, to be poured into the silver drinking cups.

Pharaoh and Nebyret sat on ornate thrones with embroidered canopies over them of silver and blue, the colours of the moon-goddess. Joseph could have been seated on his throne, two steps lower than their majesties, but he preferred to mingle with the guests, talking and asking questions in an avid search for further information about this fascinating country.

. . . .

She stood alone under a date palm. She did not desire to engage in idle chatter with the other maidens. She only wanted to look without being seen. He looked the same, yet different, she thought. He had always borne himself like a prince, but now he had the trappings and clothing of a prince. You could see by his face he had suffered. Her brow darkened when she thought of the injustice and wickedness that had caused it. No one ever knew the anguish that she had suffered, child though she was, when the servants told her that Joseph was a bad, wicked man, and had been sent off to prison. She had not known of his crime, but had wept and refused to be comforted. The day after his departure she had found, kicked into a corner, a garment that she knew to be Joseph's, and she had borne it away and hidden it, and it was still among her secret treasured possessions.

She had discovered when she grew older of what Joseph was accused, and her lips curled even at the thought. It had been a terrible thing for a girl at the age of maturity to discover her mother, who should have commanded her honour and respect, to be the woman she was. It was six or seven years ago, but the memory of Joseph, for whom she felt so much hero-worship as a child, was still locked up in her heart.

Then she was invited with many of the other maidens to attend the feast of the moon-goddess at the house of the Pharaoh. Her excitement was beyond anything the occasion demanded, honour though it was to be asked, for many said that the Grand Vizier himself was to be present. He was not seen at many of the court functions. His work for Pharaoh seemed to take him far and wide throughout the land. Something to do with storing grain, they said, though why, asked the court officials in general, should Pharaoh wish to preserve the grain when everyone knew there was so much corn in Egypt that harvesters were giving it away to anyone who would take it? The Nile was dealing bounteously with them. The god Nilus, they said, was smiling upon the land of Egypt year after year.

At last she was here, and could watch Joseph going around talking and discussing, mostly with the men, and bowing courteously to their wives. Of the many maidens, who almost gaped upon him, whispering behind their hands to each other of his handsome appearance and regal bearing, he seemed oblivious. He was coming nearer, and she would be able to look right into his face through the fronds of the date palm, to see whether in his eyes there was that same kind expression, or whether adversity and then exaltation had hardened him and made him arrogant.

They say that if the eyes of a strong-willed person stare sufficiently hard at the face of another, by some power of hypnotism the eyes of both parties will meet. Joseph was conscious that someone was regarding him, and he looked up sharply and saw the fronds of a date palm moving. He stopped short. Court officials had warned him that great personages should never be unaware of the danger of assassination. Men were jealous, and a poisoned cup or knife thrown could end a promising career.

Joseph walked over to the palm and Asenath, knowing herself to be discovered, came out and stood with downcast eyes, ashamed to be caught spying and peeping. Joseph almost laughed at himself for suspecting such a maiden of being an assassin. He saw before him a girl of great beauty, who wore fewer ornaments than the other girls, and whose eyes were not so disfigured by kohl. They were long-lashed, and as they glanced up at him now he saw the eyes of a gazelle, similar to those of his mother Rachel.

"Well, mistress," he said, "what purpose have you in hiding behind the palm?"

Asenath decided to be truthful. "I wanted to see you, great Vizier of Egypt," she said simply.

Joseph listened, astonished that she should speak so openly and not dissemble.

"Now that you have seen me, what request would you make of me?"

Then Asenath, greatly daring, forgetting to what great personage she spoke, said softly, hoping to strike a chord in his memory, "*Please*, Joseph, give me just *one* more honey date."

Joseph wondered if he could have heard aright.

"What words did you utter?" he said in his commanding voice.

"It was nothing," she said hastily.

"I command you to tell me what you said."

Asenath lifted her chin slightly at being so addressed, and Joseph, Grand Vizier though he was, added with a ghost of a smile, "if it pleases you, young mistress."

"I only said, '*Please*, Joseph, will you give me just *one* more honey date?"

Joseph called for a slave and gave a curt order. "Bring us wine and . . . er, some honey dates," and then motioning to Asenath to a seat behind the date palm, he sat down beside her.

Asenath was overwhelmed with embarrassment. He had forgotten. What must the Grand Vizier think of her for calling him 'Joseph', requesting sweetmeats like a greedy child?

But Joseph spoke softly to her. "And now, young mistress Asenath, I propose to make you eat honey dates until you are sick, to punish you for wheedling them out of the poor slave, whose master might well have beaten him to find the sweetmeat jar empty."

Asenath laughed with relief.

"Hamat would never have beaten you, Joseph, and full many times have I told you so when you made that excuse."

"Well I remember," said Joseph, "I always gave you just one more, and spoilt and indulged you, no doubt to the detriment of your character and ruination of your digestion."

"Hamat always thought the sun shone out of you, Joseph," said Asenath; then, remembering whom she addressed, added, "My lord Grand Vizier, I should have said—I was forgetting."

"Let us forget that for a little while. I grow so weary of people bowing and making obeisance, and not being able to walk without falling over recumbent forms of men bowing in my way."

Asenath gave a ripple of silvery laughter at so apt a description.

Queen Nebyret from her throne gazed over the company, and murmured to Pharaoh, "My lord Pharaoh, I never thought to see our Grand Vizier proving so entertaining a companion, and so amused with one who carries a lotus flower. They seem to be very happy. I wonder who she is."

Pharaoh, maintaining his expression of regal majesty, told his wife out of the corner of his royal mouth that she was nothing but a meddling match-maker, and should allow the Grand Vizier to relax a little without her interference.

Joseph and Asenath talked together as though they could never stop. He told her of his life in prison, not seeking to forget his degradation now that he was great, and she spoke of her new life as daughter of a priest of On.

"My father owes his promotion to you, to your generosity. It is a quiet life. My mother . . ." and as Joseph's face hardened,

Asenath realised her tactlessness, and finished in confusion, ". . . is not so happy . . . but I should not have spoken of her."

Joseph, anxious to spare her confusion, said gently, "All that is past. You did not believe that I had done ill?" he asked.

"*Never*," asserted Asenath. "Never did I believe any evil report, child though I was."

"Then that is well," said Joseph.

"You did not know me at first, did you, Joseph?" Asenath asked him.

He looked at her with a twinkle in his eye.

"Why the beautiful young maidens of Egypt think to add to their attractions by torturing their glorious hair into the most appalling contraptions, and trying to emulate lion-haired sphinxes, is beyond the wisdom even of Zaphnath-paaneah, Grand Vizier of Egypt."

Asenath laughed and pouted. "But it is the fashion," she said, "and women all do it."

"And of course, Egypt is a woman's country," said Joseph.

"Pray do not tell me, Joseph, that you plan to pass a new law saying that women must not arrange their hair so, in the eight plaits and in the large head-dress. Even the Grand Vizier would not dare to so far imperil his office. The women would rise up in a body, and seek to murder him in his bed."

Joseph told her solemnly that no such legislation was as yet planned.

"I am sorry you don't like my appearance," said Asenath.

"I did not say that," Joseph told her, "but I miss my little companion of the storerooms, with her cloud of black curls."

Then he rose. He knew that he must continue to circulate among the guests, or his absence would be noticed. They stood looking at each other, then Joseph spoke with sudden abruptness.

"Asenath, once you made me a promise."

"I made you a promise?" enquired Asenath. "And what was that? Pray tell me."

"No, I will not tell you now," Joseph told her firmly.

"*Please*, Joseph, tell me."

"*Please*, Joseph," he mocked. "That will only procure you honey dates. But no, I will not tell you of your promise yet, though some day I may remind you, and even require that you fulfil it."

He bowed low over her hand and said, "Farewell, Asenath. We will meet again, but until then I am your most obedient . . . slave."

.   .   .   .

Joseph took his leave of Pharaoh and Queen Nebyret. He thanked them for all they had done, and for inviting him to attend the festival. Queen Nebyret was consumed with curiosity, but did not care to ask too many questions.

"Did you find the company amusing? Were the men intelligent? Were the maidens beautiful?"

Joseph did not answer at first, but then he looked at the Queen and said, "You remember I told you that a little girl had promised to marry me? I think I may some day claim that promise."

25

T H E menage of the priest of On was in an uproar of excitement. The house in which he now lived was much smaller than the palatial residence that had housed Potiphar, Captain of Pharaoh's guard. His present rank was higher, though as a priest he lived in far less state. He came into his own, of course, on state occasions when, as a priest of On, he carried the Hydria, clad in the priestly leopard-skin worn over his linen robes. He was attended in great pomp by sixteen lesser priests, bearing garlands and offerings to the various deities.

But his life in general was quiet. A priest was expected to

spend much time in contemplation, offering invocations to the gods, studying all matters relating to religion and forms of worship. He had servants and slaves, for priests were given an allocation of land to till, and livestock to care for.

He was preparing now to celebrate the feast of the nineteenth day of Thoth. Those attending would eat honey and eggs, and after he had made his speech, they would all chant, " How sweet a thing is truth ".

Then a sudden upheaval shattered this quiet routine. A messenger came from Pharaoh to say that the Grand Vizier was to visit Potiphar with a request. ' A request' Pharaoh had said, but his letter was so worded that Apepi made it abundantly clear that though the Grand Vizier might make a request, Pharaoh ordered Potiphar to accede to that request. Potiphar knew well that Joseph was buying up all the grain in the land, and maybe he wished to make some arrangement with him. Or perhaps he planned to take over the little lake behind his house to form another reservoir.

Preparations would have to be made to receive the Grand Vizier. Potiphar hoped his steward would be able to do him credit. He found himself wishing for the thousandth time that Joseph were still his steward. But of course, he reflected, coming down to earth, if that were the case, Joseph would not be the Grand Vizier, and so this occasion would not arise!

Potiphar's wife would, of course, have to be present to receive the great man. It was all very awkward. But Joseph must have known that when he decided to visit him. Zadia had mixed feelings when she had been apprised of Joseph's visit. She had waited with considerable apprehension when he had at first been exalted, but no vengeance fell, only this reward to her husband for his supposed kindness. And though it fulfilled the ambition of his life, it meant banishment to her from all the gaiety of court life that made her existence bearable. She wondered idly whether Joseph knew this. However, she would not give him the satisfaction of seeing that she nourished these feelings. She busied herself in preparing to receive the great man with all the pomp that could be obtained, by hiring extra slaves, and minstrels to make music. She determined for the sake of pride to give an impression of happiness and prosperity.

. . . .

Joseph sat in his chariot, riding out from Tanis to On. It was a superb piece of irony, he thought, that Potiphar's wife, who sought to seduce him, was to be asked to become his mother-in-law. He would not show by the flicker of an eyelid that he remembered anything of what had passed, and reflected that after he was married they need never meet. The promotion of Potiphar to the priesthood had at least that to recommend it; had he still been Captain of Pharaoh's guard, his wife would constantly be at court functions.

Joseph was welcomed with all the ceremony that was possible. He was ushered into the presence of the priest of On, slaves bowing in his wake. Potiphar stood with his wife beside him, and Joseph's attendants and fan-bearers seemed to fill the large room, and made the meeting formal, robbing it of any embarrassment. Joseph bowed to Potiphar and his wife, not even looking at her face, almost as if she did not exist, she told herself angrily.

When the servants had withdrawn, Joseph addressed himself to Potiphar, ignoring his wife as though she were not present. Potiphar did not notice this, but Joseph felt that the wife of Potiphar had forfeited the right of wife and mother, not only by her behaviour with him, but by all that was spoken of her since.

" I would ask for the hand of your daughter Asenath in marriage," said Joseph, going straight to the point.

So that was it, thought Zadia—Asenath . . . he must have remembered the child.

Potiphar could hardly conceal his delight at such an honour. He not only agreed on the spot, but was about to send a slave to fetch his daughter, to apprise her of the great future that awaited her.

Joseph stayed him, saying, " I have a request. I would see her alone before any of this intelligence reaches her."

Potiphar agreed, and summoning a servant, told him to send

his daughter Asenath to the withdrawing chamber adjacent to the refectory.

"I will conduct you there, and leave you to your will, Grand Vizier of Egypt," said Potiphar formally.

Bowing to Potiphar's wife, Joseph took his leave, dismissing the servants who hurried to his side to escort him, and he made his way through the rows of bowing slaves, all curious to obtain a closer view of the one of whose wisdom all Egypt told stories and invented legends.

Asenath entered the small apartment at the command of her father. She knew Joseph was coming, and wondered much. She had lived over the conversation they had enjoyed at the festival, and wondered again at her temerity, savouring each word and look that had passed between them. Then the door opened and Joseph came in alone. She made a deep obeisance, but Joseph took her hand and raised her up, requesting her to sit with him.

"I have come today to claim a promise," he told her.

Asenath opened her eyes wide. "The promise of which you spoke at the festival—the one you wouldn't tell me about?"

"Yes," said Joseph. "When you were only seven, and you sat among the goatskins while I was checking your father's stores, you said, if you remember, that I must be a prince in disguise, and if only a princess might marry me, I would be free of the spell. You were kind enough to say that you would be willing to marry me some day, except for the fact that you were not a princess."

Asenath drew her breath, and hoped that Joseph could not hear the beating of her heart.

"And you would hold a child of seven to that promise?" she asked.

"Only if she was willing," Joseph told her. "I have no right to demand it, but I kneel at your feet and ask if you will condescend to be my bride."

"What a terrible thing that the Grand Vizier should kneel to me!" said Asenath, rising to her feet, and bidding Joseph rise also. "You as Grand Vizier can command what you will, and I have no doubt that my father will be bound to accede to any request that you may make."

"Asenath," said Joseph reproachfully, "do you think I want you by command? I seek your heart, and supplicate not as a Grand Vizier, but as one whom you have enslaved."

Asenath let down her defences.

"Oh, Joseph," she said, "these many years I have thought and dreamed of just such a time as this."

Joseph looked at her in amazement. "You have thought of me?"

"I have dreamed and wept and mourned and longed for you," she said softly, "and if you wish me to prove it, I can show you a garment which I found belonging to you. It is one of my treasured possessions."

Then they talked as only lovers can, recalling the years when he was a slave, and she was a child, speaking of their feelings for each other now. Joseph had no idea he knew so many beautiful names for a maiden, and that his unaccustomed tongue could deliver such pretty speeches.

Then it was time to part, and they reluctantly rose to their feet. Asenath looked at Joseph through her eyelashes.

"Am I to be the wife of a Hebrew, who obeys her lord in all things?" she asked.

"Of course," said Joseph, looking at her. "My lightest wish will be a command."

"I will do anything my lord Joseph commands," she said, "except to abandon my head-dress."

Joseph looked at her gloomily. "That I should saddle myself with a wife whose head resembles a beehive or a lion's mane! To what folly have I committed myself?"

Asenath dimpled. "When we are alone, I will dispense with it if you will. And now, my lord Joseph, what other commands will you lay upon me?"

Then Joseph's whole countenance changed. He looked at her sternly, his face full of purpose and determination. Asenath wondered what she had said, or in what way she had offended him.

"Asenath," he said, "I had forgotten. You have made the time fly by on wings, and I have a command to lay upon you. Dress your hair as you will. Concerning that I was but jesting. But there is one point upon which I must have complete obedience."

Asenath waited. This was a Joseph she had heard about, who made laws, commanded men, and whom men feared. She found that she feared him herself, and in a rather scared voice murmured, "Say on, Grand Vizier."

Joseph was impervious to the interruption, so earnest was he in his object.

"In my house," he said, "I will have no gods, no images, and no idols. I will not tolerate any decorations of Horus, the hawk-headed god, or jewellery with cat-gods and crocodiles. No cups of invocation said to bring good luck, no taint or touch of all the images of God's creatures, as though they had power and deity. As lord of my home and my wife, in that I must be obeyed. We will worship the God above all, Jehovah the great God, the God of my fathers, Who has preserved me in my captivity, and exalted me by His grace, Whose presence has been with me these many years."

He stopped, carried away, and looked, expecting to see opposition on Asenath's face. He saw instead that her eyes shone.

"But do you not know, Joseph," she assured him, "I have no idols and images? Have you not noticed that I am not decked out with images of cats and fishes and sacred bulls? You told me over and over concerning your God; year after year you taught me all that your mother taught you. It was all so real, and made the absurd legends of the people of Egypt sound so paltry. Search and see if any god or scarab or sacred beetle is like to be found in the apartments of Asenath, daughter of a priest though I am."

Joseph embraced her, and thanked the God of his fathers for making his way to prosper. Asenath would be a wife after his own heart, and their sons should be trained in the knowledge of God, even as he himself had been.

26

THE years of plenty were over. People had come to take prosperity for granted, and in the month if Tobi, when the inundation should come, they waited without any anxiety, for life had been so easy, and good harvests accepted as the regular course of events. It had been the custom years ago to lay up stores against a bad year, but it was now long since the Nile had not registered sixteen cubits and caused delight among the inhabitants.

But suddenly all that changed. In the month of Tobi the Nile scarcely reached twelve cubits. The year following the citizens of Egypt waited anxiously, for by now they had used up all their existing stocks. The Nile rose slowly, but to the despair of all it only reached eleven cubits. The people cried out in consternation. They faced famine and starvation. In their anxiety, they went in a body to Pharaoh to ask what should be done.

Then the decree went through the land: "Go to Joseph; he has corn for all." Everything was organised to prevent panic and confusion. Joseph had made his plans during the seven plentiful years. He had trustworthy men throughout the whole region, who were in charge of granaries and storehouses. Eagerly the people made their purchases, and were reassured to know that there was plenty for all, and none need fear, for Joseph's stores would not fail. And all spoke of his wisdom, and said did they not know that it was because of this wisdom that Pharaoh had made him Grand Vizier, and called him by the name 'Zaphnath-paaneah', for he had foretold this very situation to Pharaoh, and while many had been eating and drinking, Joseph had been preparing for this national emergency.

.   .   .   .

Joseph went to his palatial residence at the end of a gruelling day, weary and fatigued. He made his way to Asenath's apartment, where she sat with little Ephraim and Manasseh. Tired though he was, he thought what a pretty picture she made playing with her little sons, as though she were not a great lady, second only to Pharaoh's wife. Little Ephraim was just a tiny child. Joseph could never see a boy of that age without thinking of Benjamin, though reason told him that Benjamin was now much older.

He lay on his couch, and Asenath sent for refreshment. He told her that he had no need of it, but she took no notice.

"Grand Vizier you may be," she said, "but here you are just my husband, and I will care for your needs. You are tired and exhausted, and if I do not refresh you, perchance you will be evil-tempered as well. And that would be too much for an Egyptian woman to bear."

They both laughed. Joseph might be a stern ruler and an implacable Grand Vizier, but never to his wife did he show other than love and adoration.

"What has tired you, Joseph?" asked Asenath, sitting at his feet and resting her head against him.

"There is so much to see to, and so many laws to pass. The people now have no money to buy corn, so I take their land for Pharaoh, and give it back to them to plant. They cannot buy seed, so I supply them with it, and have made a law that a fifth of all the corn they grow must be given into the royal granaries. This must all be done, for Pharaoh's granaries must not fail. We have not only Egypt to feed, but the whole world, it seems. They have all heard there is corn in Egypt."

They were silent.

Asenath read his thoughts. "Think you they will come, Joseph?"

"I cannot tell. I think they must. The famine is not only here in Egypt, but the former rains have failed these two years in the land of Canaan."

Asenath knew that Joseph waited daily to see if any of his brethren would come to Egypt to seek bread. After Joseph had committed the distribution of corn into the care of supervisor and district dispensers, he insisted that all men from foreign lands should only be supplied from the granaries adjacent to his palace. So it was that day after day, men of the Philistines, of the Hivites, Hittites and Jebusites came to seek sustenance, and Syrians and men from farther afield. And daily Joseph searched the countenances of those who came, and went away disappointed.

.   .   .   .

"I never thought to be travelling to this land," said Issachar to Zebulun, as with his nine brothers he journeyed by camel to seek for corn.

When the grain situation became serious, Jacob had sent for his sons, and told them that a journey into Egypt was the only way to keep alive. There was silence. They all looked at each other nervously, and then at the ground.

"Why do you look on one another?" Jacob had said. "Hoping that someone will volunteer? You must all go—except Benjamin."

And there was no gainsaying the commands of the sheik, for when Jacob gave an order it must be obeyed. They too realised that the situation was serious. In just a few months they would see their wives and children looking little better than skeletons and dying for want of food. That strangely mysterious country in the south seemed to have magical powers of producing food. Even in the days of Abraham and Isaac people had turned their eyes towards Egypt, and travelled into the land of Pharaoh and the pyramids.

Jacob could not understand his sons' reluctance to go to Egypt.

"Is there something distasteful to you in this land?" he demanded. "Had I asked you to go to Ur or Nineveh, I veritably believe you would have been delighted to have travelled there. Has Egypt got some curse upon you, that you all look so fearful and gloomy?"

The brothers pulled themselves together. Until Jacob had put into words the reason for their reluctance, they had not realised its cause. The truth was that the very name 'Egypt' meant to them a lad with pleading eyes, who had never harmed them, but who was stripped and sent away to slavery. All took it for granted that Benjamin should remain with their father. He had lost Joseph, and should not risk losing his much-loved Benjamin.

Joseph's name was not mentioned until the brothers were actually riding into Tanis itself. An overseer in one of the fields close by the road was organising a gang of men into building an edifice. This cruel-looking man wielded a whip of hippopotamus hide, and lashed the shoulders of the slaves unmercifully at any sign of slackening in their work.

Dan broke the silence by saying, "I wonder whether in our journey we might chance to see our brother Joseph among any of the slaves."

Judah turned on him in a fury. "Be silent, fool, uttering such ill-advised thoughts. Mention not that name to us again."

· · · · · · · · · · · ·

It was more of an ordeal to buy corn than the brothers had expected. Instead of merely going to the merchant at Pharaoh's granary and making their purchase, it seemed they had to be received in audience by the Grand Vizier himself, a very mighty man with a long name, Zaphnath-paaneah, who would speak to them by interpretation. A full description of them, their names, from whence they had come, was taken from them before they were to attend his presence. They were instructed in how to behave. They would be taken into the audience chamber, then the doors would open, and the Grand Vizier himself would enter, and then they must bow themselves to the ground, and not rise until the Grand Vizier gave them permission. He was a great man, they were told, and everyone trembled at his words, and his slightest decree was law.

The brothers stood waiting, looking about them. They could not have imagined such magnificence or glory. Pillars all painted with frescos, scenes of men labouring in the fields, tilling the land, gathering the corn, gaily painted murals of men boating on the river. The canopy under which the Grand Vizier would stand was draped with dyed linen cloth of red and gold, richly ornamented with embroidery. The throne upon which he would sit was overlaid with gold, decorated with all manner of precious stones and carved jewelled legs. The whole scene was enough to take away the breath of those who had spent their lives in tents, caring for the sheep.

Then a fanfare of trumpets was heard in the distance. The Grand Vizier was approaching. There was a rustle of expectancy; everyone stood to attention. Servants walking together with a regular rhythm, hands outstretched, led the way. Other men-at-arms marched behind them, and finally, gorgeous in apparel, with a massive head-dress, such as Pharaoh himself might have worn, came the Grand Vizier of Egypt. The brothers anxiously looked at his face. It was stern, and wore an expression of implacable anger. The brothers could not know that even the servants attending Joseph were surprised to see him wearing so angry a countenance, and wondered what had put him into so obvious a state of wrath.

Joseph stood. His brothers bowed themselves to the ground, and it was well that they could not read his thoughts. Just so did their sheaves of corn bow to mine, and he let them stay bowed to the ground for a considerable time. How strange that it should all have turned out as I dreamed! he thought.

At last he bade them rise. He anxiously searched each face. Joseph eagerly recognised the brothers . . . eight, nine, ten . . . then he sighed with disappointment. He had not realised until now how he had longed to see Benjamin. He was sad, and yet relieved, for had they brought his own brother, son of his mother, his self-control might have deserted him, and made him cry out his identity, in his desire to embrace his brother.

If only he could find out if they had any remorse for the past, if they regretted their cruelty, or if they had forgotten their little brother, as though he had never been. Reuben seemed little changed, possibly weaker-looking around his mouth, but kindly. Simeon and Levi had not improved with time. Joseph wondered how little Benjamin had fared at their hands. Then he saw Judah. Joseph could not repress the feeling that Judah always aroused in him. Yet Judah, he remembered, had resisted his pleading glance, and sold him into slavery. Judah was the finest of them all, but they were all fine men, well built, and having about them that agility and good health that proclaimed them as workers under the open heaven.

Then Joseph hardened his heart, and remembered that when these men were able to behold the stars of heaven, he had been immured in a filthy cell; while they had been free to roam the hills and vales of Hebron and Mamre, he had endured Pharez's whip and servitude. He must make it his business, by assuming anger and wrath, to find out their minds, and to seek to pierce their consciences. He must stifle the feeling that arose in him, the desire to embrace them, to say, "You are my brothers, my kinsmen, my people."

He spoke roughly to them by means of an interpreter. "Whence are ye come?"

They answered him, "From the land of Canaan, to buy food."

"You lie," said Joseph. "You come on a conspiracy. You come as spies to see the nakedness of the land, to spy out our waterways and to assess our strength."

All this he snarled at them with lowering countenance, so that they trembled, and the servants of Joseph wondered what vision he had received, that the evil of these seemingly innocent men should arouse in him such suspicion and rage.

"We are all the sons of one man. Thy servants are not spies," they pleaded.

Joseph would have none of it, but repeated, "Spies, just a gang of spies."

"No indeed," they said. "Thy servants are twelve brothers, sons of one man, and behold the youngest is this day with our father, and one is not."

Joseph was hard put not to cry with joy. His father was alive, and Benjamin was with him. Little Benjamin was alive, and Jacob had not been gathered to his fathers. He must not give way and show interest. He must continue his role of suspicion and anger.

"I will have this proved," he said venomously. "You will all remain here in prison, and one of you shall go back to your father and fetch your younger brother, to see if there be any truth in what you say. For by the life of Pharaoh, I say that ye are spies.

You shall have time to reflect," and turning to the guard, he ordered the men to be taken to the prison.

So for three days Joseph's brothers found themselves in the very prison that had confined him for three years. It took much control on Joseph's part to leave them there, but he knew he was not acting in revenge or arbitrarily. He had a purpose in it all. By imprisonment and privation, they must be made to remember what they had condemned their young brother to suffer.

The brothers had no idea how long they were to be left in prison. They could gather little comfort from other prisoners, who told them that many people were placed in prison and never heard of again.

After three days Joseph sent for his brothers and appeared to relent. They were received with much less state and pomp, but with only a few servants to attend him, and his interpreter. They found the Grand Vizier in a milder mood. He had abandoned his rough manner, and no more regarded them with lowering brow, but still with stern countenance and great dignity.

"This do and live," he said, "for I fear God. If ye be true men, let one of your brethren be bound in the house of your prison. Go ye and carry corn for the famine of your houses, but bring your youngest brother unto me. So shall your words be verified, and ye shall not die."

The brothers turned to one another and, believing that he could not understand their language, spoke together.

"We are guilty concerning our brother," said Judah, not in the arrogant tone which Joseph remembered, but with a broken voice and deep remorse. "We saw the anguish of his soul when he besought us, and we would not hear, therefore is this distress come upon us."

And Reuben sadly agreed. "Spake I not unto you saying 'Do not sin against the child', and ye would not hear, therefore behold, his blood also is required."

It was too much for Joseph's self-control. To hear them admitting their fault was all that he had hoped. He remembered Reuben's kindness to him those many years ago. He withdrew hastily and wept. He had not wept all the years of his suffering, but now so great was his emotion that he was completely overcome. He recovered instantly, and returning, spoke sternly to hide his feelings.

"You may return to your father," he said, "but come not again without your younger brother to prove your words."

They turned gratefully to depart, but Joseph stopped them.

"Not all of you," he said. "That one will remain bound against your return. I would keep a hostage." And he had Simeon bound before their eyes, and led away back to the King's prison.

. . . .

"You shall not return again to Egypt," Jacob told his sons with finality.

He had listened to their recital with horror. Graphically the Grand Vizier and his harshness were described; their incarceration in the prison which, to free men, had been an unspeakable degradation; the seizing of Simeon as a hostage, and then this terrible demand that Benjamin should go back with them, his precious Benjamin.

"It shall not be. Joseph is not, Simeon is not, and now you would take Benjamin."

The story of finding their money in the neck of their sacks had made it obvious that the Egyptians had a plot against them. It was when stopping at the first inn on the homeward journey, that this shock had shattered their peace of mind. Each one found the exact sum paid in shekels to the Granary Superintendent concealed in the top of his sack. Consternation and apprehension had reigned, and now this intelligence filled Jacob with a sense of doom. If they returned, they would be seized at the frontier, accused of theft and flung into prison, and Jacob would be bereft of them all.

"Do you wish to bring my grey hairs down with sorrow to the grave?" he demanded.

The brothers were in no great hurry to visit Egypt again. The very memory was one of terror. The ate sparingly of the grain and rationed it strictly, and all went about permanently hungry, hoping that the former rains might come with promise of a good harvest, making another journey into Egypt unnecessary.

Alas for their hopes, spring came again, and the heavens seemed as brass. The land was dry, and there was neither pasture for the cattle nor food for the men. Jacob remembered again the day when Esau had gone hunting, that day when he had bought the birthright from him. He had been a strange young man then, he reflected, wanting the right things, but impetuously seeking them in the wrong way. But God has blessed me, though now I fear that great danger faces my sons. They must not return, and I will not send Benjamin—he is all I have left of Rachel. If only Joseph had lived, he moaned to himself again, and the wounds seem to open afresh.

.   .   .   .

He was left alone. They were all gone. He was utterly bereft. Not one of his twelve sons was left to care for him in his old age. He would never see them again, of that he was convinced. He had sent Joseph away gaily many years ago, confident of seeing him in a matter of days, and he still remembered that awful day when only ten brothers had returned. And now only nine had returned from Egypt. This time would any return? The old Patriarch lifted up his voice and wept. Judah and Reuben had prevailed upon him to part with Benjamin, and in the end he had reluctantly agreed. The children's bones were sticking out, and their faces were emaciated with near starvation. They would all die if someone did not go down to Egypt, did not go into the jaws of death.

It was the words of Judah that finally turned the scales. In his earnestness, Judah had sworn, "Send the lad with me, and we will arise and go, that we might live and not die, both we and thou, and also our little ones. I will be surety for him; of my hand shalt thou require him. If I bring him not unto thee, and set him before thee, then let me bear the blame for ever."

Jacob had risen to the occasion when he found that it was inevitable. His precious stores were raided, and gifts of balms, spices and nuts were sent to placate the terrifying personage who held their lives in his hand. Double money was sent to pay for the corn.

Jacob had lifted up his hands to bless his sons, saying, "Lord God Almighty give thee mercy before this man, that he may send away your brother and Benjamin. If I am bereaved of my children, I am bereaved." For Jacob loved his sons with a deep love. Their faults had angered him, but his love was beyond that now. And as they went, he yearned over them, wondering when he would see the camels coming again over the horizon.

27

"My lord Joseph, will you not sit and rest? You have paced the room for the last hour, like an animal in captivity. What are those words you keep murmuring about nine sacks of corn?"

Asenath was reclining on her ebony couch, anxiously watching her husband as he strode up and down the room, impervious to what went on around him.

"Asenath," he broke out, "how long is it since they left here, with only nine sacks of corn for my father's tribe? They will surely starve if they do not come soon. Was I right to let them go, to make Benjamin's coming a condition of their return? Did I frighten them too much? Should I even now bring Simeon out from prison, and send him up to my father laden with sacks of corn?"

Asenath was silent, not knowing how to reply. She was amazed at the depth of Joseph's love for his brothers, who had treated him so terribly.

It was as Joseph started walking again from one frescoed pillar to another that the door opened and Rahmet, chief steward of Egypt, was ushered into the Grand Vizier's presence. Bowing low, he spoke quickly to Joseph.

"They have been sighted travelling by the delta, and should be here by this hour tomorrow."

Joseph seized Rahmet's arm.

"The God of Abraham be praised," he said fervently. "Tell me, how many men were travelling?"

Rahmet paused. "Nine fully grown men, and one who is but a stripling."

Joseph breathed deeply.

"Benjamin, my own brother Benjamin is coming," he murmured, excitement surging up within him, which he knew he must suppress. How would he be able to restrain himself tomorrow from taking Benjamin in his arms, and throwing caution to the winds, spoiling his plans by overmastering emotion? This must not be; and Joseph had learnt self-control in a hard school.

He bade Rahmet come with him to his private council chamber. He had plans for the morrow, which he had devised over many months. He must not indulge his emotions, but must carry out the plan that he felt God had given him. Rahmet listened and marvelled. Joseph had already confided everything to him. He alone, apart from Asenath, knew how it was that Joseph became a slave, and that it was because of his brothers' treachery that he was in Egypt. What man could resist the temptation to humiliate, punish, and even kill, those who had so treated him? thought Rahmet. Joseph had them in his power, and his only concern seemed to be to awaken their consciences, and then care for them. Rahmet shrugged his shoulders. Joseph was surely one of the strangest and most wonderful men he had ever known—more like a god than a man in his wisdom, in unfailing kindness, and brilliant execution of his tremendous task.

Joseph returned to Asenath, and behaved more like an excited schoolboy than a Grand Vizier, until she told him that he reminded her of Ephraim before a fishing expedition, and certainly was not like a serious Egyptian statesman.

. . . .

Simeon lay in the inner prison. Time dragged slowly by. He knew to a nicety how long the corn would last that his brethren had taken home. He knew that if they did not come any day now, nothing but death by starvation faced the whole tribe. But if they came, would this terrifying Grand Vizier spare their lives? Certainly not if they came without Benjamin. He put his head in his hands, and wondered why all this had befallen them.

As the night wore on, he slept fitfully. He was neither waking nor sleeping, when it seemed as though faces were looking at him through the darkness of the night. He saw the agonised faces of the Shechemites, as he and Levi had slaughtered them in cold blood. He saw the handsome face of Shechem, and the anguish in the eyes of his sister Dinah, as before her eyes he had slain her husband in his blood-lust. He saw Joseph's eyes, as an animal at bay, when many a time he had caught him alone, baited, taunted and tormented him. He saw the eyes of little Benjamin, similarly treated before Judah had protected him. He saw again the eyes of a lad looking up from a pit, begging to be spared, and again he saw the eyes of the same lad as he was bound, mounted on a camel, and driven away into slavery. Even as he had gloated over his two pieces of silver, he had seen the anguished appeal of those eyes. Then in his nightmare, it seemed as if he had seen those eyes recently, and as he dreamt, the eyes became those of the Grand Vizier, looking accusingly at him from the face of Zaphnath-paaneah, the most powerful man in Egypt.

Simeon was terrified, and cried out for fear. Many said that the Grand Vizier had the gift of divining, and Simeon felt sure that he knew what he and his brothers had done, and when he had said, 'that one', pointing at him, 'will remain bound', he knew all about him. Simeon suddenly saw himself for what he was, and he loathed himself and his cruel ways. "God of our fathers, forgive me," he pleaded, "for I have sinned," and he cried brokenly in his cell.

Sleep had gone from him, but very early, before daybreak, the governor of the prison sent for him. He was to be given a change of raiment, and taken to the Grand Vizier's house. Simeon prepared himself with apprehension, and yet hope. He was taken by an attendant to a large antechamber, where he stood awaiting the great man's pleasure.

. . . .

It had been a considerable surprise to Reuben, Judah, and their brothers, when they had been met by Egyptian servants, and escorted right to the Grand Vizier's house. They wondered what this could mean. Did it mean death? Did it mean that they were to be accused of absconding with the money from the tops of their sacks? They waited anxiously. Then the door opened to admit Rahmet. He had dealt with them on their previous visit, but looked at them now with new interest. They certainly were a fine group of men, and it was obvious that the young one was Joseph's own brother, the likeness was unmistakable.

Rahmet explained that they were to eat with the Grand Vizier himself. This honour, instead of gratifying the brothers, terrified them. The treatment they had received on their previous visit had conditioned them to expect further harsh treatment, and kindness and hospitality were not things to be connected with Zaphnath-paaneah. Rahmet reassured them, and spoke so kindly that Judah confided in him.

"Oh sir," he said, "we indeed came down the first time to buy food, and on returning we found our money in our sacks. We cannot tell who put it there."

"Peace be unto you," said Rahmet. "I had your money. The God of your fathers must have put some treasure there for you," and turning, he said, "See, here is someone whom you all know," for at that moment Simeon was brought in to them.

The reunion was a joyous one for them all. There was much to tell, and much to ask. But many questions had to wait, for they were taken to the audience chamber for the great moment when the Grand Vizier would come to meet them. They were quite sensible of what an honour this was. Simeon particularly, having lived in an Egyptian prison, was aware of what a mighty man of importance was Zaphnath-paaneah, Grand Vizier of Egypt.

This time there was very much less ceremony when, with only a few attendants, Joseph came to them, not speaking to them from his throne-like chair, but only from a small raised platform. Having bowed to the ground, without delay they presented their gifts sent by Jacob. Joseph could not speak as he looked at the pitiful little offering of balm, oil and nuts, representing so much from the famine-stricken land of Canaan. With ill-concealed interest he asked of their welfare.

"Is your father yet alive—the old man of whom ye spake?" he asked eagerly.

They told him that Jacob was well, and all bowed again, unable to believe the change of attitude of the great one. The kindness of his tone even the interpreter could not disguise. Then Joseph turned, and allowed his eyes to rest on Benjamin, his own little brother Benjamin. The sight was almost too much for him. He could see his mother Rachel, and many characteristics of his father Jacob in this young brother of his.

"God be gracious unto you, my son." Joseph's words came in a voice quite unlike his usual tone, and so great was the yearning he felt to take Benjamin in his arms, that he went swiftly from the audience chamber to his own apartment and wept like a child. Then, conquering his emotion, he washed his face and returned, giving the order, "Set on bread."

Then there was a time of feasting. To the half-starved men from famine-stricken Canaan, it was unbelievable that such food was obtainable. Even in time of plenty, no such feast was known to them. To see ten kinds of meat, game, every variety of fancy bread and sweetmeat was something to astonish the mind, as well as gratify the body.

Joseph and his Egyptian companions sat at a table apart. It would have been an abomination for them to have eaten with the Hebrews. Joseph sat with Asenath beside him, and he eagerly pointed out his different brothers to her. Asenath noticed the affection with which Joseph spoke of Reuben, and the pride in his voice when he described Judah, and the wealth of love as he pointed out Benjamin, son of his mother Rachel. It was not surprising that, when special dainties were sent to the long table where the brothers sat, that Joseph gave orders for Benjamin to have a much greater portion than any other.

"When are you going to tell them, Joseph?" Asenath asked, as the festivity was at its height.

"Not yet," he said. "I must send them away first."

"Send them away? But why?" she asked, quite mystified.

"I shall send them away, only to bring them back for ever," was all that Joseph would tell her.

Only Rahmet knew what he would do. It was only to him that Joseph had entrusted instructions which, to the uninitiated, would have seemed inexplicable.

The feast had lulled the brothers into a sense of security. Secure in the knowledge that none could understand, they talked freely of their surroundings and the wonder of it all. Benjamin, who had never eaten so lavishly in his life, was speechless at the marvels he saw: the beauty of the Grand Vizier's wife, the wonders of the architecture of the chamber in which they ate, and the skill with which the food was fashioned and served, made everything seem like a dream. He was at a loss to understand why his brethren had conceived such a fear of the man who seemed overflowing with kindness. The man had actually made merry with them, as though he were one of themselves. It was strange, Benjamin thought, that when this Grand Vizier had come to their table and had taken wine with them, even joking and laughing with them, he had seemed just like another brother, and not like a famous Egyptian.

.   .   .   .

"I will not feel really secure until we have reached the first inn," Judah declared.

Benjamin laughed at such fear.

"Why, Judah," he said, "what can there be to fear? I have never met so wonderful a man, who showed us such kindness. What can there be to be afraid of now?"

"You did not see him as we saw him last time," said Judah.

Reuben nodded. "I felt uneasy all the time, as though there was some intrigue, some secret understanding with his steward, though Benjamin is right—he could not have been kinder."

Simeon was inclined to look furtively over his shoulder.

"I too shall be glad to be away from this land of Egypt," he said. "The great man was strangely kind to us today, but there is something that haunts me about his eyes."

Fear is infectious. Benjamin was astonished that his brothers, who braved wild beasts to protect their flock, should be riding the camels with no sense of joyous abandon, but each man was tense and apprehensive. He could not understand it. They had obtained the corn, they were headed for home, he would soon see his father, his many nephews and nieces, and Bilhah, who was more like a mother to him. And they would tell the story round the fireside of the glory of Egypt, and describe the feast in the house of Zaphnath-paaneah.

The outskirts of the city were passed. Following the road along one of the banks of the Nile streams, as it broke up to form the delta, the brothers began to feel more relaxed. Perhaps it was something about the atmosphere of Tanis that had gripped them with a sense of fear.

Then Judah lifted his head, and pulled his camel to a halt.

"What is that?" he said sharply.

The others listened too. The sound of thudding horses' hooves could be heard in the distance.

"Maybe it is only other travellers coming this way," said Reuben uneasily. "Some people of the Philistines, perchance, bound on the same errand as ourselves."

"Only the Egyptians ride horses; they rarely use camels as we do," said Judah.

With one consent, the whole cavalcade had come to a halt, each riding his own camel and leading one, bearing provisions for the journey. Each heart was beating fast, and as the fear which had receded came back in a flood, Simeon felt again the fetters which had bound him. Judah looked at Benjamin, and thought of Jacob, and his promise to protect the youngest of his sons.

As the riders drew near, Judah recognised Rahmet, attended by his servants. Gone was the kindly expression of reassurance, and in its place was one of righteous indignation and wrath. The horses were pulled back on their haunches, snorting and pawing the ground.

Without preamble, Rahmet demanded, "Wherefore have ye rewarded evil for good? Today you were highly favoured by the Grand Vizier of Egypt, yet one of you has stolen his silver cup, by which he divines. What base ingratitude and treachery is this? "

A horrified silence greeted Rahmet's accusation.

Then Judah, speaking for his brethren, declared, " God forbid that thy servants should do according to this thing. Do you not remember how we brought back the money in our sacks to thee? How should we steal of my lord's silver and gold? "

Judah looked round the astonished and horrified faces of his ten brethren, and so sure of their innocence, went on, " With whomsoever of thy servants it shall be found, let him die, and we will all be thy bondsmen."

Rahmet replied grimly, " I only need the culprit, with whomsoever the cup shall be found. He shall be my bond-slave. The rest of you will be blameless, and shall depart."

This Rahmet had been instructed to say. The brothers must show if they would once again prove callous concerning one of their number, provided they could save their own skins.

With eagerness each of them dismounted, dragged his sack from the back of the camel, and stood by for Rahmet to search, for he would not allow any man to open his own sack. First Reuben's was opened, and with relief he showed that only Egyptian corn was therein. Then Simeon's, Levi's and Judah's, and the sacks of the sons of the concubines were opened, right down to Leah's two youngest sons, Issachar and Zebulun. Only Benjamin remained. The spirits of Jacob's sons rose. They had been falsely accused, and were about to be vindicated. It reminded them of a former occasion, when Laban and his sons had searched fruitlessly for the images.

Then with a shout of triumph, Rahmet drew from Benjamin's sack a beautifully wrought silver drinking cup, and held it up for all to see.

" What is this," he demanded, " if it be not my master's cup? "

Benjamin was speechless. His brothers broke into explanations, calling upon God to witness their innocence and that of Benjamin. In their anguish, they rent their clothes and tried to reason with Rahmet. The steward remained impervious to their explanations. He must keep Benjamin, but the rest of them might proceed on their journey. Then, as instructed, he watched each one's reaction. To their eternal credit, as he told Joseph later, there was not one who even hesitated concerning his duty.

"Let Benjamin stay, while we go free?" asked Judah, aghast. "What say you to that?"

And his brothers, with one consent, remounted their camels, and set their faces to return to Egypt with their accused brother.

So far, so good, thought Rahmet. Joseph had told him his plans. He was bent upon finding out if the hearts of his brothers were changed, or if they would, as before, allow their younger brother to be taken into slavery. Would they consider his anguish, and the sorrow of their father, or would they go their way carelessly, as they had done before, when they left him in the pit to die? Then they had heartlessly sat down to eat bread, caring nothing for his cries.

These men were certainly very much changed. Judah's face looked grey and ashen, as they were ushered into the presence of Joseph. The Grand Vizier noticed that in the few hours since he had seen Judah, his brother seemed to have aged by twenty years.

Then the brothers saw the Grand Vizier, as they had encountered him on their first visit. Gone was the geniality and friendliness, and in its place was implacable wrath and anger. Benjamin now realised why his brothers had been so consumed with fear and apprehension. They fell on their faces before Joseph, making deep obeisance in their agony and anxiety.

Joseph coldly bade them rise, and asked, "What deed is this that ye have done? How do you expect to deceive a man like myself? Have you not heard that I can divine and know the truth?"

Judah, bereft of any Hebrew arrogance, bowed his head, saying, "What shall we say unto my lord, or how shall we clear ourselves?" And, speaking more to himself than Joseph, almost beside himself with remorse and fear, he murmured, "God hath found out the iniquity of thy servants. Behold, take us as thy slaves, all of us." It was as though Judah said, 'We are not guilty of this crime, but God knows how guilty we have been in the past.'

Joseph would have none of it. "God forbid that I should do so," he said. "I only require the one in whose sack my cup was found," and indicating Benjamin with an inclination of his head, he gave the order for his youngest brother to be bound.

With well-assumed indifference, he said, "The rest of you may go in peace to your father," and he dismissed them with a wave of his hand, and turned away as though they had ceased to be of any interest to him.

This was too much for Judah. He came and fell before Joseph, and rising, put out his hand as if to detain him, saying urgently, in a voice fraught with emotion, "O my lord, let thy servant speak a word in my lord's ears, and let not thine anger burn against thy servant."

Joseph nodded, hardly trusting himself to speak. Was this humble supplicant Judah—arrogant, overbearing Judah, who had once said, 'Our sheaves will never bow to yours. I shall have that coat, but not by your gift'?

Judah, being permitted to speak, tried to control his trembling voice and speak wisely, thinking that this might be his only chance to have audience with so great a person.

"Let not thine anger burn against thy servant," he said again, "for thou art as Pharaoh. You, my lord, asked, 'Have you a father, or a brother?' We said, 'We have a father, an old man, and a young brother, the child of his old age, a little one, whose only brother is dead. He only is left of his mother, and our father loveth him."

It would be difficult to say which of the brothers was the most moved, Judah or Joseph, as a vision of Rachel rose before them, Jacob, the old man, and the son of his old age. With iron will Joseph remained impassive, his finger nails cutting deeply into his hands, as he gripped them together to keep a rein upon his emotions.

"Thou didst say, 'Come not again except you bring your youngest brother.' When we told this to our father, when our supply of corn was fast diminishing, our father would not at first consent, reminding us that his other son, Benjamin's brother, was dead . . . torn of wild beasts," faltered Judah, looking quickly at Joseph's inscrutable face, and having a strange sense that the diviner of secrets knew him through and through, and even had

265   I*

knowledge of Joseph's fate. He went on quickly, "My father said, 'Do you wish to bring down my grey hairs with sorrow to the grave?'"

Judah was silent for a moment, then bowed again before Joseph. "Now therefore, I come to you, my lord, with my father's life. If I return and the lad is not with me, my father will die, for his life is bound up in the lad."

Joseph waited. What was Judah suggesting—that he grant Benjamin a free pardon, and send them all back together? No, it seemed Judah was suggesting something more than that.

"Thy servant went as surety for the lad," he said. "I will remain as your slave, only let the lad go free. For how could I return to my father if the lad be not with us?"

Joseph wondered greatly, and his heart sang within him. Judah had been content once to return, leaving another lad in captivity. No doubt his father had sorrowed much then, but Judah's whole attitude and heart had been changed. He could neither suffer his young brother to be sent into slavery, nor endure his father's sorrow.

Joseph had reached the limit of his endurance and self-control. He signed to Rahmet to clear the chamber of everyone, save only his brethren. Greatly wondering, the brothers crowded together instinctively for protection, while Benjamin remained beside Judah, one still looking with earnest supplication, and the other waiting to be led away to servitude.

There was a moment's pause, then Joseph put a hand on Benjamin's shoulder, and on that of Judah.

"Come near to me, all of you," he said, to their astonishment speaking in their own language as freely as they did themselves. "I am your brother Joseph, whom ye sold into Egypt."

The brothers were transfixed with amazement, followed by fear. As they saw tears pouring down the face of the Grand Vizier, and heard the sound of his weeping, they doubted not that this was the truth. Joseph, whom they had callously sold to Ishmaelite traders, condemned to a life of misery, Joseph exalted, as great as Pharaoh, having the power of life and death. In the hearts of all save Benjamin was the thought, what will he do with us now? Will he avenge himself upon us?

Joseph, with his heart so full of love and yearning, hastened to reassure them.

"Do not reproach yourselves, my brethren. Yours was the action, but it was the will of God that I came here. He sent me before you to preserve your lives. Two years of famine have passed; there are still five more, and there will be neither harvest nor earing. God sent me to preserve posterity. He has made me ruler of Pharaoh's house, and the lord of all Egypt."

That they well knew, and to the minds of all leapt the memory of the small boy telling of his dreams, how all the sheaves of corn bowed down to his sheaf.

Joseph could forbear no longer, but embraced Benjamin, releasing some of the pent-up love that had welled up in him since he had first seen his young brother in the audience chamber. Joseph embraced each one in turn, and the obvious love he had for them, and the joy of reunion, made them all realise what he had suffered in being separated from his family. The love of family and home is a characteristic of the whole Hebrew race, and to Joseph the joy of being among his brethren again was well-nigh intoxicating.

He bade them sit with him, and he would allow no word of self-reproach or apology to be made. He took their sorrow for granted, and told them of his plans. In the land of Goshen was wonderful pastureland, and there he would provide a dwelling place for them all.

"You must travel back to Hebron, and fetch my father Jacob, and all your little ones, for we have plenty of land here for you, and for your sheep and cattle."

It was some hours before they finished talking together. There was so much Joseph wanted to know. Each told of his family, of his sons. He learnt that Leah had died, and was buried in the cave of Machpelah. Joseph told them of his two sons, Ephraim and Manasseh, and said, "You must tell my father of all my glory in Egypt, and haste to bring him down."

Then Joseph rose, and the servants were summoned to take the brothers to the palatial apartments set aside for them until they were ready to take their departure. They remembered in time, and bowed low to the Grand Vizier. Their little brother Joseph had shown them great kindness, but he was still second only to Pharaoh in this land of Egypt.

.   .   .   .

Jacob's sons, having feasted in the special refectory hall prepared for them, set out from their brother's palatial home to see something of the great city of Tanis. Gone from their hearts and minds was the fear which had oppressed them, and made anything Egyptian seem something of a horror. They wended their way through the streets towards the river, the silver snake of water that spelt life to the world. Benjamin stared up at the painted houses, while his older brothers looked with astonishment at all the painted women with vast head-dresses. All was new and exciting.

Suddenly there was shouting, and down the street came men, clearing the way and saying, "Bow down, bow down," and everyone bowed low, like wind sweeping over a corn-field, as a magnificent chariot came into view. High and lifted up on a brocaded seat, with servants attending him, was the Grand Vizier, clad in brilliant robes. There were cheers as well as obeisance, for everyone looked upon Joseph as the saviour by whose wisdom they were fed, and by whose foresight their lives had been spared. Judah and his brothers found themselves cheering and bowing with the rest. When the dust had died down, they stood in a silent group, watching the chariot disappear on its way to Pharaoh's palace.

"What a man is our brother Joseph!" said Judah. "He would not even allow us to reproach ourselves for what we had done to him, but even made it seem that we had been instruments in fulfilling God's purpose in sending him to Egypt."

.   .   .   .

"What is this I hear, Joseph?" Pharaoh asked him. "They say your kindred have arrived."

Joseph bowed to him. "O Pharaoh, greatest of kings, how

268

swiftly news travels in this land of Egypt! I have indeed wonderful tidings."

"Anyone can see that, Joseph," said Queen Nebyret. "You look as though the Nile had overflowed its banks, and merchants had brought you many mules' burden of gold."

"It is a greater joy than that for me, O Queen. Only consider, my eleven brethren are here in Egypt, on a visit to obtain corn for my aged father." Joseph's voice was like that of an excited schoolboy.

"Tell me all about them," said the Queen, and she and Pharaoh listened while Joseph told them of the magnificence of Judah, the wisdom of Naphtali, the kindness of Reuben, and of Benjamin, his own little brother Benjamin.

"You must not send them away," said Pharaoh imperiously. "Your father must be fetched down, and some good land set aside for them. They will perish in that poverty-stricken land of Canaan. Let them not bring their stuff, but let them come with their young ones and their servants. In this way I can repay some of my debt to Zaphnath-paaneah, my wise Grand Vizier, for all that he in his wisdom has done for the land of Egypt, and indeed for the whole of posterity."

Joseph bowed as he heard the words of Pharaoh, and spoke his thanks. Pharaoh had been a friend to him as well as a ruler, and his generosity now gave Joseph great joy. How wonderfully all the past had fitted into a pattern! he thought. God had planned it all, and after fifteen years of slavery, servitude, loneliness and power, great happiness was his, and he would see his father Jacob once more.

.   .   .   .

"When will my father return from Egypt?" asked Pharez of his grandfather, for what seemed to the old man like the hundredth time.

Jacob replied, "Any day now, Pharez, my son. Take Zarah thy brother and go with Elon, Job and the other lads to the hilltop, and bring me word if there is any sign of the camels."

Off went the twin sons of Judah. Once they would have run

with energy, but when a boy feeds only on a few lentils each day, he has not the power to jump and leap, as when his belly is filled with good meat. Together the group of lads wended their way over to the hilltop, each one so thin that all his ribs could be told. Jacob watched them go, his heart yearning over their half-starved condition. He himself hardly ate at all, that the boys might have more. He was now too weak to go to the hilltop, as he had once done, and watched to see whether the boys saw any sign of life across the arid parched land.

He heard a shout go up. The boys were exclaiming and pointing. He reached for his staff; he would try to go to see for himself. Then he found his steward at his side, supporting him with his strong arm.

"Let us go and see if my sons return," he said.

"Grandfather," Pharez shouted, "only come and see. A great army is approaching." Pharez, his weakness forgotten, pointed with great excitement.

A strange sight met the eyes of Jacob and the others who crowded to the hilltop at the sound of shouting. On the skyline were not only the cavalcade of camels, but wagons, twenty asses laden with sacks of provisions. The whole tribe came out to meet the travellers. Jacob had no eyes for wagons and asses, but counted the men . . . ". . . eight, nine, ten, *eleven!*" he shouted in excitement. "They are all returned, my eleven sons," and it was with those words that he greeted Judah, who came and fell on his neck and embraced him.

"All my eleven sons have returned safe and sound," he said.

Then Judah told him, "My father, you had twelve sons; this still is true, for Joseph is yet alive."

"Joseph? My beloved Rachel's son?" Jacob asked incredulously.

"Yes, Joseph is alive, and is Governor over all Egypt."

Jacob, after the manner of the aged, was unable to take in this intelligence. He looked in unbelief at his sons.

"A likely story," he said. "Joseph, Governor of Egypt! You told me it was some Grand Vizier who treated you with harshness. Have done with this foolish talk. Whence come all these asses and wagons?" for Joseph's brothers had come home laden.

At the command of Pharaoh, Joseph had given them changes of raiment, corn and provisions, so that all the tribe could be sustained and strengthened for the journey, and fed as they made their way down to Egypt. To Benjamin, Joseph had given three hundred pieces of silver and five changes of raiment. To Benjamin it was as if a dream had come true. His own brother, of whom he had heard, was alive and treated him with love and generosity.

They showed Jacob all that they had brought.

"These are a present from Joseph, who is mighty, and to whom everyone bows the knee."

Jacob stood and considered. His sons sat round about him, and slowly, bit by bit, told their father the story of Joseph. The only part of the story which was not revealed by them was how the Ishmaelites, who had sold him into slavery, had first taken possession of him. Jacob slowly began to understand. Then he remembered Joseph's dreams—the bowing sheaves of corn, the sun, moon and stars bowing down to Joseph's star. At last he sat back against his cushions outside his tent.

"It is enough," he said. "Joseph my son is yet alive. I will go and see him before I die."

28

"THE original suggestion that you made to Pharaoh, my lord Joseph, that one-fifth of all the corn produced should be for the state, was certainly a divinely inspired one." Rahmet paused.

The Grand Vizier was pacing up and down the tiled floor of his council chamber, apparently lost in thought.

"It is consistent with your wisdom," went on Rahmet, "though surprising even then, when newly brought from the prison, you should have arrived at so wise a conclusion." Rahmet paused again. Was his lord and master listening, or calculating some figure of his own?

"About three score or maybe more," Joseph was murmuring to himself.

Rahmet was puzzled. Was it acres, grain or reservoirs which occupied Joseph's mind, as he paced on the mosaic floor, oblivious of all that went on round about him?

Then Joseph stopped, and saw Rahmet regarding him with wonder and slight exasperation. The lord of all Egypt laughed ruefully, and put his hand affectionately on the shoulder of the one whom, though his subordinate in position, he never failed to regard as his friend.

"Rahmet," he said, "I treat you shamefully. You labour and toil for me, and I reward you ill by listening with a mind wool-gathering and far away."

Then Rahmet understood. "Your thoughts are with your brethren and the joyous reunion with your revered father."

Joseph gripped Rahmet's shoulders with both his hands.

"Any day now, Rahmet," he declared, "and I shall look into my beloved father's face, whom I have not seen for over twenty years."

"Your father can be no ordinary man, my lord Joseph."

"My father is a man whom men and women love. His grandfather Abraham was one who called out respect and awe in all he met. He was a visionary, who dwelt on mountain tops with his Maker, spent all night alone with his God, and inspired my father with the great sense of destiny he never lost. But my father was so human; he was not a being far above us, but one in whom we could confide. I well remember," Joseph went on, "when we were journeying from Padan-aram to our own land, a long journey for little children and their mothers. He would never journey too fast; his loving care was like that of the tender shepherd that he was. His wives adored him, and the tribe almost worshipped him. He knew each one, and their circumstances. He would jest with us, tell stories, and yet he was wiser than all. He could calculate and reckon, and was as gifted as any of the mathematicians of Egypt. His skill with sheep and herds was far-famed, though mention that not outside these walls," Joseph laughed. "If there were shepherds in Egypt like Jacob," he said, "they would cease to be an abomination."

Rahmet listened, fascinated, as Joseph continued his reminiscences.

"The Hebrews are an amazing race," Rahmet said at last. "They stand out among their fellows as men apart. The Hittites and Ishmaelites and Midianites visit us here, but your brethren are different. It must be that they have wisdom, as worshippers of the God Jehovah."

"But for Jehovah, my people would be even as the heathen," Joseph told him. "It was because of his call to worship Jehovah at Bethel that my father remained pure and moral, and dealt with such honesty in his time of servitude at Padan-aram."

"It is not surprising that such a father produced such a son," Rahmet told his master.

Joseph waved away the suggestion, and tried vainly to turn his mind to the welfare of Egypt.

A timely interruption came. A servant brought the intelligence that a Hebrew, one Judah, sought audience with the Grand Vizier. Joseph's eyes were alight with excitement.

"They come, Rahmet, they come," he said. "I had instructed them to go direct to Goshen, and send one here to tell me of their arrival."

Judah entered, bowed himself to the ground in obeisance, and then was bidden by his impatient brother to rise.

"Has he arrived?" asked Joseph eagerly.

"Our father is in Goshen, and is yearning to see you," was the reply.

Joseph fell on Judah's neck in eager embrace, asking him a dozen questions at once: how had their father fared during the journey? Had it been a weariness to the flesh for him? Was he well? How had he taken the news concerning himself?

Judah answered the questions as well as he might, and Joseph gave immediate orders for his chariot to be made ready.

   ·   ·   ·   ·   ·   ·   ·   ·   :   ·   ·   ·

How strange it was, thought Judah, to be travelling in such state, like a Pharaoh of Egypt, and to see everyone cheering and bowing to his little brother Joseph!

"How right you were, my brother!" Judah told him. "All our sheaves bow down to yours, and the sun will soon have to make obeisance to you, a star of Egypt."

"Would that the moon, my beloved mother Rachel, could have lived to see this day." Joseph looked at Judah, and back to his mind came his childish dream that one day Judah would reverence him. "You loved my mother, Judah, did you not, though you hated me?"

"Your mother was a holy woman; anything good I ever learnt was from her," Judah told him quietly.

"I remember your smiting Levi on the mouth for speaking lightly of her."

"Joseph," said Judah abruptly, "When my father thought that you were dead, he gave to me the coat of many colours. That must be restored to you by his hand this day."

Joseph moved in his seat, and turned to his brother as they sat on the cushioned luxury of the chariot. He spoke with urgency.

"That, my brother Judah, shall not be. That coat should never have been mine. I had no desire to be my father's heir, neither did my mother wish it for me. Do you know why God sent me to Egypt, over-ruled my imprisonment, brought me out and exalted me? It was not so much to preserve Egypt or the races of the world; it was to preserve you."

"Why me?" asked Judah.

"Because from you will come the Saviour of mankind, the SHILOH. I have earthly pomp and glory, material possessions, but I have only been an instrument to preserve you."

Judah looked incredulously at his famous brother.

"You really mean that, Joseph? You really feel that sense of destiny, that God called you to preserve us for posterity?"

"Yours is a far greater calling than mine," said Joseph. "God has given me wisdom and ability to carry out His plans, but through you all the nations of the earth will be blessed. Thousands of years hence, when these houses are falling to decay, and maybe only the pyramids will stand, One will come from the line of Judah, Whom all nations will bless. Joseph and Pharaoh and all their temporary glory will be forgotten, but the names of Abraham, Isaac, Jacob and Judah will remain."

"You will never be forgotten, Joseph," Judah told him sincerely. "That which is good and divine will live on. Tell me, Joseph, you had a deep plan in your treatment of me and my brethren? Your assumed harshness and attempt to imprison Benjamin were not revengeful acts."

The chariot had left Tanis, and the cries of the people in their adulation were far behind. The river road wound on as they journeyed to the good land of Goshen.

Joseph answered at last, "I had to know, Judah, I had to find out if my sacrifice and life of slavery had been in vain. Would you sell Benjamin as callously as you had sold me? Would you, as before, shrug your shoulders and eat bread, and allow Benjamin's cries of anguish to fall on deaf ears?"

Judah covered his face with his hands.

"Even to hear of it again is like a knife in my heart," he told his brother. "Joseph, will you believe, that night after you made yourself known to us in your palace was the first for over twenty years that I slept like a little child? I have many a time nearly lost my reason; my conscience was like a hot iron in my brain. The least I could do was to protect Benjamin from harm."

Joseph's heart glowed. "I have heard that your care of him has made his life secure and happy."

As they drew near to Goshen, Joseph grew tense. The knuckles of his hands showed white with the excitement and anticipation that consumed him.

"Will my father find me changed beyond all knowing, Judah? You yourselves did not recognise me."

"When we saw you in that audience chamber, you were clad in all the glory of the Grand Vizier of Egypt. To us, you looked like a Pharaoh, and we were too much in awe of Zaphnath-paaneah to recognise little Joseph," Judah told him.

Joseph had left behind all the trappings of his state, and

275

clothed himself as much like a Hebrew as he was able, although his beardless face, according to the custom of the Egyptians, would mark him out from his brothers. Judah regarded him critically.

"You are the most handsome and comely of Jacob's sons, without a doubt," Judah assured him.

Joseph clapped his older brother on the shoulder.

"All except one. You yourself, Judah, would stand out in any company, Hebrew or Egyptian. My father has chosen well in giving *you* the coat of many colours."

. . . .

The Hebrews are by no means a cold-blooded people. Their love of family and affection for each other is one of their outstanding characteristics. When Joseph met his father Jacob, it would be difficult to decide which experienced the greater delight, and whose had been the greater suffering and deprivation over the twenty years of their separation.

Jacob had been waiting, unable to stay in the brick-built house that was their temporary resting place. His eyes, not grown dim like his father Isaac's, but keen as in his youth, watched the road for any sign of the chariot which was to bring his beloved son.

"You must remember to bow low before Joseph," Benjamin told him. "The Egyptians will expect it, and failing to bow to Joseph they regard as an act of treason."

Jacob smiled. "Never fear, I will bow before my son. Did he not dream that I should do so?"

But when they met, Jacob scarcely had time to make obeisance. As the chariot drew up, the servants of Joseph, who would have attended him with ceremony, were summarily dismissed, and the Grand Vizier leapt to the ground, ran to his father, and together they wept and embraced in a passion of joy at such a reunion.

At last Israel said, "Now let me die, since I have seen thy face, because thou art yet alive."

"That you will not do, my father," Joseph told him. "It is

to live that you have come down to Egypt. I will go to Pharaoh and tell him of your arrival, and peradventure he will grant good land for you and for your herds."

The feasting and revelry continued some days. Joseph had so much to tell. Each one hung on his famous brother's words, as he told the story of the interpretation of Pharaoh's dreams. Jacob was unable to comprehend the extent of Joseph's greatness, but his sons, who had feared and suffered under it, now gloried to be the brother of one who was second only to great Pharaoh, greatest monarch in the world.

.   .   .   .

Pharaoh and Nebyret were more than interested in the romantic story of Joseph and his brethren. When the news came that Joseph's father, the Hebrew Patriarch, had arrived, Pharaoh sent for Joseph and demanded to be presented both to his brethren and to his father.

"It will not be the first time that a Hebrew Patriarch has met a Pharaoh face to face," Apepi told him.

The story of Abraham's visit less than a hundred years before was well known to them both, and Nebyret had often gently teased Joseph, saying that he must have inherited his beauty of face from his great-grandmother Sarah, who had so enchanted and enslaved Pharaoh and the princes of Egypt.

Before presenting his father, Joseph chose five of his brothers to meet the monarch. He felt justly proud as he presented Judah, Reuben, Benjamin, and the two youngest sons of Leah to their majesties.

Joseph had been in doubt whether to divulge to the Egyptians the shameful nature of his brethren's occupation—shameful to the Egyptians, of course—and he urged them not to use the word 'shepherd', but to say rather in conversation 'we trade in cattle'. It was essential that Pharaoh should know their occupation, for he might, in the kindness of his heart, suggest giving them a parcel of land near Memphis, or in some other area quite unsuited to their trade.

The brothers bowed low to Apepi and Nebyret.

"I had never thought to see men as handsome as you are, Joseph, but I verily believe your brothers rival you in beauty," the Queen told him, while Pharaoh asked the inevitable question, "What is your occupation?"

Reuben, making no attempt to disguise the truth, bluntly said, "We are shepherds, lord Pharaoh," and though the Egyptian servants looked both aghast and horrified, Pharaoh, descendant of the shepherd kings, merely nodded thoughtfully.

Joseph sighed with resignation. Judah would have had the tact to have made their profession sound a little more honourable. But it was inevitable; the court would gossip for a day, but the scandal of the Grand Vizier's low-born and despicable relatives would soon die down. At least the women of the court who had seen them would carry a brave account.

It was well that Pharaoh knew their occupation, for he at once grasped the situation, and told Joseph, "The land of Egypt is before thee, and in the best of the land make thy father and brethren to dwell; in the land of Goshen let them dwell."

Joseph sighed with relief. It was as he had hoped; Pharaoh had possessed much land there, and Joseph could choose a fine parcel of land not far from Rameses, where the tribe could make their sojourn. Pharaoh further insisted that high appointments should be given to Joseph's brothers, as he saw fit.

The interview had taken place in a most satisfactory manner, and all that remained was to present Jacob to Pharaoh. His sons had attempted to impress upon their father the greatness of the Egyptian monarch. Jacob listened to their instructions with a far-away expression.

"He is but a man like myself, is he not, who has treated my son Joseph with great kindness?" he asked.

"Remember to bow low and call him 'my lord Pharaoh', or even 'Divinity', as the Egyptians do," Naphtali warned him.

Joseph listened with amusement to his brothers vainly trying to teach an old man, the great Patriarch, how to behave before an earthly monarch.

"Cease trying, Naphtali, to instruct one who stands before the Lord of Heaven, to stand before an earthly king. Come, Father, and meet Pharaoh Apepi, whom I am proud to call my friend."

Jacob rose, and the brothers, who had learnt their lesson, all bowed low, not only to their father, but to their younger brother, whose glory never failed to strike them with awe.

.   .   .   .

Pharaoh's meeting with the Patriarch was an extraordinary experience for him. He was accustomed to giving audience to foreign kings and dignitaries, to lesser beings, to monarchs and army chieftains. But when the Grand Vizier came in, leading by the hand an old man, who stood erect and bore himself well—though walking with a limp, that legacy of Peniel's blessing—Pharaoh found his ready speech failed him. Israel, Patriarch of the Hebrews, was giving audience to Pharaoh, not the Egyptian monarch to the visiting Patriarch.

"Peace be to you, my son," said Jacob kindly. "The God of my fathers reward you for your goodness to my son Joseph. God has blessed you, and will bless your posterity, and with long life He will honour thee."

And Pharaoh, great monarch though he was, bowed his head to receive a Patriarch's blessing. In the silence that followed, Pharaoh looked at the ageless face of one who had spoken as though he had been from the beginning, and was not something of time.

"How old art thou?" asked Pharaoh curiously.

Then Israel, the prince, became Jacob, the man.

"Few and evil have been my days," he said. "A mere hundred and thirty years. My forbears attained to much greater ages."

And they talked together as a man talks with his friend, until it was time to depart. And again, it was not the monarch who dismissed his visitor, but Israel who raised his hand in a final blessing on the man who, though the world had clothed him with majesty, was only to the old Patriarch one who had been favoured by God, and needed the Almighty's blessing.

29

JACOB lay on a luxurious couch in his dwelling in the land of Goshen. It seemed he would not end his days in a tent, but in a house—a magnificent dwelling built at the command of his powerful son Joseph.

It was good to die in comfort, thought Jacob. These last seventeen years had brought prosperity and sustenance for him and his tribe. He had been right to journey down to Egypt. He remembered his doubts as he had set off with the wagons and camels, his three-score descendants travelling with him. It had been the only way to avoid starvation, but he had thought then that to go into Egypt was a retrograde step for one of his race. Abraham's faith had failed, and he had sought Egypt's aid. His grandfather often spoke of this with regret, grieving that he had left the land of promise. His father Isaac had not been permitted to travel down to Egypt; he had been prevented by a vision. But God had been good to him, and had spoken clearly, even when he had stopped at Beersheba to sacrifice, as he made his way south.

"I am the God of thy father," the Voice had said. "Fear not to go into Egypt, for I will make of thee a great nation; I will go with thee, and will surely bring thee up again."

What cheer those words had brought, and confirmation of his plan! But God had said he would bring him back. He was too old to travel now; he knew his end was near. Would his bones lie here in alien Egypt? He longed to be placed in the family burial ground of Machpelah, where lay Abraham and Isaac. To be laid to rest in this land of embalmed mummies and scarabs and false gods was not for him. He would speak of it to his sons, to his mighty son Joseph, who could command anything by the word of his power.

.   .   .   .

Joseph's life was busier than ever. Pharaoh relied upon him more and more, and after twenty years, had never had reason to regret that apparently impulsive decision to make him Grand Vizier. Many said that though the Spirit of God had come upon Joseph to interpret the dreams, the Spirit of God had certainly come upon Pharaoh to guide him to exalt Joseph to this high position.

It was while Joseph was in audience with Pharaoh that a messenger came to him, saying, "Thy father is sick."

Joseph knew that this sickness was unto death, and bowed to Pharaoh, saying, "I think that this will be the end, and the Patriarch Jacob will be gathered to his fathers." Pharaoh was full of sympathy and concern, and commanded Joseph to prepare the finest tomb in the land for Jacob on his journey into the valley of the dead.

Joseph was ushered into his father's presence alone. He had seen, by the stricken faces of his brethren, that all knew that the passing of their father was imminent.

Jacob lay on his couch in a state of great tranquillity. So this was death, he thought; how strange that men should fear it! He felt no pain, but found that the faces around him suddenly receded, and he was in a peaceful dream between sleeping and waking. Slowly a face was coming into focus. He pulled himself together. Who was this? Those eyes were those of his beloved Rachel. Was he indeed with her already in the land beyond? No, these eyes were in the countenance of a man; it was his beloved Joseph, of whose presence he had been robbed for nigh on twenty years.

"Joseph, my beloved son," he murmured, "I have a request."

Joseph came near to his father, yearning over him with all the love that he bore him, and asked, "What can I do for you, Jacob my father?"

"If I have found grace in thy sight," began Jacob, characteristically wording his request not as a command, "put, I pray thee, thy hand under my thigh, and deal kindly and truly with me; bury me not, I pray thee, in Egypt; but I will lie with my fathers, and thou shalt carry me out of Egypt, and bury me in their burying place. Swear this unto me."

And Joseph, putting his hand under Jacob's thigh, giving the sign that if he failed in his oath, posterity would avenge it, swore unto him. After this, Jacob's mind was at rest; he could trust his son to take him back to the land of his fathers.

.   .   .   .

The next day the Patriarch seemed greatly refreshed, and the fact that his mind was at rest seemed to bring strength to his body. Towards evening, he commanded to be raised up on his pillows. The world was dim, but his mind became clear. He was shortly to leave his sons, and wished to say parting words to the twelve men whom his wives had borne him.

The room was large enough to accommodate them all, and they stood around the couch of their dying father. Joseph stood by with a cup of wine to refresh his father from time to time. Jacob's breathing was laboured, but he opened his aged eyes and looked out on the sober faces before him. So these were his sons, he thought. He had been more fruitful than his forbears; Abraham had fathered only Isaac and Ishmael; his father's fruitfulness had ended with his twin sons. But God had blessed him abundantly. There was Reuben, his firstborn. He thought of Leah and her passionate love, and later of her happy companionship with him.

"Reuben," he said, "thou art my firstborn, my might, and the beginning of my strength." Strange, he thought to himself, I was a young man when I begat Reuben, strong and mighty. "Thou art the beginning of strength, the excellency of power." The pity of it, thought Jacob, and he went on, almost thinking aloud, "Unstable as water, you will not succeed; you cannot be my heir, for you went in unto my concubine."

Reuben hung his head. He had realised many years ago that he was not to succeed his father as head of the tribe.

Jacob's eyes moved farther, and he saw Simeon and Levi, strangely like their grandfather Laban. Their little eyes reminded him of how hard had been his life at Padan-aram, and all the wrongs he had endured at the hand of Laban passed through Jacob's mind. Then he remembered that something very unpleasant had happened through Simeon and Levi.

"Simeon and Levi," he said, "instruments of cruelty are in their habitations." Yes, he thought to himself, a blood-covered sword—Dinah had told him about it; dangerous men. "O my soul, come not thou into their secret; for in their anger they slew a man, and in their self-will they digged down a wall. Cursed be their anger, for it was fierce; and their wrath, for it was cruel."

There was a deathly silence in the room, while Jacob continued to ruminate, and all could see that in his mind he was dwelling in the unpleasant past. No, thought Jacob, these three eldest of my sons could not be in the line of promise.

The Promise! His old eyes lightened. How he had longed above everything else to be the one in whom the great destiny of his people should be fulfilled! He had made mistakes; he had sought by his own will to bring it about. He had wanted the right things, but sought to obtain them in the wrong way. He need never have bought the birthright; Esau's action in marrying Hittite women would automatically have deposed him. He need not have deceived his father over the blessing, but should have demanded it openly. But it seemed that God knew his heart, and valued his desire for Him and His blessing, for five times God had said, "I will bless thee, I will be with thee." Life had been strange; he had thought to make Joseph his heir, though Rachel had ever been against this. He had ignored her instructions, and exalted Joseph above his brethren, and caused their jealousy. But God had over-ruled it all.

He brought himself back from the state of semi-consciousness in which he had sunk, and Joseph gave him a refreshing drink. He had been dreaming of the Promise, yes, that was it, and the Spirit of God seemed to fall upon him. He felt strangely refreshed and uplifted. His voice became strong; a sense of purpose came to him. He was looking into the face of one in whom would be fulfilled the Promise which he himself had sought. Judah—that son who had of late been so changed, who was one with him in the worship of Jehovah, who had helped him to erect a holy place here in Egypt, this foreign land.

"Judah," he said in a strong voice, putting out his hand, and instinctively Judah came and knelt at the side of the couch, for all could see that this was to be the patriarchal blessing.

> " Judah, thou art he whom thy brethren shall praise; thy hand shall be in the neck of thine enemies; thy father's children shall bow down before thee . . . The sceptre shall not depart from Judah, nor a lawgiver from between his feet, until . . ."

—the old man's voice reached a note of triumph, and all the brothers felt as though the ground whereon they stood was holy ground, while the old man's voice continued—

> " until SHILOH come; and unto Him shall the gathering of the people be."

The patriarchal blessing was over. Judah arose, and Jacob lay back spent. He had other kind words to say to his sons, each one bringing back memories. Zebulun and Issachar, born after Leah found the mandrakes, and settled into a happier time of life; Dan and Naphtali, sons of the concubine, Bilhah; Gad, that obstreperous young son, always in trouble : " You shall overcome at last," Jacob promised him; Asher, the fat little boy, with the insatiable appetite—the old man smiled at the memory : " You shall yield royal dainties, Asher," he said; " Naphtali will utter goodly words; he has always been like a hind let loose."

Then Jacob's eyes rested on Joseph, his beloved—not to be his heir, but always the joy of his heart.

" Yes, my son," he murmured, " Rachel was right; you were not only for us, you were like a fruitful bough; your branches have run over the Hebrew wall, to sustain the Egyptians and the whole world. Your lot has not been easy; the archers have shot at thee, and there have been those that have hated thee."

In the pause that followed, ten of those present held their breath, and wondered did Jacob really know the truth concerning their treachery to Joseph. Would it all come out now?

Reuben, Simeon and Levi had been shamed before all; were they all to be exposed, had Joseph told his father, and was it all to be revealed now? But no, they might have known Joseph better than to think that. Jacob went on,

> "But his bow abode in strength, and the arms of his hands were made strong by the hands of the mighty God of Jacob . . . even by the God of thy father, Who shall help thee; and by the Almighty, Who shall bless thee with blessings of heaven above, and blessings of the deep . . . The blessings of thy father have prevailed above the blessings of my progenitors unto the utmost bound of the everlasting hills; they shall be on the head of Joseph, and on the crown of him that was separate from his brethren."

It was a wonderful blessing, something to remember in the days to come. 'Unto the utmost bound of the everlasting hills'—what language to come from a dying man! thought Joseph.

Jacob's voice never failed nor faltered until he had made an end of communing with his sons. Then he lay back, and without effort or struggle, gave up the ghost. Joseph fell on his father's face and wept, as was fitting, for he it was who had loved his father most.

But weeping must be replaced by action. Joseph stood, and as his brothers wondered who should make the first move to go from the chamber of death, Joseph went slowly over to where Judah was standing, still dazed from his father's recent words. Joseph bowed himself to the ground, and said, "All honour to thee, Judah, the Patriarch. I am thy servant Joseph." And so did all his brethren, according to their father's words, 'thy father's children shall bow down before thee.'

   ·   ·   ·   ·   ·   ·   ·   ·   ·   ·   ·

Joseph commanded the greatest physicians in the land to embalm his father's body, that it might be taken to the cave of Machpelah. During the forty days' mourning it was not fitting, according to the custom, for Joseph to have audience with Pharaoh. So a message was sent requesting the monarch's permission for the Grand Vizier to absent himself, and take the old Patriarch to the family burying-place in Canaan. This was to Pharaoh a right and proper thing, for to an Egyptian the place of burial is of far more significance and importance than the home in which his earthly body dwells.

．　．　．　．　．　．　．　．　．　．　．　．

It was a strange experience for Joseph to travel over familiar ground after almost forty years. He felt like a small boy again, as he went through the well-known places, and saw the familiar landmarks. But it was different, for the state in which they travelled with chariots and horsemen caused no small stir. Many of the inhabitants of Canaan had never before seen a horse, and marvelled at the glory of the chariots, and the state in which these Egyptians travelled, not realising that, but for the servants, no Egyptian was among the men who mourned seven days in the threshing floor of Atad.

The burial was conducted with due ceremony. After seventeen years in Egypt, the brothers were inclined from force of habit to give place to Joseph. But he would have none of it, and accorded to Judah the place and position that his new status demanded.

Only the little ones had been left behind, while all the tribe of Israel came to do Jacob honour, as they laid him beside Abraham, Sarah, Isaac, Rebekah and Leah in the cave of Machpelah. These men who owned nothing in the land except this one burial place, bought by Abraham from the sons of Heth, knew from the promise of Jehovah that one day their children's children would possess the land and people it.

As they laid their father to rest, no one thought of him as Jacob, the wrestler, Jacob the supplanter, but as ISRAEL, the prince who had prevailed with God. He rested in the land which, in years to come, would not be called the land of Isaac, or even the land of Abraham, great Patriarch though he was, but would, for generations to come, be known as the land of ISRAEL.

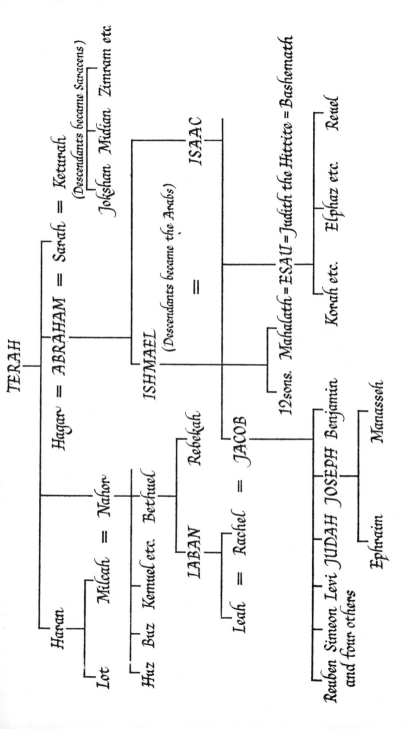

TERAH

Haran — Hagar = ABRAHAM = Sarah — Nahor

Lot — Milcah = Nahor

Huz Buz Kemuel etc. Bethuel

Sarah = ABRAHAM = Keturah

Jokshan Midian Zimram etc.
(Descendants became Saracens)

ISHMAEL
(Descendants became the Arabs)
=
ISAAC

12 sons. Mahalath = ESAU = Judith the Hittite = Bashemath

Korah etc. Elphaz etc. Reuel

LABAN Rebekah = JACOB

Leah = Rachel = JACOB

Reuben Simeon Levi JUDAH JOSEPH Benjamin
and four others

Ephraim Manasseh

BIBLIOGRAPHY

Title	Author	Publisher	Date of Publication
The Works of Flavius Josephus	Translated by William Whiston	Thomas Nelson	184?
Illustrations from Biblical Archaeology	D. J. Wiseman	Tyndale Press	1958
The Land and the Book	W. M. Thomson	Published in New York	1860
A History of Old Testament Times	R. K. Harrison	Marshall, Morgan & Scott	1957
Life under the Pharaohs	Leonard Cottrell	Evans Bros. Ltd.	1955
The Lost Pharaohs	Leonard Cottrell	Evans Bros. Ltd.	1950
The Golden Bough	Sir J. G. Fraser	Macmillan	1950
Encyclopedia Biblica		Adam & Charles Black	
Everyday Life in Old Testament Times	E. W. Heaton	B. T. Batsford Ltd.	1956
The Living World of the Bible	M. J. Steve translated by		
The Nile	D. Woodward	Thames & Hudson Ltd.	1961
They Wrote on Clay	Elgar Ludwig	Allen & Unwin	1936
Ancient Egyptian Materials and Industries	E. Chiera	Cambridge University Press	1939
	A. Lucas	Edward Arnold & Co.	1948
Marriage, East and West	D. Mace	MacGibbon & Kee	1960
Hebrew Marriage	D. Mace	Epworth Press	1953
The Ancient Near East	Ed. James Pritchard	Oxford University Press	1959
History Unearthed	Leonard Woolley	E. Benn	1958
Spadework—Adventures in Archaeology	Leonard Woolley	Lutterworth Press	1953
The Egyptians	Cyril Aldred	Thames & Hudson	1961
A History of Egypt (3 vols.)	W. M. Flinders Petrie, D.C.L., LL.D.	Methuen	1896-1905